IF I DIE BEFORE I WAKE

The Better Off Dead Series Volume 5

TALES OF THE OTHERWORLDLY AND UNDEAD

IF I DIE
BEFORE I WAKE

The Better Off Dead Series Volume 5

TALES OF THE OTHERWORLDLY AND UNDEAD

EDITED BY R.E. SARGENT
& STEVEN PAJAK

IF I DIE BEFORE I WAKE
The Better Off Dead Series Volume 5
Tales of the Otherworldly and Undead

Edited by R.E. Sargent & Steven Pajak

Published by Sinister Smile Press
P.O. Box 637
Newberg, OR 97132

Trade Paperback ISBN – 978-1-953112-12-5

www.sinistersmilepress.com

ACKNOWLEDGEMENT

Thank you to Dita Daub for her winning theme submission for this volume: Tales of the Otherworldly and Undead. You rock, Dita!

"Go then, there are other worlds than these."

-Stephen King, The Gunslinger

"Sometimes dead is better."

-Stephen King, Pet Sematary

CONTENTS

FOREWORD

Richard Chizmar

FIRST, AN ADMISSION: I HAVE not yet read the first four volumes of the *Better Off Dead* anthology series.

I've heard of them, of course, admired their flashy covers floating around online, and even skimmed a handful of positive reviews—but for whatever reasons, I'd never managed to actually lay my hands on a copy.

Until now.

I'm thrilled to say this without hesitation: after devouring, in a single sitting, Volume Five of the series, cleverly titled *If I Die Before I Wake*, I plan to correct my earlier mistake in judgment as soon as possible. Amazon, here I come.

Quite simply, I adored the stories in this book. Some more than others, naturally, but I had a genuine good time with each and every one of them. And, frankly, that came as somewhat of a surprise to me.

See, here's the thing: I've been in sort of a slump lately when it comes to short fiction. I haven't found much that I like in either the slush pile or various stacks of published works. Sure, I read a lot, so I've stumbled upon a hidden gem here and there, but as far as any sense of consistent satisfaction? That has eluded me.

Until now.

All of the folks featured in *If I Die Before I Wake—Volume Five* are talented and accomplished authors—yet none are household names. I like that. In fact, it's one of the reasons I agreed to write this foreword. It's also one of the reasons I first decided to hitch my wagon to the horror genre almost thirty-five years ago when I started a little magazine called *Cemetery Dance*. The idea of shining a brighter light on newer, or in many cases, just lesser known writers, appealed to me. Hell, back in the late 1980s and all throughout the '90s, I was one of those writers.

But, when it comes to the contributors to the anthology you are holding in your hands, I'm betting it won't remain like that for long. One of these fine writers—most likely a handful of them—won't stay "lesser known" for long. They'll keep their head down and keep writing their own unique tales of terror and the unknown. They'll take their bumps along the way and will keep going and learning. Most importantly, they won't give up. They won't even consider it. Because they can't. This is what they do: they dream and they write down those dreams (nightmares) to share with others.

And we're all the richer for their gifts.

There are a wide variety of dark tales to be discovered within these covers, and they cover an expanse of haunted ground: evil dolls, mysterious television shows, foul creatures from outer space, otherworldly demons, desperate men counting the hours on death row, serial killers, a possessed murderess, vampires, and boogeymen.

Most of the stories in *If I Die Before I Wake—Volume Five* fall neatly into the category of traditional (often times even old-fashioned) horror—but this isn't a criticism. Quite the contrary. Turn the page and read the opening story—*how can you not get excited over a tall tale called "Granny's Gift"?!?*—and you'll see exactly what I mean.

Then, keep turning those pages.

It's all here waiting for you.

Shadows and darkness; thrills and chills; mystery and wonder.

First-rate storytelling from start to finish.

I hope you enjoy *If I Die Before I Wake—Volume Five* as much as I did.

I'll bet you a bloody chainsaw that you do.

—Richard Chizmar
June 1, 2021

GRANNY'S GIFT

Renee M.P.T. Kray

JULY 10, 1999 WAS TURNING OUT TO BE an excellent day for Jezz. For starters, she had the house to herself, which meant she was able to burn as much of her Dragon's Blood incense as she wanted without her mom complaining that it made her dizzy. Secondly, she was wearing her new Fear Factory band tee for the first time, and its design of two rows of long floating teeth with the title "Edgecrusher" at the bottom was basically the flyest thing she'd ever seen.

Thirdly, Granny Nelson was still dead.

Jezz pulled on her headphones and laid back on her bed, the water-filled mattress jiggling as gently as Acid Bath's screams were loud. She was well aware that she was the odd man out in the perfect Nelson family, a family that was small-town famous due to the fact that their matriarch, Granny Nelson, had morphed from a businesswoman selling her own toys to a millionaire and local philanthropist when her "Sugar Pink Teddies" became a sensation. And boy had she taken that transformation seriously. She'd never missed a Serling County event, had started numerous charitable foundations to beautify the local parks, and was always willing to stop and graciously say a word to the press. She'd been the type to wear pearls every minute of the day whether she was going to a luncheon or taking a shit, and she'd expected her five children and eleven grandchildren to do the same.

"The Nelson name means something in this town," she'd often said. "I worked hard to make sure of it." Jezz had never tried alcohol, but she still knew with absolute certainty that she would have been fall-down-throw-up-in-your-Froot-Loops drunk if she had devoted a single day to taking a shot every time Granny said those words. She didn't deny that Granny *had* worked hard, and that the Nelson name *did* mean something to some people, but Jezz was never able to fit in with the family regardless of how hard she tried. And boy howdy had she tried. Dressing up cute, smiling big, trying to be all that and a bag of chips. But she was always just a tad too loud, her style a beat too wild, and her interests a dollop too weird, while her cousins had popped into the world from the ideal Nelson mold: poised and elegant and smart.

It was less painful to just stop trying and accept that she didn't belong, the only black sheep in a field of perfect Nelsons.

Jezz had been on Granny's shit list since childhood, but their true falling out had happened a few months back and was so explosively bridge burning that Granny and Jezz hadn't spoken since. So, when Jezz's father had pulled the phone away from his ashen face just one week ago and had announced that Granny Nelson was discovered dead in her home, Jezz couldn't have said she cared much. Granny Nelson's death was a surprise given that she'd seemed to be in decent health despite her fall earlier in the year, which had left her reliant on a cane. But Jezz's father had stressed that when a person got up into their eighties, they could go at any time.

"Literally. Any time," he'd said over and over again as he helped his siblings pick out a casket (white with chrome accents), arrange the funeral (two days from now), and pick out Granny's final clothes (a black dress with long sleeves and lace cuffs). He'd said the mantra so many times that Jezz suspected he was mainly trying to convince himself. Her hunch was further confirmed when she overheard her mom talking in a low voice on the phone to Aunt Janey about how Granny Nelson had been found sitting in her favorite chair, fully clothed and wearing makeup. Jezz thought it made sense even if the rest of her family didn't; Granny was such a tight-assed control freak that she wouldn't wait around to lose all of her faculties. Of course, she'd arrange her own death, the same way she arranged everything else in her world.

"I guess the Nelson name don't mean shit if you can't walk around and remind everyone about it, huh?" Jezz asked aloud, unable to hear her own voice under the beat of the music. She closed her eyes with a sigh, wishing she had a cigarette so that she could have released a long, dramatic drag to accent the burn she'd just given Granny.

Then the headphones flew off her head and Jezz's world went silent so quickly it was painful.

"Damn, what?!" Jezz roared, sitting up so quickly that she almost headbutted her father, who was holding her headphones in his hand and glaring at them as if the diluted thump of the music was a personal offense.

"Excuse me?" he asked, turning his disapproving glare to Jezz. Jezz rolled her eyes, but inwardly her heart sank. Her parents had left that afternoon for the formal reading of Granny's will, which Jezz had not been required to attend. Granny Nelson had made it public news that she didn't intend to leave anything to such an "unruly child," and Jezz was counting on them being gone for way longer. She glanced at her wristwatch and saw that it was only around a quarter to four, which meant that the evening was basically a bust.

"Your mother was calling you," her dad said sternly, as if his thinning hair and round glasses could intimidate anyone.

"Jessica?" Jezz's mom's voice floated in from the doorway, mousy and disembodied, and Jezz leaned over to see past her dad's shoulder. Sure enough, there was her mom with a huge paper bag nestled in her arms, shuffling into the room and glancing sideways at the band posters on the wall as if she were afraid they would literally swoop down and gobble her up. Jezz tolerated her mom better than most other members of her family, because at least she tended to yell less. But it killed Jezz the way her mom had folded in so perfectly with the family she'd married. Jezz had once discovered old pictures of her mom wearing daring colors and crop tops from back in the seventies, looking like someone who was far from the quiet good girl ideal that Granny had admired, like someone who was, well, more like Jezz. But it was like that woman had been absorbed by the ideal of Nelsonness: fifties elegance, sipping tea from china cups at two in the afternoon, and being too concerned with what everyone else thought of you. Even the clothes she was wearing that very moment—a paisley green dress with a fuzzy white cardigan—made Jezz want to vomit. She pointedly looked away as her mom sat down on the edge of the bed.

"Sorry, Mom," Jezz said, speaking so slowly and flatly that they would be able to tell she didn't mean it. "I didn't hear you."

"That's okay," her mom said, pushing a strand of brown hair behind her ear. Jezz wished she could have at least gotten that muddy brown for her own head instead of the firetruck red she'd inherited from her dad and, therefore, Granny Nelson. Red hair was "a signature" of their family according to her aunts, whatever the hell that meant. So, when Jezz had used Manic Panic on her sixteenth birthday to transform her obnoxious Ariel auburn into a sleek black, the shockwaves that had rippled up through her family had been so extreme she might as well have announced she was moving to Russia to take up ice fucking dancing.

"I just wanted to tell you that—"

"Ohhh, let me guess," Jezz said in the same flat tone, hoping they would take the hint and leave her alone. "Aunt Emma didn't get the china dishes she's been wanting for all of her existence. Drama."

"Granny Nelson left you something."

The words were so startling that for a moment, Jezz forgot

herself and looked straight at her mom. It couldn't be. Not after what had gone down between her and Granny.

"You don't deserve to be in this family, Jessica!"

A weird feeling rose in Jezz's throat, something that had to do with the way her mom was smiling so widely and the thought that Granny Nelson had actually remembered her in the will. Could it be that Granny had gone through some sort of deathbed regret? Granny had so much money that even a fraction of it to each grandchild would be more than enough to set them up nicely. Jezz could practically see herself holding a tall cup of something hot as she sat in front of an open window in a New York City apartment, studying music or poetry or something else equally interesting, something that she would, for once, be able to brag about whenever the family got together.

I could finally start my real life, she thought.

But just as the idea was getting so real she could smell it, her mom dropped the bulky brown bag into the center of Jezz's lap. Jezz stared at the bundle in disbelief, and all her big dreams rolled belly-up as she realized that this oversized lunch sack must be the thing left to her by Granny.

Not money or anything useful. A *thing.*

"Each grandchild was left a gift," her mom was explaining, still smiling that ridiculously wide grin. "According to the will, they're supposed to be distributed at Granny's funeral, but your dad and I thought it would be best if we just brought yours." The connotation was unspoken but still obvious: Jezz's parents weren't sure if they would be able to convince her to attend Granny's funeral, which was a good hunch on their part, as she had no intention of going. Sure enough, the name "JESSICA" was written at the top of the bag in Granny's tiny handwriting, and underneath, exactly the type of low blow message she expected from the old bitch: "Be mindful of how you present yourself."

It was insulting. Jezz really didn't want to open the bag, but both her parents were staring at her expectantly. If she wanted to go back to her music and sweet isolation, she would need to placate them. With a sigh, Jezz pulled open the top of the bag and glanced in, then started back when a pair of snappy green eyes looked back up at her.

"Oh, come on," she finally said as she realized what it was.

"Wow!" her mom said, reaching past Jezz to pull the doll out of the bag. "Look at this beautiful little lady."

"Beautiful" and "little" were not the first words Jezz would have chosen to describe the horrific piece of plastic in her mom's hands. The thing was uncomfortably huge, close to two feet long, wearing an ugly red and black plaid dress with a square white bib at the top. Its face was a creepy concoction of angles and freckles and diamond-shaped eyebrows, and on top of its head was the thing that had sparked the final feud between Jezz and Granny: bright red hair.

It had been two months ago that Granny had required—*required*, like she was the queen of England—her least favorite granddaughter to come to her house. Jezz had dyed her hair black less than twelve hours before, and already Granny had managed to discover the new form of insubordination like a police dog sniffing out dope.

Upon her arrival at what could only be described as the Nelson Palace, Granny had laid into Jezz immediately, whipping out insults so fast that she must have had them stored up for a long time.

"Why don't you want to be a functioning part of this family?" Granny Nelson had snapped. She was wearing a pink pantsuit with a small diamond necklace and was sitting in her favorite chair, her arms crossed, a tiny ball of cotton candy fury. Jezz imagined that the two of them must look like a demon and a unicorn facing off.

"Why don't you accept that someone can be a part of this family without listening to every word you say all the time?" Jezz fired back.

"You've always been disrespectful. Your clothes, your attitude, your hair...your hair! Why would you do this to yourself? Eh? Have you no shame? Don't you understand that people are watching? Embarrassing."

With every word Granny spoke, rage rose through Jezz like a flood, boiling and consuming and overwhelming, which was a hell of a lot easier than admitting the truth at the base of it all:

It hurt. A lot.

"Then I guess it's a good fucking thing you'll be dead soon and won't be able to see what I do anymore," Jezz had all but spat. At the use of the curse, Granny had turned as pink as her clothes.

"You don't deserve to be in this family, Jessica!" Granny Nelson had screamed, her voice breaking with the effort. "You think nothing matters. Your generation walks around without a care in the world, expecting that no one will notice you don't do a damn thing on your own!"

"You want me to do something?" Jezz had yelled back. "How's this? I'll get outta here. Kiss my ass, you raggety old hag."

The teacup of lukewarm chamomile, resting on the table by Granny's elbow, had sailed through the air and exploded at the ground by Jezz's feet. Jezz had hightailed it out of there while Granny was still looking for something else to lob, and that was the last time she had ever seen Granny or come close to any of her things. Until this very moment, that is.

The doll's eyes jiggled slightly each time it was moved, like they weren't attached firmly in its head. Jezz stared at the impish, upturned mouth laughing at some perpetual joke, and she turned cold with anger. It wasn't enough that Granny had been true to her word and cut Jezz out of the will, which she'd expected. No, she needed to leave her a piece of crap toy, something from her massive creepy collection of chachkas, so that every time she looked at it, Jezz would be reminded of just how much her own family didn't want her. Jezz's parents were babbling on and on about the doll, passing it between them like a couple of saps on Christmas. *It was a Brikette doll, a pretty thing, something she must have hand-picked, yadda, yadda, yadda.* They were probably so happy Jezz had even gotten something that they didn't notice how much of an insult it was.

"Whatever," Jezz snapped, interrupting her dad. "It's a doll.

I don't even like dolls."

"You should be more appreciative," her dad said, his voice thin and warning.

"Oh right, I'm sooooo thankful that I was given a big ugly hunk of plastic. Not."

"Jessica," her dad warned. The big vein on his head was starting to throb, so Jezz smirked and was satisfied when it pulsed even harder. It wasn't so long ago that she and her dad had been a totally gross daddy-daughter duo, the kind who hung out unironically and even had a shared favorite song—embarrassingly, it had been "Be My Baby" by the Ronnettes. But the first day she'd bought a CD from a band that actually understood what it felt like to be flawed, he'd wrinkled up his face as if the plastic case was assaulting his nose as well as his ears. From that point on, as Granny voiced her displeasure louder and louder, he'd sided with her over Jezz.

Whatever.

"Dear, please," Jezz's mom said, placing her hand calmingly on his arm. "Come on, we'll go reheat that casserole. Dinner will be in five minutes, Jessica." Jezz huffed and took the opportunity to scoop up the headphones that her dad had dropped in his excitement to handle the doll, snapping them back over her ears. The song had changed, but it was still Acid Bath, and the snarls and screams of the vocals drowned out anything further her dad might have had to say. Her mom, apparently noticing that Jezz wouldn't be adding anything further to the conversation, practically pulled her dad out of the room, and finally, Jezz was back to beautiful alone time.

Except now she wasn't alone.

The damn doll was still sitting on the corner of her bed, smirking at her with its condescending little smile, the very image of Granny Nelson, just in a plastic form. Jezz glared at it, then kicked its tiny butt and sent it tumbling through the air exactly like the teacup on her last day with Granny. It hit the opposite wall with a clack, but instead of breaking into a pile of plastic limbs, it somehow managed to land facing her, its green eyes bright and its smile still chippy.

Enough of that.

"All right, Granny," Jezz muttered as she rolled off her bed. "You wanted me to be out of your life; wish granted." She hoisted the doll up by the hair, then stopped and coughed. Whether it was because her mom's perfume had masked it or because she'd jostled something by kicking the doll, Jezz noticed a smell that she hadn't picked up on before. It was stale, the dusty stink of old Avon perfume in fancy bottles that had gone spoiled back in the days when poodle skirts were still in fashion, but with a warm and slightly fungal undertone that Jezz couldn't exactly pin down.

"Gross," she said, picking up her black and purple bottle of Anna Sui perfume and spritzing it into the room. "Figures she'd leave me something that's got mold all on the inside." Holding the doll out at arm's length, Jezz opened the door to her bedroom. By the bathroom at the end of the hall there was a laundry chute that opened directly into the basement below.

"Jessica!" her mom called from the kitchen. "Dinner's hot!"

"Yeah, I'm coming," Jezz called back. The chute door opened with a protesting squeak of old hinges, and Jezz lifted the doll to the lid. Its eyes rattled in its head the same way they had when her parents had taken it out of the bag. Jezz felt an unexpected flurry of discomfort break out on her arms in goosebumps as she looked at the toy in her hand, dangling above the open maw of the laundry chute, yet still smirking, its green eyes matching her own.

"Stop it," she told herself. "It's just plastic." And she knew it was true, but on a deeper level, the one that could raise the hair on the back of her neck, something felt very unnatural about those too-bright, too-focused eyes. An old ditty that she'd sometimes heard Granny Nelson hum came unbidden into her mind, lurching through her thoughts with the same irritating lilt of an ice cream truck's siren.

When Irish eyes are smiling, all the world seems bright and gay…

"Whatever." Jezz shook herself and dropped the doll. It disappeared down the metal throat, thudding and echoing dully until finally, she heard the crack of plastic hitting concrete. Jezz let go of the metal door and it snapped back shut.

Takes care of that.

"Are you coming?" her mom called again. Out of her peripheral vision Jezz saw her mom hovering between the end of the hall and the entrance to the main living area, clearly too impatient to actually wait the ten seconds that had passed since she'd last called. Jezz turned toward her, a sarcastic comment locked and loaded, but as they made eye contact, the breath in her throat went as dry as if she'd been sucked by the Mummy in that new Brendan Fraser movie.

It was not her mom at the end of the hall.

It was Granny Nelson.

Jezz opened her mouth to yell, but instead of forming anything intelligible, her jaw just hung with all the grace of a body from a scaffold, while a huffing wheeze came out of the back of her throat. It was Granny all right, her wrinkled mouth pinched together in a pickled leer of disgust.

She's alive, Jezz thought frantically. *She's been alive this whole time and it was all just a prank they were playing on me.*

But that wouldn't explain how the skin of Granny's face was grey and drooping from her skull in rubbery folds, the same texture as a grocery bag left windblown on the side of the road. Or how her eyes were sunken into her face, only open three quarters of the way as if she'd been half through a blink that had never come to completion. And although Jezz had seen her wear that tea-length silk grey dress a thousand and one times, she'd never before seen the limbs beneath the hem so bloated and discolored. It was as if all the liquid in her body had pooled down below the knees and was barely contained in the skin of Granny's legs, twin juice bags full of hellish purple Kool-Aid.

For a minute they both simply stood there. Then Granny's head rolled back, and Jezz saw the irises of the eyes, ridiculously bright under the colorless lids, roving until they focused in on the only other person in the hall: Jezz herself.

For the first time in months, and against all the laws of nature, Jezz and Granny Nelson were looking directly at each other.

Jezz tried to curse, but her breath was still wheezing out of her open mouth in a formless stream. It wasn't possible. It just wasn't. And yet here she was, the scourge of Jezz's life, the demon waiting in the wings. Granny lifted her hand and pointed at Jezz— one long bony finger of accusation, and that was when Jezz noticed the holes. Granny's arms were polka dotted with round cuts, each at least an inch in circumference and sliced deep enough to reveal that the layers of skin underneath her topcoat were moist and red.

Is that why they got a dress with long sleeves for the viewing? The thought flew through Jezz's horrified mind of its own accord and was gone just as quickly when Granny's swollen left leg moved, then her right.

She's coming, she's coming! Get out! But despite the terrified commands that her brain was giving, Jezz stayed rooted to the spot, staring gape-mouthed as Granny shuffled down the hallway without indenting the carpet or casting a shadow. The stink of something mildly sweet, and infinitely old, filled the space as Granny approached, and Jezz felt her legs go warm and wet as her bladder waved a flag of surrender.

"For goodness sake, Jessica, aren't you coming?" Jezz heard her mom say from what sounded like a thousand miles away, and a moment later there she was, a spatula in one hand, rounding the corner and fencing Granny Nelson in from behind.

That was the moment when her mom's expression should have broken into shards. She should have fallen away screaming from the unholy vision in the hallway. But she only looked confused as her eyes traveled from Jezz's face to the darker spot down her jean leg.

"Jessica?" she asked, her voice slow. "Are you all right?"

She didn't know exactly when it happened, but Jezz was suddenly aware that it was just her and her mom in the hallway. Granny Nelson had vanished. Jezz looked from her mom's puzzled face to the spot where Granny had been, and that was when understanding rose like bile up the back of her throat.

Despite looking directly at the apparition, her mom had not seen Granny Nelson.

"Oh shit," Jezz finally said. Every muscle in her neck felt taut enough to snap, and her voice was so thin it might as well have been traveling up from the depths of the ocean. Her mom took a tentative step forward, then another.

"What's going on?" she asked.

"I…" Jezz stammered. Her head was still swirling, and now the edges of her vision were speckled with spots as round as the bright fleshy holes that had been punched into Granny's arms.

It wasn't possible.

It couldn't be.

But it was.

"I got my period," she finally blurted. The tang of urine in the air outed her lie, but Jezz didn't wait around for her mom to react. She quickly turned back to her bedroom and shut herself in.

The moment she was alone, her throat opened up and Jezz took a gasp of air so deep that her chest shuddered. Her heart followed suit, banging a Jiffy pop morse code of fear that reverberated from her eardrums to her fingertips. How could it have happened? Granny Nelson was dead. And dead meant leaving family behind, not showing up randomly in their hallways.

But it seemed that being dead hadn't stopped Granny. Jezz looked at her room, at all the band posters of disembodied eyeballs and hovering monsters, and she wanted to laugh hysterically but couldn't manage more than a moan. The thing that had been at the end of the hallway had none of the cool aesthetics that Jezz found fascinating and her family found offensive. What had been at the end of the hallway was an abomination.

Jezz's hands were shaking so badly she could barely undo the top button of her jeans, let alone the zipper. She changed into a new pair of pants without looking at them, too overwhelmed with what she had just seen to process what her hands were doing.

Maybe you imagined it. She knew immediately that this explanation was wrong. Even after the most intense and immersive dreams, waking up made those images fade into a muted pastel story with only the occasional focused detail. They were nowhere near as real as it had seemed in the moment. But Jezz was wide awake now, and still she could recall the engorged veins crisscrossing down Granny's legs, and the way her hair had been piled tightly on top of her head the way she usually wore it when she was going to an important function, and the fact that her dead eyes were coated in peach eyeshadow that would have been subdued if her skin had still held a living hue.

Mom said she was found sitting in her chair, with her makeup all done. Jezz didn't understand how it was possible, but she knew that the Granny she had seen had been the same one her aunt Lydia had found when she'd let herself into Granny's house that day. And there was no way that Jezz could have known what Granny had looked like.

No, she hadn't imagined it. Granny had shown up and then disappeared just as quickly, that much was certain.

But it's over now. Maybe Granny had just been taking one last opportunity to ruin Jezz's life before hopping on the elevator to the hot place. It would certainly fit her M.O., showing up and terrifying the one undeserving member of the family, then probably laughing about it with all her new harpy demon pals.

"Did you see when she pissed herself? That was classic!" Yes, that had to be it. Granny just had to get in one last jab to remind Jezz that even though she was dead, she still didn't approve of her.

"Figures." Jezz felt better, but the moment she opened the door to her room and saw the hallway, her limbs tightened so severely she might as well have been a wind-up toy. She took a deep breath and then stuck her head out, looking left toward the bathroom and then right toward the living room.

The hallway was empty.

Jezz forced herself to walk slowly, casually inserting her hands into her pockets and pretending that nothing had happened as she stepped over the dark spot on the carpet.

Shit. I'll have to clean that later. She made her way to the table, where her mom was carefully spooning out a casserole that consisted of some sort of macaroni noodle with brown sauce. At the sight of her mom quietly handing out dishes and her dad adding butter to the toast, Jezz was filled with a push to tell them everything that had just happened, to let herself be comforted by their normalcy and reassured by the logic that they would certainly supply.

Who are you kidding? If she dared to tell them that Granny Nelson, their goddess, had come back as a disgusting ghost, they would either ship her straight off to the looney bin or do what they did best: side with Granny and say that Jezz had deserved it somehow, because of course she did.

Dinner was always a dull event, with her mom trying valiantly to fill in the silences by chattering about her day, or bits of exciting news she'd read, while Jezz picked at her food and her dad blabbered about politics. Tonight was no different, so Jezz was playing Edgecrusher in her head—*"Conceived in a hell / beyond your depth of perception"*—when her dad's voice brought her crashing back to reality.

"It's what Granny Nelson would want." The phrase itself was pathetically commonplace in Jezz's household, but at the mention of the name, Jezz suddenly saw the rotting, sagging face in her mind as clearly as if she were seeing it again in person, and she started so harshly that she rattled her dinner plate.

"My goodness, no need to be so dramatic," her mom chided. "Your dad was only saying you should consider it."

"Huh?" Jezz looked from one parent to the other. It was obvious from their attentive faces that they'd been telling her something and she'd missed it. Her dad sighed.

"The funeral," he said. "Granny's. I know you two weren't close, but it's a family thing. A way to start the next chapter right and pay your respects."

Pay my respects? Jezz didn't know whether to roll her eyes or gag herself with a spoon. Given what she'd seen just a short while beforehand, she didn't feel like Granny deserved any particular form of respect.

"She wouldn't want respect from me," Jezz said.

"Jessica, that's a terrible thing to say," her mom said. "She was your granny!"

"Yeah, and she hated me."

"No, she didn't," her dad broke in, lowering his fork. The polished silver hadn't even touched the tablecloth when two cold, heavy weights settled evenly onto Jezz's shoulders. She glanced down, then the breath stood still in her chest.

There were hands on her shoulders, and they were dead. The skin had shrunk so much that it was peeling back from the colorless nails, giving them the effect of hawk talons, with the tips painted a cheery pink, digging into prey. The smell was everywhere all of a sudden, crawling up Jezz's nose and watering her eyeballs, digging into every pore of her body with its awful stale rottenness. Jezz tried not to look up, but she couldn't help it.

At this close vantage point, Jezz could see that Granny's mouth didn't look pickled and wrinkled because of her expression, but because her red painted lips had shrunken so much that her teeth were imprinting through the skin. Her eyes, still frozen in their barely opened position, were fixed on Jezz's face with a gleam of cold triumph.

"Huhhhnnnnmmmm," Jezz moaned.

"Jessica? Are you all right?" her dad asked. Jezz's head felt unnaturally heavy as she looked back at her parents, who were watching her with expressions of mild alarm. The ridiculous normalcy of the moment was so shocking it was almost comedic, and Jezz barked a sharp, frightened squeal of laughter that made both her parents jump.

"Hey. What's going on?" her mom asked, leaning forward to look at Jezz's face. Granny Nelson squeezed, and Jezz gasped as a harsh coldness dug down through her, radiating inwards until her shoulders felt so heavy that they should have ripped free from her body and left her nothing more than a head on a bloody spinal column. Her parents were looking at her, looking at each other, then looking back at her, somehow managing to not see Granny, because of course they didn't. It was always just Jezz that everyone looked at, Jezz that they waited to watch as she screwed up and went down in flames.

Adrenaline suddenly kicked in, a getaway car that was late to the rendezvous point, and Jezz launched herself up from the table with a shriek. Her parents stood with her, gaping, but she couldn't even look at them. Granny Nelson's hands still hovered over Jezz's chair, twitching slightly as they looked for something else to manage, and she opened her lips in what would probably have been a leer if she could have managed to get her lips to still do that.

"Leave me alone!" Jezz shrieked, and she no longer cared whether she appeared cool and aloof or if she sobbed like a little kid. All she knew was that Granny's raw arms had rings of white mold along the cusps of the cuts, and her death stink was mixing with the smell of the casserole that was cooling on the table, and all the things that Jezz liked and that Granny had despised as classless were not nearly as fucked up as this. "I know you hate me! I know it would be better for the family if I were dead instead! But leave me alone, shit, please!"

"Jessica…" Her mom's voice sounded choked and strange, but Jezz had no time to spare for investigation. She bolted, the house blurring past in beige streaks, and the smell of Granny receding, as she raced back to her room and slammed the door behind her, locking it and then barricading it with her nightstand. Granny had never appeared in this room before; maybe she couldn't or wouldn't.

Jezz slid to her knees and gasped. It wasn't just that she was shaking; every atom from her hair through her bone marrow was trembling. It wasn't possible. It wasn't fair. And yet it was true. Granny Nelson's appearance hadn't been a fluke or a bitch's last hoorah. Granny Nelson was back, and it seemed like she intended to stay.

For a few moments, Jezz did nothing but breathe, trying to calm herself down. Her brain was tumbling with all the grace of a cotton candy machine, and she would need to chill if she was going to figure out what to do. By the time Jezz's thoughts slowed enough for her to put them in order, she'd stopped gasping but still hadn't been able to control the shaking. Her shoulders burned with cold where Granny had touched her, so she forced herself up to the mirror, where she took off her shirt to examine herself. Beside her two black bra straps, her skin appeared exactly how it always did: specked with tiny brown freckles, unevenly pink, but overall normal despite the ache that filled her arms whenever she tried to move them.

"What the heck?" she whispered, though it came out in a jumble of syllables: "wathhk." She needed to figure something out, because boy howdy did she have a problem. She couldn't live like this.

Okay. She's been dead for a while. Never showed up before. What happened today? The reading of the will? The...the doll. As soon as the plastic monstrosity came into her mind's eye, Jezz realized her utter stupidity. She was as bad as one of the white girls in a horror movie, the screaming bimbos in tank tops who'd be killed off only a half hour or so into the film. She'd accepted a gift from a dead person who'd hated her and had not only brought it into her house, she'd moved it somewhere less accessible.

"Shit!" she said, her reflection in the mirror mouthing the word back to her. What was she supposed to do now?

On autopilot, she turned away from the mirror and toward the closet to get her pajamas. She'd found the oversized green shirt and drawstring black pants at a thrift store during the winter, and for some reason putting them on always helped her calm down and think more clearly, which she certainly needed to do if she was to keep from going crazy. She pulled back the accordion door and reached for the peg where she always hung her PJs, and that was when the smell hit her.

Old perfume.

Rotten meat.

Granny.

Jezz reared away from the closet, tripping over her own feet and falling so hard on her ass that dull pain thumped up her spine.

Granny Nelson's long arm, looking more like it belonged on a moth-eaten coat than a human, inched its way from the closet opening and pushed the folding door entirely open. There she was again, the same bulbous legs and ruined hands, the same death mask of makeup stamped onto flaccid skin.

The smell was overwhelming in the closed bedroom, itching down the back of Jezz's throat and turning it raw as she inched herself backwards. Granny lifted her hand again, and this time the long, accusing finger settled on Jezz's dresser.

Jezz looked from Granny to the dresser, then back again.

"Wha…what the hell do you want?" she asked, her voice no more than a shrill exhale.

Granny's tight lips parted slightly, and though the rusty squeal that came out was no word that Jezz could identify, she understood its meaning immediately.

Granny did not appreciate her choice of words. She took a step out of the closet.

"No!" Jezz gasped, scooting herself all the way across the room until she bumped into her dresser. As the drawers rattled over Jezz's head, Granny stopped. She lifted her hand again and insistently jabbed at the space past Jezz's shoulder.

Unable to think of anything else, Jezz reached up and pulled open the first drawer she could find. She plunged her hand in and closed her fingers around the first thing she managed to touch: something cold and soft that didn't feel familiar despite the fact that it was in her drawer. Granny's eyes—*Irish eyes are smiling*—stared down coldly as Jezz pulled out a pink silky girly nightgown, which her mom had bought for her years ago and which she'd never worn.

Jezz stared at the delicate thing, so posh and ditzy and absolutely ugly against her black-painted fingernails. Why the hell did she even have it still? She looked back up at Granny, who turned her hand toward the brown paper bag that the doll had been delivered in, still crumpled at the base of Jezz's bed.

Her thoughts turned to what Granny had written. *"Be mindful of how you present yourself."*

No way. Granny didn't come back to tell me how to dress. In her mind, Jezz saw herself summoning all the disdain and rebellion she'd spent the past few years practicing and getting up, storming across the room to rip open the closet door and grab her pajamas, all while flipping Granny a nice solid bird.

Do it. Tell her she can't control you now any more than she did when she was breathing.

But in reality, her arms and legs might as well have been filled with concrete mooring her to the ground, and every hair on her head was stiff with fear. Jezz wasn't aware of exactly when tears had begun pouring down her face, but they came in earnest as she realized that she couldn't bring herself to get up.

"Hey, hon?" The sudden sound of her dad's voice, accompanied by a light knock at the door, seemed like something from another world. "Can we talk?" Jezz turned her head slowly to look at the door, her movement mirrored by Granny. It seemed like years ago that she'd been sitting between her parents, not daring to risk telling them what she'd seen.

What an idiot. Even if they didn't believe her, she should have at least tried.

Jezz rolled onto her knees, trying to move as slowly as possible, but Granny noticed. Her head snapped back toward Jezz, the thick neck beneath it popping with a wet crack that made Jezz gag. Granny took a decisive step forward, and Jezz fell back onto her butt, clutching the pink nightgown to her chest as if it were a blessed cloth that could ward off the monster at hand.

"Jessica, we're not mad or anything," her dad's voice continued through the door. "That stuff you said, I just...maybe I've been too hard on you, you know? The stress of Granny's...well, it doesn't matter. Bottom line is, I don't want you to think we hate you. I know we don't agree on a lot, but...you're a good kid."

Granny shook her head, and a wave of her dull hair flopped emphatically against the side of her head to emphasize her point: *That's wrong. We do hate you. You don't belong.* Jezz squeezed her eyes shut.

"I'm sorry if we haven't been listening very well lately. So, let's change that. Just come out when you're ready."

With that, receding footsteps told Jezz that her dad had left. For a moment she stayed as she was, listening to the complete silence in the room, and then she carefully opened an eye.

"Shi-shit!" Granny's face was right in her own, so close that Jezz could see the fluid that had dried around her eyelids. Granny stabbed her finger down at the nightgown, her meaning clear.

Jezz heard the sob coming out of her mouth rather than felt it, as she put both arms into the sleeves of the nightgown and raised it over her head. The satin was so slick and cold against her limbs that she might as well have been slipping into an amphibian's skin, and the collar was tight over her head, a younger kid's fit.

"I'm trying, Granny," Jezz gasped as she tried to shove her face out through the too-small hole. What if Granny grabbed her neck with those frozen hands? Or tried to punish her for taking too long by staying in the room all night? "I'm trying, hang on!" Finally, she managed to pop her face out to freedom.

The bedroom was empty.

Jezz stood, the pink nightgown rolling itself down across her torso as she looked around. There was no one in sight, so she slowly walked to her closet and, taking a deep breath, glanced into the racks of hanging clothes, expecting at any moment to see Granny's sunken eyes watching her over the sleeve of a hoodie.

But there was nothing. Jezz turned and tumbled onto her bed, gasping as if she hadn't been breathing for the past few minutes, which she very well might not have been. Between panting for air and all but drowning under the twin waterfalls still pouring silently down her face, Jezz found herself immersed in awful technicolor clarity. Granny hadn't been able to control her in life, so she'd worked up some horrible scheme to control Jezz from beyond the grave, something that had to do with the gift of that awful doll. If Jezz didn't always have Granny's choices and Granny's preferences at the front of her mind for each and every decision, she would risk seeing her everywhere. Could she develop a tolerance to seeing that dead face at every turn? She didn't think so, not before it drove her to a padded cell. She'd have to spend her whole life glancing over her shoulder for Granny's approval, her sanity rotting along with Granny as she eventually deteriorated from ashen corpse to worm infested flesh to grinning skeleton. Jezz's life wouldn't be her own anymore, but what else could she do?

Run away.

The thought slipped into her head as smoothly as a shot of creamer sifting through coffee. Could she outrun Granny? If she got to a place where being a Nelson didn't matter because no one knew her name, would she be left alone? It was an idea she'd toyed with before, though never with any real fire, but now the possibility opened firm and real in front of her.

I can run away. No more Granny. I don't have to be a Nelson anymore.

What other possibilities were there? To go downstairs in the dark and try to find the doll and destroy it before Granny Nelson destroyed her? Not an option unless she was crazy. It would be better this way, anyhow. She'd always been the odd man out, the screwup, the least favorite of all the members of the family. Maybe once she broke free, she could find a place she belonged, with people who actually wanted her.

Jezz got up, not daring to change out of the nightgown lest it bring Granny down upon her. She pulled on her sturdiest combat boots, slipped her wallet and a lighter she'd swiped from Uncle James into the pockets of her jeans, and grabbed her backpack. She didn't need to pack much, just enough to get her a bus ride or so away. After that, she could stop at the first mall she saw and buy some new clothes with the money she'd been saving. A sick feeling lined her stomach as she loaded the bag with underwear and socks, a few pairs of shorts, and some black tank tops. For years she'd dreamed of being on her own, free from the expectations she couldn't meet and didn't want to. She'd imagined it being empowering, a well-planned exit with her finest possessions tucked away neatly in her bag as she slipped out the window in her most daring

21

outfit. Perhaps there would be a short but impactful note left behind—*Mom and Dad: we all know it's best for everyone if I move on. Don't look for me*—and then she would walk to the bus stop with cool, determined strides.

Jezz caught her reflection in the mirror, and the sight disgusted her. There were sooty lines down her face from where her eyeliner had run, and the combination of the awful pink nightgown over her black skinny jeans was like an exquisite corpse sewn together by two completely different but equally insane people. She was a mess, plain and simple.

And it seemed like that was how she was going to leave her life behind, crawling off into the darkness with all the finesse of a wounded creature that had been tagged by its hunter. The delinquent of the family, proving correct everyone who didn't expect anything of her.

It's fine, she silently told her reflection. *You've never belonged here anyway.*

But she couldn't tear herself away from the mirror, from those big green eyes and the red roots coming in at the top of her head. She'd never be able to escape who she was, no matter how far she ran.

Bottom line is, I don't want you to think we hate you. Nothing could be further from the truth. I know we don't agree on a lot, but…you're a good kid. Her dad's words, which she'd heard but not really processed, came back, and she absorbed their impact for the first time. The backpack slipped from her hand as Jezz and her reflection stared open mouthed at each other.

Did he really say that? She couldn't remember the last time her dad had complimented her. A warmth curled in her chest, something tight and new but not entirely uncomfortable.

Holy shit, Jezz thought. The realization came fully formed and roaring in her ears, and she saw just what an idiot she was being. She'd been blaming her family for listening to Granny the whole time, but she'd been doing the same thing, letting herself be convinced that she was pointless and embarrassing and that her family would never accept her.

Why is Granny the only one who gets to decide what it means to be a Nelson? she asked herself. She had no answer, but Jezz no longer needed one.

Granny was dead. It was time for things to change.

JEZZ DIDN'T EVEN bother to change her clothes, because if she took too long to think about what she had to do, the nerve that she'd managed to scrape together would fall apart faster than a Jenga tower. So, despite the way her stomach was twisting over itself like a dirty dishrag, wringing anxiety out over her insides, Jezz opened the window to her bedroom and slipped outside.

It was still decently bright, which was typical for a summer evening, but entirely wrong considering what Jezz had to do. She knew there was no way to make it to the basement stairs inside the house without her parents seeing her, but the window above the storage room was always left unlocked and could be easily accessed from the side of the house. Jezz could slip in, grab the doll, destroy Granny's gift, and then hopefully Granny would go with it. If not, Jezz was well and truly fucked.

Jezz's heart jumped back into its machine-gun fire of fear as she snuck around the side of the house, keeping low and close to the wall just in case one of her parents happened to look outside. She knew with the certainty of a rat in a trap that Granny would be waiting for her once she got into the basement and that Granny wouldn't go without a fight.

But it's her or me. She knelt as she reached the window and slowly leaned forward to look into the basement. She would have bet all the money she owned that Granny's dead face would be peering directly out at her, or that maybe she'd be standing dramatically in a corner, but there was nothing. Jezz could easily see the entire basement, which was lined with several storage shelves filled with odds and ends that were too old fashioned to use and somehow also in too good of shape to throw away. In the center of the room was her mom's workout mat, where she sometimes followed Jane Fonda exercise routines, and beyond that, the washer and dryer. There was a pile of laundry beside the washer and the doll was on top, somehow sitting upright although Jezz was positive she'd straightened its legs in order to fit it down the hole. Of course, it was staring directly at her.

Jezz tightened the laces on her boots. She'd watched many scary movies in her time, and although every one of those had its main characters sneaking silently through killer territory, none of those villains had been a ghostly grandma. Jezz's entire plan was to get in, run for it, and get the hell out.

The window opened with a gentle creak, and Jezz lowered herself in feet first. The minute her feet hit the floor, she regretted every choice she'd made that had ever led her to this moment, but it was now or never. Before she could think about it too much, Jezz forced herself to run, arms pumping and boots slamming loudly against the floor as she propelled herself toward the doll.

One stride. Two. She could make out the doll's nasty little smirk, like it was in on a secret. The third and fourth strides brought her to the edge of the washing machine, and the fifth stride was when the familiar stink hit her.

Jezz reached for the doll, but the cold that rose up to meet her slammed into her so violently that she fell backward, too shocked to even scream. She hit the floor with a teeth-rattling thud and the world started to spin. Before it could settle, Granny appeared over her, her mouth ripped open in a wide grimace of fury that had torn back the bloodless skin at the corners of her mouth and allowed Jezz to see way too far back into the rubbery black gums. Granny pressed both palms against Jezz's chest, and the same frigid blocks that had hurt her shoulders earlier were now pressing themselves into her lungs with the painful ferocity of a thousand tiny arctic mice eating her alive. A tingling numbness rose up in answer from somewhere deep inside, and Jezz knew that if she didn't get out now, things could get a lot worse.

She threw herself to the right, rolling across the floor blindly without any sense of direction, and she barked in pain as she came up hard against one of the storage shelves. Jezz was shivering from the cold that was still holding court in her chest, but it was now or never. She got to her feet and faced the laundry pile, where Granny was standing over the doll with all the protective ferocity of a mama bear. Granny glared down at Jezz, a scowl of hatred and disgust, and Jezz gave the same look right back.

"Fuck you," she said.

This time when Granny leapt at her, Jezz was prepared for the cold and threw herself into it, gasping as the chill rolled into her lungs and scratched at her throat, but not stopping until she slid to a halt by the doll. Jezz grabbed it by its Nelson-red hair and then, without looking to even see where Granny was, broke into the only running away she planned on doing. The basement window closed in on her pounding vision and Jezz leapt up toward the opening, dragging the doll with her into the sunlight.

Jezz didn't know if Granny could follow her outside the house or not, but she didn't intend to find out. She picked up the doll and ripped its dress off to look for a weak point, then blinked in surprise. Its lower abdomen was criss-crossed with sloppy incisions that had been covered over with Caucasian putty, as if someone had broken it open and then drunkenly put it back together.

Drunk, or bleeding to death. Finally, Jezz could fit in the last little puzzle piece, the one that made the least sense of all the horrific nonsense she'd endured that day: what had happened to Granny's arms? It was a gift within a gift, a bag with a doll and a little piece of Granny at the deepest level, ensuring that she would always be able to come back.

As the cold came up again from behind, Jezz stood up and slammed the thick heel of her boot into the doll's stomach. With a sharp crack it broke along the incisions, revealing a Barbie-sized burger patty of slimy grey meat with white mold dotting the top layer of wrinkled skin. The smell of human rot came up thick and awful, a stink of roadkill and nightmares that Jezz knew

25

immediately she would never be able to forget. She pulled out the lighter from her jeans, spun the flame into life, and dropped it into the doll's open body. The piece of flesh lit up quickly, burning bright red before turning black and shriveling into nothing.

Jezz would have appreciated a ghostly shriek or dramatic scene in which Granny fell back into the ether before popping out of existence on the earthly plane, but there was nothing. The cold simply ceased, replaced by the heat of a summer evening, and when Jezz turned around, there was nothing coming up behind her. Jezz picked up the doll carefully, holding it out at arm's length. After some internal debate about whether or not to throw it out (too great a chance it might be discovered) or hide it somewhere off the property (no particular place came to mind), she took her lead from what she'd seen in *Child's Play 2* and buried the carcass underneath her old swing, which she hadn't used in years but which was still grassless from all the time she'd spent dragging her feet over it.

When it was done, Jezz sat down on the swing and rocked gently on her heels. The sun had set, so there was no worry of being seen by anyone as she focused on breathing in and out, trying to steady the shaking in her hands. She really wanted to just go inside, lie down on her waterbed, and turn up some sick tunes. But if her gift and the number of cuts on Granny's arms had been any indication, she had more work to do.

THANKFULLY, NO ONE had removed the spare key to Granny's house from the tacky garden angel statue in the backyard. Jezz let herself in and quickly rooted through rooms that were being boxed up by her parents and aunts, finally locating what she needed in the kitchen. There, on the counter, were ten brown paper bags of different shapes and sizes.

Ten? Jezz was shocked. This meant that Granny had a critique for each and every one of the cousins, not just her, which seemed impossible, as they were basically perfect. Jezz picked up the closest bag and read its inscription.

"JIMMY- Remember to practice self-control." Her cousin, Jimmy, was overweight, but Jezz had never thought it mattered to Granny because he was studying to be a lawyer, which was basically the dream of every family.

"TIFFANY- One never did any harm by applying one's self to higher ambitions." Tiffany, the nicest of the cousins and popular among everyone who knew her, was quite content in her job as a grocery store cashier.

Everywhere Jezz looked there was a critique for a cousin she'd dismissed as being Granny's favorite. And given that there was a gift to accompany each little warning, it seemed that Jezz wasn't the only one for whom Granny wanted to take corrective measures. She smiled to herself. It probably wasn't the nicest thing for her to be glad that her cousins were just as big a disappointment to Granny as she was, but given the favor she was doing for them, Jezz was pretty sure it was justified.

Jezz carried the bags one by one to a big metal can outside that Granny had used to burn leaves during the autumn season. When everything was inside, she lit it up, then sat a good distance away and watched as it burned, breathing through her mouth to avoid the smell. Her aunts and uncles would surely wonder what had come of the gifts from Granny, but they'd get over it.

Jezz only left when she was positive that there was nothing left in the can except for ash. As she walked back to her own house, she saw that the porch lights were on, and she was about to sneak through the darkness to her bedroom window when she decided against it.

I'll never actually belong if I continue behaving like I don't.

Jezz opened the front door and let herself in. Her mom and dad were watching television, their faces glowing pale in the darkness, and as she entered, they looked at her as if they'd seen a ghost.

If only they knew what *that* was like.

"Jessica!" her dad said, his voice high with alarm. He looked toward the bedrooms and then back at her. "Where did…did you sneak out?"

"What are you wearing?" her mom asked, then seemed to think better of her question. "Are you all right?"

There was too much to explain, and Jezz had no idea where to begin. But for the first time in a long time, she didn't think she would entirely mind sharing.

THE MAGENTA ROOM

Jeremy Megargee

"HI KIDS, SEDGWICK SUGARPLUM HERE, and how I love to see you all visiting me in the Magenta Room!"

It's a warm and vibrant room, the walls that special blend of red and purple, and there are flowers all over, huge and intricate floral arrangements to add additional life to the scene. Tulips, daisies, orchids, all manner of sweet-smelling growing things, and Sugarplum cavorts among them, bending down to smell each one, greeting the flowers like old familiar friends.

Sugarplum is dressed in a canary yellow zoot suit with a silky black bowtie, and his hair is a shining platinum blond color, glossed back on his head with some kind of gel or product. It's immaculate, almost too perfect, looking a bit like some shiny helmet plastered across his scalp.

His skin tone fits his name, for it's plum-like, his cheeks rosy with rouge, a layer of dewy foundation beneath, and his lips are big and red. When he smiles, his teeth look just a little big in the gums. They're incredibly white and artificial, like a new pair of dentures fitted just a tad bit improperly.

His eyes are like marbles, and they're expressive, rolling around in the sockets, and when the lighting of the set touches them, the irises look golden. He cuts quite a figure, shimmying from side to side, big hands covered in little white theater gloves, and once his introduction jig is complete, he settles into a firm stance in front of the camera with his hands resting on his hips.

"We thank the sun for shining, we thank the flowers for growing, and we thank the sky for being so perfectly blue! It's good to appreciate life, children. Life is precious. We only get one life, and we have to make it count. Can I share a fun thing with you all that I love to do?"

He smiles that big wholesome grin, and he kneels down, taking a rose into his gloved fingertips. He brings it to his nose, and the camera zooms in. He has large pores, and for a split second, we can see a fly crawling across one of his eyelashes. He blinks, and then it lifts off and is gone.

"I like to smell the roses. I like to get down low with the growing things and spend a special moment just letting that fragrance drift up into my big ol' nose! It's a nice feeling. It's like smelling the world. Smelling all the things in the world that are alive…"

Sugarplum stares at the camera pointed at him. He is smiling, and his eyes smile too. The eyelids are creased, and little wrinkles jut out across his face when he grins, cutting furrows into the stage makeup that coats his features.

"Every single one of my little Plum Pals watching this right now, always remember that you're a person, and it's pretty darn neat to be a person. Take a breath, and feel your lungs! Press a thumb to your wrist, and you see that blue thing there, that snaky thing under your skin? It's a vein, and it's full of blood! You're all full of blood, children. It's the red water of life…"

He rises, and we pan backward, seeing more of the Magenta Room. There's a large oak tree puppet in the corner, and it sways from side to side. It has huge sad puppy dog eyes, a frowning mouth across its trunk, and roots that curl up like the ends of a tapered skirt.

"Isn't it swell to be alive, Agatha Oak?"

The oak tree puppet opens its mouth, and from the vast blackness, a sweet child voice emanates.

"Are we really alive, Sedgwick Sugarplum?"

There's the slightest twitch in Sugarplum's smile. It fades out like a flickering lightbulb. The fly is back, and it crawls across Sugarplum's slicked back hair before darting off again. When the smile returns, he turns up the wattage even more, making it especially bright.

"Of course we are, silly goose! I'm as fit as a fiddle and how about I climb up into your branches and give you a shake? Maybe that would make you less glum, Agatha Oak."

There's a sigh from the tree puppet. Long and deep, almost wistful.

"Sorry, Sedgwick. It is very fun to be alive."

"Sure is. Indubitably! Well, children, that's all the time we have for today. Won't you do your buddy Sedgwick Sugarplum a favor and skip through a meadow for me today? Smell the daisies! But you must never ever pick them! To pick a flower makes it dead. Dead things are glum, and they never have fun."

He starts his dance again, this time an outro jig, and there's the slightest rattle from the inside of his zoot suit. It sounds like old bones shifting together, clacking and brittle. It's hard to tell how old Sugarplum is. With his thick makeup and his garish clothing, he seems ageless.

The feed fizzles out, and the Magenta Room becomes white noise.

I THINK I was about six years old when I first saw that show. It came on some local cable access channel that no one ever watched, and it only lasted a few minutes each time. It always started with the host in that room with the magenta walls, all those pots full of flowers, and there'd be some little lesson or moral, and then the episode would end. There was never a schedule for when it would come on, and I don't even remember ever seeing it in the TV guide when I became a teen. If memory serves, it would often be on the old dinosaur of a television set we had in our living room when I'd wake up to pee at around two a.m. My dad would be asleep in the recliner with a few Guinness bottles next to him after a twelve-hour shift at the paper mill, and the show would be on. I'd sneak over and watch it for a bit before going back to bed. There were never any commercials after, and no other show would come on to replace it. It would just fade out into gray static.

The episodes were meant to be lighthearted and cheery, but certain little details would stand out to me, and they always appeared out of place. There seemed to always be a fly or two buzzing around Sugarplum. Sometimes his skin wouldn't look so good, like the makeup artist didn't fully cover it, and the flesh beneath was jaundiced.

Other times, the puppets he would talk to would not talk back, and one time, when he tried to banter with a puppet called Turtle Tim, it started to cry from within the puppet suit.

It was a weird show, and when I got older, I started to think about it again. There are times in life when you become an adult and get that burst of nostalgia to seek something out that you remember from your childhood. Sedgwick Sugarplum and the Magenta Room happened to be one of those things for me. So I started doing internet research about it, but there was literally nothing online. There wasn't a Wikipedia page, an IMDb listing, or any information at all that I could readily access. I tried searching for the identity of the actor who played Sugarplum, and that was a total dead-end. Almost every search engine failed me.

But then I tried TOR, and I explored the dark web. I came across a single post on some obscure forum. It seemed to be from this nutcase of a woman, and she must have been a little girl back when she saw the show. She said that she received a letter to be a member of the studio audience about thirty-seven years ago. The invitation provided her with an address, and her mother and father drove her there when she was just a kid. The address took them to a cemetery outside of the city limits. The place was overgrown and seemingly returning to nature. There was a rickety caretaker's house practically rotting down to nothing in the center of the cemetery, shutters busted, front door splintered halfway in, and graffiti marking the skeletal drywall in the hallways. Her dad did a walkthrough of the house, and he found it to be totally empty, not a soul in sight. They assumed it was a prank and left.

This woman claims that she kept getting letters from the show after that. Vicious and cruel letters, the tone fully changed. Her post states that she still receives them sporadically, about one letter per decade. Mocking her for not being in the audience. Calling her cowardly and small of heart. Telling her that she missed her chance and that the Magenta Room is only for those that truly believe. Kids that don't hide under the shadow of parents. Kids excited about life and adventure. Special children who know to smell the tulips without picking them...

It all read like paranoid nonsense to me, something a conspiracy theorist would write, but I noticed that on the thread, some anonymous user had left a link with a few video files uploaded of old episodes, and I wasted no time in downloading them. It was just about satisfying a curiosity.

I started to watch them, and it opened forgotten gates in my head, memories that had fizzled and faded into static during my boyhood.

"WHY DO FRIENDS leave?"

Sugarplum looks sad, a frown causing deep grooves to attack his face. There are so many creases across his skin, and the makeup is very noticeable, almost blotchy.

"We have petunias, and birdsong, and we're safe here, so why go anywhere else?"

The camera is zoomed in on his face, almost uncomfortably so. For a brief second, it looks like something white squiggles in his nostril. He brings up a silken pink handkerchief, and he blows his nose before making it vanish into an inner pocket of his suit. It had to have just been a little dollop of snot. That could not have been a maggot...

"I don't like being alone, children. Time is long when you're alone. You'll stay with me, won't you? We'll walk hand in hand through the bluebells. Wouldn't you like that?"

The camera pans backward, and we see that he's brushing his fingertips against a large teddy bear puppet's head. The puppet doesn't move or react to his touch, and the fur looks rough, slightly moldy. The limbs droop at the puppet's side, and Sugarplum lifts them, shaking them from side to side, trying to dance with it. He chuckles to himself, letting the arms drop, and he skips back to the forefront of the set.

"I always love to meet new Plum Pals. And if you come, guess what? You can have Bradley Bear's honey! It's fresh and gooey and yum yum yum, and he left it behind, so he won't need it anymore. Stick out your tongue, here comes heaven!"

Sugarplum rubs his belly, and there are some liquid noises from inside. It's like a barrel sloshing full of water. A quirky sound effect, perhaps?

He waves, exaggerating his hand movements, ears flopping from side to side.

"Bye! Hope to see ya, and remember, there's always magic in the Magenta Room!"

I'VE BEEN BINGING the old episodes. There's a reoccurring theme where Sugarplum will talk to one of the big puppet suits, and it won't talk back. Sometimes the puppet suits will look old and musty, like they've been sitting there unattended for years. When he goes to a puppet that does talk back, it sounds scared; almost like the little kid voice coming from within is warbled and fake. Someone trying very hard to sound like a child…

There's this element of the bizarre that I just can't shake. It's literally eating at me. I've always been the type to want to unravel a mystery, and I feel like this is calling to me for some reason. I keep pausing it at that part where I saw the white thing squirming in Sugarplum's nostril. What the fuck was that? Like, seriously?

I thought about it a bit, and taking what I know from that post on the forum, I was able to piece together the location of the cemetery the woman supposedly went to. There are two active cemeteries in the city, both normal and kept in serviceable shape, but the map of my area shows one green section on the outer rim that I've driven past before but never explored. It's on a little backroad that doesn't really go anywhere, and all you can see from the road is a busted gate grown over with kudzu. If you're passing by, you wouldn't even realize there were headstones or a house beyond it, as the foliage is just too thick and wild.

I never do stuff like this, but I have to go there. This thirst for curiosity feels like it's not going to abate until I've seen the area for myself. I know this is real life, and I'm not going to find anything but a few forsaken graves and maybe a derelict house, if it hasn't already collapsed in on itself since the last time this woman claims she was there. There can't be anything beyond that gate that actually pertains to some odd kid's show that barely anyone has seen or would care about, but why not check it out?

I want to know why most of those puppets don't move or talk. I want to know why Sugarplum's skin doesn't look right sometimes. Where is the Magenta Room? Where's the actual set?

Too many questions, but I can't help myself…

I ARRIVED AT night, thinking that lurking around during the daylight hours might draw attention if there actually is someone monitoring the property. I expected the gate to be locked, but it was corroded and choked in vines, no chain or padlock in sight. There was a shower of rust flakes when I pushed it open, but it yielded easily. I allowed the beam of my flashlight to guide me down a tangled path, noticing occasional weathered headstones jutting up out of the weeds, but for the most part, it was like traversing a dark jungle instead of a cemetery.

I could make out the outline of the house somewhere up ahead, the whole area like a wilderness, requiring me to take up a stick and bushwhack my way through thorns and crooked branches. The house was on a hill surrounded by weeping willows that had all grown together, their trunks knotted into each other, and it would be quite an uphill climb to reach it. I was breathing heavily and working against the elevation change when I noticed the figure standing next to an angel statue with a crumbled stone face.

It appeared to be a young boy, but I couldn't see him too well in the weak illumination cast by my flashlight. I could make out a plaid shirt, suspenders, and an uncombed nest of curly black hair.

I didn't get too close because I didn't want to scare him.

"Hey, kid! How's it going? I'm out here doing some research about a show called *The Magenta Room*. You ever heard of it?"

The boy nods, his curls bouncing.

"Do you know if there's a set around here? Maybe a place where the crew did the filming?"

"There's no crew. It's just Sugarplum and his puppets. There's an old camera on a tripod, but I never saw a tape in it. I used to be on the show…"

The boy's voice is incredibly shy and hard to hear, almost like he's worried that if he says the wrong thing, he'll be hurt physically.

"That's awesome! Well apparently, I found the right person to talk to. But, uh, how's that possible? If there's no crew and the camera doesn't work, how does he broadcast the show?"

The boy shrugs. "I don't know."

I point to the house, scrubbing a hand against my jaw while trying to get a better look at the boy. There's some ground mist in the cemetery, and he's standing partially obscured by vines, so it's difficult to see all of him. He almost looks transparent at times. Trick of the light...

"Is that the house where he films it?"

He nods again, but there's reluctance in the nod.

"Not in the house. The house is just the gate. There's nothing in there but dust and graffiti. But if Sugarplum likes you and wants you on the show, he'll take you to the Magenta Room. It's in another place. A bad place."

I'm starting to think this kid is fucking with me, but I figure I might as well humor him...

"Why is it a bad place?"

"It just is. He sends letters to kids, trying to lure them to the house. He wants companions. He's really lonely, and he's been around a long time. He usually only takes the kids that show up alone. The ones that walk or ride their bikes to find him."

"Okay, and what happens to the kids he takes?"

"He makes them wear big puppet suits. Forever. You become part of the cast. But sometimes he forgets to feed his puppets, and the kids in the suits die. Others get really old and aren't kids anymore, but he forces them to talk like children for the show. That's not the worst part."

"What is...the worst part?"

The boy looks down, his arms crossed on his frail chest. He kneads his elbows, clearly uncomfortable to be talking about this, but powerless to stop the confession.

"He's dead."

"You mean like a ghost?"

"No. He's just dead. He's a corpse, but he can still talk, walk, sing, and dance. I don't know why. I don't know how he is what he is. I think maybe he made a covenant with something greater than himself once, and now he lives even when he's dead. He pretends that he is alive, and he doesn't like to be reminded that he's not. He smears makeup on his face for the show, but underneath, it's all saggy and decomposed. He is rotten, and he hates to smell his own rot. So that's why he brings in all the pretty flowers. He wants the sweet fragrance to cover up the smell of his own decay, but it doesn't help much. I know. When he leans in close, you can see the worms inside him, and the flies, and the bloated tissue under his foundation…"

The boy is scrubbing at his own elbows, clearly traumatized by the memories that are circling in his head.

"Sir, I don't know you, but don't go there. His organs are all rotted out inside of him, just a stinking brown soup, and when he dances, you can hear it sloshing around within his body. That's how he feeds his puppets. There's a wound that never closes under his suit, and he sticks a wooden spoon into it, and he makes us eat what comes out. He calls it Special Stew for his Plum Pals. It's like tasting rot. Tasting deadness."

The boy is weeping, deep snuffles that travel through his entire body. This is some of the craziest shit I've ever heard in my life, and I'm convinced that it must be a prank. Telling tall tales to spook the stranger in the abandoned cemetery.

"I'm free of him now. His puppets aren't like him. When they die, they're just dead. They don't keep walking and talking and singing. He's different. He's tainted and rotten and eternal. Stay away, okay?"

I scoff. I gotta give it to this boy, he's pretty damn creative, and he can spin quite a yarn.

"You've got one hell of an imagination. What's your name, kid?"

"He called me Bradley Bear."

I'm about to respond, but when I lift the flashlight, the kid is gone. It freezes me in place for a second, because it's like he just blinked out. One moment there and the next vanished. He must have crouched down and quietly run off. There's no other explanation for it.

I exhale, a little flustered, but I'm here, and there's no way some weirdo kid is gonna keep me from investigating the house. The prankster had his fun, and I hope he got a good laugh about it.

I start back up the hill, the beam of the flashlight trembling a bit in my hand the closer I get to the house.

THERE'S NOTHING VERY special about the house on the inside. It's a derelict ruin, a few pieces of sagging furniture in the corners, mildew on the floors, moss growing across a staircase that drips with water from the shattered latticework of the ceiling. I check every room, my boots creaking across the floor, but there's not much to be seen. There's a little office that has waterlogged documents and binders on the floor, obviously the cemetery caretaker's workspace at one point. I flip through a few pages, seeing plot locations, grave marker information, miscellaneous stuff like that.

There's graffiti everywhere, most of it the usual uninspired crap you see in bad areas. Crude genital drawings, forgotten gang tags, and names and dates so blurred that they're no longer visible.

One piece catches my eye, though...

It's near the end of a long, winding hallway, smeared across the walls in a dark violet shade of paint, the font jagged.

"He is deep in the deadplace, among the tulips and the daffodils. The TV man. The lonely man. And rot calls to rot..."

It makes me curious, so I follow that hallway again. The last time I checked, it ended in a dead-end, but maybe I got myself turned around, because this time there is a door...

It's a magenta door, and it's open just a crack.

I can't resist, and I enter. There's a rusted spiral staircase, metallic and rickety, and it leads downward. The chamber is like one big cylinder, and I can barely make out anything even with the flashlight. There's the slow plink of water droplets from above, and the echo in here is loud as hell. I've come this far, so why not?

I begin my descent. I walk and I walk, and soon I lose track of time, and I realize that I've been descending for hours. The staircase looks exactly the same. My calf muscles are tired and my knees are sore, and it feels like I've been walking for miles.

When I look back up to see any sign of the place where I entered, there is nothing up there but swirling gloom. I literally can't get the flashlight beam to cut through the darkness, and it's impossible to see anything that isn't a few feet in front of me. It's like the dark is inky and alive, not willing to show too much of itself.

I'm going to collapse if I don't take a break, so I sit down on the steps and let my head flop down into my hands. I'm dizzy and sleepy, and nothing seems entirely real.

I let myself go.

I drift away…

"YOU CAME. YOU'RE all grown up now, but it's okay, the Magenta Room will still have you…"

I must have fallen asleep, and that familiar voice jars me back to life. The staircase is gone. The first thing I become aware of is the smell. It's the overwhelming aroma of rot, dead tissue breaking down slowly, and it's overlaid with the perfume of flowers. That somehow makes it worse. I'm gagging before I even open my eyes, struggling not to vomit and choke on it.

My eyelids feel crusty like I've been asleep for a long time, and I open them slowly. Magenta walls, magenta ceiling, and a garden of fresh flowers all around me: pots, vases, wreaths, and bouquets.

Sedgwick Sugarplum is seated in a corner on a leather chair, in front of a large vanity mirror with several bulbs lighting him, a few of them dim and dark. It's a section of the Magenta Room that is always out of frame, never seen on camera. His back is to me, and I'm slumped into a sitting position against the wall.

He's not wearing his zoot suit. He's shirtless, and the skin of his torso seeps with suppurations, boils, and the bloat of decaying flesh. Flies hover over him, buzzing and landing on his flesh, slurping from little pools of pus with their proboscises. He's using a dirty old brush to apply his makeup, and it looks like his blond hair is a wig, for it sits on a mannequin head in front of the mirror. He's bald, and his scalp is sloughing off, crusted over with necrotic flesh.

I can't believe I'm seeing this. It's a nightmare. I fell and bonked my head on the staircase, and this must be a nightmare...

"There are no doors in or out of the Magenta Room. You have to be a very special child to gain entry. I have to sense that you're loving and loyal. You must cross the schism to reach me. And you, sweet boy, have crossed..."

I rotate my head around, and I see other puppets here and there. Some are just lying on the floor with their limbs sprawled out, the flies making feasts of them. Others move sluggishly. I see Agatha Oak, and she rocks back and forth like a mental patient, self-soothing and deranged.

"What the hell is this?"

"It's what you sought. A forever friend. A smile in the night. Isn't that what we're all seeking? An innocent place where you'll never be too busy to bend down and smell the wildflowers. You're one of the lucky ones. Some never make it this far..."

He spins around in the chair, and I wish that he hadn't. I only see half of his face, the half not covered in thick gaudy makeup, and it's raw, dripping meat, a butcher's cut, the skin a mixture of fatty yellow and lusterless gray. He offers me a cadaverous grin, and there's nothing to see but gums, confirming that he wears dentures for the camera. His mouth is full of maggots, and he clears his throat, swallowing them down before he can continue to speak.

"And what shall we call you, my new Plum Pal?"

"My name is Dave, and I need to leave here. I have to get home. Please, I need to not be here..."

I'm full to the brim with a mixture of panic and confusion. I cannot be talking to a corpse right now. This is not happening. The smell is driving me mad, and I've only been here for a few moments. It smells like roadkill that's been baking for weeks in the sun.

"You are where you're meant to be. You flew here on fern wings and you landed in a honeysuckle grove. Your home is the deadplace. Your home is with me."

Sugarplum rises to his feet and he shambles closer to me. It's clear that he takes great pains to appear agile on camera, but now that he's not performing, he's more noticeably a cadaver that shuffles on creaky legs with wasted ligaments. He wears stained undergarments and nothing else, and I notice a festering wound in his abdomen. It's putrid, and it seems to burst with infectious corruption that drips down in messy dollops as he walks.

He's unsettled the flies, and they all buzz angrily around him, waiting for the moment when they can land again and have their supper.

"From this day until your last day, you are Lionel the Lilac. You will be a happy boy when the camera rolls. You will shake your lilac petals and giggle when I tickle your chin, like all happy lilacs do. Do you understand?"

Now that he's in close proximity, I'm fucking horrified. He's death given some semblance of artificial life. His rot turns my stomach, and his eyes are just drooping jelly in the sockets. I fear if he leans too close, they'll fall out of his head and splash against my face. I can think of nothing else to do except give him the answer he wants. I nod emphatically.

I lift my arms, and I'm not entirely surprised to see that I'm wearing a big puppet costume, my limbs covered in light purple petals. I am what he said. I am Lionel the Lilac…

"If ever you are not laughing and wonderful and full of sunlight, I will leave you in a corner with no sustenance, and you will starve. You'll go unfed, and you'll be dead. It's no fun to be dead. It's no fun at all to feed these ones here…"

He lifts his fingertips, twirling them for me. The flesh has split in several places, fetid briny hotdogs left too long in the pan, and the flies cover them, lapping at the juice, eating alive the parts of him that are still wet and yummy.

"But I know that you'll be good. You'll be a loyal lilac and you'll perform with me until your time is through, and we'll invite new friends to the Magenta Room. We'll do it together. And I will care for you, in my way, as I care for all of my children…"

Sugarplum produces a wooden spoon. It is covered in teeth marks and a few splintered bits. He begins to dig it into that wound inside of him, and I hear all the corruption sloshing around, that rotten brown soup, and then he's pulling it free, and he's mashing it against my mouth, the wood clattering against my teeth and some of the rot spilling down my chin. My lips part in a shock response, and he's spooning his deadflesh into me: squirming insects, decomposed organs, all that nasty nourishment that waits in the cauldron of his gut…

"I feed what's mine. You'll never go without."

I can literally feel my mind slipping off some normal sane track in my head as I'm forced to suck the foulness from the spoon. I start to disassociate, and my body begins to rock. This cannot be real. I am not here. I am not in the Magenta Room.

I shiver and I shake, a happy little lilac, and Sugarplum grins in approval.

"Soon, we'll start the show…"

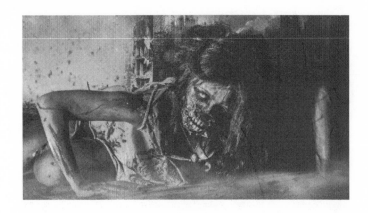

THE FIREBALL

Scotty Milder

"Coming straight down upon us/from the black depths of sky/Nowhere to run to/No place for us to hide…"

— Dead Oath, "World on its Knees" (from the album This Poisoned Earth, ©1991, Massive Metallium Records).

IT CAME FROM BEYOND THE Kuiper Belt. It hurtled through space at forty-three thousand miles per hour. It was seventy-nine feet across at its widest and, once caught in the well of the earth's gravity, it would weigh over eleven thousand tons. It entered the upper atmosphere at almost exactly 7:00 pm, just above the town of Medicine Hat, Alberta. By the time it was over Grand Forks, North Dakota, it had slowed by half and become a flaming superbolide more than twice as bright as the sun. Windows exploded in Duluth, Minnesota, mildly injuring one eighty-five-year-old retired schoolteacher and one sixteen-month-old boy. Cars ran off the road just north of Watertown, New York. A thirty-six-year-old single mother from Deer River named Marianne Jenkins died after she rolled her leased Ford Focus under the tires of a tanker truck while gazing in wonder at a night sky that had just exploded around her.

The meteor began to break up north of Lebanon, New Hampshire, and anyone looking skyward for the next twenty seconds or so saw what appeared to be a green, flaming crab screaming across the night, followed by a school of equally green, and equally flaming, shrimp.

Eventually, the meteor blew past the North American continent, where the largest piece finally disintegrated seventy miles southeast of Maine's Cape Elizabeth. After cruising for untold eons through the cold black nothing of space, the entirety of its final journey from Medicine Hat to the Atlantic took a minute and a half. Most of what remained plopped harmlessly into the ocean.

The only piece to touch land was less than twenty-five pounds and eleven inches across. It slammed into a junkyard in South Portland at a hundred seventy miles per hour, punching a hole through the bed of a rusted-out 1958 Dodge pickup and leaving a three-foot crater underneath.

The yard was closed at the time, and to this day that truck remains buried in a stack of ancient junkers near the back fence, right next to a 1977 Chevrolet Caprice with a very large—and very empty—trunk.

Even now, no one knows what's in there.

CARLTON HUGHES COUGHED himself awake. His head pounded. His guts made an ominous bass rumble.

He opened his eyes and immediately shut them against the sun, which came at his retinas like ground glass. He groaned and rubbed a hand up his cheek.

A girl lay next to him, all hard angles and swampy, post-sex heat. She made a noise and rolled over, pressed up against his side, and her hand flopped against his chest like a dead fish. He squinted at the chipped maroon nail polish. He half-remembered seeing those fingers last night, wrapped around the shaft of his dick. He just couldn't remember the face they were attached to.

He forced himself to look around the room. A sick, startled feeling thumped into his stomach, made his guts go all slurpy again. It was the room of a little girl. Pink walls and a cartoon unicorn poster tacked to the door, a cheap Wal-Mart dresser/vanity spackled with glitter, a pile of dirty clothes shoved up against the closet door, lumpen and misshaped like some dark Lovecraftian toad god.

Oh Christ, did I—?

But no. His eyes fell to the Roadrunners pennant on the wall above the vanity, and it all flooded back. Her name was Patty, she had been at the show, and he remembered her letting him into the apartment by the university in…was it San Antonio? The apartment she shared with two girlfriends. She was a junior majoring in, uh, was it public administration? Whatever. Some boring shit like that. Luckily, she hadn't talked about it much. Her mouth tasted like raspberries and vodka, and the skin between her stomach and her pubic mound tasted weirdly like cinnamon. There was a little heart tattooed on her left hip.

Patty made a thick snorty sound and looked up, sleep-gummed and smiling, lipstick smeared, her thick auburn hair corkscrewing every which way. She looked younger than he remembered, but definitely legal. He tried not to breathe a sigh of relief.

"Hey?" she said. "You want me to make some breakfast? I think I got eggs, maybe even some waffle mix."

"I, uh…"

He remembered stumbling up the steps after her, not-quite-playfully grabbing her ass as she jutted the key into the lock. If he dug a little, he could probably remember at least some of the sex. But he didn't remember the cab ride over from the Rock Box, and he had no idea where her apartment was in relation to the hotel. And he vaguely remembered having lost his phone somewhere.

He looked over her shoulder at the digital clock next to the bed. 10:47. Now his guts churned like something alive and caught in a thresher. Dead Oath was playing a late show at the Arkansas State Fair that night. A nine-hour drive. The band was supposed to be on the road and headed toward Little Rock by no later than ten.

She *harumphed,* but she was grinning. She could read the scrawl of his thoughts all across his face and—thank Christ—she got it. "No time for breakfast, I guess."

He smiled and kissed her forehead.

"How do you get back to the Interstate from here?" he asked.

THE THING CRAWLED out of the hole and flopped into a cluster of plants that were long and straight and unlike anything it had encountered before. The smell and feel of them—cloying and pungent, slick and soft—drove it mad with fear and a queer hunger it didn't understand. They made a papery sound as it wriggled its narrow, gelatinous body through them.

The first thing it needed was darkness. It had no eyes as we understand them. But the soft scrum of pinkish tissue across its rippled forehead was sensitive to variations of light. Having gestated in a place of absolute cold and utter darkness, even the cloud-choked night sky drove a hot lance of pain right into the center of its being. It had no vocal cords and only a narrow proboscis through which to voice its displeasure. That displeasure was considerable, and it came out in a series of agonized clicks and squeaks. It thrashed back and forth in the muck, finally scrambling through the weeds until it found something hard and metal and oddly curved.

The fleshy tip of the proboscis opened like a flower. Instead of petals it displayed a circular array of needle-like teeth. It had no ears, not yet, but through the vibration of the teeth as they sawed through the metal, it could sense the contours of the empty space beyond—an air bubble inside a cocoon made of iron and carbon and myriad other substances it could not identify.

The teeth spun and bore. Metal shrilled and squealed. Within minutes a perfectly circular hole exposed the bubble.

It gathered its many legs beneath it and crawled inside.

FUCK THIS, CARLTON thought as the van banged and skittered over some backwoods dirt road south of Coffeeville, Alabama.

It was just Carlton and Cody. The rest had taken the other van and the box truck up I-59 from Hattiesburg, where they would hop onto Route 80 and follow that all the way to Montgomery. Cody insisted this was a short cut, and Carlton stupidly agreed to ride with him. Turns out that, as usual, Cody didn't know what the fuck he was talking about. Somewhere along the way he turned off 84, and now here they were, bouncing their way through deep ruts and clattering over washboard roads no wider than a footpath. Farmhouses flitted by, dark windows yawping at them like the toothless mouths of old dogs.

Cody insisted he knew where they were. The junction to 43 was just ahead, and that would take them right on back to 84, *"slicker'n a virgin cheerleader's dewey pink asscrack, just you fuckin' wait and see, my man."* Carlton didn't believe him, and the GPS on both his phone and the dash couldn't find them. That's how goddamned lost they were.

They called Cody their "Road Manager," and he'd been with them since the short tour with Exodus and Lääz Rockit in '86. Back then he'd been a vital member of the crew, but these days he was a burnout and basically useless. They only really kept him around because he had that good coke connect down in Anaheim. He was always getting them into shit like this.

The van hit another rut. Something seemed to explode beneath the vehicle with a metallic rattle. The ash tip fell off the end of Cody's cigarette, splattering across his stained cargo shorts. He never even slowed.

Carlton felt the slosh of last night's whiskey working its way through his belly, coagulating with bile and a half-eaten breakfast burrito, steadily turning itself to vomit. His head thrummed. He shut his eyes.

His phone beeped with a new text. He pulled it out of his pocket and looked. It was from Rex: "We r here. Where r u guys?"

Cody laughed at something, no doubt a reminiscence of ancient road pussy puddling around that smack-fried brain of his. Carlton shot him a side-eye and swore to himself that after this tour the motherfucker was gone. Connect or no connect, and history be good-and-goddamned. It was probably time he got himself clean anyway.

IT DIDN'T EXPERIENCE time the way we did. It couldn't tell one day from the next. It had no frame of reference to tell how long it stayed in the metal cocoon. It knew that the hole through which it entered sometimes blasted light, and whenever the light came, it turned its head away and made those same clicks and squeaks, until the light vanished and the darkness returned. It scrabbled around the space, came to know it. The bottom of the cocoon was soft and fibrous, scratchy and unpleasant against its belly and legs. But beneath that was the same hard metal, as cool and comforting as the rock it had ridden across the cosmos. After some time, it couldn't take the fabric anymore. The proboscis flowered, and the teeth shredded the pliable lamina until it was nothing but tufts of billowy tissue. It worked its legs and shoved the tissue into the hole, finally managing to block out the intruding light.

It drank the air inside the bubble, tasting it like a glorious wine. Its body hadn't evolved for atmosphere, and the crash of gasses inside it—mostly nitrogen, some oxygen and carbon—made its nerve endings erupt in remarkable new sensations. It became giddy and drunk on it, its carapace rapidly expanding and contracting as parchment-thin lungs knitted themselves together, then began to fill out and toughen.

It molted once, then twice, devouring the slick wet dermis as soon as it wriggled free of the mucosal sheath. After the second molting its skin began to harden and scale over in broad, spade-shaped segments.

It felt itself growing.

"HEY, BABY!" CARLTON waved at the laptop screen, feeling like an idiot. "Hey, precious girl!"

Imogene blinked at him in that stupid way babies did, then her chubby lips flapped into a gummy smile. She giggled.

"Oopsie, she needs changed," Trisha said and plucked Imogene out of the highchair. She bent and grinned at Carlton. "Better go before she gets diaper rash."

"Hold on a sec," Carlton said. "Lemme just look at you."

She shot him a look, a bit long-suffering but mostly amused. "What's this, you getting sappy now?"

Trisha wasn't his girlfriend. She wasn't exactly a groupie, either—she hadn't even heard of Dead Oath before he told her the name. She listened to a few songs off the first album (*The Temple*, ©1988, Massive Metallium Records) and pronounced it "not really my thing." She was just a waitress in Columbus that he partied with occasionally, whenever the band gigged there. She was fifteen years younger, funny in a dry sort of way that mostly confused him, and not at all clingy. Rex would have called her the perfect slice of road pussy before he went and married his own.

Then she called him out of the blue two years ago and told

him that A) she was pregnant, B) the baby was his, and C) she was keeping it. The paternity test bore her out. He panicked, thinking there was no way in hell he could be a dad. And knowing—after nearly thirty years as rhythm guitarist for a third-string thrash band, with four mostly-forgotten records, a couple busted Econoline vans, and an ancient box truck for the constant touring—he didn't even have any money to offer. Then Trisha told him she didn't give a shit about any of that, just thought he should know. And when she emailed him a .JPEG of the sonogram a couple weeks later, none of it mattered anyway. Trisha was a good shit, and he supposed that if he absolutely *had* to knock up a girl on the road, he was glad it was her.

"Nah," he said. "Just...let me look at you."

"You okay, babe?"

"Yeah, totally."

She arched a skeptical eyebrow. "Where you at tonight?"

"A Ramada in Durham. If I stuck my dick out the window, I could piss right onto the interstate. Heading up to D.C. in the morning. We're headlining at The Pinch tomorrow night." *Headlining* made the gig sound significantly more impressive than it actually was. It was a Tuesday night show, after all, and the opening band was a bunch of high school kids.

Trisha seemed to get it. "You'll be fine," she said. "How's Ricki?" Ricki was Dead Oath's lead singer. He was white-knuckling six miserable months on the wagon.

"He's all right. What he's giving up in coke, he's making up for in middle-aged mom snatch." It came out a bit nastier than he'd intended. He rather didn't like the knife edge he heard in his voice just then.

She mock-scowled from the laptop. "Classy," she said.

"Always."

"So how much longer is the tour?"

"About a month. We're doing a string of gigs up the East Coast, circling through Maine and New Hampshire, then closing with two shows in Pittsburgh before flying back to Burbank." An idea occurred to him. "Maybe I'll rent a car and drive out to see you guys for a day or two, have the label book my return flight out of Columbus instead of Pittsburgh?"

"Okay, well, I really gotta go change her diaper. It's getting rank."

"Okay," he said, hearing the pout dribbling into his voice but unable to cork it. He was disappointed that she hadn't sounded more—or, really, *at all*—excited by his proposition. "Hey, give me a little somethin' first."

She cocked her head. "I thought we weren't doing that anymore."

"Oh, come on. I'm stuck in a Ramada in Durham, and they don't even have any pay-per-view porn on the tube. Just a little peek."

She laughed, again with that half-annoyed/half-amused look on her face and pulled down her tank top. Her breasts lolled out, still so perfect and round, even with a year of breast-feeding on them.

Carlton found himself clutched by a sudden and unfamiliar desire. Not for sex, exactly. Not really for love, either. Just for…closeness. It occurred to him, not for the first time, that he was lonely and not having much fun anymore. The future unspooled before him like a big black wind tunnel. And there Trisha was, halfway across the country with his baby in her lap. She'd let him talk to the kid on Skype and she'd give him a peek of her tits now and then, but the moment he fooled himself into thinking it was ever going to be more than that for her, was the moment he should just put his gun in his mouth and get it over with.

He tried to push that away and forced his lips into his best rock-star leer. "*That's* what I'm talking about," he said.

She laughed again, less annoyed this time, and pulled her tank top up. She blew him a kiss. "Be careful," she said. "Don't get AIDS." It was her standard sign-off, meant to be funny. He let her think it was.

"I'll do my best, love."

She killed the connection. He closed his laptop and rolled over onto his back. He stared up at the water-stained ceiling and listened to a couple arguing in the next room, the crackle of their voices mingling with the drone of traffic on I-85, just outside his window. He thought about jerking off before realizing he was too tired to do the act any sort of justice. It occurred to him that, once upon a time, he had thought fifty was old.

CYCLES OF LIGHT and dark. The tissue blocking the hole still let in some illumination, but as time went on, the lances of pain waned and then ceased altogether. The pink strip of flesh on its forehead began to dry out and flake away, finally revealing a set of eight bulbous, red/black eyes.

It grew and it grew and it grew, coiling over itself again and again, until it filled nearly every inch of the metal cocoon. And with each spurt of growth, a new sensation: pain. Not the same spike of agony as when it first met the light, but a dull ache in its guts, like a swallowed ember. It burned away in there, growing hotter and larger with each passing day. Whatever was in there *swelled*, pulling its soft underbelly taut and nearly translucent.

It mewled and clicked, kicking its legs feebly in the dark. It explored the bulge on its stomach with its proboscis, licking the raw, bone-white skin with its many flitting tongues.

When the spasms came, it welcomed the clarity. The urgency. The pain churned inside it, turned spiky and toothful.

It shrieked, arching its back against the top of the cocoon, deforming the metal with its sudden bestial strength. As it screamed, it heard an answering squeal from the cocoon itself, and then the cocoon burst open like a seed pod, spilling the crying thing out into the dirt. Legs scrabbled against the weeds and shattered glass, twisted, then snapped like twigs and tore off the thing's body as it tried to eel away from the sudden explosion of light and sound.

It had no lids with which to shut its eyes; the pain in its guts only grew and grew—churned and bore, thrashed and cut—and this sudden rush of new visual and auditory information was overwhelming. It wanted the blessed cool darkness of the cocoon in which to die, for surely that was what was happening. Torment like this could end no other way…

Its lower half was still thrashing inside the cocoon, and it was that lower half that suddenly exploded, expelling…*something*…across the metal floor. The pain dribbled away so quickly, it almost forgot it had been there at all.

It lay there, half in the cocoon, half-splayed upon the dirt. Its chest heaved as it gulped at the air and took in all these new smells. Smells from inside the cocoon, smells from whatever had come out of it, smells from…*out there.*

Out there. This was an interesting new concept, one that had barely occurred to it before. Because there was an *out there.* It could see it, lights twinkling along the bottom of a black, star-crusted sky. It could hear it, a meaningless clatter of mechanical drones and roars whizzing past, and an odd, rhythmic *thud thud thud* from somewhere in the other direction.

And it could smell it…the smell of *out there.* Metal and dirt and vegetation, yes, but something else as well. Something hot, and fluid, and tangy. Something akin to itself, akin to whatever it had left in its cocoon, and yet, something wholly different altogether.

It had felt hunger since it first crawled, larva-like, from the meteor fragment. But that sensation had heretofore been meaningless, simply a part of it, only a buzzing desire attached to no action it could fathom.

But these smells…

It raised its proboscis, let it flower, flicked its tongues across its teeth, tasted the air and what the air bore upon it. Its hunger turned suddenly cold, hard, dagger-like and…*understood.*

It would find the source of the smell, which came from the direction of that *thump thump thump*, less a sound now than a beacon, far away from its now-useless cocoon and from the things that had burst from its belly—things that were already squirming and squealing and clicking and tasting the night for themselves.

Yes. It understood.

It would find the source.

And it meant to bite.

To rip.

To cut.

To hurt.

…TO EAT.

THUMP THUMP THUMP…

Carlton stood at the bar, drinking his whiskey (always Jameson, none of that Protestant shit for him), and trying to place the song—not because he was really interested, but just for something to do before Cody and the others were done, and he had to go onstage. The Deftones, he thought. Something off *White Pony*. Not one of the later albums, where they became so arty he couldn't listen anymore. Whatever it was, it spilled out of The Fireball's PA system, all cracked and broken, buzzing and near indistinguishable beneath the clatter of bottles, the bray of the pinball machines, and the shimmery squeal of feedback, as somebody did something unforgivable to the soundboard.

Thump thump thump…

Not the Deftones, he decided. Just some knockoff. All those 90's bands sounded the same, anyway.

Dead Oath was playing the middle of one of those bills that only made sense to phoning-it-in promoters and tiny clubs in shitsplat little cities like this. Clubs like The Fireball, which was tucked down a South Portland back alley and flanked by an abandoned warehouse on one side and a massive junkyard on the other. The opening band was a bunch of kids from New Hampshire called Hot Knife on Lover's Lane. They were doing what, a few years ago, was called "metalcore," but, to Carlton, sounded like the same shit Dead Oath had been playing since the 80s, only technically better and a whole lot prettier. The lead singer flounced and purred around up there in leather pants and mascara, his emo-flop of dyed hair seeming to move of its own dark volition. Sometimes the guitarist—who looked fifteen and only a little less prancey than the singer—did some death-metal growls into the microphone. Carlton got bored and went for the bar.

Dead Oath was up next, for a quick forty-minute set, to be followed by the headliner, which was some broody, beardo three-piece out of Boston called Storm Season. Ricki had called them "post-metal" and played a few tracks for Carlton on Spotify. Low, doomy guitars and swirling synths. No vocals. Ten-minute songs that all bled into each other like watercolor. Carlton had seen them come stomping out of their tour bus (an actual bus!) before The Fireball opened its doors. They looked like either lumberjacks or philosophy students.

The Deftones, or whatever, faded out, and Marilyn Manson started screaming about cake and sodomy. Someone behind the bar loved their 90s playlist.

Carlton finished the whiskey and looked dismally around the club. Usually, Dead Oath could be counted on to turn out a few 'pushing-fifty' weekend warriors and slightly puffy soccer moms pining away for their misspent youth. Not tonight. Carlton didn't see anyone who looked over thirty. There were hipster girls in cat-eye glasses and babydoll dresses (he couldn't tell if they were there for Storm Season or Hot Knife), and lithe young guys with spiraling neck tattoos and faces studded with piercings. The girls laughed easily, the guys smirked mysteriously, and occasionally one would glance curiously over at Carlton, obviously wondering what the hell a dinosaur like him was doing there.

This show wasn't going to go well.

He turned back toward the bar and waved his glass at the bartender. She was small and skinny, maybe Trisha's age, but with a ragged, rode-hard look that made her more than a little sexy. Her tattooed arms were ropey with muscle and deeply tanned. Her hair was long and mouse-brown but luxuriantly thick. Her eyes danced with a chaos he recognized. She smiled and nodded, showing a row of small, very even teeth, and as she approached and reached for the bottle of Jameson, he caught himself looking down at the small diamond on her ring finger and thinking *I bet I could still fuck her.*

The depression, when it fell upon him, was like a cold, wet blanket. He watched her fill his glass and shoved the feeling angrily away.

THE HUNGER CHURNED inside it, but even so it took the time to seal the mewling things back into the cocoon. It didn't quite know why it did that, only that it had to. The mewling things squirmed and writhed and gnashed against each other, their needle-teeth slashing. Black ichor leaked from dozens of wounds. One or two would survive, it knew, and that would be enough.

Thud thud thud thud...

Once the cocoon was shut, it turned and moved toward the sound. Sights and smells danced within and around it, making it tingle from its head to its hundreds of feet. Its body pulsed and rippled, began to secrete something thick and acrid.

The dirt and papery weeds fell away, and now it was skittering across a rough, flat surface that was remarkably cool. There was a bright light up ahead. Swaying beneath it were four creatures. They stood on two thick appendages, waving two shorter ones before them in strange, indecipherable gestures. They made peculiar sounds out of holes that writhed and flexed within a fifth, bulbous appendage that protruded from soft, barrel-like torsos.

Soft. That was the overwhelming sense it had of them. Soft, and warm, and full of juices.

One of the creatures was fairly large—almost as large as it was itself—and it stood with its back against a flat, rectangular barrier. The others were much smaller. They faced it, made their strange sounds and gestures, and then one threw back that bulbous fifth appendage and made a sharp, trilling sound that split the night.

Beyond the barrier, it sensed another cocoon, this one much vaster than the one it had sprung from. And within the cocoon, there were more of these odd jelly-like creatures. Many, many more...

Carlton would have recognized the larger creature with its back against the barrier. His name was David, and he was The Fireball's doorman. Nearly forty, once a star college linebacker before he blew out his knee, now a part-time slam poet who won contests all across New England and had self-published two slim booklets of hard-edged verse. He had an ex-wife and an eight-year-old daughter, both of whom lived in Hartford. He managed to get down to see them every couple weeks or so.

The girl standing in front of him laughed at one of his stupid dad jokes, and he decided he liked her and that he would let her in, even though her ID was about as genuine as a three-dollar bill. Her friends looked on, coolly indulgent, infinitely patient.

It gathered its legs beneath it and hurled itself forward. The proboscis irised open. The teeth gleamed wetly in the sudden blast from the streetlight.

David caught a whir of movement over the girl's left shoulder, looked up, and had just enough time to strip the gears of his sanity before the thing was upon them.

WHEN THE SCREAMING started, Carlton was gazing at the back of Ricki's head and thinking about Imogene. Nothing profound, just picturing the way her eyes bulged whenever she giggled, remembering the way she clutched his callused finger the one time he saw her in person, three weeks after she was born.

Ricki was wailing into the microphone, pumping his hips seductively against the mic stand. It was an act that had worked well for him over the years, scored him lots of tail, but Carlton didn't think it would work tonight. The kids in the front row stared up at him like he was some kind of slightly embarrassing alien. His long blond hair was getting thin on top, his waist was getting thick, and there was a gleaming bald spot, half-covered, that Carlton never noticed before.

Carlton's fingers danced mechanically over the frets, his other hand pistoning thoughtlessly against the guitar body. The song was "The Temple," and he'd played it so many times he didn't even have to think about it anymore. Instead, he thought about Imogene, the tinkling wind-chime sound of her baby laugh, the ice-blue eyes that had been his only apparent genetic gift to her.

The screaming came from back by the bar. Carlton's eyes snapped away from Ricki's bald spot and instinctively scanned the crowd. Probably nothing more than a drunken bar fight, although the note of terror that cut through the crash of guitars and drums sparked an unsettled ember in Carlton's throat. After what happened to Dimebag, you could never be too—

A girl was pushing her way through the crowd, shrieking and covered in blood. Carlton blinked and saw she was missing her left arm beneath her shoulder. The socket pumped jets of blood that looked black under the shifting strobe lights.

Nobody was helping her. They all backed away as she staggered toward the stage, collapsed first to her knees, then tipped over onto her face.

Carlton's fingers still danced. His arm still pistoned.

More screams. First a scattered few and then a wave of them.

He looked up.

No, he thought.

Because the thing that was sidewindering through the crowd, its movements made stuttery by the strobe, simply could not exist.

Carlton kept playing as the thing came forward, its black scales glistening wetly. The crowd just stood there, gaping, as it cut through them like a saw. Sinews of flesh speared from its tubelike mouth, grabbing anything and everyone in its path, yanking them, shrieking, toward its spiral of teeth.

Carlton played. He realized, in some dim way, that he was the only one who was still doing so, but he couldn't seem to stop. Ricki was gone; Carlton saw him tumble from the stage and scramble for the back door.

The thing was in the middle of the pit now. It sort of looked like a giant millipede and Maybe a little like one of Giger's big, fleshy cock paintings. In most ways, though, it looked like nothing even the most demented artist could have imagined. The bartender—she with the even straight teeth and the sexy ropes of muscle—half disappeared into the long beak of its maw. The other half fell away, severed, chewed and pumping blood.

Carlton played.

The thing turned its eyes toward him, seemed to mark him, and then it was slithering up onto the stage.

No, he thought.

Carlton stopped playing. His eyes fell on the bottle of Jameson that sat, three-quarters full, on the Marshall stack next to him.

The thing made a hungry clicking sound as its snout wriggled toward him like an elephant's trunk. Carlton batted it aside with the guitar, and feedback erupted through the speakers, melding with the screams of the crowd that had bunched itself up against both the front and the back doors.

The proboscis swung around, jabbed toward him again. He felt a blast of the thing's fetid breath.

The proboscis opened. Teeth unfurled.

Carlton grabbed the whiskey bottle and hurled it. He had been a more-than-fair baseball pitcher in high school, and his aim was true. The bottle exploded against the hard ridge of the thing's forehead. Whiskey dripped down in its carapace in thin rivulets. It made a strange, cat-like sound and backed off a step. He saw that a shard of glass had impaled one of the thing's rapidly deflating eyes. Milky white fluid spurted from the cavity like semen.

Carlton's hand dipped into his pocket and found his lighter. It was a cheap thing, a knockoff Zippo he'd picked up in some truck stop or other, but he had just refilled it that morning. Thank God.

The creature turned its remaining eyes back toward him as he thumbed it open and spun the wheel. It guttered flame.

The thing lunged.

He threw the lighter.

From the Boston Globe:

"PORTLAND, MAINE — Tragedy struck Portland, Maine, late last night as The Fireball nightclub was engulfed in an unexplained fire.

Portland Fire Capt. Russell McGilroy estimated that at least thirty people perished in the blaze, which occurred during a heavy metal concert featuring popular New England acts, Hot Knife on Lovers Lane and Storm Season.

The band, Dead Oath, had just begun its set when the fire started. Among the dead are Dead Oath's drummer, Rex McClane, and rhythm guitarist, Carlton Hughes, the band's management confirmed.

Reps for Hot Knife on Lovers Lane confirmed that the band had already departed the venue before the start of the blaze. A spokesperson for Storm Season said that the band was still on its tour bus warming up and that all members and crew are "shaken but fine." Both bands have offered condolences to the victims' families.

McGilroy declined to comment on the cause of the fire, although several witnesses have claimed that an unidentified animal found its way into the club and started a panic.

"I don't know, is there a zoo or something around here?" Dead Oath road manager, Cody DeWitt, asked. "I mean, I didn't see it—I was outside—

but I heard it was like an alligator or something."

Officials at both York's Wild Kingdom in York and the Maine Wildlife Park in Gray have confirmed that no animals have gone missing…"

From the CryptoMonsterBlog Podcast:

"…okay so here's the thing, guys, I've talked to at least six people who survived that fire, and every single one of them says there was something in there and that it wasn't a bear, a tiger, or an alligator. This one girl, she asked me not to give her name, so we'll call her Katie, and this guy, Frankie Shannahan, they both said it was like a big centipede or something. I know it sounds nuts, but come on. Too many people are describing the same thing. But the officials are covering it up and blaming that Carlton guy, saying he was drunk and started the fire as a prank…"

COMMENT ON THE YouTube video *monster attacks dead oath at the fireball (cell phone vid)*:

"Obvs a hoax, guys. You clearly see that asshole throw the whiskey and then light it, but the rest is such painfully bad cgi I can't believe any of you are falling for it. Super tasteless that anyone even made this thing, and I'm glad that motherfucker's dead, goddamned murdering piece of drunk shit—"

From the Portland Press Herald:

PORTLAND — The family of Darryl Arsenault, 52, has announced a $20,000 reward for any information concerning the missing South Portland man's whereabouts.

"We just want to know where he is," Arsenault's wife, Deborah Arsenault, 48, said during a tearful press conference this morning. "I know Darryl's done some bad things, but he's got a wife and kids who love him."

Arsenault, owner and operator of Arsenault Auto Recyclers, went missing last Thursday while closing up his business for the night. He was last seen walking through the junkyard, on his way to close the back gate.

Speculation has arisen about Arsenault's connections to organized crime elements in Providence, but, as of now, those connections remain unconfirmed. When asked about Arsenault's possible mob ties, Portland Police Detective Lawrence O'Bannon declined to comment…

EVEN NOW, NO one knows what's in there.

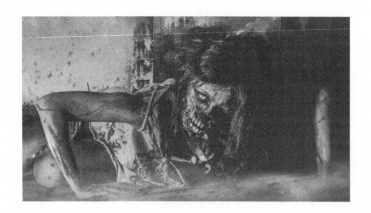

FALLEN EARTH

Steven Pajak

AGENT JERRY RAFFERTY STOOD BEHIND THE thick
pane of the two-way mirror, staring at the gray being sitting on the other side of the glass. He shook his head again, still unable to believe what he was seeing—or, rather, his mind could not fully comprehend—even though he was looking at it with his own eyes.

He placed one hand against the polycarbonate barrier, the only thing separating him from the otherworldly visitor. As soon as his fingers touched the surface, the gray looked up and seemed to lock eyes with Jerry, as though it somehow knew he was there looking in. A sudden chill ran down his spine, from neck to ass.

Without shifting his gaze from the gray, Jerry asked, "Do you think it can see us? Through the mirror, I mean."

Head Agent Dale Hunter, Jerry's partner and senior agent, was sitting across the observation room, perched on the edge of a sturdy metal desk. Earlier, they'd cleared the sheriff and his deputies from the building, before commandeering it in the interest of national security. Currently, Dale and Jerry were the only two, in the great state of Nevada, with clearance high enough to allow contact with...the prisoner.

Prisoner.

Dale didn't like that word because he didn't feel it was accurate in the current situation. The alien was in their custody, yes. It was being held in a locked room, behind impact-resistant glass and cinderblock walls, yes. Yet Dale had the feeling the gray could escape their custody whenever it chose, in the same way it arrived. This raised Dale's hackles and put him in a foul mood.

Looking up from the file he was reading, Dale fixed Jerry with red-rimmed, tired eyes. It was three in the morning in Nevada, and just two hours ago, Dale was snug in his bed in Encino, sleeping soundly next to his wife of twenty years, when his smartphone woke him. Just one hour ago, he was in a chopper speeding across California in ink-black darkness, through the desolate Mojave Desert, heading toward the small town of Searchlight, Nevada. He was briefed on the satellite phone—by none other than Deputy Director Stevenson, the man in charge of Directorate X, the secret division of the NSA—about a sudden and unprecedented threat to national security.

Now, just past three in the morning, because he had the distinction of being the most senior agent in closest proximity to the event with the right clearance, here he sat in the cold observation room of the Clark County Sheriff's Office, trying to prepare himself mentally for a conversation with a being from an unknown universe. He couldn't wrap his head around this, yet in just a few minutes he would be conducting an interview to assess if it was a threat to the country. To humanity.

"How the hell should I know?" Dale retorted, his anger flashing to the surface. Normally, Dale was the strong, silent type who always kept his composure. Obviously, this situation had him on edge.

"Sorry," Jerry said in a subdued voice. "I just thought maybe you'd done this before."

Dale fixed his partner's reflection with a cold stare and furrowed brow. The vein just above his right eye twitched, and he felt the beginning of a migraine starting to throb at the base of his skull. He reminded himself that this was all new to the kid, too. The difference was, Jerry approached all this with excitement and wonder, while Dale could not shake the overwhelming feeling of dread that formed, like a squirming ball of snakes, in his belly.

After a moment, his anger simmered, and Dale said, "No one's done this before, kid. We're navigating in unchartered territory without a fucking map or compass."

"Right," Jerry said. He continued to look at the thing behind the mirror. For the first time since getting off the chopper, the immensity of what was about to transpire dawned on him. Slowly turning away from the interrogation room, he said, "Dale, you and me, we're going to be the first people in history to talk to an extraterrestrial."

"Yeah, I know, kid."

"You know what's amazing? How much he looks like all the descriptions everyone, who ever claimed to see an alien, said they look like. Maybe there is some truth to the claims after all."

"No, there's not. You know as well as I it's all bullshit."

"Then how else do you explain how close the descriptions are to the real thing, sitting right there?"

"I can't."

He could certainly understand the kid's enthusiasm, and he wished he could share in the wonder and awe of the moment with Jerry, but right now, Dale needed to collect his thoughts and get his head right before going into the room. This moment was the most important in his entire career, and he wasn't about to screw it up because he was awe-struck and not prepared.

He tossed the file down onto the desk and stood up. "Listen, kid. The President and the Joint Chiefs want to live stream our interview. Why don't you get the audio and video equipment from upstairs and start setting it up, huh? Then we can go in there, the two of us, and make history."

"I'm on it," Jerry said. His excitement was palpable. He turned away from the mirror and exited the room, on his way up to the sheriff's conference room to gather the equipment, leaving Dale alone with the extraterrestrial.

When he was alone, Dale resisted the urge to stand in front of the two-way and stare at the being. Instead, he returned to the desk and resumed his review of the file. According to the sheriff's after-action report, the gray appeared in the lobby of the sheriff's office just past midnight. The eyewitness, Deputy Hawkins, who was manning the front desk, stated there was a bright flash of light, which caused him to shield his eyes with his arm. The flash was followed immediately by a strange sound, like all the air was being suddenly sucked out of the room, followed by a sudden pressure in his ears, like when flying at high altitudes. When Deputy Hawkins peeked out from behind his arm, the flash faded, and the alien was standing there in front of him, quote, "naked as the day he was born, well, if aliens are even born...I don't know."

Dale could only imagine Hawkins' initial shock upon seeing the gray materialize in the lobby, like something out of a *Star Trek* movie. One second nothing, then the next, an almost six-foot humanoid is standing in the empty lobby looking at you with those giant, black eyes. Dale got goose-flesh on his arms just thinking about it.

DALE SAT ACROSS the table from the gray, no more than an arm's length of inch-thick stainless-steel tabletop separating them. Dale found it difficult to get over the initial shock of seeing the alien in the flesh. Rafferty was right: it looked just like he would have imagined, based on "eyewitness" accounts, what he'd seen plastered on TV screens, in theaters, in magazine spreads, and on the Internet.

The alien was humanoid in its appearance, with a large, upside-down, oval-shaped head and large egg-shaped eyes. It had nostrils, though no protruding nasal trim, columella, external nares, or nasal tip. Its mouth appeared as just a slash without any upper or lower lips. It stood about five-feet-six-inches tall and its physique was slender, with rope-like musculature on the appendages. The epidermis appeared slick and non-porous, almost rubbery, like that of a dolphin. The alien seemed docile and appeared sympathetic, though its face did not seem structured to adequately portray emotions.

"My name is Head Agent Dale Hunter, and this is my partner, Agent Jerry Rafferty. We are with the National Security Agency, a federal agency for our government."

"And yes, I am named after the famous singer," Jerry said, his attempt at humor falling flat, and he immediately regretted it. He could feel Dale's eyes on him. In a loud voice, as though he were addressing someone with impaired hearing, Jerry asked, "What's your name?"

"Jesus, Jerry, I don't think it's deaf."

"We don't know that. We don't know how his hearing works."

"I'm sure its hearing is fine. Now lower your voice. We don't want to give an impression of aggressiveness."

"I wasn't being aggressive," Jerry said, lowering his voice.

Before Dale could respond, the alien spoke, if you could call what came out speech. The sounds that issued from the thin slash of mouth were a series of clicking, popping, and buzzing sounds that resembled nothing either of them had ever heard before. The alien's voice was guttural, with a vibration that seemed to resonate from deep within its chest cavity.

The agents looked at each other for a moment, exchanging stunned glances. Jerry said, "That's not English."

Frustrated by Jerry's habit of stating the obvious, Dale said, "No shit, Sherlock? How'd you figure that out?"

"I'm just saying, how are we supposed to communicate with him if he's not speaking our language?"

"With *it*," Dale said.

"Dhalgroi Baenets Dhees'ars," the alien repeated.

"We don't understand," Jerry said, resisting the temptation to raise his voice again now that it had been brought to his attention.

"My name does not translate in your language," the alien said.

Jerry grabbed Dale's arm and squeezed it. "He speaks English, Dale!"

"I can hear," Dale said, pulling his arm away from Jerry's grip. To the alien, Dale asked, "If your name does not translate, what should we call you?"

The alien considered the question. "You may call me…ALF."

The alien's voice sounded robotic yet still primitive and guttural, something like a cross between human and animal. But the alien was communicating in English, which just made their job a whole lot easier.

Jerry laughed again, the reference dawning on him. "Your name is ALF? Like from the TV show? You've got to be shitting me."

Dale turned and gave Jerry that stern look he usually reserved for when Jerry spoke out of turn or said something incredibly inappropriate, but the younger agent took no notice. Dale fully realized the weight of being the first humans in history to interview an extra-terrestrial life form, yet the concept seemed completely lost on his partner in the moment.

Contrary to the conspiracy theorists and other popular beliefs, no alien species had ever visited Earth, at least none of which the U.S. government was officially aware. The UFO sighting by Kenneth Arnold at Mount Rainier, the infamous UFO crash at Roswell, the Lubbock Lights, the incident at Rendlesham Forest, hell, every story of alien encounter ever spewed was bullshit. There were no aliens housed at Area 51. There was no advanced alien technology being reverse-engineered at Mount Weather. In fact, the whole Directorate X division was built on theories and conjecture, their agents trained for theoretical encounters.

The gray sitting across from Dale and Jerry was the first and only alien ever discovered on Earth, or anywhere else, for that matter. The top brass at the NSA, even the president and vice president, were sitting under the east wing of the White House in the Presidential Emergency Operations Center, watching this very feed, and his partner was cracking jokes.

"I have adopted the name ALF from your popular television show of the mid-1980s. You can call me something else if you choose," the gray said.

Jerry laughed again. He looked like a kid on Christmas morning, ready to open his presents. "I much preferred *Mork & Mindy* to *ALF*, but you don't really look like a Mork, so we'll stick with ALF. Your planet wouldn't happen to be named Melmac, would it?"

Dale elbowed his partner and nodded toward the two-way mirror where the cameras were rolling, streaming a live feed of the interview to NSA HQ and wherever else those, with high enough clearance, were gathered while the threat was assessed. Dale wasn't completely up to speed on that protocol, didn't have that clearance.

The alien's face did not change or react in any way to Jerry's response. In the monotonous, humanoid-animal-like voice, ALF said, "My planet does not translate in your language. You may call it Melmac, Agent Jerry Rafferty of the National Security Agency."

"That won't be necessary," Dale said and glanced at Jerry, as if defying him to follow that trail of conversation any further.

"Very well, Head Agent Dale Hunter of the National Security Agency. My planet shall remain unnamed in your language."

"Is your planet like Earth?" Jerry asked.

"My planet's atmosphere is quite different than Earth, with no similarities other than the fact that our planet also has vast oceans."

"How do you survive here, in our atmosphere?" Dale asked.

"Our physiology is extremely enhanced by billions of years of evolution, Head Agent Dale Hunter of the National Security Agency. Our ability to adapt to atmospheric variations has allowed us to travel to many planets in many galaxies. This characteristic of adaptation is typical of most extraterrestrial space travelers, at least those with superior technologies and many tens of thousands of years of evolution."

"Travelers other than your kind?" Jerry asked.

"Yes, Agent Jerry Rafferty of the National Security Agency. There are unknown numbers of life-forms that are capable of deep space travel."

"Jesus," Jerry said, awed by the thought of unknown numbers of species on star ships, cruising across the galaxy. "Have you been in contact with other species of travelers? Are there others out there, like us?"

"Hold that thought," Dale said, silencing the younger agent for the moment. "We'll come back to that in a minute. For now, let's stick to you and yours. How long have your…kind…been traveling through deep space?"

"We have travelled through space for eons, Head Agent Dale Hunter of the National Security Agency."

"I don't understand that term of measurement. How many years does an eon represent?"

"I do not know the exact number, Head Agent Dale—"

"Please, just call me Dale. And call him Jerry."

"Very well, Dale and Jerry."

"So how long?" Dale persisted. "Just an estimate."

"I estimate eleven billion years, Dale," the gray said.

"That's almost as old as space itself," Jerry remarked.

"Space is far older than your scientists estimate. Regrettably, your science is quite in its infancy, and you are not able to comprehend inter-galactic time and space in any way but linear. You have no understanding of how space and time actually interact."

"And you do?" Dale asked.

"My presence on this planet is irrefutable proof of that fact, Dale."

Dale suddenly felt a chill, as though someone opened the door and let a draft into the room. Dale did not like the way his name sounded vibrating up the alien's vocal cords and out the slash of mouth. He certainly did not like the sense of superiority in that response, either.

"Granted, your science is far more advanced than ours, but how can you survive an eleven-billion-year trip? Surely no life form, no matter how advanced, can survive that long."

"That is correct, Dale. Although there are many life forms that can live millennia, no single entity could survive in physical form for billions of years."

Dale was silent, considering. When he spoke, he said, "Are you saying that certain life forms…can survive longer in some form other than physical?"

"That is correct."

"In what form? Spiritual?" Dale asked.

The alien regarded Dale inquisitively. Its eyelids blinked horizontally over its black, onyx-like eyes. The slash of mouth moved very little when it spoke. "Not in spiritual form."

"Okay, then what else is there?"

"Consciousness," ALF said. "Memory."

"You mean like hive-mind?" Jerry asked. He sat forward now, suddenly more interested in the conversation.

ALF's head swiveled toward Jerry, his movement robotic and over-exaggerated. "I understand your reference, though it's technically incorrect. Your species would describe it as a collective conscious mind."

Dale said, "Please explain this collective consciousness...or whatever you call it, to those of us not familiar with the term."

"Collective conscious mind," ALF corrected, now focusing its massive black eyes on Dale. Those damn eyes reminded Dale of the shark in the movie *Jaws*. Dead, cold eyes that seemed to see right down into your soul, where your deepest fears resided.

"Yes, okay. Explain, please."

"Simply stated, it means all knowledge learned by my kind, throughout our history, is accessible to us all, even after our physical forms cease to exist. Although my physical form is much younger than all who have come before, I have access to all memories of my kind since our beginning. So, in this sense, I have lived eleven billion years, Dale."

"How old are you?" Dale asked.

"My physical form is more than one thousand years old."

"That's incredible," Jerry said.

Dale was silent, considering his next question, when there was a knock at the door. Dale stood and went to it. He opened it, stuck his head out, and was surprised to come face to face with Deputy Director Stevenson.

"Agent Hunter, I need a moment," Stevenson said.

"Yes, sir," Dale said.

He closed the door and crossed the room casually. Leaning over, he whispered to Jerry, "We need to step out."

Jerry looked up at him and then stood. "Excuse us a moment," he said to ALF.

ALF said nothing but watched them with those large black eyes, which seemed deep enough to fall into, like two black-holes, waiting for you to get sucked into their gravitational pull.

Outside, Deputy Director Stevenson sat perched at the edge of the desk, where Dale sat earlier. He wore a blue gingham dress shirt under a navy-blue sport coat and a pair of dark blue jeans. His white hair was combed smartly into a side-part. He smelled of Old Spice and V05 hair cream. He looked at both men with crisp blue eyes that hid behind puffy eyelids. He'd grabbed a quick nap on the flight from Washington, but he was still jet-lagged.

"Give me a sit-rep, Agent Hunter."

"Well, sir, we've only just started to interview the subject."

"You are able to communicate with it?"

"Yes, sir. It speaks English."

"Interesting," Deputy Director Stevenson said. He looked over Dale's shoulder at the alien behind the glass. It sat looking forward, as if oblivious of the three men. "What do we know about it? Preliminarily, of course."

"Well, it claims it is one of many species of extraterrestrial space travelers. It claims that it has been traveling through deep space for eleven billion years to reach us and that space is much older than our science can determine."

"Eleven billion years you say?"

Dale nodded. "That's right, sir."

Stevenson whistled through his teeth.

"He says that his kind can survive millennia in physical

form," Jerry chimed in, "but that they have the collective knowledge of their entire history that passes along to them, even after the physical form passes."

"I'll be damned," Stevenson said, taking in the information and trying to digest it. "Collective conscious mind."

"You've heard of it, sir?" Dale asked.

"I've studied it," Stevenson said. "Wrote a paper on it."

Like Jerry, Dale could see that Deputy Director Stevenson was in awe of the creature, rather than fearful. Dale felt in his bones it was a mistake not to fear the thing in the other room. They had no idea how many of them were out there or why they were here. The latter concerned him deeply.

To Dale, Stevenson asked, "Did it say why it was here?"

"No, sir. That's where I was going next, sir."

Stevenson stood and walked forward now. He stopped in front of the two-way, hands clasped behind his back, a look of child-like wonder spreading across his face. He spoke to them without turning around.

"In my thirty-seven-year career, I never thought we'd ever make contact. At least not in my lifetime. And look at this son-of-a-bitch, sitting right there behind this glass."

Jerry joined the deputy director. "It's incredible, isn't it, sir?"

"It is," Stevenson said. He turned to Jerry now. "What does he call himself? Does he even have a name?"

Jerry laughed. "He calls himself ALF."

"You're shitting me."

Jerry laughed again. "That's what I said!"

"Is that his true name?"

"No, sir," Jerry said, a stupid grin spreading across his face. "He told us his name, but it was gibberish. It doesn't translate."

Stevenson looked at Jerry, his white eyebrows raised. "I'd like to hear him speak. Can I get sound in here?"

"Uh, yes, sir," Jerry said. He stepped forward and switched on the wall-mounted intercom system. "This knob controls the volume. You can hear us, but we can't hear you unless you push and hold this other button to speak."

"Thank you, Agent…"

"Rafferty, sir."

"Excuse me, sir, but we'd better get back to it," Dale said.

"Right," Stevenson said. "Carry on, Agent Hunter. I'll monitor the interview from here. Is the video running? The president and his cabinet were promised a live stream."

"Yes, sir," Dale said and indicated the equipment with a quick jab of his index finger.

"Excellent. Let's find out if these gray men come in peace or if we're going to have to nuke their asses back to wherever it is they come from."

"Yes, sir," Dale said. "Agent Rafferty, on me."

Together, they left Deputy Director Stevenson and entered the interview room again.

"MY APOLOGIES FOR the interruption," Dale said, taking his seat across the table from ALF.

"Is the elder your commander?" ALF asked. "The man in the room beyond the glass?"

Dale and Jerry glanced at each other.

"Yes," Dale said.

"Is it he who decides my fate?"

Now, Dale looked toward the two-way mirror, as if awaiting direction from Deputy Director Stevenson. After several seconds, he looked back at the alien.

"We're not here to decide anyone's fate," Dale said. "We're just here to learn more about you and your kind. To learn about why you're here."

ALF turned to face the glass. The alien stared at the

two-way mirror for almost a minute, making Dale uncomfortable. He wondered briefly if the alien was trying to reach out to Deputy Director Stevenson using some sort of telepathy. That was foolish, he knew, yet Jerry wondered the same thing earlier, too—if the alien could somehow see through the glass. He'd meant mentally, of course, because Jerry knew how two-way mirrors worked.

Breaking the silence, Dale said, "You've traveled a long time to reach Earth. Tell us why you're here. Why now? And why make your presence known?"

ALF refocused its attention on Dale, fixing him with those damn void eyes. In its strange voice, ALF said, "We have come to save the planet."

"Why do we need saving?" Jerry asked, leaning forward again. He folded his hands on the table in front of him, clasping them tightly. "Is something coming to harm us?"

Dale put a hand on the other man's shoulder, giving him pause. Jerry sat back in his chair and deferred to the senior agent.

To ALF, Dale said, "Please, continue."

"This planet is in peril. In the very near future, global thermal-nuclear war will destroy much of the planet's surface and ecosystem, annihilating all species, including mankind. No humans or animals will survive the aftermath. The only creatures that survive will be mutated abominations that will roam the planet for the next million years."

The room grew quiet, as if all the air had been sucked out, creating a vacuum. Dale could hear his heart thudding in his ears.

"You're talking an extinction-level event," Jerry said.

The alien did not respond but rather stared blankly at the two men. Although its face was expressionless, Dale couldn't shake the feeling that there was a coldness beneath the surface.

"We're not at war with anyone, not one that would lead

to nuclear annihilation," Dale said.

"You will be," ALF responded.

"Who will we be at war with?"

Again, ALF did not respond.

"What country attacks us?"

"It is not your country that is attacked."

Dale and Jerry looked at each other, confused.

"What does that mean?" Dale asked.

"Your country is the aggressor. The catalyst that destroys this planet."

"You're saying we start the war?"

"That is correct."

Dale felt the gooseflesh on his arms again. The whole vibe in the room seemed to change, become darker. The room suddenly felt too warm, stifling.

"When does this nuclear holocaust happen?"

"September 23 of your year 2025," ALF said.

"Who do we attack and why? We must have been provoked."

"Your president and that of Russia will form an alliance. Their desire to control the planet, to exert their dominance over the lesser, will lead them to the brink of war. The oppressed will rise, form their own alliance. War will become imminent. The desire to control and the desire to be free will shade all logic, and both sides will launch their nuclear arsenals, knowing they will destroy the world, yet still they cannot step away from the brink. Still, they push their buttons."

"Assuming what you've just said is true, how could you know this? How can you know our future?"

ALF was silent.

"How do you know about events that haven't happened yet?" Dale pressed.

"This is not the first time we've visited this planet."

"That doesn't answer my question."

"In two hundred years, we will visit this planet, only to

find it destroyed, uninhabitable," ALF said.

"What do you mean, will visit our planet?"

"In the future."

"What does that mean?"

"I think he's saying he traveled back in time," Jerry said.

"In two hundred years, we passed through this galaxy and learned the fate of this planet. Our council of elders determined we must travel back in time to prevent the events of September 23 of your year 2025."

"Okay, hold on," Dale said. He rubbed his throbbing temples. This conversation had somehow gone sideways, fallen off the rails. "First, you tell me you traveled eleven billion years to get to Earth. Okay, I'll buy that. Then you tell me that space is older than we think. And now, you're telling me what? That time-travel is also possible?"

ALF nodded.

"Time travel is not possible," Dale stated.

"It is difficult for you to comprehend. Yet, it is possible."

"Our science has cured diseases, created new technologies, launched men into space. If our science says time-travel is not possible, then I believe it is not possible."

"Your science is elementary. Crude at best."

Dale scoffed. "Okay. Explain it to me."

ALF said nothing.

"How is time-travel possible?"

"You would not understand. What is important is that time-travel has allowed us to return to this planet. To save it from destruction."

"Returned from the future?"

"From the future and the past," ALF said.

"What does that even mean?" Dale asked.

"As I said, this is not the first time we've visited this planet."

Deputy Director Stevenson's voice addressed them

through the intercom system. "Agent Hunter, I need to speak with you."

Ignoring his boss, Dale asked, "When have you been here before?"

"We were here during this planet's evolution, from the time it was just a ball of molten rock, forming in cold space, to when the great beasts walked its surface, to when your species first evolved."

Now a knock at the door, but Dale ignored it. He held up one finger—*wait!*—toward the two-way mirror.

"Why does your kind have such an interest in us? Why keep visiting us throughout time?"

ALF did not respond. He seemed more interested suddenly by the knock at the door. The alien turned its head, looking toward the direction of the sound.

"You know, I've been listening to you for about twenty minutes now. I hear you say you're interested in saving the planet, but not once did you talk about your interest in saving humans," Dale said.

When the alien did not respond, Dale slammed his fist down against the metal tabletop. ALF turned his head back, fixing Dale with its void eyes.

"This planet is of great significance. Humans are not."

"You care about our planet, but you don't care if humans live or die?" Dale asked.

Silence. Then, "No."

Jerry swallowed hard. Dale could now see concern on his partner's face when he asked, "I don't understand. How do you save a planet and not the people?"

"Millions of life forms thrived on this planet for billions of years before your species evolved. This planet was home to countless species, some from here...some not. It has been a waystation for space travelers who have crossed thousands of light years in intergalactic travels. In the short time that your species has dominated this world, you've caused nothing but destruction and devastation. Not just among the people, but the planet. Humans have depleted it, and its resources, more than any other species, and in a very small amount of time."

Again, the intercom buzzed. "Agent Hunter, step out now."

Dale held up his hand impatiently toward the two-way.

"Sea ice is vanishing due to a rise in global temperatures, causing rising sea levels. Overpopulation is causing immense pressure on the planet's natural resources. Deforestation and the destruction of habitats is further affecting climate change. And on September 23 of 2025, you will destroy the planet's ecosystem and population, making the planet uninhabitable, not just to Earth's own species, but to those from beyond the stars who rely on this way-station for intergalactic travels."

The intercom buzzed a third time. "Damn it, Agent Hunter—"

Suddenly, an alarm sounded within the building—a sharp buzzing interspersed with bright flashes of light. Water sprayed down from the building's fire suppression system, soaking them. The door to the room opened suddenly, and Deputy Director Stevenson stood at the threshold, beckoning them to come to him. He was speaking, but they could not hear his voice above the ruckus. Both agents stood, and Jerry moved toward the door and stopped when he realized Dale did not follow.

"Dale, we have to go!" Jerry shouted to be heard above the bleating of the alarm.

Dale stood firm, his fists planted against the stainless-steel table, eyes locked with the alien. They both stared at each other for a moment, then Dale shouted, "Tell me why you are here!"

"We are here to save the planet."

"How? By stopping the war?"

ALF shook his head.

"Tell me how!" Dale insisted.

"I have read your thoughts, Head Agent Dale Hunter. I think you already know the answer to your question."

Dale gasped. The gray's intention was not to stop the war by diplomacy. Instead, this was an invasion aimed at killing all mankind, a pre-emptive strike to destroy them before they could destroy the planet.

Dale turned toward Jerry and Deputy Director Stevenson and tried to yell something, but before he could exhale, a large spike pierced through his back. He stared uncomprehendingly at the sharp point that exited his chest. Suddenly, his body was lifted several feet off the ground, before the spike retracted, and his lifeless body fell to the floor.

ALF stood, his face no longer emotionless. His nostrils flared, and his slash of a mouth was now replaced by a jack-o-lantern-like mouth full of razor-sharp teeth. His body seemed to double in both size and girth, transforming into a creature found only in children's worst nightmares. One of the creature's hands appeared to melt together, again reforming.

Jerry watched in wide-eyed horror as ALF's arm shifted into a six-foot-long pike. Jerry screamed, and he tried to shove Deputy Director Stevenson out of his way—"Sir, get out!"—but ALF attacked, spearing them both like a shish-kabob with the pike. Just as suddenly, the pike retracted and ALF's hand reformed into five elongated fingers.

Across the planet, from portals buried deep beneath the sands of Nevada, from vast caverns hidden within the mountains of Nepal, Egypt, and Russia, from the darkest fathoms of the sea, the alien beings, hidden for millennia, emerged. The invasion of Earth had begun.

CROAKER

Barry Charman

SITTING IN THE BAR AS IT BURNED, Croaker knocked back a pint of ashes and wondered if he'd heard right.

"You want me to go back? Up there?"

He knew better than to ask too many questions. He'd been asked to pull up a seat; he shouldn't presume anything. The man sitting across from him drank, then paused to blow a small flame off the cuff of his sleeve.

"I want you to go for a walk," he said. "Take a look."

"Okay, sure. But…why?"

A sigh. "I haven't been up there in some time. It's depressing, to be honest. But every once in a while, I like to make an…assessment."

"What am I assessing?"

The other man leaned forward. "Are they any closer to finding peace?"

Croaker tried not to lean back. Was the guy afraid he was losing his edge or something? "I can do that."

Nodding, the man opposite got to his feet. Around them, the

bar was burning, but like them, the few remaining patrons didn't care. They were damned if they were going to let that come between them and a drink. There were places to burn and places to feed the fire.

"I expect you to be thorough. And I expect you to know what will happen if you're not."

Croaker thought of the Church of Nails. He gave a pained nod. "What if I, uh, need to contact you?" The job was already making him uneasy.

A black card was dropped on the table. "Use this."

Croaker picked it up. *The Saint Who Ain't*. He smiled thinly. When he looked up, the other man was gone. Croaker sighed. He hadn't known what to expect, but he hadn't expected this.

Christ. He was going home.

WHEN HE WOKE, he was face down in a puddle. Someone was screaming. Croaker slowly pushed himself up and looked around.

It was midnight; he was in an alley made of cracks. The moon had washed everything the color of bone. A man was standing over him with a knife, while a pale woman was staring at them both in shock. Someone had messed up—he should have come back without any witnesses.

Oh well.

He got to his knees and noticed it was raining. Closing his eyes, he turned his face to the sky. The sensation was so cool, so alien. He was amazed at how different it felt. Had he forgotten?

"How the hell are you still alive?"

Croaker's eyes snapped open. He jumped to his feet and cracked the man's neck before he could become a problem. The body dropped, limp. He turned to the woman, but she was sliding down the wall, a red necklace already spilling from her throat.

He stood over her for a moment. Two lovers had come

adrift, picked clean from the night by some desperate knife. So it goes.

Leaving the alley, he went to the nearest streetlight and inspected himself. A red wound in his side had stopped bleeding. The creature that walked in this man had nothing to bleed. He carefully adjusted the shirt, zipped up his coat, and walked on.

Croaker checked himself in a shop window as he passed it; he looked normal enough. This body would endure.

The process of death could be deferred, for a time.

Walking over to a bench, he sat for a while, until people started to pass him by. He wasn't sure what form this assessment needed. Perhaps all that was required were his observations…his thoughts?

So, he started by letting the world walk past.

The skirts were shorter than he remembered, the men taller. There was more volume and less patience. The temperament seemed much the same as ever, though.

Are they any closer to finding peace?

Croaker got up, picked two men who were talking animatedly, and followed them discreetly. He allowed himself to be pulled along in the current of their conversation.

"She doesn't know?"

"Nah, don't think it would matter if she did. You get me? I keep her keen."

The first man laughed. A sharp, cynical rush of breath, it was the sound of gunfire braying into a slab of meat.

"Thing is, they crave affection," continued the second. "They like how you treat them, however you treat them. Shows her who she belongs to, right? And if she steps out of line, you just let her know, get me?"

"Quick jab?"

"Not too quick."

That got a laugh. "Yeah, never think of a girl as anything other than an unruly pet." They continued talking, exchanging notes about women they'd wounded. They only paused to accost new ones as they passed them.

Their ugliness was coarse and brittle, forged in ignorance and cruelty. He'd known their kind. He listened as they unpacked the word "no" and reinterpreted a "yes." It was fascinating, the narrow corners which they inhabited and infused with their concentration.

He let them go, knowing his assessment had to take a broader form.

For the remainder of the night, he crossed the city. Hiding in doorways, traveling night buses, walking in shadows. He traversed race and class, sex and age. He found people fueled by alcohol and apathy. Desire still made its puppets, greed still had its sway.

The sun would rise on little new.

THE NEXT MORNING, the first thing he did was steal a paper and read about the world around him. Religion, terrorism, politics, liars with interchangeable masks. Was there nothing new? Was the world at least more, or was it less?

He read an article about a young woman in Central America. She miscarried a baby she hadn't even known she was pregnant with, and then woke up handcuffed to her bed. The hospital reported her, and she was sentenced to thirty years for aggravated murder.

She never saw her baby.

Hidden away in the back pages, he discovered a car bomb had killed scores of people, but the country was just far enough away for it to be barely deemed newsworthy.

Reading between the lines on another page, he understood this government had turned on its people, distracting them while it carved into every infrastructure for profit.

The rest was gossip and sex, the famous and the reckless. The vile and the veil, that comforting lullaby of lies.

This is such an old world, Croaker thought. *It changes so much, yet changes so little.*

HE DECIDED TO sit on a street corner, seemingly down on his luck, to see what the world would make of him.

As expected, it ignored him.

The world walked by, heads down, hands in pockets, eyes fixed determinedly on phones. He was that sharp context that made them take sudden comfort in their own weathered existences.

Eventually, his mind began to drift, and old faces began to swim up from long-still waters. He studied them for a moment before flinching away. Soon names would ebb to the surface, and other things best forgotten: sensations, whispers. Dreams.

Unsettled, Croaker was pondering his next move when a figure walked out of the crowd and came over to him.

"Are you okay, honey?"

He looked up. A woman was standing over him, looking down with a concerned expression. She radiated warmth and a level of concern that he found surprising.

"I've been better."

"Look, I volunteer at a place; there's food, it's warm. Why don't you let me show you?"

Bemused at this sudden ray of sunshine, Croaker pulled himself carefully to his feet and gave her a cracked smile through cracked lips. "Just lead the way…"

HER NAME WAS Louise. Curly blond locks kept escaping a practical hairband, framing a round, ruddy face that seemed as cheerful as it was tired. She took him to a small soup kitchen that had been set up in a community center. People were lining up to get food and then wandering over to rows of tables. Croaker got some coffee, then sat by himself to do some more people watching.

There was something ever truthful about the ragged community that wandered by. The story of any society was told by the people that slipped through its cracks.

He was contemplating this, when a thin girl, dark-skinned, and dark-eyed, sat down across from him. Her hair was long, and she pulled it away from her eyes while she picked at her food. When she started to eat, she didn't pause between bites, or even look up, until she'd cleared the plate. When she had finished, she looked around and noticed him.

"You look hungry," Croaker said, warming his hands around the cup while she studied him.

"You look ill," she said.

He gave her a faint smile. "I'll be fine."

She scowled. "Well, good for you." Her gaze darted away from him—she couldn't settle.

"You're running from your parents."

It wasn't a question. She glanced savagely at him. His eyes could read more signals, more sorrows, than she could imagine.

"What?"

He shrugged. "Rule of running: don't stand still. You know what will happen if they find you." Her eyes went wide. He fixed her with an unblinking stare. "Honor is more important than anything else. Their love has reached an end."

She opened her mouth to question him, but nothing came out. Her eyes dropped, and she looked desolate, as if the truth would destroy her in the end.

At that moment, Louise joined them. The girl glanced up at her, took in the smile, the face full of questions, and walked away just as Louise sat down.

She watched the girl go, then gave Croaker an appraising look. "How are you feeling?"

"Warm."

She smiled, used to the stoic and the withdrawn. "Glad we could help."

Glancing around, he took in the number of people looking

rough. "Are there more people on the streets, do you think?"

"More than summer." She looked concerned. The leaves were falling, discoloring, autumn was blowing through everyone. The older people looked punch-drunk, as if they knew winter was waiting in the wings. They wore strained expressions of concentration, perhaps hoping they could think themselves out of the gap they'd slipped into.

The dreamers would thin this herd out.

"Nobody doing anything about it?" he asked casually.

She laughed, which was answer enough.

A slight, fair-haired girl joined them, sitting next to Croaker with an exaggerated sigh. Louise gave her an appraising glance. "Something to eat?"

The girl was fumbling for something in her pockets. She looked up and nodded animatedly. "And a coffee."

"Please."

The girl looked at Croaker, thoughtfully; she turned and gave Louise a smile. "Please."

The word seemed sweet enough, but it had been dragged through some harsher notes. Louise hesitated, long enough to realize she couldn't refuse the girl, then stood and left the table.

The girl offered Croaker her hand. "Paige."

He looked at the hand, then shook it.

"Jesus, did you die out there?" She pulled away from his cold touch, wincing.

He shot her a smile as dark as his coffee. "Could be. Think I'd notice?"

She continued to rummage in her pockets, then paused to look up and stare into space. Something about her mannerisms amused him. Eventually, she yawned, and thrust her hands back into her coat.

"Lost something?"

She shook her head. "Nothing to lose."

They sat in silence until Louise returned. She gave Paige some sandwiches wrapped in foil, and a steaming cup. Paige thanked her with a big smile. They watched as she tugged the wrapping open and devoured the food without saying anything. She probably wasn't even tasting it. She angled the foil wrapping below her, so she could catch any crumbs that fell, then tipped them into her mouth when she was done.

Finished, she warmed her hands on the coffee, blowing on it occasionally.

"Been on the streets long?" Louise sounded tired.

Paige shrugged. Louise sighed and walked away, but Croaker picked up the weight behind the silence. She'd been on the streets long enough that time meant nothing to her.

She was so utterly disconnected from the world around her that she was perfect.

"Where's your spot?"

She scowled, and her eyes went to her feet.

"I'm not muscling in…just wondered if you were doing okay."

"Worry about yourself." She gave him a brief look, like she wasn't going to waste a second trusting him just because he looked as ragged as her.

Her hands were small, covered in tattered mittens. Everything she wore seemed thrown together, but it was all black, save for a turquoise shirt that had turned as dark as dusk.

"What are you staring at?" Her voice was emptied of anything aggressive. When he looked at her, she was almost smiling.

He pointed at the mittens. "Just wondering what's holding them together."

"The holes. What holds anyone together?"

He heard a sadness in her voice…She probably hadn't intended to be as sharp as she was. She tried to minimize it with a rueful expression, but they'd both caught it.

"How long do you think the streets will keep you?"

Paige was staring into space again. She snapped out of it, forcing a smile on her face. "Keep me warm until I'm cold."

Her life was a series of ever-ready maxims, each one keen to deflect more attention than the last.

"Get a man," he said. "Someone would take you in."

"Do you think I'm pretty?" The smile had turned wry; she'd put a lilt into her voice to disarm him.

But without a pulse, his blood did not run her way.

"Not anymore. Might have, once."

She looked surprised for a second. He watched her slump slightly. "Whatever."

"Get a man," he repeated, "and get a blade. Use him to lose him. You should look after yourself. Kindness won't end the streets."

His voice was quiet, insistent. She leaned toward him, as if drawn by the low certainty, the brutal clarity. Abruptly, she pulled away, looking frightened. "What's wrong with you?"

He mimicked her disarming smile. "All the same things that are wrong with *you*."

She inched away from him then. It amused him, the uncertainty of dazed prey.

Bored, he turned his head to take in the latest people that were filing in. A convention of silhouettes.

After a while, he looked back. Paige was gone.

Not a crumb remained.

CROAKER SAT HUNCHED in a corner, watching people as they interacted, argued, and pleaded. They came for food and shelter. Heat, both human and functional. All of them adrift in a sea of life. They would find harbor for a while and then be turned back out. He could learn a lot from their faces: whole lives were carved in the worry lines. He watched, reading it all.

When he'd had his fill, he slipped away at dawn.

ARE THEY ANY closer to finding peace?

Croaker broke into a flat to watch television. The world began to come into sharper focus. The greed was all it ever was, the appetite undimmed. The wars rolled over the world and back again, mainly out of some mutilation of religion. One half of the planet gorged while the other starved. Everything was suspended in some web of politics that he could tell no one would ever untangle.

There was little value in being good.

That was the clearest indicator. Those who became wealthy forgot they were ever poor, and those who were poor aspired to dreams they could not realize.

The narrative of man was as clear as ever. Judge the weak for being weak, if possible. Support the wealthy, chip away at the helpless. Allow one class to disintegrate, so another might gawk at the spectacle.

Man invented the wheel, and nothing else.

FOR A DAY, he walked the city, from the towers that scraped the sky to the slums they dwarfed. He crossed sullen faces and slumped figures. There was laughter, true, but that was simply a release, an abandonment of worry.

These people drank, copulated, fought. They reveled in everything that kicked their blood into another day.

At one point, he sat in a park and watched some children play. It was the first time he'd felt a sense of innocence, of something clear and unmuddied. He closed his eyes to listen to the laughter. When he opened them again, he looked around to see two women huddled together, pointing at him.

They were watching him while they watched their children. Speculating, perhaps. He knew there were men, and women, that walked this world with an appetite for innocence. A stain that seemed to have deepened considerably since his day.

He thought then, back to his own, distant, childhood. For a moment, he considered revisiting the old house, seeing if the door was still white as he remembered. The people he'd known would have had grandchildren by now, great-grandchildren, in fact. Would he recognize the old faces in the new?

He allowed a brief smile, but no, he would not look. He had no interest in that life, or whatever faded echoes it had spilled.

The women watched as he got to his feet and walked away. Innocence existed, but it did not last long.

A CHURCH SPIRE appeared in the distance. Croaker wound through some narrow streets toward it. If Heaven were overflowing or emptying out, the tell-tale signs would be obvious either way.

He watched the point of the cross as he got closer. That wild stab into the sky always said so much.

When he turned a corner and found it before him, he almost recoiled at the dense and fetid accumulation of dust. There were churches in Hell, but they were places of song and sex. Books were written, not read.

Croaker thought of the ecstasy he had seen, the abandon. Congregations of flesh and delight. The demons joined in sometimes. Reptile silhouettes, transgressions of love. Poetry made from exquisite corpses. Thinking about it all, it was difficult for his mind not to snag on the Church of Nails. The blackened tower, east of all the rest. The Saint sometimes took mass inside, punishing those that had forsaken his charity or failed his tasks. There were no animals in Hell, only the screams of men that had been reduced to their level.

Quickly dismissing the memories, Croaker walked up to the doors. They were locked, so he ripped out a nail and used it to carve some filth into the wood.

When it began to rain, he sought shelter under a tree across the road. There he watched, waiting for someone to arrive. He would not intrude uninvited; you had to be cordial about these sorts of things.

He smiled through a dead man's face, amused by himself.

Eventually a man walked up to the doors and unlocked them. He hesitated, as if he'd noticed the crude words etched into the door and was startled. For just a moment he stood frozen in the doorway, then walked inside.

Croaker counted to a hundred, then crossed the road.

AT THE END of the room, the cross leaned over the altar, while dust mites danced in a weak stab of light beneath. Croaker sat in darkness until the vicar noticed him, one dead man eyeballing another.

"Can I help you?"

Holding out his dirty hands, Croaker revealed his frayed cuffs. "A little charity. But not too much—I don't want to get soft."

Something in his tone stopped the vicar. He looked like he was going to step forward; instead, he just looked his visitor over. "Have you been in an accident? Perhaps I could call you an ambulance?"

Croaker laughed. "Too late, son." He glanced around. "Something tells me it's always this empty, am I right?"

"Well, it's early…"

The vicar was a tall man, approaching crooked. Stale as an idea, he seemed ageless and sexless, undefinable. The grave yawned every time he opened his mouth. Croaker studied him in a way that made him pause.

"What is it you want?"

Something of Croaker's bearing had given him away. He shrugged, irritated with himself. "How's the flock? Are the numbers swelling? Are they healthy?"

"What does that mean? Again, what do you want?"

Croaker let the silence teem between them. He wasn't breathing and wondered if the other man could tell. He held him with a look of contempt, unblinking, unfiltered.

"If I could tell you a little of Hell, would you want to hear?"

The vicar's face became tired. "Absolutely not."

"You picture a lake, perhaps? A fire that cannot dim. A choir that screams for mercy. A creature that bathes in the shadows." He curled a mocking tongue around each word. Unsettled, the vicar looked at him as if he almost understood why.

"But it is a pleasant place," Croaker said, smiling. "Full of the truest pleasures and the mass of all who've walked the world. Tell me—when Heaven is empty, will the last that remain come knocking on Hell's door for company?"

"What…what is this? What are you?"

Well. Perhaps even the sightless could see.

"I am a witness. Not unlike yourself, in a way."

"A witness to what? For what?"

Croaker reeled it in. He wanted to tip his hat, not his hand. He shrugged and casually got to his feet. At the end of the room, the carpenter hung from some wood. Croaker gave him a nod. "People have turned to other things to fill them. Weakness traded for weakness. There's an apathy out there without name. A callous pulse. Can you hear it?"

The vicar stared at him but said nothing.

"You try not to, I suppose."

"I think you should leave."

Ignoring him, Croaker walked to another pew and wiped his finger through the dust gathered on the seat. "To think he was afraid Hell would be empty. He wondered if mankind might find peace. Maybe there's a part of him that'd like that. I mean, it's almost depressing." He was goading the other man, but there was something about the words he found hard to rejoice in.

"There is always hope."

Croaker shrugged. "Not up here." He turned and walked to the door, uninterested now in the other man's reactions.

He had already told him enough.

AFTER SEEKING A man that was better off, he sought one that wasn't.

Creeping in some alleys, Croaker found a man stooped in a puddle of his own creation. His head was rocking, and a rain had begun that would be the end of him. Croaker was intrigued. At whose gate would he soon be knocking?

He crouched and shook the man lightly. Something fell loose from the man's sleeve. Croaker watched as the rain washed a needle into the gutter. He reserved judgement as a matter of course.

The white gate would not part for this. This was a deed of sinful selfishness, a coarse act. At the black gate, one of the creatures would open up and throw him a blanket. They'd hunker by the nearest fire and exchange stories. Punishment would come— they were compelled to enforce that—but the man would understand it, value it. He would know what waited on the other side.

He would, most likely, ask if it were the white gate. Someone would find him a job then, maybe even hook him up with some woman, or man, who'd fallen through a similar crack.

Croaker remembered the first night after his trials ended. He'd been introduced to a woman who looked just as he felt. They'd talked all night, then when they realized there was no day, they moved on to something else.

Waking up with someone as forsaken as you is no Hell.

He thought about her for a while longer, then walked back into the rain.

CROAKER STRODE INTO a bar, said something that should have been unspeakable, then waited for someone to buy him a drink.

"You're right, mate, got to say this stuff," his new friend said, slapping a beer down in front of him. Hadn't been hard to win him over: just the usual them-and-us rhetoric. Could it be possible there were more prejudices?

"If they want to live like that, they should go back home. Who do they think they are? People bend over backwards for them. What about our values, our jobs? If you stand up for the working man, you're racist or something!"

Some working-class hero, Croaker thought. *A lesser Lennon.*

"We need to just line 'em all up, you know?"

Croaker smiled thinly. "You want to shoot them?"

Lennon gestured expansively, gave him a broad smile. "No, line them up, kick them out, make them someone else's problem."

"That all they are? A problem to be pushed away?"

"It's not our problem, that's all I'm saying."

"Ah." Croaker nodded, as if it all made sense now. "Of course. Their lives are not your concern."

"Exactly."

Croaker pulled the humor out of his smile. That was where they'd gone wrong. That disconnect, that apathy that had slid over empathy like a black glove. Your problems were your own in this world.

"Little selfish, don't you think?"

Lennon put his hands up, frowning. "Hey, I'm not a racist, but I'm just saying. Everyone has to look after their own first."

"Don't help people if they can help themselves?"

"Sure."

"What if they can't?"

Lennon shrugged irritably. It wasn't his problem.

Croaker laughed. "Hell, you're right, man. Those kids come here and expect a new life to be laid out for them—it's pathetic."

"Too right."

"They're trying to flee the bombs—bombs we sold—but they should just make something out of the rubble. Whining that strangers have ripped apart your land, well, it's obnoxious, isn't it?"

Lennon laughed, awkwardly. It was like he wanted to agree but suddenly felt he needed permission. As if he didn't know who they were laughing at anymore. Poor lamb. Poor bloody lamb.

Croaker stopped laughing abruptly, just to make the man uncomfortable.

Strange man, that needed his venom validated, almost as if he knew there was something wrong with its focus.

"Got kids?"

Lennon nodded. He didn't say anything more. They just let the silence speak, as it often did.

A BRIGHT MOON came up, watchful like a skull. Croaker admired it. There were levels in Hell that were pure ash; the moon felt like an old friend.

"Had fun?"

The 'Saint Who Ain't' walked out of the shadows, his pale face grinning in the somber light. The skull leered beneath.

"I don't think anyone here's having fun."

The Saint grimaced. "Oh, that's not true. Lots of fun is being had at a lot of people's expense."

Croaker nodded. He tapped the card against his leg, anxious. He hoped he'd done enough. "So, you want to hear what I think?"

"Sure." The Saint was expressionless.

Croaker still wasn't sure exactly what the Saint was going to do with his assessment. Did he want some theory confirmed? Some philosophy validated?

He wondered if he risked a question. "You wanted to know if man were any closer to finding peace, but you must have known how little they'd changed?"

The Saint lightly brushed at his suit, a wry smile visiting him briefly. "I never really thought it would come to this," he said. "That it's possible they'll never find peace. There's a lot a man like me can do with knowledge like that if you think about it." The Saint looked away into the night—he didn't seem either triumphant or troubled. There was a dark glint in his eyes, but that was always there, a small fire lit in the darkness that roamed before the world was anything like this.

Croaker gave him his assessment. "They're scattered, selfish, every one of them isolated in their own meager struggle. The world is smaller than ever; they're all interconnected but dragging each other down. The planet's getting hotter, doomed to fail, and none of them can agree to care. They're all cornered in tawdry escapes. The wars are more, and increasingly for less, because it's the same story, told over and over."

The Saint nodded. "Peace?"

"Not even a glint in their eyes."

The Saint paced for a moment. He stopped suddenly and fixed Croaker with a cold look. "How does that make you feel?"

Startled, Croaker shrugged. "I...I don't know."

"Upset?"

He realized he didn't even know how to answer the question. "I'm not surprised, I guess."

The Saint sneered. "Not what I asked."

"No..."

The Saint tilted his head, an animalistic motion that looked like a predator sensing prey. "Been up here too long?"

"What? No—"

"Been down there too long?"

Croaker hesitated. He gave a half nod, a concession.

"I want you to bring me something. Up to it?"

Croaker sensed a shift in the mood between them. He

nodded, quickly. Afraid not to.

The Saint relaxed. "Good. Bring me the blood of an innocent."

"The—?" Croaker cut himself off. He didn't query, just nodded. He felt that a further assessment was now being made.

Would there be a steeper price for failure? He didn't need to ask.

The 'Saint who Ain't' studied him, as if following his quickening blood. Not that this blood would run any more. He parted with a smile that was a wound exposing bone, and then shadows draped him.

There was a lingering smell of ash, of smoke. Croaker breathed it in, feeling that sweet bitter taste he'd come to call home.

In many ways, it was a world that made more sense to him than this.

INNOCENCE.

It took Croaker a while to realize the task he'd been given came with a difficulty he hadn't considered, though no doubt the Saint had.

Who was truly innocent, here? Where did you find something as pure as that?

He began by seeking acts of kindness. Few had seen him when he was begging, which was enough to tell him acknowledgement was exceptional. He listened to the night and heard a scream he could use. There was a body in some bushes, some young woman that had been followed and assaulted. It was still night, though the sun was a dim pulse somewhere distant. Croaker dragged her body to a soon-to-be busy road and waited.

The first car braked when it saw her, reversed, paused, then slowly drove around. The next vehicle was a large truck. Here was a man tied to a deadline, bound to a quick turnaround, wired by the night, run to a thin nerve by the workload.

The truck waited. Slowly it backed up, the many wheels pointed at an angle, and then it slowly made a turn that took it round the body.

When a car finally did stop, the act meant nothing to Croaker. This was no longer innocence but guilt. Light stabbed accusingly through the dawn, and acts could no longer be conveniently ignored.

Croaker walked away, knowing he had to be more precise.

He found himself retracing his footprints, hoping to see a certain smile, an act of kindness, a spark. Thinking of the lives he'd crossed, he thought back to Louise at the soup kitchen and wondered if he hadn't already seen what he was looking for.

When he found her again, she was still there, helping out a different crowd. He looked around, wondering what had happened to the faces he'd seen passing through just days ago.

Croaker paused in the doorway before he went inside. This body had been dead when he first tapped on its shadow; a process had begun that he couldn't ignore. He found his reflection in a brass panel and studied himself. Patting his hair down and adjusting his suit, he breathed in and realized no one here was as fresh as they once had been.

His hand hovered over the door handle. What would the Saint do with the blood?

Did it matter?

He found Louise handing out clean shoes and socks to newcomers. She looked startled when she saw him. "You look terrible."

"Feel worse, if you can believe it. Couple of kids jumped me, bit banged up."

She led him to a seat and tried to fuss over him, but he deferred any treatment. "I just wanted some place quiet to sit down for a bit."

"You're so pale. You could have an infection…"

He sighed heavily. "I'll be honest. I'm ill, but I've made

peace."

The news seemed to deflate her momentarily. She froze as if she didn't know what to say next.

"I'd take a coffee, though."

"Sure…" She gave him a tight smile, then left to get him a drink. While she was gone, he scanned the room. So many of the new faces were young. How'd they hit a dead end this quickly?

Before he could unravel that, Louise came back with a coffee. She put it down and sat with him, looking him over. "I'd offer to get you something clean," she murmured.

"Don't waste it."

Louise nodded, the gesture bound in sadness. It was her, had to be. There was nothing selfish in her bearing. How much time did she give to this place, to these people? Did she get any reward, expect one, even?

Spilling her blood would give him little satisfaction, which told him she was perfect. She talked to him for a while, though seemed distracted by the shadow he'd draped over them both. Abruptly she got up and started to clear a table near them, carrying plates to some kitchen or storeroom.

He watched as she patted the shoulder of a boy as she passed him and paused to smile at someone else reassuringly.

When she disappeared through a door, he counted to fifty before following her. He fingered the Saint's card in his pocket. With any luck, he would be done here shortly, then he could go home. Maybe he could go and find Rebecca. He hadn't spoken to her in some time; caught up in his death, he'd forgotten to go on living. The notion made him smile. He would find her in the labyrinth. Most chose to wander in there at some point. To compare dead ends, to navigate how lost they could become. He would find her, give her a reason to come out.

Walking through the door to the storeroom, Croaker paused. There was no sign of Louise, but her laughter was trickling down a hall to the right. The volunteers kept their spirits up however they could, he guessed. She was vital to this place—he imagined handing her over to the Saint would be like stealing from the bottom of a house of cards.

The laughter ended abruptly as he nudged the door open. He paused, wondering if he'd interrupted something, if he should wait, but when he entered, he realized they couldn't see him.

Louise was in the corner, standing over one of the boys from out front. He was sitting on a stool, staring down at his shoes.

Her voice carried softly across the room. "Come on. It's Billy, right?"

He mumbled something.

"Come on, Billy. Be nice. You liked that meal, didn't you? Were those gloves nice? Eh?"

Croaker watched from the doorway. Louise ruffled the boy's hair, then took his arm and brought his hand up to her leg. She tilted his head to look in his eyes. "Fair's fair, eh?"

The boy looked away, while his hand began to move. She lifted the hem of her dress, then steadied herself with a hand on his shoulder, moaning as she squeezed it tight.

She stroked the boy's hair, pulling him close, so his sobs were muffled. Croaker watched them for a moment, then turned and walked out.

HE GAVE HIMSELF back to the night. Walking, watching, listening. Each time he thought he'd found what he was looking for, he realized he was further away than ever.

A taxi driver who'd taken sympathy on him and ferried him across the city without charging used the time to lecture him against the perils of foreigners and the lies of women. A young couple who seemed bright eyed and full of the raw rush of love, openly laughed when he walked over to them for assistance. An elderly woman walking her dog brushed past him as if he were invisible. When he called after her, she threatened to drop the leash.

He even went back to the church, but the vicar was gone. Where had his disappointment taken him?

Tired, Croaker walked to a park and sat in the shade of a tree. The card dug into his leg, and he wondered if the Saint ever grew impatient. A hymn from the Church of Nails came jarringly to mind...

But then, if there was no innocence to be found, perhaps that was the point. Croaker grimaced. He imagined a world reduced to good intentions and shallow gestures. Was there anything real left?

Had the lie dressed itself up and thought itself real? A dead man's heart rolled in his chest, and he nodded.

Such a world was and is.

He was reaching into his pocket when he heard the beat of a familiar heart. It was distant, but that meant nothing to this body; it was not limited.

Wondering, he clawed his way to his feet, and then he ran.

THEY LISTENED TO many heartbeats in Hell, a curious diversion, like so many. Hers was so clean, like a bright pulse calling through the darkness.

He didn't hold back as he ran, didn't pause or use caution. There was only the thudding of her heart, getting clearer and clearer.

She was close.

He stopped, allowed his failing body to recover. If he pushed it much more, he feared parts might start to give way. He laughed and felt his jaw detach, swinging loose. Trying to push it back just made it click weirdly. His legs felt odd, like his hips weren't right anymore. Well, it was too late to worry about it all now.

Paige was sitting on a bench, eating chips from a bag. Approaching her, he cleared his throat. Startled, she looked up and saw him.

He smiled. "Hey, you all right?"

She was on her feet before he'd finished speaking. Time on the streets had sharpened her flight response. She was already looking over his shoulder, wondering how he'd snuck up on her, wondering if he was alone. Also, he must have looked messed up as all hell.

He held up his hands, the simplest unthreatening gesture he knew. "I was just walking past. It's all right." His mouth didn't feel right, but the words were still getting out okay.

She cautiously returned to her seat. He limped closer and sat next to her, leaving a clear space. "Nowhere to go?"

His sudden appearance had clearly unsettled her, but she gave him a weak smile. "What do you think?"

"Thought you might've listened to what I said."

"Use a man?" She shook her head. "Christ. No."

"Was pretty sinister advice, I guess." He grinned. She ignored it. Good girl. She might not last long out here, but she deserved to.

"I won't live like that," she said, though she didn't have to say anything.

"Like what?" He held his breath.

"Like…" She sighed, glanced away, and then looked at her feet. "Like the only way up is to claw someone down. I don't want to hurt anybody."

Was that aimed at him or the street?

"Even if it means being lost?" he whispered.

The night was cold: he saw it wrap around her. She could have made a fire out of anything, especially bad advice. He reached out and helped himself to one of her chips. They were stale, probably fished out of the trash.

"If I told you how to make it, but that meant someone would get hurt…"

She shot up to her feet. He lashed her into place with a tone of voice so cold even the night flinched. "Listen. If someone else suffered, just a little, in some small way you'd never even know, and it gave you the chance to prosper in their place, would you take it?"

"No."

"You didn't even think about it."

She looked at him, as if she somehow knew him for what he was. "Think about what?"

"Saving yourself."

Her jaw dropped. The cold blew through them both for a moment. Her sleeves were pulled down low around her small hands. She looked pale, frightened perhaps, that there was something in the words worth hearing. A salvation made of that most terrible thing, the easy answer.

"Well, some people don't deserve saving."

He laughed. It had been a long time. He coughed and felt something loose roll around inside him. "Good for you."

Paige must have picked up on something because she stepped away. Her eyes were roving over him. She knew there was something wrong but couldn't pick up what. She looked agitated, but there was something else. She hesitated. "Are you all right? Can I..." She didn't know what more to say. Clearly, she wanted to offer something but had nothing.

She could have run, but she didn't. Croaker looked her over and sighed. His jaw drooped and he shoved it back into place. Just then, it felt like his whole body was coming apart. His scalp itched, he rubbed it, and a chunk of hair, and more, came away in his hand. His flesh felt paper thin; his bones felt like they knew it and were trying to stab through him from the inside. He clenched his eyes shut, for fear they would weep out of their sockets. He had to hold out just a little longer, see this through...

After a deep breath he looked up at her, face drawn and pale, a mask pulled over bone, no more.

Paige took a step back from him, disturbed. "What is this? What are you doing here? How did you find me?"

Questions. He'd come here to answer one that refused to be.

In one pocket was the card. In another was a knife, picked up on his first night from the man that had "killed" him, but not touched until now.

He knew what he had to do.

"Can I go?" Paige's voice was low, though she didn't know why she was scared.

Croaker looked around. It was a late hour on a less-traveled street. There were no houses, just boarded-up shops and alleys that conversed in whispers.

"I'm not stopping you."

"Will you?"

He looked up at her. "I might."

For a second, he thought she'd run. There were tears in her eyes but nothing left to pour out. To his surprise, she sat back next to him, and picked at the remaining chips.

"Why are you here?" he asked, voice as low as hers.

She shrugged. "Never knew Dad. Mom drank. I went into foster care, took myself out."

"What did you think would happen?"

Her eyes were the blue of a drowned world. "This."

Across the road, a streetlight flickered, as if unwilling to witness anything further. *We are all made of old roads like this*, Croaker thought. He smiled. Hell had made poets out of them all, but that didn't mean they were any good.

Paige saw the smile. "Does this have to happen?"

"What do you think's going to happen?"

She groaned. "Please. Just…just say something real."

The card was in his pocket, but he hadn't read the name. He didn't know why.

"Croaker."

"What?"

"That's my name. I died across the city, can't remember the year. There was a war, somewhere. Bet that narrows it down…" She was just staring at him, confused. She tried to smile, so he gave her a look that erased it.

"There's a man I know, watches from the ashes…Ah, it doesn't matter."

He watched as she chewed her lip. She was afraid, but he

hadn't moved, hadn't raised his voice. There was something perfectly still between them, a concession of defeat, an awareness of futility. He was already dead; she was barely living.

The card sat. The knife sat.

"You should go," he said, releasing the words that had been pent up inside him.

"Where?"

She had given up; as good as any soul he'd crossed, yet she couldn't see it. Croaker took the dead man's wallet out from his pocket and counted the money. He threw it down and nodded at it. "No good to me, not where I'm going."

"I don't—I don't want charity."

"Why not? You won't steal it, and you won't accept it when it's given to you? How long will you last? You deserve to. You know that, right? You've proved that."

"To whom?" Her eyes lit up.

"I'm not saving you. I'm helping you save yourself."

She crouched down and scooped up the wallet, then sat with it in her lap.

Croaker studied her. "Don't thank me."

"Why not?"

All the lights in the street were now flickering. He glanced around. How long had it been happening?

A dry voice suddenly joined them. "Because the deed is enough, I imagine."

Croaker's head whipped left, and he saw the 'Saint who Ain't' standing in the entrance to the alley. He was staring impassively at them, wearing a white suit that was stained with streaks of ash.

"I'm sorry," Croaker said, quietly.

Paige had also seen him, and she knew something was wrong. She'd gotten to her feet, but the Saint was in front of them before either understood how he'd moved so fast.

"It's perfectly all right." He was smiling at her, his voice so smooth, so reassuring, it was almost unreasonable to be afraid.

"Please…" Paige was begging, and she probably wasn't sure why.

The Saint continued to watch her. He sniffed the air for a moment, as if cherishing the blood in her veins.

Croaker got to his feet. He felt dizzy, and he didn't understand why he'd done what he'd done. "I should have called you," he mumbled.

"But you didn't."

There was nothing to say. Croaker just shook his head, frowning.

"Doesn't matter. I was watching all the same."

Paige looked from one man to the other. She'd noticed the smoke in the newcomer's footprints. Perhaps she'd sensed more, a strange tint in his eye, a trace of sulfur when he spoke.

The Saint waited. "Take your time."

Her hand went to her mouth. Somehow, she knew. We all do when the time comes. Her voice was cautious, cowed. "Are you the devil?"

He spoke with a voice like velvet draped over bone. "I'm only the devil if you name me."

She moaned. It was the sound of a child torn from a parent.

Croaker didn't want to see what would come next but felt he should watch. He just wanted to go home, but not like this.

The Saint had come even closer, seemingly without moving. He was at Paige's side; his hand had lightly dropped to her shoulder. He seemed to drink in her tiredness, her fear.

Her head jerked away, seeking Croaker, but the Saint's voice cut through the motion. "Don't look at him."

She looked back to the Saint. He watched as she swallowed, bit her lip, blinked. Each motion seemed compelling to him. "I've been making an assessment." His gaze slowly turned to Croaker. "Do you think you've passed?"

Croaker's eyes closed. He should have known.

When he looked again, the Saint had stepped away from Paige and she had begun to take faltering steps away from them.

"Wait!" The Saint's voice froze her. He nodded at the wallet, which had fallen from her hands to the ground. "This is yours now.

Take it."

She could have continued walking but seemed more frightened of not obeying him. Stooping down, she quickly snatched up the wallet. The Saint turned his back on her, and this time, she didn't hesitate to run.

Croaker watched until she'd gotten to the end of the road and turned out of sight.

"So, what was the assessment?"

The Saint ignored him and sat at the bench. "I asked for her blood. Did you think she was an innocent?"

"Yes," he admitted.

"So why didn't you kill her?" The Saint bared his teeth. "You didn't do your job. Even though you knew the things I'd do to you."

"It took me so long to find someone who was actually innocent…" Croaker trailed off, almost apologetic. It was hard to make words. It wasn't just the state of his jaw, but the state of his nerves. Soon he would be kneeling in the Church of Nails. Joining the flayed choir…Oh God…

"You couldn't bring yourself to hurt her?"

"Something like that."

The Saint nodded. "I wondered if there was anyone left who could turn a demon from his path and what it would mean if there was."

Croaker didn't understand. "I'm sorry."

The Saint darted him a wry smile. "Look at you. You've come far, you know that?"

Feeling uncertain under the gaze, Croaker gave him a vague shrug and looked away. The Saint laughed. "You've been better served by my world than this one. You're a better man for your time spent down there than up here. Dwell on that."

Croaker tried.

Sighing, the Saint looked up into the starless sky. "I will never make an accord, you understand? Heaven will wither, this is all as you've made it. But I'll keep Hell open to everyone. Can't you see?

It's the best of all possible worlds. It's where we all belong. There is innocence there..." He looked back at Croaker. "I never doubted these people would endure. I know them so well."

Croaker sat, exhausted. His mind reeled. He'd begun to doubt, but Paige had shown him something. Even so, it seemed like a glimmer, no more. "So, you still think they're innocent?"

The Saint shrugged. "Of course. They're children."

Croaker nodded. There was too much to that for him to think about right now.

"Makes you glad, doesn't it? The dark has no value, no purpose, without the light. You could see that, having lived in the dark so long..."

Weary, Croaker felt relieved, but he didn't know how to express it anymore. He felt as if his body was on the verge of finally abandoning him.

"How do you feel?" the Saint asked him, softly.

Croaker didn't answer. He felt tired, elated, drained. Eventually he simply said, "Alive."

They exchanged rueful smiles, as demons did. The Saint got back to his feet and helped Croaker stumble over toward a nest of shadows.

"Are we going home?" Croaker asked.

"Come on, I'll buy you a drink."

He nodded and followed the Saint until the darkness flickered and a familiar light beckoned.

They drank ashes, to ponder the fire. It had always seemed apt.

INFECTIOUS GLOW

Red Lagoe

BETELGEUSE WENT SUPERNOVA. THERE WAS never any guarantee that it'd blow in his lifetime, but then Chuck caught word through this astronomy club's social media group that it happened. Pushing eighty-four years old, Chuck couldn't risk letting his heart give out before seeing it for himself, so he popped an aspirin and took some calming breaths to quell the excitement. The other side of the planet witnessed it hours before. Images on the news, and online, of a bright light in the evening sky, almost as bright as the moon, washed out the glow of the stars. Folks in Russia and Europe had been treated to a nebulous bulge against the backdrop of the night. Reports and astro-images described brilliant reds and purples. Just Chuck's luck. Colorblind, he'd never been able to distinguish reddish hues—not even the supposed ruddy color of the super giant before it went supernova. Just a faint gray-white light, devoid of color.

Despite the lifelong inability to see those reds, Chuck took a liking to astronomy, as a hobby, from a young age. In his lifetime, he'd dumped thousands—tens of thousands—on equipment to catch photons from millions of years ago. Glimpses into the past. Little gray, fuzzy blobs of light, reaching him from eons ago, whispering that all was right in the universe, even when all on earth went to shit.

This evening, as the city rotated out of the sun's light and into the darkness of space, the constellation of Orion would be rising in the east, along with what was left of its star Betelgeuse.

He wished Marian could be here to view it with him. Not that she cared much for bundling up in winter coats to peek through an eyepiece at the little fuzzy blobs that Chuck loved so dearly. But for this, she would have been right by his side.

His gear was packed into the cart. His twelve-inch Dobsonian. The Takahashi for imaging. Binoculars. A reclining lawn chair. Chuck wheeled his cart into the hallway of the apartment complex. Fourth floor—closest to the roof. It wasn't exactly dark skies up there, but the elevator made it convenient, and the landlord gave him a key to the rooftop lights so he could shut them off as he pleased. He'd considered moving away from the city to darker skies after Marian passed, but he couldn't bring himself to leave her.

His neighbor, Devon, walked down the hall, head down. Oversized headphones sat on top of a slouched knit hat. Skinny jeans so tight, Chuck was surprised he could walk in them. The kid's backpack was slung over a shoulder while a free hand thumbed at his phone.

Devon raised his eyes as he approached Chuck. "Got a big night planned?" His slow, stoner-like voice irritated Chuck.

"Ha! Are you kidding?"

Devon stared, mouth hanging open, and shrugged.

"Betelgeuse blew!"

"No way!" Devon staggered back a step.

"How have you not heard this? Don't you get news on that thing?" Chuck nodded to the kid's phone.

"I've been working all night." Devon's bloodshot eyes spoke of his exhaustion.

"Come up for the show as soon as it's dark. I'll let you look through the scope."

"Most definitely." Devon nodded. "Got some homework to do, and then I'm there."

Devon pulled his headphones back over his ears and continued down the hall. Devon wasn't the only oblivious one. So many people had no idea what was going on over their heads every moment of every day. Billions of galaxies swirling, burning, dying. Stars collapsing and exploding. Remnant clouds of gas expanding and contracting, and yet the people kept walking, eyes on the ground, eyes on their devices, never caring to look up until the news told them to. And the news was almost always wrong about when to look up.

But now, the headlines were everywhere.

Red Giant Goes Supernova!

Massive Stellar Explosion Visible from Earth!

Alien Life Sends Signal Across the Stars!

The End is Near!

Some of the headlines were ridiculous, and Chuck laughed them off. For every astronomical event, there was always some yahoo thinking the world was ending.

Chuck rolled his cart to his spot on the roof with a view of the southeast sky. Beyond the two-story building next door, Chuck had a view of the campus quad and the west hill where the sun had recently set. Beyond that hill, though out of view, was the cemetery where his dear Marian was buried.

"It's going to be quite the night, Marian," he whispered to her.

Behind the atmosphere's twilight, the archer, Orion, was sparkling against a black backdrop. The shoulder star, Betelgeuse, would rise above the horizon soon.

An hour passed and the sky darkened. The faint glow of a cloud-like structure rose. Another half hour passed, and the bright glow shone into view. It was larger than the moon, which was below the horizon this evening. The most beautiful naked-eye object he'd ever seen. The nebula shifted gently against the darkening sky like the aurora borealis. He'd never seen anything like it.

"What the hell?" Chuck laughed with delight, or maybe insanity. It shouldn't have looked this way. Other astronomers had to be losing their minds over this, but there were no new notifications from his astronomy group.

On the street below and on rooftops across the way, people left the comfort of their homes to look at the magnificent sight. Clad in robes and flannel for a brief glimpse at the supernova, they stared with rapt and silenced awe. Chuck had never seen a non-astronomer so fascinated by the sky. Sometimes, the public would be wowed by the craters of the Moon, the rings of Saturn, or Jupiter's moons. Occasionally, folks who truly appreciated the heavens would be dazzled even by the dull, little, fuzzy blobs that were entire galaxies. This moment—with masses of the general public enjoying the sky—brought a spark of joy.

Chuck's Takahoshi was set to automatically take photographs. With the shifting light, there'd be a good chance he'd get nothing but streaks and blurs. He gazed through his Dobsonian, but the central star where Betelgeuse had collapsed was far too bright to view. A wide field-of-view eyepiece would allow him a better look. He traced the nebulous dust as it shifted through the sky. There was something strangely magical about it. Something living and breathing about the way it streamed and swirled upon the air—this wasn't light from hundreds of lightyears away. It was atmospheric.

Another half-hour passed. He always lost track of time at the eyepiece. The rest of the world around him fell away, and he was part of the universe.

A few neighbors from downstairs opened the rooftop door, drawing Chuck's attention back to earth. Mrs. Gent, with her two kids, approached.

"We saw the news and thought you'd be up here," she said.

They were not strangers to looking through Chuck's eyepiece whenever he set up for the evening. Mrs. Gent gave a friendly smile and a wave, then ushered her children closer. He gestured for them to take a look while he fumbled with his phone, calling his astro-buddy, Mike. Chuck rubbed his itchy eyes and waited as the phone rang.

No answer.

Nothing posted in his group yet, either.

"I'm not sure what the heck that glow in the sky is, but it can't be from Betelgeuse." He looked up from the phone. The eyes of Mrs. Gent and her children were locked on the sky. Curtains of glowing, moving light reached from five hundred light years away and somehow appeared to enter our breathable air, hypnotizing the family of three. "Mrs. Gent?"

She stared intently, slack jaw, eyes unblinking, arms dangling loosely by her sides. Her children did the same. On the rooftop next door, others stood without movement. Upright, facing the east, but everything about them looked asleep.

The glaringly bright Betelgeuse rose to forty-five degrees over the horizon. The gray-whites and blues of the nebulous cloud expanded outward.

Chuck grabbed Mrs. Gent by the shoulders and tried to break her gaze. "Mrs. Gent?"

No response as he gently shook her. The woman's spine and knees were locked steady. Gabby and Trey were in the same state. Chuck knelt down, bum knee trembling before landing on solid ground. He tried to lock eyes with Gabby—the smallest—who was in kindergarten, if he remembered correctly. Her brother Trey's hand dangled beside hers. He stood a foot taller, but Chuck had no clue how old the boy was. He had Marian for remembering that stuff.

Dark eyes reflected the hypnotic dance of photons in the sky.

Chuck slowly turned his head back to the sight. Back to the mysterious light. Dry eyes irritated Chuck to the point of breaking out his moisturizing drops. Sirens in the distance sounded. He wasn't sure how long they'd been going.

On the streets, people stood on sidewalks, gazing upon the sky.

Nobody moved.

Chuck pulled up his news app for information and the headlines appeared immediately. Reports of people in a hypnotic state. Thousands, tens of thousands, had been affected. He clicked a video. A shaking anchorwoman sat before the camera. "We're trying to reach an expert—*anyone*—about what may be happening. For now, whatever you do, do NOT look at the supernova. Stay inside."

Hours-old reports flooded his search feed. European nations locked down while their people stared to the skies. It was everywhere. Happening to everyone—everyone but Chuck.

Chuck unplugged his computer and camera and gathered them under his arms. With a moment of hesitation, he left the cart, the refractor, and the Dobsonian behind. He backed under the awning to the elevator and pressed the button. His heart pounded and his head scrambled for answers, but nothing made sense.

Back in his apartment, Chuck closed his blinds, squeezing one more peek between the slats. The number of people on the street doubled. They all stood deathly still, faces following the light in the sky. Their bodies turned as Betelgeuse and its strange nebula slowly trekked higher into the southern sky. Most of the cloud stayed with the photons of Betelgeuse's bright center, but some trailed behind, leaving a strange arc along the ecliptic path.

Chuck paced the apartment, scratching his head, shaking himself as if from a terrible dream. Maybe it *was* all a dream. Losing Danny when he was so young. Marian's battle with cancer. The years of sickness. Moving to the city where she could be closer to the center. The years of giving up his love of the night sky so he could be by her side whenever she needed him. Then after her passing, the insomnia. The endless nights where nothing but the stars brought him light. Maybe, just maybe, he was finally asleep. But this dreadful reality was no better.

Chuck lay down on his bed, blinds drawn shut. He squeezed his lids together until tears eked out of dry eyes, soaking his lashes. Ragged breaths shuddered his heart. An ache in his left arm forced him to sit up. Calm, relaxing breaths. He reached for his bedside bottle of aspirin and popped a couple in his mouth to ward off another attack.

"Not now," he whispered to his failing heart. "Not now." But he wasn't sure why not. Why not let his heart go so he could be with his family again?

Looking at the news would only exacerbate his condition. He needed rest. He needed relaxed nerves and a cool mind, then he'd figure it out. His head hit the pillow. Marian's side of the bed had been empty for a while now, but he liked to imagine her laying there beside him.

Sleep evading him, he forced his eyes closed and repositioned himself at least a dozen times. Upon opening his eyes, giving up on the attempt to sleep, the clock on the nightstand read 6:00. He'd slept after all, but it didn't feel like it. The nerves in his body trembled as he peeked out of the blinds to the lamp-lit streets below. Dawn's light barely kissed the horizon in the east. Hundreds of people now stood outside on the sidewalks, some in their street clothes, some in scrubs, suits, or robes. Everyone faced west, where Betelgeuse would be setting soon.

All of his gear was hopefully still on the roof, untouched, and safe from any accumulating dew. It was a ridiculous thought to have in this moment, to be worried about dew on his gear. But his gear was his window to all he had left to live for.

Chuck turned on the television—digital TV with rabbit ears—Marian and he could never find anything good on cable or satellite. None of the usual major network channels came through. He popped another aspirin for preventative measure, then searched his browser for information on Betelgeuse and strange human behavior. Conspiracy blogs and unclear, unsubstantiated news reports. It was as if the reporters who were left unaffected couldn't get answers as to what was going on. Speculation flooded the screen.

Then he found reports out of South America and Australia where Betelgeuse was not visible. The southern hemisphere shared stories out of Russia, India, China, and the U.S. Folks were in a "zombie-like trance." Upon sunrise, the people seemed to wake up and wander in a daze. Many were violent upon awakening.

A viral video out of Russia showed a man walking barefoot down a desolate road. The camera person stood on his porch, recording the white-out conditions and what appeared to be blistering cold weather. When the man with the camera approached the barefoot straggler, the straggler turned to face him. Lurching shoulders and awkward knee jerks moved him forward as if he was learning to walk. The camera man backed up as the man drew closer, asking something in Russian that Chuck couldn't understand. The straggler closed in with startling speed and the camera jerked away, falling to the snow. White nothingness covered the screen, but the distinct sound of gasping and gurgling tortured Chuck's imagination.

The sun would be up any moment. If these reports of people waking in a violent state were true, he'd need to get his things.

Chuck donned a thick, fleece-lined flannel and poked his head into the hallway. He hurried to the elevator.

Mrs. Gent and her kids remained standing on the roof, now facing the opposite direction to the west. They must've followed the ecliptic path of Betelgeuse all evening. That eerie curtain of light trailed the entire southern sky, from east to west, like a colorless rainbow. It moved above and below sparse clouds. Whatever it was, it was here on earth. Chuck's eyes burned, and he rubbed away the sensation.

"Mrs. Gent," he said, voice shaking. "Gabby? Trey?"

No response. Their skin had turned a faint shade of blue. Fingertips whitened. The rooftop people across the way suffered in the same state. Frost-bitten and hypothermic.

Chuck hurried to his cart and began to disassemble equipment, but breaking down his gear would take too long. Who knew what would happen once the light from Betelgeuse set? He disconnected the Takahoshi from its mount and laid it in the protective foam—now damp from dew and plummeting temperatures.

Movement below caught his eye. He peeked over the side of the building to the people on the street. All of them, at once, spanned out different directions. None of them bothering to say a word to another. Their movements were awkward. Several tripped and crashed to the ground, as if learning to walk after being frozen solid all night. From their vantage point, Betelgeuse must've been out of sight. They woke up after it set…and if the reports were true, they would turn violent.

Chuck backed away from his equipment. Betelgeuse kissed the top of the hill.

Mrs. Gent and her kids remained still, but not for long.

Chuck hurried for the elevator doors. He left his precious equipment behind. The doors opened quickly, and Chuck entered, rapid-firing at the close-door button.

Before the doors shut, little Gabby woke from her trance, and her blank eyes met with Chuck as the bell dinged. Trey did the same, then their mother. They all held his gaze. As the doors closed, Mrs. Gent pushed past the children, stumbling toward Chuck.

He thought to hold the door. Maybe they weren't a danger. Maybe they needed help. He could've taken them to the hospital. All these thoughts rushed out as quickly as they galloped in. The elevator doors shut.

The bell dinged and the doors parted. Chuck pushed through unforgiving knee pain and crept quietly back to his apartment. The moment he closed his apartment door, a banging vibrated through the wood.

"Chuck!" a voice said.

The door vibrated with pounding from the other side. "Chuck!"

Heart racing, Chuck grabbed the baseball bat by the door and faced whoever was out there.

Devon stepped back, wide-eyed. Phone clenched tight in one hand. "I heard the elevator and saw you go in your apartment."

"What the hell is going on?" Chuck said.

"I fell asleep early last night. I didn't see." Devon aimed his phone's screen at Chuck. The headline from the Australian news source read *The World Stops*.

The elevator dinged. Both Chuck and Devon turned as the doors opened. Two small figures stepped into the hall—Trey and Gabby. Their mom, Mrs. Gent, followed. All three stood in the hall, knees wobbling, arms stretched to brace themselves on the walls. Gabby stumbled to the left and fell to the floor, quickly righting herself with a leap to her feet. The family's eyes fixed upon Chuck and Devon. Mother and children retched from the shoulders up, as if they were stretching out their necks to throw up, retracting, repeating. Eyes wide and bloodshot, Gabby stepped forward first. Her arms wavered, catching her balance. Trey took the next step, then all three sped closer.

Devon pressed into Chuck's apartment, both men keeping their eyes on the family coming toward them. Limbs chaotic and awkward, like a pack of wolf pups learning to run. Hunger in their eyes, Mrs. Gent and her children closed in.

"Mrs. Gent?" Devon's voice shook as he shoved all the way into Chuck's apartment, away from them. Chuck shut the door. Bodies slammed into the other side.

Chuck's trembling hand locked the deadbolt. A hammering heart warned him to breathe easily. It thump-thumped and sputtered, chugging to keep up with his mind and body.

Banging, thrashing, and scratching ensued at the door. Sweat dripped from Chuck's sparse white hair and dribbled into his eye. Salty perspiration seeped into chapped lips. He kept his weight pressed against the door.

"What's wrong with them?" Devon held his stance, bracing the door with his arms, leaning into it.

Every bang against the door sent an interruption into Chuck's steadying heart.

"Everything okay out here?" a voice called from farther down the hall.

Devon's eyes widened as the banging ceased.

"Ma'am? You okay?" The man's voice drew closer.

Mrs. Gent and her children were silent. Footsteps shuffled away from the door, drawing their shadows from under the gap.

Chuck rolled over and fought his knees to get up.

Devon carefully twisted the deadbolt, which clicked like a shotgun blast no matter how slow it turned. Devon's eyes met with Chuck's briefly before twisting the knob. He opened the door only a crack, and they squeezed their faces close to get a peek into the hall.

"Hey!" the man at the end of the hall said. "You need help?"

The man in the robe—Chuck forgot his name. Brian or Bryce or Braxton or whatever, according to the mailbox. He moved in a week ago.

Instead of veering back into his apartment, the man drew closer to Mrs. Gent and the kids.

Devon stepped into the hall. He stood like a man ready to run…or maybe ready to fight. His feet were planted solid, one foot in front of the other, elbows bent, prepared for whatever was to come. Chuck wasn't sure if the kid was going to try to dash after them and play hero or if he was ready to throw punches if they turned around and came back.

It was absurd that Mrs. Gent and these kids seemed like such a threat. They were harmless. Innocents. Not a bad bone in their bodies. Chuck had high hopes for little Gabby, who was the most impressed person to ever look through his telescope. She could name all of the Galilean moons. That was unheard of for a girl her age. Hell, most adults couldn't even identify Jupiter.

His mind raced through so many thoughts as the awkward clumsy family crashed into Braxton-Brian-Bryce at the end of the hall.

The man's eyes latched onto Chuck as he fell to the floor with a grunt. Gabby crawled over him as he flailed. From Chuck's angle it was hard to see, but she hovered her face over his.

Gabby's mouth opened wide and a pink substance spilled forth. A vomit akin to rice and raw meat spewed onto the man's face. He screamed, thrashed, and threw Gabby into the wall.

A screech from the stairwell drew Mrs. Gent's attention away.

Chuck's pulse pounded between his ears as he stood petrified, watching. All he could do was *watch*. His muscles, his will to run to the man's aid, it all froze solid—as stiff as the people who couldn't stop staring at the supernova. Mrs. Gent and Trey stepped over the squirming man on the floor and headed to the stairwell after the screams.

Gabby climbed to her feet. She gazed down the hall for a moment as Brian—Chuck decided his name was Brian—writhed on the floor.

Chuck and Devon backed into the apartment before being seen. Another piercing shriek from outside. Sirens blared in the distance.

Gabby stumbled forward, hit the button on the elevator doors, and stepped inside.

At the end of the hall, the new tenant, Brian, sat upright. His head twitched from side to side. Arms fell limp to the floor. His spine was slumped, sitting like a ragdoll coming to life.

Spying from the cracked door, Devon whispered, "We should check on him."

The squirming larva-like pink rice on the floor climbed Brian's body, disappearing beneath fabric and into his hairline. It squiggled down his face and entered his eye sockets, ears.

Chuck's stomach lurched and he quickly covered his mouth to hold back the contents. He choked it down, then snatched a wad of Devon's shirt between his shoulder blades to keep him from going into the hall. The same grab he made for his boy, Danny, when he was a toddler. About to run into traffic, or plow through someone at the mall, Chuck would snatch Danny's shirt to keep him from utter catastrophe.

"Wait," Chuck said, his fingers clenched tight to the fabric. "Something ain't right."

Brian climbed to his feet. His body undulated, wormlike

for—Chuck counted—six, seven, eight seconds. Brian stood still, lifeless, any sign of humanity scrubbed clean from his face. The stairwell door flung open, and a woman ran screaming from inside.

"Help me!" Outstretched arms reached for Brian.

Stomping feet on the stairwell followed her.

Brian opened his arms, grabbed the woman in a bear hug, and pulled her to the floor. Pink excretions poured like a deluge from his mouth, over her face. More blank-faced people entered the hall.

Chuck yanked Devon back and closed the door, securing the locks.

His fingers were still clenched tight to the fabric of Devon's shirt. Knuckles ached as he loosened his grip.

Devon paced. "What the fuck?" His voice trembled as he met eyes with Chuck. "What..." He gestured toward the door. "...the...fuck." Devon sat on the recliner, elbows propped on his knees, head in his hands, squeezing tufts of black curly hair between his fingers.

Chuck opened his laptop. There had to be more information out there, somewhere. He scoured the search engines again for additional news. But major networks seemed to be silent. Hours ago, they made their last reports. Australian, Brazilian, and South African news sources remained online. Speculation was all they had to go on. And all they knew was that everyone who gazed upon the supernova was affected.

"Did you see it last night?" Chuck asked.

Devon rocked in his seat, clinging to his phone like a lifeline, scrolling.

"Hey, kid!"

Devon snapped to attention. "No! I think that's why I'm okay. They're saying if you looked...but *you* looked." Devon stood, right foot slid in front of the other, prepared again to either run or fight.

Chuck nodded. "But nothing happened to me."

"Why?"

Chuck went back to the screen for answers—or at least ideas that could lead to some kind of reasonable explanation. His eyes itched. "I don't know."

"It can't be the supernova," Devon said. "If you were looking at it…"

"Then what?"

"Parasitic," Devon said. "Those things that Gabby threw up all over that guy's face. It got into him. I don't know any parasite that works that fast, though." Devon's demeanor changed. He paced, but less frantically. He paced as if he were contemplating. Furrowed brow. Hands tightened into fists, biting his lip. He went to the window and paused.

Chuck's eyes scanned his screen.

"But they all—every one of them—the moment they saw the light in the sky, froze. They were in some kind of trance," Devon said. "I only saw the reports."

"It's true," Chuck said. "I saw it myself last night with the Gents. As soon as the glow of Betelgeuse was above the horizon, everyone stopped and didn't move again until the light set this morning."

"Light…information…parasites and light?" Devon whispered random words.

Chuck feared the poor stoner kid was losing it.

"And what's this cloud in the sky?" he said. "The streaky blue and red glow—like northern lights. What is that? That's not from Betelgeuse. It can't be."

Chuck joined him by the window. "It's in our atmosphere. I saw it move in front of a cloud. But it trails Betelgeuse's path along the ecliptic." Chuck made an arc with his hand from east to west.

"It's dissipating." Devon leaned closer to the window.

"Or daylight is washing out its glow…no. I think you're right. The cloudiness of it does seem sparser now. I see some faint blue hues—but the gray in-between spaces don't seem as bright. That's the red, right? Is there any more red?"

Devon glanced to Chuck.

"Colorblind." Chuck squinted out the window.

Devon shook his head. "No. There's hardly any red wisps at all. What if that cloud is carrying the parasites?"

"Aerosolized parasites? Like a bio-weapon?"

"I don't know…" Devon chewed his bottom lip, then felt the frame of the window. "These windows are solid right? Not too drafty?"

Chuck stepped away from the window. The thought of an aerosolized parasite squeezing between the cracks, into the vents, and into his bodily orifices made him shudder. Those rice squigglies wriggling into his mouth, taking over his body until he was nothing but a shell of a human…Chuck's neck tensed, and he focused on a deep breath to relax the muscles.

Devon jumped. "A hoax—a diversion. A bio-weapon let loose across the world. But to get more people exposed, they staged a fake supernova explosion. Made it look like Betelgeuse blew so that more people would be infected as they looked up to the sky."

Chuck shook his head. "Betelgeuse definitely went supernova. Amateur astronomers all over the world were looking through backyard telescopes, taking astro-images and uploading in real time. I must've seen hundreds of images of auto-uploaded raw images before they went silent. I saw it myself. You can't hoax something like that."

Devon growled. "Supernova. Light. Information. Parasites…Some bacterium are photosensitive. They need light."

Chuck raised an eyebrow, surprised by the stoner kid. "What do you go to school for, Devon?"

"Microbiology. I just earned my bachelor's in biology, and I'm now going for a PhD. So, it's kind of my thing."

Chuck was taken aback. "I just thought you were a dumb stoner."

"That's funny. I just thought you were a miserable old man."

Chuck huffed and scrolled his screen again. "It's all impossible. None of it adds up."

"But why not *you*?" Devon stared intently at Chuck. "Color-blind."

"How does being colorblind have anything to do with infection?"

"It doesn't."

"My cones don't process red light."

"So, what is it about the red light?" Devon's eyes darted back and forth. "Red light...Parasite." It was like watching an AI calculate information in some terrible sci-fi movie.

"Red light carrying information?" Chuck asked. He wasn't sure where the kid was going, it was all very far-fetched, but grasping at straws was all they had. "Maybe that's why I didn't get all hypnotized. My eyes were bugging me last night. They were itchy. What if those things were sending information on the red light?" Chuck burst out laughing. "Nevermind. I sound like a quack!"

"And then there's Schrodinger's Bacterium."

Chuck waited for more. He'd heard of Schrodinger's Cat, but never this.

"Okay, hear me out." Devon paced, rubbing his hands. He chuckled a little "This is insane."

"So is everything we've experienced."

"There was a study done years ago—2018 or 2019, I think. I remember reading the article. This study linked a connection of some bacterium and light and quantum physics. They suggested the possibility of quantum entanglement between photosynthetic organisms. *Organisms!* These green sulfur bacterium live in the deep ocean where there's, like, no light. But they photosynthesize somehow—and quantum biology is one of the theories. Being in two places at once. Where there is light, and where there isn't."

Chuck sighed. "This is all..."

"Theoretic, and completely bonkers. Yeah. I know." Devon held up a finger. "But what do we know? Betelgeuse went supernova. That's a fact, correct?"

"Yeah."

Devon's eyes were wild, wide and excited. "And it's a fact

127

that when Betelgeuse went supernova, there was also an appearance of a cloud in our atmosphere—the glowy red and blue stuff, right?"

Chuck nodded.

"So, we don't know if this is causation or correlation, but it's feeling really fucking causation-y, you know?"

Chuck interjected. "Even at the speed of light, it would take five hundred years for anything to get here. Nothing travels at light speed, other than light. And if some bacteria could travel at the speed of light, nothing survives five hundred years in space."

"But hear me out. *If* there is microbial life out somewhere near Betelgeuse, which isn't an outrageous thing to believe, and *if* that microbial life is dependent on—let's say—*red light* to somehow do a quantum entanglement thing—"

"Quantum entanglement thing?" Chuck's confidence in the kid's theory waned.

"Look, man. I'm not a physics major. I don't know a damn thing about the quantum realm. I'm just brain-vomiting here…What if this is some kind of bacterium—or in this case, some kind of parasite—that was threatened with the blow of its life-giving star, and in its last desperate attempt for survival, it quantum-jumped here?"

"Quantum jump? Like that old TV show *Quantum Leap*?"

Devon rolled his eyes. "I don't know what that is. But there's a cloud of red light that hypnotized the world, hijacked some brains, and let in some potentially aerosolized parasites. And now everyone is infected. Except for the folks who didn't look. And except for the folks who didn't have the proper receptors to process that red light, initially…still doesn't add up." Devon rubbed his forehead.

"They traveled here by some red light quantum leap. But they're here and spreading. We can see the wormy little bastards ourselves. Those aren't aerosolized. I bet if those little larva guys got inside me, I wouldn't stand a chance, colorblind or not."

Devon shook his head. "Probably not…" He let out a

maniacal laugh. "That's so crazy! That can't even be what happened. It can't! That's...there has to be a less crazy idea." He looked to Chuck.

"Sorry, kid, I've got nothing."

Screams in the street drew their attention to the window. A shriek gurgled into silence before they could spot what had happened. Scattered people shuffled down the street. Arms limp. Legs chaotic, over-corrected steps, like their limbs had fallen asleep and they'd forgotten how to walk.

"They're like fucking zombies, man," Devon said.

Chuck hated that the kid was right. They *were* like zombies. Every one of them. Mindless. Bodies driven by some other inhuman force. Some raging infection from those little pink squigglies, eating away at their brains until they were nothing but walking carcasses, intent on spreading themselves among the human population.

For a moment, he was relieved that Marian left this world before this happened, but he also wished she were by his side to calm his nerves. She had a way about her. She'd press two fingers into that little divot at the back of his neck, just under his skull. She'd press and hold, almost like she was slowing the rush of blood to his head, slowing his mind, slowing his pulse.

Devon checked his phone. "He's alive." His eyes gleamed with hope. "My friend at the university. I have to get to him."

Chuck shook his head. "Son, please. Don't think about going out there."

"The red glow—I can't see it anymore." He gestured out the window. "The aerosolized stuff is gone. I can risk it."

"But why?"

"It's the university. Food. Shelter. Strong doors."

"And thousands of people, probably throwing up that pink rice all over campus."

"This all went down overnight. Only a handful of people are in the building overnight. Everyone else is on the other side of campus at the dorms. My friend is in the lab with a few others…maybe we can figure this out. We have one of the best labs in the country."

"What are you going to do? Gather up some of those worm things and go do tests on them?"

"I don't know. Maybe. *Someone* should."

"I think it's best if we wait it out here for a while. Let's see if the government is doing anything."

"The government doesn't give a shit about us!"

"I think it's smarter if we give it a couple days."

"I'm not leaving him alone for a couple days!" Devon said. Tears reached the rim of his lower lids. Rage swirled in his desperate eyes. The kind of rage that bubbled up when a man was kept from the one he loved. Chuck had felt the same anger fill his heart, his soul, all the way to his eyeballs, when he'd learned of his wife's terminal illness. Angry with the doctors, angry with his wife for letting it go for so long, angry with God…

"He's a good friend?" Chuck asked.

"Yeah…" Devon stared out the window. "He's my boyfriend."

"Casual or serious?"

"What do you care?"

"Because if this is someone you barely know, it's not worth the risk. But if he means something to you, then that's a different story."

"He means something."

"Okay then." Chuck slid his arms into his fleece-lined flannel and began to button. "I'll go with you." What the hell did it matter? Chuck couldn't live out his last days starving to death in his apartment. In the depressing one bedroom where his wife succumbed to the cancer inside her. The place where his son never spent a moment of his life. Danny never got to see anything beyond the age of eight because of Hodgkins. What was left to do in this miserable world other than look at the stars, then die? There was nothing left for Chuck. But he could at least help this kid try to do something. Try to save the world, or whatever he thought he was going to do. Save his love. Be with the one he needed to be with. That's all people have—their loves. Of life, of each other, of art and nature…

"You don't have to do that, Chuck."

"I know what I do and don't have to do. You said it yourself. The university has food and a lab. And no doubt one of those departments has a communications system and, of course, backup generators. It's a smart call."

"Maybe we should wait until dark? Sneak through the shadows, you know?"

"When it's dark, Betelgeuse will be rising again. What if it throws off some of that light stuff again? What if gets in you?"

"What if I go out now and it gets in my eyes?" Devon said.

"You could close your eyes…"

"And what? Bird Box my way to the lab in a blindfold?"

"What?"

"It's a movie."

Chuck gazed out the window to the building across the street. Below, fewer and fewer people could be spotted walking. "Where are they going?"

"Probably to find more hosts? The zombie-ant fungus gets into an ant and hijacks its body so it can reproduce. The ant walks around under control of the fungus."

"They're finding more people? *What* people? Half the damn planet has laid their eyes on the supernova by now. The major network news stations aren't reporting. What happens when everyone is gone?"

THE VANTAGE POINT from the roof gave a view of the streets with straggling souls wandering below. The chill of the crisp air bit Chuck's nose. The crowds thinned. Beyond the next building, the campus quad had few people, unlike the hundreds from earlier. Chuck's breaths amplified in his gas mask. Devon wore Marian's old mask from the twenty-twenty pandemic. The masks were equipped with goggles and ventilators. Chuck had saved them all these years, just in case.

"Do you think they're in the buildings?" Chuck asked.

"Ryan says the main building is secure."

"Where the hell did they all go?"

Devon shook his head. "If they're looking for more people, maybe they're leaving town. Maybe they've gotten everyone here and they're moving on…to other mammals? Crossing the equator and spreading into the southern hemi? It's all a guess. Until we know more about this thing, everything is a wild guess. One of the guys with Ryan lives on the coast. It's not that far. He's got a boat…like, a yacht, I guess. They're talking about sailing south."

Chuck nodded and tried to comfort himself. "I've never seen the southern hemisphere's sky. That might be nice."

The path straight to the school would leave them wide open. Driving would only attract attention. Devon assured Chuck they could slip through the park down the street under the cover of high hedges until they reached the fringe of campus. From there, they'd climb the west hill and follow the ridge, down the other side to the lab.

Devon's backpack was strapped on, packed full of supplies, which Chuck helped him curate for the short but dangerous trek across campus and beyond. A lighter, flashlight, utility knife, dry clothes and socks, typical backwoods camping gear. He held a baseball bat in one hand in case he needed to protect himself. It reminded Chuck of sending Danny off on his first day of kindergarten. Shoving him out into the cruel world to survive.

"Ryan's expecting us. They have the main entrance doors barricaded, but the back entrance to the lab will be easy to get to. They'll be there to let us in."

CHUCK AND DEVON hurried along the sidewalk, close to the

buildings, tucked in long shadows as the evening sun fell behind the structures. Betelgeuse would rise again soon. Overhead, songbirds soared, flitting around as if nothing had happened, unaffected by the crumbling world.

They turned into the small park, staying low, concealed by hedges. Behind them, a click drew their attention. They paused and crouched as a straggler stumbled into a vehicle. The woman studied the door, head unstable on her shoulders. She grabbed at the car door handle and pulled.

"What the—" Devon whispered.

The straggly woman flung open the door, nearly falling over. She corrected herself and dove headfirst into the vehicle's driver side. After sitting right, she put her hands on the wheel, staring forward. No key. No ignition. No attempt to shift. She rocked forward and back, in some mindless attempt to drive. Some small motor memory of how things worked allowed her to open the door and try to drive somewhere. Just like earlier with Gabby, opening the elevator doors.

Chuck's masked breaths echoed in his head. His speeding heart joined the song. Devon raced forward, young legs carrying him with ease. He looked back frequently and slowed his pace to allow Chuck to keep up.

Good kid.

The hill was torture on Chuck's knees. He weaved to remain in the shadows, tucked close to the shrubbery as they climbed. Nearing the crest of the hill—the ridge that divided the campus from the cemetery—a grunt came from below.

Falling sunlight skimmed the gravestones and the heads of hundreds of people.

Devon dropped to the ground on his belly, propped up on elbows, and crawled to the edge of a bush.

Chuck crouched as low as his bad knees would let him and joined Devon.

Below, dozens amassed. Some wandered aimlessly. Some propped on hands and knees over the gravestones, using their bare hands to dig at the earth.

A mound of soil at the bottom of the hill piled high. Loose, fresh soil in a mountain beside fresh flowers. A recent burial.

Clawing arms ripped through cold soil; bloodied fingers didn't slow them down.

Chuck looked beyond to the sprawling oak where Marian laid in peace, along with Danny's ashes. For now, none of the bastards were bothering them.

Three people hovered over the grave below. One fell into the hole and pried open the casket. He bent over, spewing the pink larvae onto the corpse. The suited old man, eyes closed, lay lifeless beneath the deluge of parasites.

"How do they know?" Devon whispered.

Chuck was speechless. His mouth hung open.

Devon's breaths became louder through the mask.

Chuck's eyes were glued. He couldn't look away. He counted…one, two, three…

Time slowed while they watched intently.

"…eleven, twelve…thirt—"

The body in the grave jerked upright into a sitting position. Eyes pinned shut, body devoid of blood, it sat up and used its atrophied arms to lift itself out of the grave.

Chuck gasped. His neck tightened.

"Reanimation…" Devon got to his feet. "We need to leave."

A sharp pain in Chuck's shoulder forced an unexpected yelp from his lips. He grabbed at the painful area. The ache stopped him from getting up. *Focus on breathing.* He popped an aspirin, which was floating loose in his right breast pocket, then swallowed it dry.

Devon didn't tell him to hurry. He didn't ask what was wrong. The boy knew. He looked Chuck in the eyes and figured it out. *Smart kid. He'll be all right.*

One of the stragglers below heard the yelp and began its ascent up the west slope.

The ache traveled down Chuck's arm and spread across his chest. *Breathe.*

Devon hurried to his side and flung Chuck's arm over his shoulder.

"You better get going," Chuck said.

"Shut up and move."

But the pain paralyzed him. If he kept moving, his heart would give out. Chuck dropped to his knees. The sun slipped below the horizon, shifting the contrasting black shadows and sunlight into a steady even shade of gray.

The straggler closed in. Chuck held out an arm to hold him off, but he was too close.

Devon drove in with a blow to the person's head. The bastard's neck twisted, a crack. A spray of pink dusted the air and the straggler fell, rolling down the hill.

Devon dropped to Chuck's side. "Can you walk?"

Down the hill, none of the others seemed to be aware of their presence.

The aspirin worked at thinning his blood, at helping his heart keep beating. Chuck wiped a bead of sweat from his brow. When he lowered his hand, a pink thing wriggling on his thumb caught his attention. Before he could swat it away, it burrowed beneath his fingernail.

Chuck flailed, then squeezed his thumb to keep it from going farther. Beneath the skin, he felt it squirm. It dug deep, slipping into his veins.

"We'll dig it out," Devon said, breaths becoming more frantic.

"There's not enough time for that, son." Under his skin, he felt it spread through his arm.

"Come on!" Devon said.

"You should get going."

"I'm not leaving you here."

"And I'm not going into that building with this thing inside of me," Chuck said, raising his voice.

Even through Devon's gas mask, there was a hitch in his voice. "Jesus, Chuck."

A wave of numbness swept over his left arm. Inside, he knew the creature was multiplying, spreading, taking over his body. His nerves sparked in protest, and Chuck let out another outburst.

This time, the living corpse, who had just risen from the grave, rose to his feet and ascended the hill. Another straggler followed.

"Time to go, Devon." Chuck removed his mask and handed it over.

Devon accepted it with reluctance in his eyes.

"Go save someone that can be saved." Chuck slid his pack from his back and tossed it to Devon's feet.

Devon looked to the sky, defeated, then back to Chuck before taking off with the supplies. He disappeared beyond the crest of the hill. It was a short trip to the side door, where a group of brilliant young people, just like Devon, would be waiting to let him in.

Chuck lay on his back in the cold grass, as the corpse man worked his way to the crest. Overhead, the sky darkened to a deep blue. The orange horizon melted into purple.

A star shone above, piercing the twilight sky. Capella. To the east, the brilliant, exploded Betelgeuse rose again.

Corpse man stumbled over the top of Chuck. His heart pounded with anticipation, but the man continued his course, uninterested in Chuck, whose body had already been taken.

Chuck let out a sigh and stared back to the sky. To his love. To the only reason worth living anymore. A wave of nausea coursed through his body, but his heart slowed. His heart calmed. At the back of his neck, where that little divot at the base of his skull was, he felt pressure. The gentle touch of loving hands. Marian's two fingers pressed against him, calming his heart and his mind. Existing here with him in this moment, while simultaneously decomposing at the bottom of the hill. He took one deep breath, knowing that they'd exist together always, no matter where they were. Chuck exhaled one last time—one final escape into the universe.

MADE IN HELL

Richard Clive

CHAPTER ONE

FRANK D'ANGELO HANGS UPSIDE DOWN in the dark hotel room, eyes focused on the door.

The neon blush of downtown Miami glows faintly from between the Venetian blinds. In the neighboring room, the headboard thumps, and Frank can hear the thick beat of two hearts hammering toward climax; he can hear every ragged breath. He can hear somewhere, too, a cockroach scuttling for cover; the chink of glasses on the ground-floor bar far below; the distant hum of an ascending elevator.

His heightened senses are tuned to every whisper, scent, thought, every rhythmic dilation of a human pulse contained within the high-rise.

The elevator's mechanical doors ping and swish, birthing a rabble of noisy drunks into the corridor maze of the third floor. His floor. He inhales greedily, tasting the vaporized currents from the air-conditioning vent: Perfumed skin. Gin-tinged breath. Sweat. It is intoxicating.

He's waited thirty years to kill the old man who will soon emerge from the corridor; he can wait thirty more. Time matters little now. Because back in the void, eternity has its own doors, and Hell is as close as the stifling Florida heat.

The fabric of existence is thin, indeed, like the papery skin of the elderly.

He extends his claws.

The lift's former occupants pass the room by, their echoing voices fading as they trail away along the corridor, searching for another numbered room.

Roosting, one hundred and fifty feet above the city streets, Frank D'Angelo closes his eyes and remembers the faceless boy, remembers Tony La Rosa—the old man he's come to kill—and remembers the life he once lived.

He waits, knowing another familiar name will soon be inked on the scabrous surface of his skin.

CHAPTER TWO

17 August 1991

"SO, THE PRICK asks me for another week," said Tony, snorting more cocaine from the tip of his bandaged index finger. "Kike motherfucker refused to pay."

Frank drove the silver Dodge. Tony told his story from the passenger side, while Jimmy Pileggi snickered, hanging on his every word from the backseat. All three men wore crinkled suits and loosened ties, their faces roughened by two-day stubble.

"What you do?" asked Jimmy.

"What did I do? What do you think I did?" said Tony. "I put his head right through his fuckin' till—that's what. Ka-ching, motherfucker. The customers, you should've seen their fuckin' faces."

Tony and Jimmy burst into another bout of unrestrained laughter. "Customers? You went when he was open?" said Jimmy, lighting another cigarette.

"He's a Jew. He's always open. Anyway, I said, Jacob, you know the deal. You can sell all the bagels you want, but you don't pay, we can't offer no protection."

"He paid?" said Jimmy.

"Course. Gave the tight-assed fuck a free nose job, too."

More laughter.

"Is that how you got the Band-Aid?" said Jimmy. "Trapped it in the Jew's till?"

"No, his kid bit me, the ballsy little shit."

"You beat him in front of his kid?" said Frank.

"Kids," corrected Tony.

"Jesus. Come on, man," said Frank.

"Hey, the kids learned a valuable life lesson."

Frank scowled. "And what was that?"

"Don't fuck with Tony La Rosa."

Jimmy laughed.

"You need to drop the wise-guy routine," said Frank.

"Eh?"

"It's embarrassing," said Frank. "You're a fuckin' cliché. You know that?"

"Bada-bing."

"I'm serious."

"Fuck you."

The car sped west.

Frank's bloodshot eyes bulged in the rear-view mirror. The car reeked of male sweat and cigarettes. In the last twenty-four hours, he'd slept for just three on the car's backseat when they'd rotated drivers.

They had left Brooklyn yesterday morning for a business trip to Chicago's south side. Arriving late that evening, grouchy and disheveled, they'd eaten at an associate's restaurant, where they'd discussed a potential construction opportunity. But forty-five minutes and two glasses of Valpolicella into that meeting—after a twelve-hour straight drive—the waiter had interrupted their meal. They'd received a call: *Go. Drop everything. Drive.*

Sick of the sight and smell of each other, the three men were still chewing steak and mopping their chins when they got back in the car, but the order had come from the top. And Frank had been made a promise: do this job, and you'll be made. It was all he'd ever dreamed of—everything he'd worked toward for two decades. Names on planes, though, could be traced, so they drove—again.

The destination? Some hick college town in rural South Dakota. But if the town wasn't familiar, their target certainly was: Lorenzo Russo.

"Way he pinned that hit on Paolo, Russo has this coming," said Jimmy.

"Fucker knows enough to shut everything down," said Tony.

The cops had brought Russo in a year ago. It was a matter of time before they raided every crew member under the Marino family's control. Protection rackets, narcotics, illegal gambling, the pigs would get it all.

"He's cut a deal," said Tony. "Mark my words, Paolo won't be the only guy who gets pinched."

"Then what's taking so long?" said Jimmy. "How long does it take to build a case?"

"The more he's told them, the longer it'll take," said Tony. "But if the pussy thinks he can hide behind witness protection, he can think again." A warped grin spread across his pock-marked face.

Russo had a new name now: Charles Muller. But someone wanted him dead, because his location and new identity had been leaked.

It was Saturday morning. Since leaving the Windy City, they'd crossed two state lines and were approaching the Minnesota/South Dakota border after passing the tiny town of Porter.

"Forty minutes," said Frank.

Tony loaded bullets into the cylinder of his revolver.

"We need to talk about his wife and kid," said Frank.

"Talk about what?" said Tony.

"We leave them out of this, okay?" said Frank.

On the backseat, Jimmy fed bullets into his pistol's magazine. Jimmy and Tony exchanged a wary glance in the rear-view mirror.

"I'm fuckin' serious," said Frank. "We go in, we get out. We do this clean."

Silence.

There were rules. You didn't kill a guy's wife and kids. Although special circumstances arose. The reality was, though, innocent people died all the time, and Lorenzo Russo was a rat, the lowest of the low.

"The kid and the wife stay out of this. Do we have a deal?" said Frank.

The other two men nodded. Both avoided his searching eyes in the rear-view mirror.

Frank sighed. "There's something I haven't told you," he said. "If we do this right, I'm going to be made."

Both Tony and Jimmy ceased playing with their weapons.

"No shit," said Tony.

"No shit," said Frank, fixing his gaze on the road ahead. The car's open windows allowed a ruffling breeze, but he felt the air stiffen, the silence grow.

Tony's blue eyes might have turned green; he had similar aspirations, and Frank knew the likelihood of both men being made was remote. It was one or the other. He guessed Tony knew that, too.

Jimmy broke the silence. "We can't leave any witnesses, Frank," he said. "You know that, right?"

"Course I fuckin' know that," said Frank. "But we do this right. Okay?"

"Sure," said Jimmy.

They headed west along South Dakota's Highway 30, passing cornfields and the occasional dairy farm. A radio report interrupted Bryan Adams. A storm was on the way—a possible tornado. All they needed.

At just before ten a.m., they reached their destination:
Brookings, SD. Population: 16,428

They cruised along the town's main street—a succession of
low, flat-roofed, red-brick convenience stores, sports bars, and
sandwich shops. The roads were eerily quiet. Then they headed east
and toward the leafier suburbs where Frank pulled over to check
the map. The sky was clear, the morning sun already causing the
hot air to shimmer above the baking asphalt.

"Can I help you gentleman?" asked the young woman, bending from the sidewalk to the car's passenger window.

Jimmy grinned at the view, acknowledging the cleavage that
spilled from her pink halter-neck T-shirt.

"Are you guys lost?"

She was pretty, mid-twenties and blond. Everyone was. Every
cyclist, jogger, and roadworker was either red-headed or fair-
haired. The place epitomized small-town America where the dom-
inant ancestry was clearly Scandinavian or German. The young
woman smiled, chewing gum, the sun brightening her golden hair
while she stared into the car occupied by the three dark-haired, ol-
ive-skinned Italians. None of the men had seen a shower in days.
The New York license plate, at least, was fake, but that could attract
unwanted attention, too.

"We're just fine, lady," said Frank.

"If you're sure," she said. "You guys have a good day."

Tony gave the woman a lewd wink, and she walked on. But
Frank noticed she glanced back over her shoulder.

"Every route out of this town is a long road to nowhere,"
said Frank. "Nothing but cornfields in every direction."

"Point being?" said Tony.

"Someone sees three suspicious wops out here and decides
to call the local sheriff's office, there's no way out," said Frank.

They followed the map three blocks east, arriving at a small
cul-de-sac of large, wooden houses, built in the typical midwestern
style, with steep-gabled roofs and overhanging eaves. The pavement
was well shaded by enormous elm trees. Of the seven homes on the

street, three had American flags mounted on their immaculate lawns.

A small boy rode his BMX up and down the spotless pavement, narrowly avoiding a little dog. A mailman waved at an old lady who was standing on her doorstep with curlers in her hair. A floppy-haired teenager wearing a Guns N' Roses T-shirt skateboarded around the corner and out of view. So far, nobody appeared to have noticed the car with the false plates.

"That one there," said Tony, holding the map, pointing to the largest house on the street. As if hearing his cue, a dark-haired woman walked out of the home's front door, followed by a boy, aged about eleven.

"That's her. That's Maria, Russo's wife," said Tony.

"You sure?" said Frank.

Squinting, Tony watched the woman and boy get into a red Ford parked in the driveway. The car started, the engine little more than a gentle purr. He nodded. "She's cut her hair, but that's her. I went to the kid's christening. Must've been ten years ago."

"You went to that kid's christening?" said Frank.

Tony nodded. "Sure."

The red Ford pulled out of the shadow of the large house and into the glare of the midwestern sun. The woman—Maria—turned and waved back toward the direction of the house. The front door remained ajar. From the shadows behind the door, a hand returned the gesture, then disappeared. The door closed.

"He's in there," said Jimmy.

"We have to do this now," said Frank, watching the red car disappear down the street. The crucifix Frank wore around his neck glinted in the sun, flashing in the rear-view mirror.

The mailman got on his bike and rode away. The old lady patted her curlers and retreated into her home.

"It's broad fucking daylight. Are you out of your fucking mind?" said Tony, pronouncing every syllable. "We stick to the plan. Scout the place now and return after dark."

"When the woman and kid will likely be back home," said Frank.

Tony scowled. "And?"

"And...we leave them out of this, remember?"

In the passenger seat, Tony wiped his palms on his knees and pinched the top of his nose. "Frank..."

"This is the only way," said Frank.

Jimmy made eyes at Tony, then Frank, his gaze settling on one man then the other. Finally, Tony nodded, conceding defeat but still holding the bridge of his nose as if warding off an aggressive migraine. "Okay," he said.

Russo's house had two adjoined garages. Both were empty—the doors open. Frank started the car and sailed soundlessly up the slight slope of the drive and into the shaded garage nearest the house.

Quietly the three men exited the vehicle, emerging into the cooler climate of the shaded air. Outside, crickets chirped. A sprinkler fizzed on the neighboring lawn. Nearby, children played, their distant voices innocent eruptions in the thick heat. Frank hit the switch to close the garage door, sealing them in near darkness.

There were two doors at the garage's far end on opposite walls: one leading to the second adjoined garage, and the second into the house. They took the second.

The three men had been here before, not in this town, not in this affluent midwestern home, but in the moment that preceded a hit. Frank's lips were suddenly dry, his knees weaker. But this was their line of work, and fifteen hundred miles away, in the shadow of Manhattan skyscrapers, cops fished bloated, crab-nibbled corpses from the sediment of the Hudson River, discovered bodies rotting under steel stairways amongst restaurant rubbish and rising sewer steam. Most often, though, remains were never found, except by the scavengers of the Catskill Mountains. Death was dealt in silent understanding. The men understood each other unequivocally, without the need to speak. They communicated with a series of curt nods and eye gestures, moving through the house and across its polished floors with deadly stealth.

Outside, a warm wind was picking up; it had arrived suddenly, the still of the day turning, whistling in the pipes.

Despite the house's spacious architecture and high ceilings, Frank rounded every corner with a deep feeling of claustrophobia, his heart thumping hard. His head throbbed. If the police were alerted, this was over. There was no escape from this Godforsaken blot amongst hundreds of miles of corn.

Guns poised, they reached an expansive kitchen with marble worktops where a newspaper lay strewn:

DEVIL-WORSHIPPING RAPIST SENTENCED TO DEATH, read the headline.

Murderer Murphy to face needle after guilty verdict

On the windowsill, in a silver frame, three ghostly faces smiled in a photograph. The picture was bleached white, like a negative, by a bright shaft of sunlight.

Frank left the kitchen and emerged into a hall. Tony and Jimmy split, veering in the opposite direction to scout the large hallway and other rooms.

Alone, Frank entered a lounge.

He found the man standing before a large TV, drinking from a mug and smoking. The man turned, and his eyes widened. Coffee trickled on the lush carpet. Back in New York, Russo had been dark-haired and clean-shaven. This man had light brown hair and a heavy moustache. But Russo's features were undeniable. The TV was turned on, the volume low. On the screen, a red-headed woman was forecasting an imminent storm.

Frank aimed his 9mm at Russo's chest.

"Please," said Russo. "I have money. We can talk."

Russo reached for the weapon concealed beneath his jacket, and Frank fired three times. The silencing suppressor did its job, and aside from a dim whistle, the only sound was the dull thwack of the bullets sinking into middle-aged meat. The large man groaned, then collapsed, shattering a small glass table and scattering a Monopoly board and its pieces.

By the time Tony and Jimmy entered the room from the hall, Russo was dead. Tony scowled, looking genuinely aggrieved that Frank had killed Russo before he could.

"We need to go," said Frank, looming over the body, the gun at his side, the silencer still warm against his leg.

As the three men turned to leave the room, the woman stepped through the front door in a wash of bright sunlight. Fumbling with her rattling keys and pushing the door behind her, she stood in the now duskier light of the hall and said, "You wouldn't believe I forgot my—"

Her eyes widened as she saw them through the gap in the door. For the longest of seconds, Maria Russo stood rigid. Then a terrible grimace of understanding formed on her delicate features. While the door behind her was still ajar, it blocked her chance of a quick escape. She darted into an adjacent office.

It was Jimmy who reacted quickest. He followed her with his gun at his side. That mistake was fatal because the thundering clap of the woman's handgun sent Jimmy staggering back from the office into the hall. A second bullet ricocheted above Frank's head, splintering the wood of the door frame. A third skimmed his thigh.

The woman emerged from the office with a wild look of horror possessing her pretty face, wisps of dark hair plastered to her cheek, teeth clenched in fury, the gun's barrel raised as she fired.

Frank raised his pistol and shot.

The woman's head spun as a bullet punched through her neck and severed her spinal cord, splashing the white gloss of the door with blood. Maria Russo fell dead in the doorway, her head hanging loosely by its sinews. Blood spread in a glistening pool on the polished floor. Her dead eyes remained open.

Both men turned toward where Jimmy had collapsed, holding his stomach, white shirt turning a deep red from the blossoming wound. "I'm going to fucking die," he said, panting.

"You're not going to die," Frank lied.

"Mom?"

By the time Frank turned, the boy was already crouched at his dead mother's side, a tear running down a cheek as pale as marble; then he looked up at them with inconsolable, questioning eyes.

Tony lifted his revolver, aiming at the distressed child.

"No," shouted Frank.

Tony hesitated, the gun dropping slightly. "He's seen us. We don't have time."

"I don't care," said Frank. "He's a fuckin' kid."

The boy stared at them, frozen by grief and fear.

Tony further relaxed his arm, letting the gun drop nearer to his hip, as if Frank had perhaps altered the course of his murderous intent.

The hall grew darker. Outside, the wind rose.

Tony scowled. "You know they have the death penalty here?"

The boy was still holding his dead mother, crying.

"We need to get Jimmy out of here," said Frank.

"Jimmy's as good as dead, and he knows it."

Jimmy looked up and met Tony's eyes, the color draining from his face.

Tony gestured to the dead woman and the cowering boy. "What else would you have us do, Frank? Her shots would have been heard three blocks from here. We need to go."

"He's a child," said Frank.

"Made man," said Tony La Rosa, his face a scowl of disgust. "Don't make me fuckin' laugh." He casually lifted the gun, and with the blood-soiled band-aid hanging from his trigger finger, he fired, spraying the boy's pretty face across the polished floorboards in an oatmeal plume of blood, skin, and brains.

Frank roared.

Tony turned the gun on the two other men. When he had finished firing, the air was acrid with the tang of propellent. Frank tried to speak, but his chest was too tight, and only blood bubbled on his quivering lips.

Tony grinned his wolfish grin and said, "What's a-matter, Franky boy? Cat got your tongue?"

Frank lay on the hard floor, listening to the howling wind, praying he bled out before the sirens arrived.

CHAPTER THREE

Twelve years later

WARDEN JEFFREY OLSON entered the small holding room abruptly, looming over Frank, who sat at the table with his hands and feet shackled in chains. "Mr. D'Angelo, I have news."

Frank met the gaze of the silver-haired prison warden in the grey suit. Olson was clean-shaven, in his mid-fifties, and had maintained an athletic physique. The warden sat on the plastic chair on the table's other side. "You're obviously an influential man, Mr. D'Angelo," he said.

"What do you mean?" said Frank.

"Oh, I think you already know," said Olson, squinting slyly in contempt. "You people are all the same," he hissed.

Frank shook his head. "What?"

The warden straightened in his chair. "I've been ordered to inform you the US Supreme Court has ordered a stay of execution, following a motion from your family's attorney."

Though Frank heard the words, he almost failed to believe them. He'd refused any legal representation. He'd spent months preparing for this day psychologically, emotionally, and spiritually. He'd sent his final letters, cleared out his cell, put his shit in order. He was ready to die and embrace oblivion; indeed, he welcomed that—anything to escape the waking nightmares the doctors called psychotic delusions. But when they'd moved him from the holding cell minutes ago, his niggling suspicion had grown.

"You can't be serious," said Frank.

"Deadly, if you'll excuse the pun." Olson flashed an insincere smile, then repeated soberly, "Your execution has been stayed."

"No, please. I'm ready," said Frank. "I want this over."

"As do I. But I'm afraid that's impossible," said the warden, shuffling a pile of papers.

On the wall, a clock ticked too loudly. The small room smelled of disinfectant. The sterility was spoiled, though, by a fat bluebottle, which buzzed about, zipping into the fluorescent panel lighting. Minutes ago, Frank had speculated that the fly would out-live him if it could avoid the swatting hands of the two correctional officers stationed at the door.

"Why?" said Frank.

"The attorney submitted a petition for a writ of prohibition. It was granted."

"On what grounds?" said Frank.

"Your mental health."

"Fuck you."

"You will not be executed today."

He'd escaped death by minutes.

"Most prisoners are pleased when this happens, Mr. D'Angelo."

"Well, I'm not most prisoners."

"Don't pretend you're some kind of…criminal aristocrat. You're a common thug and nothing more. You deserve the needle—worse."

"The only difference between you and me," said Frank, "is that when I say I'm going to kill someone, I fuckin' kill them. And listen to me, you piece of shit…I never killed no one who didn't either try to kill me first or who didn't deserve it."

"Like the boy?" said the warden.

"You know I didn't do that."

"Then who did?" asked the warden.

"If I was a fuckin' rat, I wouldn't be on death row, would I?"

The warden smiled benignly. "That's not for me to speculate. But the consensus seems to be you were never fit for trial."

"Bullshit."

"All this, you waiving appeals, acting the lunatic, it's all part of a larger game, isn't it? To avoid justice," said the warden.

"No—"

"The Supreme Court has ordered a re-examination of your case," said the warden. "The attorney has a forensic psychologist attesting you were coerced into carrying out your crimes, that you were manipulated by high-ranking mafioso overlords, that you were intellectually vulnerable due to an existing mental health condition."

"There's nothing wrong with my state of mind, not then, not now. Give me a gun, and I'll do it myself," said Frank. "The only thing that is affecting my mental health is the prospect of having to go through this again. I want this done. Today."

The warden averted Frank's gaze and looked toward the officers guarding the door. "Escort Mr. D'Angelo back to his cell," he said, straightening his paperwork for the third time in as many minutes.

FRANK NEVER WAS "made." That particular honor went to the bastard who'd left him bleeding out on the floor of the house in that deadbeat Midwestern town. He remembered how that had felt, too, dying. Lying on that polished floor, sirens nearing, the storm building, the smell of blood in his nostrils, he'd watched La Rosa step over him. The motherfucker had then pressed the cannon he'd used to shoot the boy into his limp palm.

It was his senses that had faded first. He'd been vaguely aware of the insectile buzz of a pestering wasp; aware of his tongue resting against the dry roof of his mouth. Then time had ceased to exist. His perception had been reduced to something dreamlike. He might have been lying on the floor minutes, hours, or centuries. He understood now. His brain had all but shut down. He'd been reduced to nothing but his sentient core. In the end, though, nothing mattered. You simply shrank back into the same oblivion from which you were birthed. Then a distant electronic hum had whined on the fringes of his unconsciousness.

Adrenaline.

Clear.

The jolting thud had lifted him from the floor, his senses

rushing back into existence, the light flooding his eyes.

Pulse.

The first thing he'd noticed was the smell of latex, the gloves busy about him. The second thing he remembered was the faceless boy. In the blood-soaked hall, the boy's actual body was covered with a white sheet, as was Jimmy and the woman, too. Yet there the boy had stood amongst the paramedics, bodies, and commotion, pointing at Frank.

The kid had been shot at point-blank range by a high-caliber revolver. The structure of his face had been obliterated. His mouth, nose, and chin had been replaced by a gaping, ragged hole, the surrounding layers of ruined flesh exposed like an open flower. Despite the pressure of the electrode paddles on Frank's chest, the drip inserted into the back of his hand, the sponge plugging his bullet wounds, it was the grotesquely mutilated boy he'd never been allowed to forget. The boy and his accusing finger.

Everything else had been a blur: his substantial weight—minus three pints of blood—being lifted by a stretcher. Sirens. White corridors. White scrubs. The raging storm outside. He'd died three times on the operating table after he'd gone into hypovolemic shock. But in the end, his life was saved—just so he could be sentenced to death for first-degree murder. The jury had been unanimous, the sentence a modern brand of frontier justice. A deadly solution of barbiturates, paralytics, and potassium would be injected into his veins until his heart stopped.

But twelve years later, Frank no longer trusted the legal system, because it had failed to end his misery. Twenty-three hours a day, he sat in his six-by-nine cell at the South Dakota State Penitentiary and contemplated death alone.

He'd considered cutting a deal and ratting on La Rosa. But what good would that do? La Rosa was now a gangland capo, with the capability of extending his considerable influence into any prison in the US. Life without parole, amongst the general prison population—if his lawyer could have negotiated that—would have condemned him to a permanent state of hyper-vigilance. He had family on the outside, too. No. Frank craved death—but he wanted it on his own terms, not bleeding to death at the hands of some hired convict armed with a toothbrush shiv. Suicide was not an option, not without a gun.

"How are you, Frank?"

Lying on the mattress of his bedstead, Frank glanced through the blue, steel bars. The prison chaplain's large frame was a silhouette. It was late, after lights out. Father James Williams stepped into a pool of dim light from a solitary lighting panel. He was a large black man with a shaved head, goatee beard, and little round glasses. He wore a tweed jacket over his black shirt and clerical collar.

"Been better," said Frank.

"You wanted it, didn't you? Death?"

Frank nodded.

He had never really accepted Father Williams' religious counsel. Instead, he'd welcomed the big guy's occasional visits and used the allotted time to discuss the Yankees or Giants. The one thing they'd never spoken about was Frank's case, until now.

"I didn't kill the boy," said Frank. "I tried to stop it."

"But you killed the others?"

Frank nodded. "Do you believe in ghosts? In Hell?"

"I believe in the Holy Ghost, if that's what you mean."

"I see the boy's face…every day."

"Conscience is what makes us human," said Father Williams. "When your conscience speaks, we hear God's voice."

Frank wasn't speaking metaphorically. The boy's hideously disfigured face was everywhere. When the lights went out, the boy materialized in the shifting gradients of darkness. He saw the boy's faint, distorted reflection in the stainless steel of his toilet. He saw him in the crackling static of the television. Once, he'd reported this to the prison doctor. He'd swiftly been diagnosed with depression and post-traumatic stress disorder, leading to peduncular hallucinosis. The truth was, though, no one gave a shit when the guy on death row was going fucking insane. Not until now.

"No, I'm not talking about God," said Frank finally. "I'm talking about ghosts."

"You have your Bible," said Father Williams. "Embrace God, and he will be your savior. Admit your sins. Find peace. You can be redeemed before the end."

The prison chaplain's footsteps receded down the corridor, leaving Frank alone in the dark. From the hard mattress of his bunk, he stared through the bars of his cell at the space the priest had vacated and waited for the boy; sure enough, the kid stepped forward, his face a bloodied ruin.

He had spent years avoiding the sight of him. If the boy appeared, he'd look away toward the light or close his eyes, and sometimes that small distraction was enough to allow his sanity to prevail. But it had been a long day, one he'd thought would be his last. He'd accepted his fate, and fate had betrayed him.

He decided to challenge insanity. He stared at the hole where the boy's face should have been, between the flaps of rotting skin. The darkness contained by the wound was rich and shifted with liquid consistency, like deep water—like the rippling Hudson River where bloated bodies stared into their own cold oblivion, putrefying.

Peduncular hallucinosis.

Though Frank craved death, he feared that Hell awaited. He understood, too, that all men were doomed. Didn't every man have an execution day? Somewhere, a piece of marble or granite existed for everyone, waiting for a name to be inscribed. The void awaited. You chose your own Hell.

"The priest can't help you," said a gruff voice in the dark. "But I can."

At first, Frank was confused as to where the voice had come from. Then something fluttered through the bars of his cell like a black moth. The card landed on the floor next to his bunk.

Dwayne Murphy had been on death row twelve years. Only a string of appeals had kept him alive. Despite the two men being separated by mere feet and one thin wall, Frank sometimes forgot he existed. He was reminded by the occasional blatt of a fart or the sound of the other man masturbating. That he didn't like to think about, because Murphy was a rapist convicted of killing three teenage girls.

"I can help you."

Frank picked up the white card. Scrawled upon it, in red ink, was an equilateral triangle containing an open eye that was surrounded by lines representing rays of light.

"I heard the priest. He's lying," said Murphy.

"Don't fucking speak to me," barked Frank.

"Suits me. But know this: you are going to Hell. Might as well embrace it."

Frank looked at the crudely drawn eye on the card, then outside his cell toward the boy that Tony La Rosa had murdered in cold blood over a decade before. But the boy had gone. Only the bars of his cell remained, casting long shadows in the murk of the still, remorseful night.

"HERE, WE'D LIKE you to complete this."

From her plastic chair, the psychologist handed Frank the papers through the steel bars of his cell. The young woman had red, shoulder-length hair and was probably no older than twenty-seven or twenty-eight.

"It's a questionnaire," she said, her glasses perched on the end of her pretty nose. "I have a few primary questions of my own before we can begin."

Frank nodded in agreement.

"How is your general health?" said the young woman.

"You have my notes."

"Yes, but I'm asking you for your opinion."

"Fine," he said.

"Many prisoners, especially those on—"

"—death row?"

"Yes—experience depression, anxiety, and stress disorders, that sort of thing," she said. "Do you suffer from chest pains, profuse sweating, increased heart rate, anything like that?"

"No."

"Any recurrent bad dreams or nightmares?"

"No."

She scratched her pen against the form on the clipboard. Then shuffled her papers and picked out another sheet.

"It says here you have suffered hallucinations. You were diagnosed with acute depression six years ago."

Yes, he thought, *because I'm on death row, because a dead boy with a hole in his fucking face follows me around my cell twenty-four hours a day.*

"No," he said. "That was a…a cry for help. I made it up."

"You made it up?" she said, her eyes narrowed in suspicion.

"Yes."

She looked at him as if in contemplation. "I see. And have you ever abused alcohol, narcotics…prescribed pharmaceuticals?"

"I wish."

The questions went on: Had he experienced physical abuse as a child? Would he change the decisions that had led to his incarceration? Did he have violent thoughts? Did he think about his crimes, relive them, fantasize about the moment preceding him pulling the trigger?

After enduring three months of psychological assessment and screening, he'd convinced half a dozen forensic psychologists and criminal psychiatrists that he was of sound mind.

A new execution date was set. He had three months left to live.

What really clinched it, though, Frank believed, was the letter he'd addressed to the Supreme Court. He'd never been a man of words, and he'd scrawled the testament on a notepad with a cheap biro. It had done its job.

I, Frank Alessandro D'Angelo, confess to killing Lorenzo Russo and Maria Russo in a cold-blooded, premeditated attack at their home in

Brookings, South Dakota, in the summer of 1991. I had full possession of my faculties when committing the crimes.

Against his lawyer's advice, he had added:

If I could dig them both up and shoot them again, for nothing but the idle sport of it, I'd do it in a heartbeat.

He refused any blame for the boy.

Frank was taking a shit when the second card fluttered through the bars of his cell. When he picked it up, he again discovered the same crudely scrawled triangle containing the unblinking eye.

"You think I'm impressed by this shit," shouted Frank. But no reply came. His lingering question echoed in the empty corridor.

Later that night, Frank sat in the dark, trying to avoid the sight of the boy. But the sound of a funneling wind erupted from the bloody hole in the boy's face. In its varying howl, he thought he could hear the faint scream of a child and the low-frequency hum of a wasp, forming an insectile harmonic of words: "Made man. Don't make me fuckin' laugh." Then a racket of gunshots exploded in his ears, awakening his memories like a stirred cloud of bats.

"Peduncular hallucinosis," Frank told himself. That's all this was, the slow, degenerative onset of psychosis, his mind playing cruel tricks, his guilt surfacing. But the boy stood resolute, pushing the ruined flesh of his face against the steel bars.

Frank looked away—and saw one of the cards thrown from Murphy's cell. The unblinking eye stared at him from the top of his waste-paper basket. When he dared to look back toward the bars, the boy had disappeared.

"The cards, what are they?" shouted Frank into the unyielding darkness of his cell.

A brief silence.

"Think of it as a calling card," replied Murphy finally, his voice gruff with sleep.

"The symbol?" said Frank impatiently.

"The Eye of Providence," said Murphy.

"What does that mean?" said Frank.

"Depends on perspective."

"Fuck you—and your riddles. Tell me."

"Christians believe the symbol represents the all-seeing eye of God," said Murphy.

Frank remembered Murphy's disheveled appearance. He was a rapist and a child molester if ever he'd seen one. He remembered hollowed eyes, sun-faded tattoos, and lank hair that stuck to a pallid face so thin it was near skeletal. Murphy had the grizzled look of an outlaw battling a twenty-year dope addiction. He was no Christian.

"And what do you believe?" said Frank.

"The drawing represents the third eye, the truth. You're haunted by the past. We all are, by the things we've done," said Murphy. "You crave death, don't you?"

"What's it got to do with you?" said Frank.

"I have a day, too, for my execution. A date with death," said Murphy.

"You deserve it, you piece of shit."

A soft laugh echoed manically in the hollowed architecture of steel and brick. "You have a dark heart, Frank. We are bad men. Nothing good awaits us. But there's a choice."

"What's that supposed to mean?" said Frank.

"I've heard you, talking to the priest, crying out in your sleep. You've already seen Hell, haven't you? It waits for you. Your only hope is to serve it."

"You're a fuckin' lunatic, you know that?" said Frank.

"I can save you," said Murphy.

When Frank lay back on his bunk, movement caught his eye. The boy had returned, his ruined face dripping blood that pooled on the hard floor, coagulating in the cold night air.

He closed his eyes. Hours passed before he fell into a restless sleep.

"I'M GOING TO enjoy watching you die," said Sofia Greco.

When the woman spoke, her nostrils flared and her spit sprayed, like venom hitting the sheet of the Perspex glass that separated them. The woman sat rigidly, her dignity rehearsed, her fury repressed. Her unblinking eyes, though, burned with a fire of hate.

"I have heard of it going wrong, you know, the lethal injection," she said. "One prisoner took half an hour to die. The pain was, apparently, excruciating." She smiled, revealing perfect veneers. "I have a good Chianti in the cellar, a sixty-seven. In two weeks, after I've witnessed your life snuffed like a candle, I'm going to go home, pop the cork, and toast your arrival in Hell."

"Mrs. Greco—"

"Don't interrupt me, you bastard. My sister did nothing to you. My nephew, Leo, he was eleven."

"I'm sorry."

"Are you fucking serious?"

"I never intended to...hurt your sister." He sighed. "And I didn't kill the boy...Leo."

"Don't you say his name, you son of a bitch."

"Please—"

"*Figlio di puttana,*" she cursed and slammed her delicate fist against the glass, alerting a watching guard; he did not intervene.

In the Perspex, a familiar reflection appeared from behind him. The lines of the boy's ruined face were a tracing shadow over the woman's hateful scowl.

Back in his cell, he contemplated his reasons for agreeing to meet Greco. Perhaps, after inflicting so much violence on her family, he had wanted simply to allow her to express her anger, to relish in his demise. He thought he was incapable of demonstrating true penitence. Perhaps the last kindness he could offer was to be the monster that she wanted to be slain. He'd never felt this hopeless, this alone.

Later, Frank lay on his bunk with his troubles. After hours of enduring a sleepless torment, he shouted out in desperation to the neighboring cell. "You said you could help me. Tell me how?"

A brief silence. "You're a Catholic?" answered Murphy in his southern drawl.

"Yes," he answered, realizing the very idea of him being affiliated to any respectable religion was ridiculous. There was no road to redemption; he'd burnt those bridges.

"You're in a kind of purgatory."

"What?" said Frank.

"Do you see them, the demons?"

Frank hesitated, then said, "I see a boy."

"The third eye—you see the truth, the choices you've made."

"I don't understand—?"

"You carry your sins. We all do. Demons are parasites. They feed on your misery, your guilt. You're being eaten alive. Even a blind man could see there's little left of you."

Frank remembered the last time he'd seen his gaunt reflection. Murphy was right. He looked tired and old, a hollow man with grey skin and whitened hair, his humanity cut out, his lifeforce faded.

"It's a bit late in the fucking day for metaphors," said Frank.

"It's not a metaphor. Men are architects of their own hell. You build it, brick by brick. But that needn't be. You can take strength from your sins if you own them."

"What the fuck?" said Frank.

"Hell needn't be a prison; eternity can be your domain. But first you must confess. Choose."

"Choose what?"

"Darkness."

"What—?"

"You were a gangster, a wise guy?"

"No," said Frank honestly. "I was never...made."

"You're going to Hell," said Murphy. "You can either go as a victim and suffer eternal fucking damnation, or you can seek affinity."

159

"With whom, the devil?"

"A deity of many names."

"You really are a crazy fuck, you know that?"

"I'm offering you a chance," said Murphy.

"Why am I even talking to you?"

There was a brief silence.

"Because," answered Murphy finally, "I've seen the boy, too."

Frank lifted his head from his flat, unfluffed pillow. For a fleeting second, he dared to glance in the direction of the bars of his cell. Indeed, the boy was there.

"He's standing at the bars outside your cell," said Murphy. "He has no face."

"You can see him?" The words left Frank's lips desperately.

"His face is gone," said Murphy, "and in two weeks, you will be gone, too."

Am I sane? thought Frank. The possibility terrified him.

"I can help you," said Murphy, his voice a thin whisper. "Eternity waits for the anointed, for the ordained."

Frank had no idea what he was talking about—perhaps Murphy was even crazier than he was—but he had little time for contemplation because a metallic clang startled him. He looked to the floor where the noise had originated and saw Murphy had tossed an old tobacco tin through his bars; it was painted with the Confederate flag. Anxious that a guard could have heard, he peered out into the corridor outside his cell. Nobody. Nothing. Only shadows…and the boy. Always the boy.

He picked up the tin and opened the lid. Inside was a bare hypodermic syringe and a small plastic bottle containing a dark liquid.

Ink?

"Frank—D'Angelo, that's your name, right?"

The rapist addressing him by his full name made him somehow uncomfortable. "Yes," he answered.

By then Murphy had already begun his canticle. His voice was near indecipherable from the other side of the cell wall, but the chant was delivered in a pitch several octaves lower. By the prosody and precision of his intonations, Frank guessed the crazy bastard was reciting classical Latin verse.

"What are you doing?" said Frank.

"Do you remember the names of the people you've killed?"

Lorenzo Russo. Maria Russo. There had been many more; scores of them. But he'd never killed indiscriminately. It had always been with cold, business-like efficiency. He was assigned. It was professional. There was a name and a bullet. Rarely had it been personal. Most deserved it.

"Well?" harried Murphy.

"I guess I could remember most if I—"

"Inscribe the names of your victims on your body."

"What?"

"Every one of them. I have heard a lot about you, Frank. I know there were many. Leave your face and hands until last."

"Are you insane?"

"I can see the boy, Frank."

"Tattoo myself?"

"Confess. Own your sins."

"With a dirty needle?"

"Worried about infection?" Murphy sneered. "You'll be dead in two weeks."

Frank picked up the needle, inspected it.

"There's something else," said Murphy. "You must not sleep. Wait until they pump your veins with poison."

"Are you serious?"

"You must purify your soul. You came into the world naked. You'll leave in the same skin. Pledge yourself. Free yourself from mortal concerns, their trappings. No food. No sleep. Conceal the needle. Recite the names. Work at night. Prepare for sacrifice."

Again, Frank dared to glance at the faceless boy on the fringe of his cell, blending to the shadows.

How could Murphy know?

While the prospect of insanity had terrified him, that fear was insignificant compared to eternal damnation. He'd never believed in the prospect of Hell. But that was then, and this was now, when his imminent death was a stark fact.

I can see the boy, Frank.

On the other side of the wall, Murphy's bizarre chant continued.

He remembered visiting a church as a child, the books, the crude medieval paintings, the depictions of Hell: naked humans entwined by serpents; horned demons lancing bodies; cauldrons of screaming sinners cooking in flames.

A ridiculous fairy tale…

Perhaps the doctors were correct in their diagnosis: he had simply succumbed to mental illness after years of solitude and regret. But maybe insanity was all Frank had. He tore off the crucifix that hung around his neck and tossed it to the floor.

He rolled up his trousers. He unscrewed the top of the ink bottle, dipped the needle, and began to carve names on the meat of his calf. As he did, he imagined a hundred rotting eyeballs rotating in their cadaverous sockets, looking up from the tenebrous murk of the Hudson, stirring from the depths in acknowledgement of their killer. The sharp pain of the needle, though, was a comfort. That, at least, was tangible, something real he understood, to pin down his scrambling sanity. He recited the names, whispering as he worked, owning every life he'd taken, making his confession.

And one by one, they did appear. The corridor outside his cell became busy, filled with those he'd butchered and maimed, faces that had haunted his conscience for decades. As if summoned by the ritual of his litany, they pressed wet flesh against the bars of his cell, wounds smearing, filling his nostrils with the rank stench of decay.

His world was a grey place. But there were still two distinct sides: good and evil; Heaven and Hell; darkness and light. Frank D'Angelo had chosen darkness. The anointment took minutes, and that night he was ordained, made a member of The Order Abaddon.

By morning's dull cast, thirteen days remained until the lethal injection. Already black ink scaled his shins like ivy, crawling up his limbs toward his beckoning torso.

"Made man," said Tony La Rosa from the deepest recesses of Frank's sleep-deprived mind. "Don't make me fuckin' laugh."

He'd never been made. That honor had been stolen, the initiation that set you for life. But there were other ceremonies—Murphy had promised—ceremonies that set you for eternity.

With each night, the needle punctured, the pigment spreading like sepsis, his blackened soul poisoned beyond antidote.

The air soured, and something that blended with the dark whispered unseen in the quiet of his cell.

The nights passed in a frenzied blur, Frank's soul in utero.

"WHAT THE—?" Through the bars of the cell, the warden stared at Frank's naked body, his eyes wide with amazement.

Buttocks bared, limp cock shriveled, rib cage exposed, Frank stood in the cold confines of his cell with his arms at his side. He'd completed his work with seconds to spare, leaving his hands and head till last as Murphy had instructed. He'd worked by night and in stealth, and every inch of his reachable body was now covered with the names of his victims. On that final night, he'd shaved his head with a blunt razor and tattooed his pale skull. Rivers of blood ran down his face, blinding his eyes. The needle had been so blunt he might as well have carved the names with a spoon. The pain, though, he'd savored; it had kept him awake.

An overweight guard opened the cell door, the sliding mechanism like sudden thunder. The warden entered, followed closely by a correctional officer with his hand placed on the taser attached to his belt.

"My God, you're fucking insane after all," said the warden, Jeffrey Olson, squinting, circling Frank, and bending to read the words on his graffitied body.

Olson turned to his inferior officers. "Look at him. Has nobody been watching him?" The men shrugged in apparent confusion.

"You know that's contraband, don't you?" said Olson, pointing to the empty bottle of ink and the needle that Frank had placed carefully in the tobacco tin on the floor a minute before.

Frank ignored the question. He staggered with exhaustion, wiping blood from his lips. He'd left his eyelids and tongue till last. That had been a delicate job for his butchered, bleeding hands because he shook with the effects of sleep deprivation and hunger. He'd feared to press too hard, in case the needle—even blunt as it was—penetrated the thin skin of his eyelids and blinded him.

"Names?" said Olson, reading the words scrawled on Frank's body. "What is this, a confession? Stalling tactics? You have been a busy boy." He sighed. "If you think this will delay things, you are out of your mind." He tapped an expensive-looking wristwatch. "Twenty-four hours."

The itinerary had been planned with military precision. Frank was given a clean white uniform. He was escorted to a holding cell. He'd refused final visits with family and friends. Even though hunger burned in his gut, he'd refused his last meal, too. He spent his last mortal day on earth sitting on a bunk in a bland room, fighting sleep, staring at his uncut, brittle nails, and reciting the names of the dead.

At 9:20 a.m. on Saturday, the twentieth of September, 2003, the door to the holding cell opened. Frank was dressed in a white gown and slippers, handcuffed, and led down a sterile corridor.

His head spun. He swam in a sea of nausea and dizziness. With every step, his heart pounded in his ears. He feared dying but thought it might be a relief to finally sleep. He was so tired. He'd refused the sedative they'd offered, but his reflexes were out of kilter, and every second unwound too slowly. His blurred, watering eyes burned. Colors appeared too stark. And when he looked up from his chained and shuffling feet, he saw the dead, the buzzed heads of the prison officers mutating into the butchered faces of his victims.

They arrived at the death chamber.

Dressed in grey shirts, three correctional officers led Frank into a small, white room, together with the warden. The air smelled clinically tinged. The walls were bare apart from a simple clock. In the center of the room was a padded gurney, with unfastened straps, next to a small medical table. A black phone stood on a second table in the corner.

Father Williams stood in his clerical clothing, clutching a Bible and staring at Frank's newly tattooed face. The priest nodded curtly as he passed.

Frank caught sight of his reflection in a large, mirrored screen. He was unrecognizable. He was a bald, thin man, older than his years. He'd not slept for so long, and he knew that caused him to hallucinate, because the tattoos covering every inch of his sallow skin squirmed like maggots. The ink shifted and reformed, the words reading as others than the names he'd scrawled.

He was uncuffed and helped onto the gurney where he lay flat, his heart hammering in his chest, his breath escaping him in desperate bursts. His arms placed by his sides, the officers fastened buckled straps at his wrists, torso, and ankles. He was trapped. He could blink, and that was all.

"Try to relax," said the officer nearest, his sulfurous breath tinged with coffee. Didn't prison officers receive standard-issue toothpaste? He was living out his final moments, yet that was the thought that occurred to him. These were people putting him to death, people with petty concerns and small lives. What qualified any of these wage slaves to end his life with such medical meticulousness? It was true Frank had craved death, but now that the moment had arrived, he resented these people. He thought he'd prefer a more brutal death, something less intimate—a firing squad, maybe—because this clinical façade somehow made it worse.

A female officer clipped something to his gown. "A microphone," she said. "For your final words." Her voice was soft and maternal. Another officer taped a heart-monitor sensor to his tattooed chest.

A man wearing a white coat entered the room from a second door and put on latex gloves. "Stay calm," he ordered, his kind blue eyes sparkling. The man took a sachet from his pocket and tore, producing an alcohol swab. He wiped inside the hinge of Frank's left arm. Frank stared at the ceiling, the jaundiced, unnatural light blurring his tired eyes. He was terrified.

A sharp prick.

The doctor sighed.

Another sharp prick.

"Vein's constricted," said the doctor. "This man's dehydrated." He gripped his arm hard and tried again, face lined in a frown. "There, all done," he said, patting Frank's arm as if he was a young child frightened by a tiny needle. He inserted an intravenous tube, taping the drip secure. The doctor repeated the process, inserting a second IV into his right arm. This time, two tries was all it took to find the vein. Then lines were attached from behind Frank, feeding into his arms from the room with the mirrored screen.

The officer at Frank's rear turned a mechanism that altered the angle of the gurney from nearly flat to forty-five degrees. He now faced a second screen concealed by a mechanical curtain, exposed in his gown for all to view, his dignity and absolute vulnerability laid bare.

Apart from Father Williams, only two officers remained stationed at each end of the gurney: the woman and the man with the bad breath. Everybody else had cleared the room.

Up the curtain went, revealing a second mirrored screen he knew concealed the witnesses who looked on: Sofia Greco waiting to watch him die.

He faced his tattooed reflection.

"Frank Alessandro D'Angelo, you have been sentenced to death for the murders of Lorenzo Benito Russo, Maria Francesca Russo, and Leonardo Antony Russo on August 17, 1991," the female officer said with unwavering authority, all trace of maternal warmth gone. "Now you have the opportunity to make a final statement before we proceed to carry out your sentence."

Frank tried to speak, but his lips were too dry. He wet them with his sandpaper tongue. "Tony La Rosa," he croaked, desperately trying to catch his breath. "I'll see you in Hell."

There was a brief silence, and the gurney was lowered back down so he was again horizontal. He was staring at the ceiling, his heart beating so hard it felt like it might burst out of his chest. Here he was—this was the time. The end had come.

"Release Syringe A."

He felt the sedative enter his veins. Immediately his heart slowed, and his thoughts became muggy and thick, his fear dissipating. Father Williams bent over him and put a firm hand on his shoulder. But in the blurring glare from the ceiling's light, Williams' head morphed. The priest's face became that ruined atrocity of the boy's, ragged flaps of skin hanging around a cavity that resembled some huge, bloodied maw.

Frank felt himself receding, and his eyes closed.

"Syringe B."

The pain arrived in a bolt of agony, like acid burning every molecule in his body, abruptly waking him. He writhed in his binds, convulsing in frenzied spasms.

"He's still conscious," shouted the doctor who was again at his side. Panic filled the room.

The mechanical curtain descended, obstructing the witnesses' view of the ensuing chaos.

Another blistering stab of pain hit Frank, and he felt his muscles tighten as if his body might enter a seizure. And that's how he died, facing sin, staring into the gaping wound of the boy's face that had become a cavernous black hole where a storm raged within. The void swallowed him like a tornado. His memories flew around him within the vortex amongst whirls of debris.

In the great, iridescent gloom of the sky, the moments of his life were projected on the sullen clouds by eruptions of sheet lightning, every gentle moment, every act of wickedness lit in violent fulmination: baking oatmeal cookies with his mother; kissing a pretty girl; beating a man to death with the bloodstained butt of his revolver; watching as Tony La Rosa killed an innocent child.

Deafening thunder roared with Old Testament fury. He roiled in eternity.

When the storm abated, Frank found himself kneeling in the hot sand of a vast desert where fires burned on the horizon. It was dusk. He watched the flames lick the air, backlighting endless rows of inverted crucifixes. In the distance, men screamed amongst the incessant hum of swarming flies.

Somewhere, he knew, Sofia Greco toasted his arrival with a glass of vintage as blood red as the crimson sky. But not Frank. No crucifix awaited him. Damnation was a blessed kiss. He was ordained.

Made Man—Don't make me fuckin' laugh.

It would be Frank who would have the last one.

CHAPTER FOUR

THE MIAMI SUNRISE paints the hotel room in a luminous haze, the light beaming through the Venetian blinds, illuminating constellations of swirling dust motes.

The alarm clock reads 6:38 a.m.

In the long corridor, two drunken figures stagger, falling into doorways and clipping a fire extinguisher, knocking it on its side. Frank detects their meandering approach from the hotel room with sonar-like precision.

"I can do this thing with my tongue," says La Rosa, his voice thinned by age.

"Shush," says the girl, hiccupping. She sounds like a child. "You'll wake the…sleepy people."

Laughter.

"Fuck them. If they're not awake now, they soon will be, way I'm going to make you scream."

The girl laughs. "Well, we're not breaking any laws…as such."

"Not yet, sweetheart."

The girl giggles. By the smell of her, Frank surmises she is young enough to be La Rosa's granddaughter. He can smell the Jack Daniel's on La Rosa's breath. He can smell the ink on the thick wad of dollars contained in the old man's wallet. He can smell the banana-scented condom coating that clings to the girl's labia from the last client she'd fucked.

The handle turns, and the door opens. The old man stands at the edge of the room, the hooker a foot behind, the sunrise now blinding the room in a wash of warm light.

Squinting, La Rosa pauses for a second as if he's caught the whiff of danger, a rat sniffing poison.

Hidden by shadows, Frank remains poised on his powerful haunches, an apex predator waiting to bring about death, waiting for the prize of La Rosa's tarnished soul.

Finally, the old man enters the room in an arthritic shuffle. The Tony La Rosa of 1991 had never walked like that. But Frank has no doubt that this is the same man who shot him and left him bleeding out so many years before.

"Welcome to my humble abode," says La Rosa, gesturing for the prostitute to enter the room, a manic grin scarring the grey flesh of his elderly skin.

Frank moves like a glitch in time, a stir of flickering shadows ghosting in the glare of the burnt hue of dawn. He propels his solid mass toward the door; it slams, sealing the old man in the room. He grabs La Rosa by the lapels, throwing him across the floor like an unwanted toy, tearing the jacket of his expensive suit.

La Rosa falls against the bed, bones audibly snapping; he cries out in pain. The girl is knocking on the door's other side, oblivious.

"You okay, Tony? Tony?"

Cowering, pissing his pants, La Rosa looks up.

The names of the dead scroll Frank's skin like digital rain, and he looms over the old man, his huge wings extended, his horned head casting a forked shadow across the brightly lit room.

Shaking, La Rosa regards him with narrowed eyes, a glint of

recognition forming. "You," he says and produces a revolver from inside his jacket. He points it uselessly, his aim wavering.

At seventy-eight years old, La Rosa no longer resembles the ruthless killer who put so many men to death, and in his last moments, his sharp wit and quick mouth fail him. He looks frightened and old.

Frank rams his fist down the old man's narrow throat, rips his tongue from its root, and holds his glistening trophy aloft.

La Rosa's bloody body lies still on the floor, a brittle pile of bones. His soul, though, is a heavier thing, burdened by decades of hate and murder and sin.

In the lonely, barren desert, where the sky is scorched red, a cross waits for La Rosa, a cross and a faceless boy whose ragged flaps of skin surround a hole as black as the darkest of hearts.

REFLECTIONS OF US

David A. Anthony

"TRY THE NEXT ONE!" Rai shouted over their frantic footfalls. "Right there! Hurry!"

Tyler Pierce rammed his shoulder into the front door, and it flew wide open. He paused for only a moment, letting the long coppery rays of the setting sun illuminate the small entryway of the old house, listening carefully, wary of any shouts or commotion or signs that someone was home. He expected to hear nothing, not now, not in this neighborhood, but he could never be too careful. After several seconds he waved the others over. "We're good!"

They rushed inside the house, and Tyler slammed the door behind them.

They were immediately engulfed in a thick semi-darkness, with only a few sharp orange blades of light cutting through the heavy boards on the windows to offer them any illumination. Ava was saying something to him, sounding agitated, but he ignored her. He and Rai slid a heavy bookcase in front of the door and then braced a dust-covered couch against it.

"Tyler, are you listening to me?" Ava screamed. "We can't

stay here! I won't do it!"

The light was fading fast. The orange blades had darkened to a bruised purple, quickly going to black. They only had seconds left. "Ava, I need you to calm down. We can't go back out there. Not at night. You know what's there. Just take a deep breath and lower your voice."

But she wouldn't. She was getting louder and more hysterical. Too loud.

"You need to chill, Ava!" Rai cut in. "You're gonna get us killed."

"That's not helping!" Tyler snapped at him. "Ava, listen to me. It's just for a few hours. Just until sunrise. Then we'll be on our way back home with the supplies." He tossed his backpack down onto the couch, sending up a plume of dust. "It'll be okay."

"You're not listening," she shouted. "It won't be okay! If we try to spend the night here, we're not going home! We'll all be dead!"

Before he could respond, the light vanished, plunging them into uneasy darkness.

The group fell silent, listening. Something moved outside, over by one of the windows. Ava opened her mouth to speak, but Tyler slapped a hand over it, silencing her. He pulled her closer to him, holding his breath as his heart beat loudly in his ears. He thought he could hear hers, too. There was another noise, over on the other side of the house…the sound of movement. There were several of them out there, surrounding them, trapping them.

Something knocked on the front door.

Tyler met Rai's eyes, and he could see the panic there. None of them moved. None of them made a sound. Tyler had the sensation of a tall, hulking form just on the other side of the door, listening for movement inside, hungry. They stood there like that for several long minutes, petrified, waiting for something to happen. Tyler tightened his grip on his shotgun so hard he thought he was going to break the bones in his hand. Any second now they would break the door down, or smash through the boarded windows, and then it would be over for them, after all of these years of running and hiding and avoiding the night. But then, suddenly, he could sense them moving away, hear their movement, on to other houses, in search of other prey. They were safe.

For now.

He waited another full minute to make sure they were gone before releasing his hold on Ava. She immediately stepped back a few paces and glared angrily at him. He could barely make out her features in the gloom, just her voluptuous figure in those tight jeans and that form-fitting top, a figure that drove him crazy. Her silky black hair cascaded over her shoulders and spilled halfway down her back. He couldn't see her dark brown eyes in the dimness, but he could feel them burning on him, the anger radiating off her. And there was something else there, too, something primal and dangerous: fear. She was visibly trembling, but strangely, he didn't think her fear was exclusively for the creatures outside. It was something else.

"What the hell was that about back there?" Rai hissed at her, still keeping his voice low. "You could've gotten us all killed."

"What was it about?" She barked out a harsh, sarcastic laugh and flicked on her flashlight, shining it around the room. "This is what it's about."

The beam of light seemed to be everywhere at once, bouncing from one wall to the next, and the next, all at once. Tyler frowned as he was overcome with light and confusion, and then realized what was going on. "Mirrors. Holy shit, they're everywhere!"

The observation was an understatement. Mirrors of all shapes and sizes had been affixed to the walls around them, covering nearly every available space. There were no family photos, paintings, artwork, or any of the normal décor one expected to find in a home, only mirrors. They were square, oval, rectangular, and diamond-shaped, small and large, modern-looking and antique, with gothic styles. Tyler tilted his head back and found them on the ceiling as well, long nails driven into their frames to secure them. One or two appeared to be held in place with duct tape. Ava turned off her flashlight and Tyler flipped a switch by the door, but nothing happened.

Rai noticed several candles lined up on the mantle above the fireplace, each embedded in decorative metal holders. He scooped one up, along with a book of matches, and lit the candle. He held it up, allowing the soft glow to penetrate the shadows so they could see the assortment of mirrors more clearly. "Why the hell would they do this?"

"I think I know," Tyler answered. "When the Lurkers first appeared, some people mistook them for vampires or demons. There's an old folklore that mirrors allow people to see the hidden truths inside themselves and others, but also to see supernatural creatures hiding inside seemingly normal folk. When this thing started, a lot of people were paranoid, suspecting their friends and relatives of being undead. This family probably thought putting up all these mirrors would help them identify who was undead and who wasn't once they stepped inside."

"I wonder how that worked out for them," Rai said, glancing around uneasily.

"That's not how it works," Ava said. "Not even close."

Tyler turned his eyes back to her. In the wan, flickering light of the candle, her trepidation was even more apparent. He'd never seen her like this before. Her body shook violently, her eyes darting around the room from one mirror to the next, a sheen of perspiration on her brow. Tyler had known Ava Cervantes for almost two years now. They'd met shortly after the Lurkers had arrived, taking over the night and killing a large portion of the population. Most everyone fled the big cities where the Lurker presence seemed most concentrated. Tyler and Rai Tanaka, his best friend for almost fifteen years, had been attending the University of Washington at the time, and they quickly fled Seattle to an abandoned Navy base outside the city that had become a safe haven from the creatures. It was there he met Ava.

She'd been one of the first people he'd interacted with upon arriving at the base, sucked in by her beauty but held fast by her charm and inner strength. Like a lot of people there, she'd become separated from her family and friends and, with cell phone reception inexplicably down, she had no idea how to find them. She, Tyler, and Rai became an inseparable trio. When supplies started running low, they joined a scavenging unit, going out during daylight hours into nearby neighborhoods and businesses to search for food and supplies, first with others, and then on their own, venturing farther and farther from base as the supplies within their vicinity gradually depleted.

Somehow, during all of this, things had become intimate between him and Ava. She was the best thing to happen to him even before the Lurker nightmare began. They started spending a lot of time together, just the two of them, doing chores or finding a secluded spot for lovemaking. Rai had been noticeably jealous, even though he'd been seeing a few other girls inside the base himself. Tyler suspected it was all the time he spent with Ava, rather than Rai. It made their scavenging outings uneasy. They never fought, exactly, but there was a tension in the air between them, something unspoken, but palpable. Tyler had wished things would just go back to normal; that whatever unspoken conflict there was would be spontaneously resolved. And it had. Nothing had been discussed, to his knowledge, and no big blowup or fight had occurred. But lately, the companionable feel had returned, and everything seemed normal. At least until tonight. In all their time together, he had never seen Ava like this, so terrified and out of control. It was starting to scare him.

"What do you mean?" Tyler asked. "That's not how what works?"

Ava let out another laugh, a small sound of exasperation. "The fuck do you think I mean, Tyler? You're not listening to me! You never listen to me! It's the mirrors! The goddamn mirrors! They don't just show you things, people's secrets, or whatever. They're doorways. That's how they get in." And, in a barely audible voice, she added. "That's how they got her."

Tyler took a deep breath before replying. They'd had this discussion before, about what had happened to Ava at Midnight Mel's Traveling Carnival when she was seven years old. About the haunted house, with its maze of mirrors and scary, knife-wielding clowns, and the giant spider that came down from the ceiling. About getting separated from her mother and what she thought she'd heard and seen in the mirrors. But, of course, most of it had just been her imagination, her way of rationalizing what had really happened, what her mother—the person she'd idolized and who'd meant the world to her—had done. He'd been kind when they'd spoken about it in the past, tried to appear understanding, but tonight, it was time to rip off the Band-Aid. She had to keep it together and overcome this fear. They needed her to be calm and keep quiet—to keep her head on straight—if they wanted to survive the night.

"I'm sorry, Ava," he said. "But there was nothing inside the mirrors at that haunted house. It was just special effects, actors, and illusions."

Her eyes shot to his, sharp and piercing. "What are you saying? That I'm crazy? That I imagined that hideous face, and those long claws, reaching out and pulling her in?"

"Come on, guys," Rai cut in. "Let's take a break for a second. Before we say something we don't mean."

But Tyler pressed on. "I think…" He paused, considering his words carefully. "…that some people struggle with the concept of being parents; that the responsibility can become too much for them. Eventually, they just leave and never look back. I think your mother had it planned. She used the confusion of the haunted house to ditch you, sneak out an emergency exit, and leave you there on you own. It was an awful thing to do, and she probably regrets it now, but—"

"That's not what happened," she said, cutting him off. "I was there. I saw it."

"You were young. And scared. Fear can do strange things to people; make their minds play tricks on them. It's why we have to keep our heads on straight tonight, with the Lurkers right outside."

"I can't believe you're saying this." She sounded a bit choked up, and her eyes were watery, yet somehow, she kept from crying. "You always acted like you believed me before."

"I never said I believed it. I just...tried to understand, to be there for you."

"Well, you're wrong. About what happened back then." She gestured around. "And about what's going to happen here tonight. I'll stay here, because it's too late to go back outside. But this is a mistake." She turned and strode off angrily down the hallway.

He started to go after her, but Rai stopped him. "Don't. Just let her go."

Tyler sighed tiredly. "Damn it. I shouldn't have said any of that. It was stupid. I was just trying to snap her out of it, get her to see these mirrors are no threat so she'd calm down and handle staying here for the night. But all I did was make it worse."

"It's okay. Let me go talk to her. I'll smooth things out."

He sighed again. "Thanks. But then we need to get started securing this house. Make sure there are no other ways in. Make sure we're alone here."

"Got it. Be back in a few." The orange glow of Rai's candle receded down the hallway, casting its flickering light from one mirror to the next, until Tyler was left in darkness.

He went to the mantle and lit the rest of the candles, placing them around the room, keeping one for himself. He could hear their voices down the hall, engaged in heated debate. He felt like an asshole for saying the things he had. He'd never intended to hurt her, but opening someone's eyes to the truth often had that unfortunate side effect. He should have expected it.

Ava and Rai were gone for a long time. Their voices became much lower, less intense, until he couldn't hear them at all. As he stood there in the living room, a strange, oily feeling of dread slid down into the pit of his stomach. He didn't like this house, or these mirrors. His reflection appeared oddly distorted in them, almost hostile, and it gave him an uneasy feeling of being watched. Now and then, he'd sense movement out of the corner of his eye, but when he turned to look, he only saw his own startled reflection staring back at him. Once or twice, he thought he heard movement outside the house and became deathly still, utterly silent, until that feeling of someone, or something, standing there and listening from the other side of the wall had passed.

After a while, Tyler grew tired of waiting and ventured down the hallway. The house was old and very large. The mirrors that began in the living room, continued throughout the hallway, on both the walls and ceiling. They were also in the kitchen, dining area, and the small, main-floor bathroom. He didn't see Rai or Ava anywhere, and he didn't dare call out to them. He couldn't risk the Lurkers hearing. But that wasn't the whole truth, was it? What was the rest of it? The mirrors? Was Ava's irrational fear of them somehow infecting him? The terror of someone, or something, hiding behind them, watching and listening, waiting to reach out and grab him? Or was it something else? Something more real and infinitely worse.

At the end of the hallway, a staircase led upstairs to the second level. To his right, he caught a glimpse of flickering candlelight emanating from behind a partially closed bedroom door. As he approached, he heard voices, low and urgent with emotion. He could make out Ava's voice but not her words. When he nudged the door open, what he saw stopped him dead in his tracks. It had to have been a hallucination, or some trick of the light, playing upon his nervous mind by the omnipresent mirrors. Ava and Rai stood close to each other in the center of the room—a little too close for Tyler's liking. Rai had one hand on her waist and was speaking softly to her. Ava appeared to have calmed down considerably and was leaning in toward him, almost melting in his arms. The thoroughly ridiculous notion occurred to Tyler that Rai had been about to kiss her. But that wasn't what had frozen Tyler in place. It was Ava's reflection in the mirror on the other side of them. The image he saw there wasn't of a voluptuous, young Hispanic woman, but something else: a vile, contemptuous thing from the darkest depths of a nightmare. Perversely, the beast had Ava's figure, her perfect curves and form-fitting clothes, but its skin was charcoal grey and covered in festering sores. Its face was grotesquely misshapen, with a crooked nose and filthy, matted hair. The creature's head turned slowly to look at him, the lips splitting open in a hideous grin, revealing rotting green teeth. Its searing red eyes burned into his, scalding him, like the fires of hell itself.

"Tyler!" Rai called out to him.

Whatever dark spell had seized the room a moment before vanished. Ava and Rai broke their embrace—or maybe that had never happened to begin with; Tyler couldn't be sure anymore. The nightmare-woman in the mirror was gone, Ava's reflection back to normal, and Tyler found himself unsure if it had really been there, either. Maybe he was going mad.

"Hey, man. You okay?" Rai asked. Tyler thought he detected something in Rai's voice—fear, perhaps...guilt? Or maybe there hadn't really been anything there, either.

"I'm fine," Tyler answered, his throat dry. "I just thought..."

Rai frowned. "You thought what?"

Tyler shook his head. "Nothing."

An awkward silence fell over the room.

Ava stepped over to Tyler and pressed her body up against his, wrapping an arm around him. "Hey, what do you say we go check out the rest of the house? Make sure it's secure." There was something off about her voice and the look in her eyes, but he couldn't put his finger on what it was. He thought about that horrible grinning thing in the mirror, and it sent a shiver down his spine.

"Okay," he said. "Let's go. Rai, you stay down here. We'll check the upstairs."

Rai just nodded. But there was something in his eyes Tyler didn't like.

179

TYLER HELD HIS shotgun at the ready as they ascended the stairs, its mounted flashlight scanning for movement. Ava followed closely behind with her Glock. Mirrors lined the staircase and upstairs hallway. They were inside both bedrooms, the bathroom, and thick heavy boards covered the windows, but there were no people or animals; no signs of recent habitation. They were alone. The wind whistled in the eaves and rain pattered softly against the windows as a storm brewed outside, the beginnings of a violent one.

Inside one of the bedrooms, Tyler checked in the closet and under the bed, finding nothing unusual. He turned off his flashlight and lit another candle. "Looks safe enough. You and I can stay in here tonight."

She hesitated a moment, then nodded. "Okay."

There was another awkward silence, tension in the air between them. Tyler broke it. "Listen…I'm sorry about earlier. I shouldn't have said those things about your mother, about what happened to her. I know how traumatic that was for you, and I wasn't trying to hurt you."

"I know. I get what you were trying to do, help me to accept…" she gestured around the room, at the mirrors, "…all of this. But you're wrong. I know what I saw that night."

"Okay," he said, not contesting her claim further.

There was more he wanted to say, not only about this, but other subjects. He wanted to ask just what the hell he had walked in on between her and Rai. Was something going on between them? When had it started? How far had it gone? He wanted to ask if she'd seen the thing in the mirror, or anything else unnatural inside this house. He wanted to say that maybe she was right, that there was something dangerous about the mirrors, that maybe they should make some attempt at covering them up or taking them down. Or, maybe they should just get the hell out of there and take a chance on the night, the storm, and the horrors awaiting them outside. But he said none of these things, just let the tension linger, and the moment soon passed.

"We should regroup," Ava said. "We don't want to keep Rai

waiting."

Tyler nodded weakly. "Yeah. Good idea."

She exited the room and he turned to follow, but out of the corner of his eye he noticed something watching him, his own reflection, bizarrely distorted and facing the wrong direction. It looked directly at him, rather than toward the doorway. His breath caught in his chest.

"Chicken-shit."

Tyler whirled around at the voice, pointing his weapon at the mirror, his pulse pounding rapidly in his throat. He could hear Ava spin around with him, her pistol coming up and aiming at the same mirror. But there was nothing off about it now: just an oval, full-length mirror reflecting his wild-eyed startled look back at him, shotgun leveled menacingly at himself.

"What?" Ava nearly shouted. "What the hell is it, Ty? Tell me! What did you see?" Her voice was frenzied now, the panic from earlier returned to it, that near-hysteria back full force.

Tyler waited several seconds to see if it would move or speak again, but the mirror mimicked his movements perfectly, as it should. He lowered his weapon. "I don't know. I thought…just nerves, I guess. Sorry."

Her eyes seared into his, alarm and terror blazing there again. "Bullshit. You saw something. What was it? Tell me!"

"Nothing. Really. These mirrors are just putting me on edge."

She stared at him a moment longer. "You're fucking lying. You saw something. There's something in this house with us." She shook her head angrily. "We never should have come here." Before he could say another word, she spun and disappeared through the doorway.

THE RAIN STARTED coming down in earnest as the night wore on, hammering loudly on the shingles above them and on the darkened streets outside. The three of them sat in the mirror-covered living room and ate a cold dinner of canned black beans and beef jerky they'd found in one of the other abandoned houses. Their search of this one had proved less fruitful, yielding only a half-empty box of some kid's cereal, a couple cans of peas, and a refrigerator full of spoiled meats and vegetables, which caused a gut-churning stench that made them quickly close the door. They ate with plastic spoons and drank water from plastic bottles and spoke in hushed voices about the Lurkers and what they knew of them or, more precisely, what they didn't know.

"Has anyone killed one of them yet?" Rai asked. "That we know of?" No one answered. "See, that's just it. I don't think they can be killed. Bullets pass right through them. No wooden stakes can touch them. Not even chopping off their heads or burning them works. They just can't be killed."

"I don't believe that," Tyler said. "I can't. There has to be a way; we just haven't found it yet. We have to have something to hold onto, a reason to keep going. There has to be hope."

Ava shook her head. "There's not. Hope died with the old world. Now there's only surviving. Running and hiding and doing whatever we have to do to still feel alive. Most days I don't feel that way." Her voice was flat and lifeless, her eyes carefully avoiding the mirrors.

Tyler didn't know what to say to her. There was still something in the room, something unspoken between the three of them, something dangerous.

They went to bed soon after that: Rai in the downstairs bedroom, Tyler and Ava upstairs. She resisted Tyler's attempts at lovemaking. She was still too scared—of the mirrors, of the house—but also, he suspected, still angry at him from earlier. He drifted off to sleep, eased from his own fears, and led down that nighttime path to slumber, by the staccato sound of the rain drumming heavily on the roof and rolling down the gutters like a fast-moving river. He dreamt of corrupted, un-killable forms whispering to him from the mirrors, creatures that looked like people he knew, telling him things he didn't want to hear, ideas that threatened his very sanity.

Something jerked him awake.

Night was at its darkest point, morning still a far-off dream. The storm raged furiously outside, and his rational mind told him it had been a crash of thunder or a bright flash of lightning that had brought him back to wakefulness. But he knew it was something else. Ava's spot on the bed next to him was empty and cold. She'd been gone a while. He picked up his shotgun, resisting the temptation to light a candle or turn on his flashlight, and crept down the stairs in the dark.

Tyler felt the electricity in the air as soon as he reached the bottom stair, fiery and passionate. He could sense it even before he saw the candlelight radiating from behind that partially closed bedroom door, before he heard their hushed moans or the dull slapping of skin on skin. He could just barely make out Ava's voice, uttering the dirty words and urgent requests she usually reserved for him. Tyler felt anger and arousal dueling within him.

He took a step forward, but something inside begged him to stop, to just go back to bed and deal with this in the morning, that if he went any farther, a terrible thing would happen, something that none of them could ever take back. But something else inside him—primal and demanding—pushed him forward. It was as if a fuse had been lit within him, burning with fury and on its way to exploding. He simply could not let this go.

Tyler nudged the door open with the barrel of his shotgun. Rai and Ava were naked on the bed, facing toward the door. Rai had his hands on Ava's hips and was taking her from behind in the doggie-style position, pounding his pelvis against her bare ass, again and again, in an aggressive rhythm. From this angle Tyler could see Ava's face, her eyes closed and features crimpled in ecstasy, her large breasts swinging freely with their movements. They were both moaning and grunting in excitement and didn't see him, but something else did:

The thing in the mirror.

It was where Rai's reflection should have been, but, like Ava's earlier this evening, his was horribly distorted, with the same charcoal grey skin and hideous, oozing sores. The creature was naked, muscular, and had a salacious grin on its face. When it turned its head to look at Tyler, its red eyes blazed into his. A long, forked tongue slid from between its lips, impossibly long, and dipped between Ava's legs, making her moan harder.

Tyler kicked the door all the way open. "You son of a bitch!"

They saw him and immediately stopped what they were doing. Ava sat up with a look of pure horror on her face, awkwardly trying to cover herself. "Tyler…baby. This isn't what it looks like. Let's talk about this." They jumped off the bed and pulled on their clothes.

Rai struggled to stuff himself back into his jeans, forgoing his plaid boxers in his haste. "Hey man, just give me a second. Let me explain!" The grinning beast was still there in the mirror, its forked tongue hanging out and dripping thick strands of mucus—or some other bodily fluid—onto the floor. "Fuck you," it mouthed at him.

Savage rage throbbed in Tyler's veins. He fought against the urge to raise the weapon.

"You gonna let him do that to you?" Tyler's reflection asked, casting its red-eyed glare upon him from the mirror to his left. "Bang your girl and then say that shit to you?"

"No," Tyler said. "I'm not."

He leveled his shotgun and fired.

Thunder boomed outside at the same instant the weapon went off. Rai dove at Ava and tackled her onto the other side of the bed, as mirrors shattered on the wall behind them, showering them with shards of broken glass. Tyler could hear the thing to his left shouting joyously, encouraging him to kill them both. He pumped the weapon and fired at the wall again, sending more glass down on them. Hatred was a drug in his veins, pushing him onward.

Rai peeked his head up over the side of the bed. "Are you crazy? We're your best friends and you're gonna kill us! For what? Some stupid fling on a night like this? She was scared! And mad at you! She just came down here to talk. We didn't plan for this to happen!"

"Then it shouldn't have." Tyler pulled the trigger again, and Rai was just barely able to get his head down in time before a section of the mattress exploded, spraying out a cloud of stuffing and more shards of glass from the broken mirrors. The thing to Tyler's left brayed with laughter. Tyler pumped the shotgun again, feeling good about what he was doing. Very good.

"You're right, fuck this shit." Rai's voice came from the other side of the bed, and he seemed to be responding to someone, though Tyler hadn't heard Ava say anything. This was followed by a sharp metallic click, barely audible over the storm and the ringing in Tyler's ears from the gunshots, but he knew what was coming next. He ducked back outside the doorway just as Rai sprang up and started firing shots off from his pistol. Mirrors in the hallway shattered; broken glass and splinters of wood rained down onto the floor.

Tyler popped out and fired again, shattering more mirrors. The shot sent one of the lit candles tumbling off the nightstand and onto the carpet, starting a small fire. Ava appeared from behind the bed, clothed now in just her tight-fitting shirt and panties, beating at the flames with one of the pillows, trying to put it out. Tyler saw this as his opportunity to take the treasonous bitch down. He pumped the shotgun and took aim at her, but before he could fire, Rai was on his feet, shirtless and screaming hysterically. Tyler ducked back into the hallway as Rai stalked toward him, firing shot after shot. The gun empty, the slide locked back just as he reached the doorway.

Tyler swung around and tried to press the barrel of the shotgun into Rai's belly, intending to blow out his guts. His former friend caught the weapon and used it to shove Tyler backward into the hallway, banging the back of his head, as his back was pushed against the wall. They both held onto the weapon, and Rai used Tyler's momentary disorientation to gain leverage, forcing Tyler down onto his knees and pressing the shotgun to his throat, trying to crush his windpipe.

Rai leaned in close as he shoved the shotgun down, an intense hatred burning in his eyes that Tyler had never seen there before. "You never deserved her, Tyler. I saw her first! She was always meant to be mine. But you just had to go and steal her from me. Always sneaking her away and fucking her while we were supposed to be working. You devious bastard!"

Somewhere in the back of his mind, Tyler was dimly aware that none of this was natural, that somehow their emotions were being manipulated and turned against them. He looked up and saw more of the ghoulish, charcoal grey creatures staring at them from the mirrors: his own twisted, nightmarish reflection, Rai's, and many others. He had an odd sense of certainty that some of them were perverted images of the people who had once lived in this house. Their red eyes blazed as they chanted strange words in a language Tyler had never heard before. Then, suddenly, Ava was there, wrapping an arm around Rai's neck and trying to pull him off.

"Stop it! Both of you! Look at what you're doing. This isn't right! This isn't us!"

But Rai didn't stop. Trying to dislodge her, he pulled a hand off the shotgun, and Tyler felt Rai's weight shift from him just enough to strike out.

"Here's what you deserve, asshole!" Tyler landed a vicious uppercut into Rai's groin, and his former best friend howled in agony, his eyes bulging from their sockets. Rai dropped the shotgun to grab at himself, and he and Ava toppled backwards onto the floor.

Tyler scurried over to grab the shotgun, but Ava cried out and kicked it away from him, sending it clattering down the hallway. He climbed to his feet and ran after the weapon. Just as he bent to pick it up, Rai crashed down on top of him, driving them both to the living room floor. The gun slid under the couch, out of reach.

Rai turned Tyler over and started raining blows down onto

his face. "You always thought you were better than me, thought you were so special just because your parents had good jobs and paid for all of your college while I had to take out loans! Who's better now, punk?"

Something was going on in the room around them. Tyler caught brief glimpses as he held up his arms, warding off the blows. Every mirror held one of the strange creatures now, all of them different, all of them chanting. An eerie blue light emanated from the mirrors while a thick, silver fog swirled about behind them. Inexplicably, in some of the mirrors, that fog actually appeared to be spilling out into the room with them, like a 3D photograph come to life.

Tyler tried to tell him to stop, to take a look at what was going on around them, but he couldn't get so much as a word out with the violent blows continuing to come down, and Rai had no intention of stopping. Blood was running down Tyler's face onto the floor. He felt woozy, like he was going to black out very soon.

Suddenly, Ava was there again. She jumped on Rai's back, screaming at him to stop and trying to pull him off. Rai's eyes lit with fury again, this time directed at her. He twisted around, clawing at her arms and trying to pull her off. When that didn't work, he threw an elbow back, connecting with her mouth. That did it. Ava let go and stumbled backwards, bringing her hand up to her bleeding mouth. Her eyes registered shock, disbelieving. But that didn't satisfy Rai—this violent, raging bull who had once been their best friend. He drove his fist hard into her abdomen, nailing her in one organ or another. Ava gasped in pain, her hand going to her abdomen as she fell backward, crashing into a large square mirror. This time, there was no broken glass. The glass didn't seem to be there at all anymore. Instead, one of the charcoal grey creatures leaned through the mirror, wrapping its long arms around Ava and trying to pull her inside.

Alarm exploded through Tyler. Whatever dark hold these creatures had over him shattered, and he knew he had to save her. Ava was holding onto the sides of the mirror frame to keep from being pulled through. Tyler attempted to climb to his feet and go to her, but dizziness overcame him and he crashed back down to the ground. Rai had also recovered and dove for the creature, trying to pull Ava from its arms. When that failed, he offered it the same 'punching bag treatment' he had given Tyler. Dark, blackish blood erupted from the creature's nose and mouth, and it became enraged. It let out an ear-piercing shriek, louder than the thunder outside, and swatted Rai off with a massive swipe of its long arm. The thing hissed as its nails began to elongate, becoming savage claws. Before Tyler knew it, they were three inches long, and then six, and suddenly, they were razor-sharp nine-inch blades. The creature dragged the blades up Ava's torso and across her chest. She screamed in agony as blood welled up across her upper body, soaking through her shirt, as clothing, flesh, and muscle were shredded with terrible ease. Blood ran down her bare legs to pool on the floor beneath her, like red rain rolling down the house's gutters.

Rai roared in anger and horror as he rose to his feet, preparing to dash at the creature again. But another monster, leaning out from a circular mirror, grabbed him from behind. The creatures were coming through all the mirrors now, including those on the ceiling. One of them was crawling toward Tyler, its body stretching out like a snake, hissing at him with a long, forked tongue. Ava was right; this was how they got in! Maybe they had gotten her mother this way. But it was also their weakness.

He dove for the couch, stretching his arm out and grasping for the shotgun. His fingers curled around the familiar grip, and he snatched it out. Ava was a bloody mess now, barely conscious, but she was somehow still holding onto the frame, preventing it from pulling her all the way in. Tyler pressed the barrel of the shotgun against the creature's forehead. They locked eyes, and he could see something there besides anger and hatred:

Fear.

"Go back to hell, you bastard!" Tyler pulled the trigger and the thing's head exploded. He and Ava were splattered with hot, blackish blood and small chunks of skull and brain matter. The bulk of the gore was sprayed inward—not into the mirror itself, but into whatever dark dimension the mirror had become a doorway to. An ear-piercing scream flooded the room, as all the creatures screamed in unison. They seemed to be connected somehow, sharing a hive-mind and collectively feeling the first creature's agony. They retreated through the mirrors from which they had come, quickly and fearfully, as the one holding Ava released its grip on her and collapsed lifelessly back inside the mirror-dimension. Tyler caught Ava as she fell forward, easing her onto the floor.

The eerie blue light and fog disappeared, thrusting the room back into darkness.

RAI SCRAMBLED OVER to where Ava lay in a thick pool of blood, shouting to Tyler to take off his shirt and use it to put pressure on the wounds. When they peeled up the sticky, tattered remains of *her* shirt, however, and saw what had been done to her, they knew there was no hope.

She gave them a forlorn smile. "At least you know how to kill them now."

Tyler returned her smile, wanly. "It wasn't worth the cost."

They knelt on the floor with her like that for the rest of the night, each of them holding one of her hands and whispering soft reassurances to her, until she was gone. The storm outside had died down, and Tyler couldn't tell if the soft, pattering sound was rain hitting the puddles out in the street, or their tears mixing with her blood on the floor.

Soon, the long purple rays were slanting in through the boards on the windows again, thickening to gold. Tyler released her hand and stood.

Rai looked up at him. "What do we do now?"

Tyler took a deep breath, thinking it over. The air carried a coppery scent to it now. "I think I saw a shed out back when we were running here. Maybe there's a shovel inside. We can use it to bury her in the backyard, pull down some of this plywood to make a grave marker."

"And then?"

"Then we go home."

Rai slowly stood, eyeing him with uncertainty. "What about…everything else?"

"The rest we can figure out as we go. But Ava was right; we found a way to kill them. Maybe that can be our hope. Maybe that can be what keeps us going. Without her."

"Maybe," Rai answered.

Together, they shoved the dusty couch and heavy bookcase out of the way and opened the door. They said nothing as they picked up Ava's lifeless body between them, descended the rain-slicked steps, and crossed the wet grass to the gate that led to the backyard. Soon, they would begin the long journey home.

CURIOSITY

Kristal Stittle

SARA SPAT OUT HER TOOTHPASTE and noticed there was a bit of blood in it. She'd been having gum problems. If she were lucky, it was the kind that would go away with some focused brushing and wouldn't require another trip to the dentist. She missed her old dentist, Dr. Frisby; the new guy always seemed to be distracted. It probably didn't help that Sara always thought of him as the new guy, even though he'd been running the town practice for nearly eight years now. Dr. Frisby was well into retirement, just like Sara herself.

"At least I have teeth," Sara reminded herself in the mirror. In a glass beside the sink, Bill's dentures grinned up at her. She checked the glass to make sure Bill had put in the cleaner. Every night she checked, even though he'd only ever forgotten once back when they were new.

Finished in the bathroom, she stepped into the bedroom and paused. Bill wasn't in bed. For decades, Bill used the bathroom first and then Sara. When she was done, she'd step out to find him lying in bed with his nose in a true crime novel, the pages all battered and bent. The book was there, opened up, face down on the mattress, but there was no Bill.

"There's a light outside."

"Oh!" Sara jumped, not expecting his voice to be so close. "You startled me." To the left of the bathroom door was the tall dresser, and just beyond that, Bill stood at the window. He'd been just out of eyesight.

"There's a light outside," he repeated, his voice less flat this time, more inquisitive. More like he was talking to her than himself.

"What do you mean a light?" Sara made her way over to stand beside him at the window.

Bill shrugged. "I mean a light."

Sara peered out, and yes, there it was, a light. She could see it even without her glasses on. It was hard to miss, frankly.

Out past their backyard was a field. When they'd first bought this home, forty years ago, it had been a working farmer's field, but for over a decade, the new owners had just let it lie fallow, sprouting weeds and ferns, grasses and wildflowers. Sara quite liked it that way. It drew in even more animals than before, especially deer. Her favorite days were the ones when she spotted the fox mother with her cubs.

There was only a split rail fence between their yard and the field, giving them a clear view all the way to the trees on the far side. There, in the middle of that patch of darkness, was a light. It was small, but bright. *An LED*, Sara thought. As she and her husband watched, it slowly shifted colors. Green, then blue, then yellow. Green, blue, yellow. Sometimes it changed a little faster, then it would go really slow again. Sara kept expecting to figure out the timing of its pattern but could not. Then it skipped a color. Sometimes, during the shift, there seemed to be a fourth color for a split second, like purple, but it was so fast she couldn't be certain.

"What do you think it is?" she finally asked Bill.

"Don't know." He shrugged.

"Probably some kid left a toy out there."

"It wasn't there when we came into the room."

"Teenagers?"

"Maybe." What he meant was "likely," but "maybe" was his go-to word for a lot of things. Teenagers always found their way into the field, where they would smoke pot and drink underage. Sometimes they'd have bonfires or set off fireworks. Sara didn't like calling the cops on them, but sometimes they forced her. A bonfire could burn down the whole neighborhood, and fireworks were not amusing at two in the morning.

"I can't see any," Sara commented, squinting her eyes although that did nothing. It was like looking into the beam of a flashlight in the dark: everything behind it was hidden.

"We should get to bed," Bill commented but made no move to leave the window.

"Think it's a projector of some kind? Maybe they're watching a movie."

"And projecting it on what? There's nothing out there."

"Like a hologram."

"Those don't exist yet. At least not like they do in the movies. Also, we'd see it, wouldn't we?"

"Could be a drone."

"Drones are huge."

"Not a military drone, a toy one." Sara rolled her eyes even though he wasn't looking at her. "One of those little buzzing things, like Jack has."

"Then why aren't they flying it?"

"Maybe it's still booting up."

They waited in silence, but the light remained on the ground.

"What made you get out of bed to look?" Sara wondered. When lying in their beds, the only things they could see through the window were the sky and the tops of the pine trees that flanked their yard.

"I heard a thump," Bill told her. "I thought it came from the backyard. Wanted to make sure it wasn't a deer breaking the patio furniture again."

They didn't have much in the way of a deck, but they'd put

down a stone patio after Liz had moved out and spent many an evening watching the sunset and having drinks back there. Sara glanced toward the loungers and the table between them, but saw that they were upright and intact.

"We should go to bed." This time it was Sara suggesting it.

"You're right," Bill sighed. "It's probably nothing. Just some teenager with a new gadget."

Sara got beneath the covers and picked up the historical fiction book she'd been enjoying, while Bill returned to his crime novel. Despite the story being quite riveting, Sara found her mind continuously wandering to the strange light. It bothered her that she didn't know what it was. It even bothered her that she hadn't been able to pin down its pattern. The chapter she read was a short one, but she struggled through it, taking much longer than she normally would. Sticking her bookmark back in place, she looked over at Bill and found that he wasn't reading, either. His novel was lying on his chest the same way it had upon the bed earlier.

"Think it's still there?" Sara asked.

"No idea."

"Should we check?"

"I don't see the point."

"Let's check."

All Bill needed was permission. He was up and walking to the window even quicker than Sara.

"What is it?" Sara asked, knowing Bill didn't have any answers. Nearly half an hour had gone by, and it was still there, glowing away, changing its color.

"Probably a kid's toy."

"What if a teenager stole it from one of the neighborhood kids, played around with it for a bit, and then just abandoned the thing out there?"

"Then they littered."

Sara sucked in her cheeks for a moment. "I want to go check it out," she finally admitted.

"It's past midnight," Bill pointed out.

"I know, but I'm not going to be able to sleep unless I find out."

"And if it's just teenagers?"

"Then I'll ask what they're up to. Maybe I'll learn something new, and maybe they'll finally realize that we can see them from our house."

"Well, I better come with you then."

Sara knew that Bill wanted to go even before she had admitted that she did. The two of them split up to get partially dressed. They both donned socks, Sara pulled on a pair of comfy pants beneath her nightgown, and Bill put on a sweater.

"I'll get your boots," Sara offered, heading for the front closet. Bill went to the kitchen window.

The field could sometimes get really muddy, so Sara grabbed their rubber boots along with her jacket and Bill's hat. As she passed the darkened living room, Mitz meowed at her from his favorite chair. The old cat was wondering what the people were up to, but not enough to leave his comfortable spot, where the heating from the floor vent could reach him.

"We'll be right back, Mitzy," Sara cooed at the feline. She treated it like her baby, even though her real baby was grown and had recently become a grandmother. The thought was mind-boggling. Sara had felt like she was in a dream at her grandson's wedding. A great-grandmother? How could Jack have gotten that old? How could she have?

"Thanks," Bill said, accepting the boots and hat. He always wore a hat outside, no matter the weather. His hair had gotten very thin, and he was self-conscious about the spots that had appeared in recent years. The doctor said they were nothing. Sara thought they were from too much sun in his younger days, but he debated her on that point. He used to have a thick head of hair that protected his scalp from such things. He did, however, concede that his habit of smoking—one he had quit long ago—had probably contributed to his bad teeth.

From the kitchen, the light was still clearly visible. The new angle offered no new information, however. It just shifted through those same three colors. Or was it four? Five?

A brisk wind blew in when Bill pulled open the sliding glass door.

"Maybe I should've gotten you your coat as well," she commented when they stepped outside.

"I'm fine," Bill huffed. "I have my warm sweater on."

The nights never used to feel so cold. Only during the height of summer did Sara not feel a chill when she stepped out into the dark. On those nights, she liked to look up at the stars. She'd been so disappointed when Liz moved to the city. But then, Liz had always been a difficult, disappointing child. Sara wanted to be close to her—her grandson, Jack, even more so—but there was no way she'd abandon this sky for the stifling lights of the city.

"You really need to fix this fence," Sara commented stepping over a section that had fallen down.

"Then how would we get into the field?" Bill responded.

"You could always build a gate."

"That sounds like work."

"It does, doesn't it?"

This was the usual banter between them. Sara couldn't remember when it had started, but whenever there was something that she needed Bill to do, he would comment on how it sounded like work, and she would agree. It would always get done, though. Eventually.

"Careful, it's squishy out here," Bill commented.

"I noticed," Sara replied, just one step to the right of him. "It only stopped raining this morning. Hasn't had time to dry out yet."

Neither of them brought up the fact that the teenagers tended to avoid the field when it got soggy like this.

Mud squelched under their boots, threatening to slide away and take their footing with it. It wasn't as bad as trying to walk on ice, but a fall was still a concern. They were getting to that age where even landing in soft mud might wreck more than just their clothes.

The light didn't change when they approached it, but it

seemed smaller than it had from their bedroom window. It was strange. Up close, Sara thought it was too bright to make out the object giving off the glow, but at the same time, it barely lit its surroundings. She held up her hand to block it, hoping her eyes would adjust to the dark, but squinting at shadows failed to reveal any people, even ones who might be lying on a blanket on the ground.

"Hello?" Bill called, having done the same thing. "Is there anyone out here?"

Only the wind answered, telling him to shush as it moved through the forest ahead.

"Someone must have left it behind," Bill decided.

"Strange thing to leave behind," Sara commented. "You'd think it would be hard to miss if you dropped it." So far, neither of them had made a move to pick it up.

"I can't see what it is," Bill said.

"Me neither. Think we should just leave it? Go back inside?" Sara may be old now, but she'd been a child once, and that part of her wanted to go. It didn't think they should be out here.

"What if it's worth something?" Bill wondered.

"What if it's dangerous?" Sara countered. "We might be being irradiated as we speak."

"It's not irradiated."

"How do you know?"

"Why would it be out here? A thing like that wouldn't be carried through this field, and it definitely wouldn't be left behind."

"Maybe it fell from the sky?" Sara suggested.

Bill gave her a look but didn't respond.

They both stood staring at the light, watching its ever shifting, impossible to predict pattern.

"So, are you going to pick it up or am I?" Sara finally said, knowing one of them was going to do it eventually.

"I'll do it."

"Should you use your hat? Or your sleeve? In case it's hot."

Bill's knees popped when he crouched down beside the mysterious thing. Only partially heeding Sara's advice, he poked at it with a finger. Whatever the light was hiding, it was solid and round, rolling slightly on the ground.

"Not hot," Bill reported. "Cold actually."

"How cold?"

"No colder than I would expect, it being out here." Bill finally picked it up off the ground. No mud clung to it, but neither of the senior citizens noticed that.

"What is it?" Sara asked for what felt like the hundredth time.

"A ball," Bill told her, sounding more confused than ever. He rolled it around in his hand, squinting as he peered into the light.

"What are you doing?"

"Looking for how the hell you turn it off."

"Let me try."

"Hold on, I got it." Bill poked and prodded, the very tip of his finger nearly disappearing with its close proximity to the light source.

Sara simply held out her hand and waited. Bill finally huffed and passed it over.

It certainly felt like a ball, but heavier than Sara had anticipated. She'd assumed it was made of cheap, transparent plastic, but this was more like a large ball bearing. She commented on the weight to Bill as she conducted her own investigation.

"Yeah. It's also not as smooth as I'd thought it would be," he added.

It was smooth, but not like glass or plastic. More like the way a river rock is smooth. Or an egg.

Sara tried gently twisting it in various directions, wondering if that's how it turned off, despite not having felt any seams.

"Be careful, don't break it." Bill's hands twitched as if to take it back.

"I'm not going to break it." Sara rolled her eyes. It didn't twist, it didn't turn off, it didn't do anything but shift its colors. Sara huffed, frustrated.

"Let's take it inside," Bill suggested. "No sense standing around out here."

Sara agreed, and they turned to head back to their house. The bedroom and kitchen lights glowed, islands in the sea of darkness. One day a developer would come and scoop up all the land that surrounded them, but for now, their oasis remained untouched. Neighbors were close enough to call on, but far enough to ignore. Their perfect little home.

"Do you want me to carry it?" Bill offered, holding out his hand toward the orb.

"No, I got it, it's not that heavy." Besides, she kind of liked the feel of it, especially now that it wasn't so cold thanks to the warmth of her hand. She tried holding it out ahead of them to light the way, but its strange glow couldn't reach that far, even though it seemed bright enough to pierce through to the back of her eyes.

They stepped carefully over the fence, crossed their large backyard, and re-entered the house.

"Mitzy! We're back!" Sara called in greeting as she stepped out of her muddy boots.

His meow of acknowledgement came from the living room. He hadn't left his chair. Since she was up, Sara thought she should go and give him another goodnight smooch on his furry little head.

The moment Sara stepped into the living room, Mitz lost his mind. His whole body shot up into an arch, and he hissed like she had never heard him hiss before. With a screaming yowl, he bolted from his chair with a speed he hadn't shown in years and took off down the hallway with all his fur standing on end. Sara was so startled that she dropped the orb. Despite its weight, it made barely a sound when it landed on the carpet.

"What's wrong with the cat?" Bill asked, having heard but not seen.

"I don't know." Sara scooped the orb back up. "He just took off."

"Maybe a mouse bit his tail." Bill walked over to the chair to investigate.

"Wouldn't that be something." But Sara wasn't really paying attention. She was worried about Mitz. That had been very strange of him. Was he sick? He was certainly getting up there in age.

Heading down the hall, Sara searched for her fur-baby. She couldn't find him in the guestroom, the main bathroom, or her own room. Wherever he had chosen to hide, he had also chosen not to come out.

"We'll find him in the morning," Bill said, attempting to soothe her. "It's not like he could have gotten out."

"I just don't know what's wrong with him. He's never done that before."

"Maybe that toy makes a high-pitched whine we can't hear. You know, like a dog whistle. Only a cat whistle in this case. Guess Mitz didn't like it."

"I suppose. Maybe I should get his treats and lure him out."

"Mitz's fine. He's a cat. Cats do weird things sometimes. Leave him alone and he'll be all right. I don't know about you, but I'm exhausted."

Sara was feeling rather tired herself. When she glanced at a clock, she saw it was much later than she'd thought. It wasn't like they had anything to do tomorrow, but Sara found it increasingly impossible to sleep in these days, and knew she'd be waking up at the same time as always. If she didn't get to sleep now, it was possible she'd be awake the whole night and then wouldn't be able to function all day.

Since she couldn't turn the glowing light off, she stashed it in her fluffy housecoat pocket, where it hung over the back of the chair in the corner. Only a faint glow of shifting colors emerged from the pocket's opening to paint the fabric above. Sara watched it for a little while until she couldn't keep her eyes open any longer. It distracted her from worrying about Mitz.

She dreamt she was young again and running. It wasn't like running in a nightmare, where you seemed to go nowhere; this was true and proper sprinting. In her dream, she was young and healthy and moved with a grace that had long since abandoned her. Like a deer, she practically flew through an infinite forest, bounding with ease over fallen logs and streams. She was free.

When morning came, Sara found that her gums didn't ache

anymore. When she brushed her teeth, there was no pink mixed in with her spit. Whatever had been wrong she must have fixed with last night's brushing. It healed faster than the previous times she'd had a problem, but that certainly wasn't anything to complain about. When she donned her housecoat to go make the coffee, she wrapped her hand around the orb in her pocket. The batteries hadn't died, it still glowed, and that smooth weight between her fingers provided a strange sort of comfort. Like a child's plush toy.

When she entered the living room, however, her heart broke in two.

Mitz was dead.

His little body was sprawled on the carpet and completely stiff with rigor mortis. He looked smaller somehow, almost withered. When Sara cradled him to her, his skin seemed to slide too easily over the bones and muscles beneath. That's how Bill found her, sitting in the living room, soothing her dead cat.

They held a little funeral in the backyard. Bill made an appropriately sized coffin, not making a single comment about how much work it was or bringing up the fact that a shoebox would do just as well. He even fashioned a cross. While he didn't show it as much outwardly, he mourned the death of Mitz just as painfully as Sara did. The cat may have liked sitting with her more when they read or watched TV, but he was always accompanying Bill when he fixed up something around the house and purred extra loud when he wanted whatever Bill was eating. Mitz had been a fixture in their lives, and now he was gone.

"I knew something was wrong last night," Sara wept.

"I know."

"We should have found him."

"I know."

"Should we have brought him to the vet?"

"In the middle of the night? I'm not sure they'd have been open."

"No, I mean before we buried him. To find out why he died."

Bill shook his head. "That would be a very expensive trip for very little gain. He was old. In cat years, he was older than us. Ancient, even. It was just his time."

Sara spent the day grieving. It was especially hard having to call Liz and tell her, but this seemed like it required more than just a text message. Liz didn't really know the cat all that well—he tended to hide from visitors—but understood how broken up her mother was. In the most tactful way possible, Liz suggested getting a new cat the moment Sara thought she was ready. Or maybe even a dog; they certainly had the space for one.

The whole time, Sara had the orb on her. She'd dressed in one of Liz's oversized hoodies and kept the light in the belly pocket. Of course, the hoodie hadn't belonged to Liz since she'd moved out. It had spent more years in Sara's closet than hers, but Sara still thought of it as Liz's. She only wore it when she needed comforting.

The fox family didn't make an appearance that day.

When night came, and Sara had cried herself to sleep, she again dreamt of being young. This time she was on a bicycle, racing through the streets. It wasn't like any dream she had ever had before. She could feel the powerful muscles of her legs pressing down on the pedals, and her hair, long and waving instead of the short bob she wore these days, flapped out behind her like a copper flag. The air filled her lungs with ease, and her heart beat strong and steady in her chest. She rushed down a massive hill, headlong, without any fear about what could happen when she reached the bottom.

As usual, Sara was awake before Bill. All her crying yesterday had drained her, but otherwise she was feeling pretty good. As she combed her hair in the morning, she swore it was thicker than when she had gone to bed. The pain that usually inhabited her knuckles had also abated for the time being.

Shuffling about in her housecoat and slippers, the orb in her pocket, Sara put on the coffee. The aroma alone did wonders for perking her up. She was thinking about how Mitz really had been a very old cat, and how she should have expected this. It was better than a long, drawn-out illness or having to decide to put him down. Maybe she'd look for cats up for adoption today. Kittens. She told herself she wouldn't get one, it was much too soon, but she'd just look.

With her mug in hand, she glanced over at the sliding glass door, hoping to spot the fox family. She saw one fox, but not where she expected, nor in the condition she had hoped for.

On the tiny wooden porch, near the glass, lay one of the kits. For a second, Sara hoped it was just sleeping, but that hope was quickly snuffed out. Its eyes were only half closed, and the visible parts were a milky white. Its tongue hung out awkwardly between its jaws. There was a thinness to the little creature, a sunken quality to its coat. It reminded Sara of Mitz, quite frankly.

"Oh. Oh no. You poor thing." Sara eased herself down to the kitchen floor beside the door for a closer look. It wasn't breathing, but at least there weren't maggots. She wondered what happened to the cub. Illness, it looked like, since she couldn't see any injuries. Maybe that's what had happened to Mitz? Maybe he had somehow contracted the same thing?

There was movement on the stone patio, and Sara was afraid to find the mother fox mourning. What she saw was much worse.

"Bill!" she screamed. "Bill!" She couldn't think of another word to say as she shot up onto her feet, firing off pain through her legs.

He came rushing down the hallway, still half asleep, banging into the walls as he stumbled.

"What is it? What's wrong?" His voice wavered, his eyes darting up and down her body fearing she may have injured herself. When he saw the baby fox, he frowned.

Sara couldn't find any words so she merely pointed. Bill's eyes followed.

"Is that…?" He struggled for words as well.

"Mitz," Sara finally managed to gasp. "It's Mitzy."

"Impossible," Bill shook his head. "We buried him yesterday. He's dead, Sara. That must be a cat who just looks the same."

"The exact same? Look at him, Bill. That's Mitz. The patterns are identical."

Bill just kept shaking his head. It was impossible, but he had to agree he could see no difference between this cat and the one he'd put in the ground. Mitz was a black and white cat—a cow cat, Sara liked to say—and bore some rather distinctive markings because of it. The fur around one eye was all white, and around the other it was black with a tiny white eyebrow. His nose was pink, the surrounding muzzle covered in white fur except for a black smudge around the base of his right whiskers. One paw white, three black, and one of those had a single white toe. Black tail, white belly. A black smudge on his chest that formed a heart when he was sitting and you squinted at it just right. All these things were on the cat outside.

"Mitzy!" Sara called, pulling open the sliding glass door.

The cat responded with a meow. Mitz's meow. It sounded just like him, although maybe a little hoarser.

Stepping over the dead kit, Sara attempted to rush to her cat, but Bill grabbed her arm.

"That's not Mitz," he insisted despite what he was seeing.

"Of course it is! Look at him!"

"Mitz is dead! Even if we somehow made a mistake, how did he get out of his grave? Out of the coffin I made?"

That gave Sara pause. Bill was good with his hands; he'd helped build many of the homes in this area and others. Even though he hadn't had to build anything as serious as a house in many years, the box had been sturdy.

Mitz was lying on a lounger, basking in the sun. He didn't seem to care about the humans' argument.

"I have to know," Sara begged. "I have to."

Bill let go of her arm.

Sara walked up to the cat with more caution than she would have if Bill hadn't brought up the coffin. Mitz looked up and meowed at her, giving his head a little shake at the same time. It had always been his way of greeting both Sara and Bill. It was him. Sara let him sniff her fingers, but then he thrust his head into her palm, wanting to be petted. It was him, but he was also somehow wrong. His fur was dirty and matted, but it was also loose. Loose like when she'd found him on the carpet, stiff with rigor mortis. And he smelled. He stank of dirt and spoiled meat.

"Sara?" Bill called to her.

She looked over and found him by the grave. The soil had been freshly turned, and he held up the box he'd buried. It was broken and empty. The cat nuzzling into Sara was definitely Mitz.

Without a word to her husband, she scooped up the cat and brought him inside.

"Sara!" Bill protested, but then she was through the door.

Mitz was still dead. Sara knew it. Her hands were wrapped around his body, but she couldn't feel him breathing. She couldn't feel his heartbeat. This didn't matter. Her fur-baby was back. Bill wouldn't understand.

She locked herself in the bathroom with her cat. Filling the tub a small amount, she placed Mitz inside and began to clean him. Normally the cat would detest such treatment, but this time he didn't seem to mind. He behaved like a perfect gentleman, letting Sara scoop up water and run it over his head. He purred as she brushed the dirt out of his fur.

"Sara?" Bill knocked on the door. "Can we talk, please?"

"Later."

She heard Bill huff and return to the kitchen. She didn't join him until Mitz was clean and dry. An odor still clung to the cat, and his body didn't feel right, but Sara didn't care. Somehow, he was back.

"Let me see him," Bill said gently, holding out his hands.

Sara hesitated but then held Mitz in his direction. Mitz did not want to be held by Bill. He hissed loudly and swiped at him.

"Yow!" Bill cried out, thin red ribbons appearing on his hand. Mitz had never tried to draw blood before, but there it was, forcing Bill to stick his hand under the tap.

"Mitzy!" Sara scolded him, pulling him back to her chest.

"Bad cat!"

He purred and nuzzled her with his head. As he did, his lip pulled up, revealing blackened gums.

"Sara."

She looked at Bill, who still stood at the sink.

"Sara, that's not Mitz."

"It is," she insisted.

"No. That's Mitz's body, but that can't be Mitz. Things just don't come back from the dead like that. They don't break out of coffins and dig themselves free of the earth. I don't know what that thing is, but it's not our cat."

"Then what is it, huh?"

"I don't know, but Mitz never would have done this." Bill held up his hand for her to see. He was going to need a couple of Band-Aids.

"Maybe you scared him." But Sara knew her argument was weak.

"Sara. Please. Just…put him back outside for now. Until we figure out what's going on."

Reluctantly, Sara agreed. She opened the back door and placed Mitz on the porch. He was an indoor cat but loved to get outside when he could. Instead of running off to explore, however, he just sat there beside the door, looking like he wanted to come back in. That was definitely not Mitz behavior.

"Where's the fox cub?" Sara had noticed its absence.

"I put it by the field, just on the other side of the tree," Bill told her. "I figure it's part of nature, and so we should let nature decide what to do with it."

Sara nodded. The foxes weren't the only meat eaters around. Perhaps one of the turkey vultures would make a fine meal of the creature, or even a raccoon. Gruesome to think about. Sara wished the body had been placed farther away.

All day, Bill and Sara went back and forth about Mitz. The cat spent the day on the porch, sleeping in the sun, or watching them through the glass door. He meowed if either of them made eye contact. The quality of the meow differed depending on which one of them it was: pleading to Sara, angry at Bill.

Going online they found only unproven stories and wild conspiracy theories. Nothing like this had ever really happened before, or else they would have already heard about it. There were plenty of tales of lost pets finding their way home or illnesses that were miraculously overcome. There were even some stories of families who'd thought their beloved pet had died and buried it, only to have the pet come home perfectly safe and sound the next day. In those cases, the family had buried a stranger's pet. They had mistaken a mangled roadkill kitty for their own. They didn't have an empty coffin.

"Are you still carrying that thing around?" Bill asked when he saw Sara sitting on the couch, rolling the orb around in her palm.

"I like it," she told him. "It comforts me."

"It's irritating. That light hurts my eyes after a while."

"You're welcome to take your phone to another room." All their research was being done on their mobile devices. Liz's husband worked in telecommunications and always made sure they had the best.

Bill grumbled but remained seated. The next best place to sit was in the kitchen, and he wasn't about to go in there where the corpse of Mitz could watch him.

"Maybe we should take Mitz to the vet," Sara suggested.

"That's an option, but not just yet. I don't want to ride in the car with that thing if I don't have to."

Sara held her tongue. That thing was their Mitzy as far as she was concerned. But she knew Bill and knew what he was really thinking. Bringing the cat to the vet would cost money, but it was also possible that the vet would take Mitz away. Not that Bill didn't want him gone in his current state, but if there was money to be made, he wanted in. It was the thing that bothered Sara most about Bill. When it came to money, he didn't always consider that the cost of something could be more than just dollars.

When they went to bed that night, there was tension between

them. Sara hadn't liked the idea of leaving Mitz outside all night, but Bill didn't want him in the house. The compromise was to move his litter box and food into the guest bathroom and keep him locked up in there. Sara didn't mind carrying Mitz, but Bill made his disgust about it known. As for what they would do with the cat in the morning, that remained undecided.

Sara dreamt of dancing. Not the kind she was used to, with the slow swaying, or the distance between bodies. No, in her dream she was in a nightclub and was moving the way the young people of today did. Her body was pressed up against strangers, their expressions revealed only when the light flashed, but their intentions and desires were clear from their movements. She felt hands run across her, feeling her flesh through the tight dress she wore. Her hips pressed up against the tightened pants of men who wished to be alone with her. Even other women trailed their fingers down Sara's arms, in a way that wasn't undesired. So wrapped up in how good she felt, she didn't notice that the light didn't pulse in time with the thumping music. It shifted in an unlearnable pattern between blue, and green, and yellow.

In the morning, Sara saw clear changes in her face. Her lines had smoothed out some, and there was even a tiny bit of color to her roots. Spots that had appeared on her body over time had faded. Even her old caesarean scar was practically gone, and it seemed her glasses prescription was off. When she weighed herself, she'd lost ten pounds. Also, her skin was firmer than when she'd rubbed in her moisturizer last night.

It was a bright and sunny morning, and Sara felt so great, she didn't feel the need for coffee. Instead, she hurriedly got dressed without waking Bill, pocketed the orb, and went to grab Mitz.

The cat was in the same condition as when she'd put him in the guest bathroom. The food in his bowl remained untouched, and his litter box was unused. He was happy to see Sara and happy to be picked up.

Outside, there were three new bodies on the porch. The rest of the fox cubs had succumbed to the same thing as the first. And yet the first seemed to be doing just fine now. As Sara stepped down onto the stone patio, it crept out from beneath one of the loungers. Once Mitz was on the ground, the cat and the kit began to play as if they were the best of friends. It delighted Sara to watch them.

"What the hell?" Bill grumbled from the doorway.

"Good morning," Sara greeted him, feeling like the sunlight was inside her.

"The cubs are dead."

"I know. It's such a shame. But look, the first one came back."

There was a paleness to Bill's face. "Sara, come inside please."

"Why? Look how friendly it is." She bent down and pet the baby fox, its skin moving loosely over its bones.

"I don't care. Come inside."

"I'm just going to move these dead ones first. I'll put them over by the field like you did."

"Sara!"

"Just a second!" She picked up the babies and crossed the lawn with them. One by one, she laid them in a row next to a big pine tree. Walking back, she wrapped her hand around the orb in her pocket.

"What's wrong with you?" Bill asked her once she was back inside and the door had been shut between them and the resurrected animals.

"Nothing. I feel great, actually."

"You just carried three dead fox cubs over to the field without any gloves and without even batting an eye."

"I suppose I should wash my hands."

"Sara!"

"Bill!" she mimicked his tone as she stepped over to the sink. "Maybe I'm just a little less concerned than you. I mean, clearly there's some sort of illness going around that makes these animals seem dead to us at first, but then they bounce back. I don't think we need to worry."

"Yeah? You really think that?" Bill directed his gaze to the door where both Mitz and the first fox kit were watching them through the glass. "You think that's totally normal behavior, do you?"

"Well, what do you want to do?"

"Call someone."

"Like who?"

"You suggested the vet yesterday."

"I did, although now I don't see the point. What are they going to tell us that we don't already know? It would be costly, and we'd get nothing out of it. Hell, they might even want to come out here and run some tests. Probably ruin your garden while they're at it."

"Maybe the media."

"And what would they do? If they even believed you enough to come out here, they'd just take some pictures or video, then write up a story that makes us sound like kooks. Or worse, they'd put this place on the map, and then those developers would show up for sure. Goodbye, neighborhood."

"So, what are you proposing?"

"We do nothing. Just let them be."

"I don't like them."

"And I don't like the way you pick your nose and wipe the boogers under the table when you think I'm not looking."

Bill flushed a bright red.

"We should get rid of them," he decided.

"What do you mean? Put Mitz up for adoption? No way. And who's going to take a wild fox kit? Pretty sure that's illegal."

"That's not what I mean."

Sara's mood finally darkened. "No."

"Sara…"

"No! Mitz is just sick. He'll get better."

"Sara."

"You touch one hair on his head, and I'm going to go stay with Liz." Now she was angry. "Just because you don't understand what's going on doesn't mean you have to get rid of it. That's Mitz!

He's staying right where he is!"

"I don't want him in the house."

"Fine, he'll stay outside. He likes it out there anyway."

"What's gotten into you today?"

"Into me? You're the one threatening to kill our cat."

"I can't deal with this. I'm going out."

"Yeah, run away. Good plan."

Bill scowled at her, but that didn't deter him. "I'm taking a drive."

"Maybe you can pick up a gate to install in the fence while you're out."

"Maybe." He threw up his hands and stormed off. He hadn't even had breakfast.

Sara spent the day out in the backyard, the big umbrella between the loungers protecting her from getting too much sun. Sometimes Mitz sat with her, and sometimes the kit did as well. She'd left the back door open and didn't find it at all strange when she asked Mitz to go inside to get her book and he actually did it. It just felt natural somehow.

She knew when Bill came home because she heard the car door slam. He didn't say hello, not even when he shut the sliding glass door. It didn't seem likely that he'd bought a gate, considering he hadn't taken any measurements beforehand. It was unlikely he'd have bought one even if he had. Why get a really nice pre-constructed gate when he could make one himself that was much more utilitarian? She knew he could make some pretty fancy-looking work—she'd seen it at other people's houses—but to get him to do the same here was like pulling teeth. It was probably because after working all day elsewhere, he didn't want to do the same at home, but Sara decided it was because he was cheap. If he wasn't being paid for it, why bother?

When Sara returned indoors, she could hear the power tools buzzing away in the garage. Maybe he was making the gate after all, measurements be damned.

"So, did you have a nice drive?" Sara asked once they had sat down for dinner.

Bill muttered unintelligibly.

"Come to any decisions?"

"Yes."

"And?"

"I'll leave them alone. For now. If they hurt anyone or break anything, however, they're gone. Understand?"

Sara nodded, pleased. She knew Mitz and the fox kit would behave. They were perfect little angels.

"Can you leave that outside, too?" Bill asked about the orb in Sara's hand.

"Why?"

"I don't like it."

"It's just a kid's toy."

"You're obsessed with it. You spent most of the day just staring at the thing."

Sara was about to object when she realized he was right. After Mitz had brought her the book, she'd only read maybe a chapter and a half for all the hours she'd been out there.

"I'm not obsessed," she insisted. "If it makes you feel better, I'll keep it out of your sight. The batteries are probably going to die soon anyway." But she knew better. She knew that it wasn't being run on something as mundane as batteries. There was no way the orb wasn't connected to what happened to Mitz and the fox kit; that would be too much of a coincidence. She hadn't told Bill about what it seemed to be doing to her as well. About the dreams, and how she woke up without any pain. How her hair and skin were both healthier. How even her organs felt healthier. Maybe if he'd noticed, if he'd commented on it, she would've told him, but he hadn't said a word. Apparently, he didn't look at her anymore, not really. He didn't see the changes. It broke her heart a little.

That night, Sara lay awake. She was tired and she was excited, anticipating what her dreams tonight would bring, but she refused to close her eyes. While Bill snored softly in the other bed, she lay on her side and watched the pocket of her housecoat. Her eyes were so heavy, and it was kind of boring just lying there, but she refused to give in. Finally, just before three in the morning, something happened.

The light grew a little brighter. It then floated up and out of the pocket. No longer did it possess the shape of an orb, but something more like a bird or butterfly. It didn't flap its wings to fly, simply floated up as though pushed by a gentle current. There was no definition to the thing, just a smooth outline filled with that glowing, shifting light. Sara stared in wonderment. It was so beautiful. Her eyes remained locked on the creature as it floated over to her window and then passed seamlessly through the glass as if it weren't even there.

Nearly another hour ticked past, but by this time Sara was wide awake. She stared at the window, waiting for the light to return. And she knew it would. It had all the previous nights.

When it came back, it was different. The shape was the same, but the light was not. It was red. Solid red, no shifting, no pulsing. It had never been red before. Sara didn't think she could avert her eyes even if she wanted to. The bird shape came over to her bed. To her face. Its wings folded around her, covering her eyes.

She dreamt of a man. Not Bill, someone she had never seen before. He was young, fit, even more handsome than Bill had been back in the day. And God, did he know what he was doing. When Sara orgasmed, she thought she might die of pleasure and would have been perfectly okay with that. To wake up alone was a disappointment.

Sara had expected to find herself tangled up in the sheets with a dampness between her legs, but neither of these things were the case. She was in the same position she had been in when the light had attached itself to her. Now, it was back in her housecoat pocket, and Sara felt better than ever as she got out of bed. She dressed quickly, plucked the orb—it was an orb again, shifting through green, and blue, and yellow, and never red—and hurried to the kitchen.

The vixen was dead on the porch. Before Bill could wake up

and find her, Sara scooped up the fox and hurried away with it. She stashed the body beyond the edge of their property, near the Stones' place next door. The Stones had a large lot, and at the end that abutted theirs, they'd set up solar panels on gimbals to follow the sun. Bill hated them. Not because they were solar panels or because of what they looked like, but because the Stones didn't bother to take care of the yard that grew around them. The grass was long and, much to Bill's consternation, full of weeds. Sara knew the vixen wouldn't be found there.

She ran back to the house—actually ran, without any pain in her knees!—and was inside making breakfast before Bill emerged from the bedroom. Through the window above the sink, she watched Mitz playing with the kits. There was a full complement of them once more, all four back together. Their mother would rejoin them soon enough.

"You're not going back outside now, are you?" Bill said after the breakfast dishes had been cleared away.

"Why?"

"I thought today was your shopping day."

"Oh, that's right." She always went shopping on Thursdays. "Totally slipped my mind. Are you coming today?"

He shook his head. "My stomach isn't feeling too great."

"Poor dear." She kissed his head. "You've been rather stressed lately. Maybe you should just go back to bed."

"Maybe."

"Do you want me to pick up anything for you? Soup from Merdi's?"

"Yes, soup might be nice. Thank you."

"Just go back to sleep and you'll feel better in no time."

"Are you bringing the orb with you?"

Sara had been careful to keep it out of his sight. "Why?" she wondered, suddenly suspicious.

"Because I want you to leave it here."

"Why?" she asked, this time more aggravated.

"So I know that you can."

Sara scoffed and rolled her eyes. She made a show of putting it away in a cupboard. When Bill was back in bed, she slipped it into her purse and headed out.

Mitz and the fox cubs had come around the side of the house and gathered around the car.

"Sorry, dearies," she told them. "No pets allowed at the grocery store. You stay here, okay? Go on now. Back to the backyard."

All five heeded her command. So pleasantly obedient.

It took fifteen minutes to drive to the grocery store from where they lived. Sara spotted Mr. Jackson out on a jog, and as she drove past, she waved in a neighborly way. He nodded his head in return, not breaking his stride. He looked rather dashing with his salt and pepper hair. No pot belly on that one.

Sara browsed the aisles, deciding on a whim to pick up a few things that weren't on her list. Things like popcorn and chocolate, food she normally bought only as a special treat because she had to watch her waistline. That didn't feel so important anymore. Her tummy was thinning itself.

She was two-thirds of the way through her trip when it hit her.

Something was wrong. In an instant, she knew Bill didn't really have a stomachache. He was up to something, something he wanted her out of the house for. He was doing something to Mitz and the kits.

Abandoning her entire grocery cart in the middle of an aisle, Sara ran for the exit. She sprinted, drawing startled looks and concerned shouts from familiar neighbors and strangers alike.

"No, no, no, no, no," she mumbled on repeat as she scrambled into her car. She could feel it, like someone was squeezing all her limbs and scooping out her insides. Bill was doing something horrible.

Horns were leaned on as she raced down the streets back toward home. She blew through stop signs and even a red light. In only seven minutes, her car bounced over the curb next to her driveway when she took the turn too sharply, and the tires squealed as she hammered on the brakes. She jammed the car into park and leapt out, not bothering to turn the engine off or even shut the door behind her. Racing around the side of the house, she knew something terrible awaited her.

"Bill!" she shrieked.

He stood on the stone patio, with a bloody hatchet in his hand. Next to him were a pair of shattered wooden boxes. He hadn't been building a gate, but cages for Mitz and the fox cubs. They hadn't co-operated with him. Blood ran in rivulets from Bill's arms and legs, but he'd fared a lot better than they had. The stones were awash in crimson, bits of orange fur mixing in with the larger clumps of black and white. Mitz and the kits were in several, un-moving pieces.

"What did you do?" Sara screamed, running over to the scene. She badly bruised her knees as she dropped down among the little corpses.

"What I had to!" Bill screamed back at her. "They weren't right! They weren't right, and you would know that if that orb weren't twisting up your mind!"

Her purse sat at her side, only one strap hanging off her arm. It was propped open, the orb visible. Bill snatched it out.

"No!" Sara tried to grab it back, but he pushed her. Pushed her! She couldn't get to her feet in time. He was already in his garden, next to the quaint little well that Sara loved. He had already dropped the orb inside.

Sara cried uncontrollably. Bill finally tried to comfort her. She kept pushing on him, but he just held her tighter and tighter until she gave in to his embrace. He whispered soothing words. He wiped the tears from her cheeks.

"It was changing you, honey," he told her.

"For the better," she mumbled.

"No. I love you just the way you are. I don't want anything to change about you. There is no better."

It was sweet, but sweet wasn't what Sara wanted. She wanted what her dreams gave her. She wanted strength and beauty. She wanted youth.

She allowed Bill to take charge. *Let him have this*, she thought. She moped and cried, watching him bury all the little bodies together and hose down the stone patio. She even helped him clean and bandage his wounds. There was a little pleasure to be had in watching him wince with pain from the antiseptic.

"I hadn't intended on killing them," Bill explained. "I just wanted to take them somewhere. To a research center. Somewhere a scientist could look at them."

Sell my babies, you mean, Sara thought but didn't say. *And to think I was going to buy you some soup.*

That night, she lay awake again. She waited and waited and waited, her anxiety mounting. But it came. The light bird floated through the window. It could not be contained by something like the well. It wouldn't let itself be contained by anything.

It wasn't red when it showed up. It hovered in place, seeming to look at Sara although it didn't have any eyes that she was aware of. Then it turned toward Bill.

"Yes," Sara whispered.

It landed on his face. He made not a sound, completely unaware. The light shifted through its colors, red showing up more and more and more until there was only that scarlet wash. Bill didn't make a sound. He was no longer snoring. His chest no longer rose and fell, and in the dark, Sara could see that he had withered. His skin no longer fit him.

Sara waited for the light to come to her. To give her dreams and youth. Tomorrow she'd have the vixen for company. After that, Bill would be back. He'd be back and he'd be obedient.

Maybe she should invite Liz to come visit for the weekend.

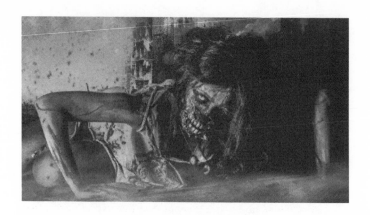

BOOGEYMAN NIGHTS

Scott Harper

"That is my ambition, to have killed more people—more helpless people—than any man or woman who has ever lived."
— Jane Toppan, American multi-murderer.

THE BOOGEYMAN STAMPEDED THROUGH THE WOODS, his breath fogging in the chilly evening air, as he breathed heavily through a burlap mask. Cold menace blazed from the twin openings he had punched in the material for his eyes, pinpricks of spite floating amid the night's shadows. The moonlight glinted off the razor-sharp KA-BAR knife he clenched in his bloody right hand. The Boogeyman felt strong and invincible, his strides long and confident, as he smashed brush and small trees aside.

He heard the panicked woman running ahead of him, the pistoning of air through her lungs, and saw the brief puffs of condensation form as her hot breaths struck the cool night air. The full moon showed through patches of black cumulous clouds, illuminating the forest and making it easy for him to see the path she had taken. Even if it had been a moonless night, his heightened senses would have allowed him to follow her with more skill than a pack of bloodhounds.

His hands were covered in blood. He'd found the couple camping near a copse of trees, the sounds of their lovemaking, from inside a tent, echoing in the night. The noises accompanying human fornication always enraged him. In his former life, before he had been chosen and elevated, he had never experienced such intimacy with another person. His self-esteem was dismally low. Since childhood, he'd always been looked down upon and made fun of by others. His own mother constantly belittled him, lecturing him that he was ugly and should never leave the house, that every time he went out in public, he embarrassed the family. His father behaved similarly, mocking his lack of interest in sports by calling him a girl and suggesting that he play with dolls.

But that was another life in another time. He had been remade into something far superior to the cretins he now slew with such ease and frequency.

His shadow had loomed large over the tent as he stepped in front of the fire the couple had made earlier in the evening, an open bag of marshmallows and oily roasting sticks lying forgotten beside the smoking pit. He heard the woman scream in terror as his sharp blade diced through the green nylon tent. The man swore loudly as the Boogeyman stepped in through the opening he had made.

He took note of the naked young woman on the ground before him, of the erotic darkness of her summer-tanned skin, offset by white lines, where a bikini top had covered her. Her ample breasts were pale and supple, jutting over her firm belly. The Boogeyman was able to see a small thatch of blond pelvic hair descending to her womanhood before his view was interrupted by the cover of the violet polyester sleeping bag in which she lay. The heady smell of sweat, splooge, and vaginal liquids hung heavy in the air.

Her naked lover stormed to his feet, his erect member still covered in the residue of his most recent ejaculation. He was young and strong, with rippling, dark-haired pectoral muscles and chiseled six-pack abdominals. The Boogeyman took brief note of the lover's questionably fashionable man bun hairstyle. The muscles on the man's neck corded as he balled his fist.

"You freak, what the fuck do you think you're doing, coming in here!?" Man Bun bellowed.

The man punched the Boogeyman in the jaw with a vicious roundhouse. The bones of his fist broke with an audible cracking sound. Man Bun winced in pain and cradled his broken hand, retreating into a standing fetal position. The blow had caused the Boogeyman as much harm as would a passing breeze.

Anger filled the Boogeyman at the mention of the word "freak," a fire building deep in his gut and flowing out into his sinews, threatening to explode. "Freak" was a word he was quite familiar with—he could not count the number of times he had been so labeled in his previous life. But now he had the power to do something about it. He had the power to ensure that this man never used that word again.

He gripped the man by the throat, his long fingers wrapping around the neck and cutting off air to the windpipe. Man Bun struggled to free himself, pounding at the Boogeyman's head with his fists and kneeing him in the groin, but the blows were to no avail.

The Boogeyman became aroused as he felt death coming for the man. His erect member strained against his pants as Man Bun's face turned an exquisite red. When he could wait no longer, the Boogeyman squeezed his fingers together, crushing the man's throat. A cataract of blood exploded from the ruptured flesh, a wash of gore covering the interior of the tent. The air filled with the stench of death and shit as Man Bun's bowels released. The Boogeyman dropped the body, letting it slip to the tent floor as he lunged for the woman.

She barely evaded his outstretched hands and reached into her purse. She retrieved a .357 magnum black revolver and shot him five times in the chest, the sound of the gunfire echoing in the night. The lead rounds seared through his torso. The Boogeyman staggered momentarily, absorbing the impacts, then stood straight. He tilted his head to the side, silently rebuking the woman for her actions—conventional weapons could no longer end his life.

The woman dropped the empty weapon and ran off naked into the night, the pale cheeks of her ass compacting and bouncing as she moved. He ran after her with his tireless stamina, savoring her screams of fear as he followed.

After a few minutes of running, the Boogeyman realized the woman was at least as fast, if not faster than he was. Judging by the tight muscularity of her body, she was an athlete and skilled runner. She slipped once, her bare feet losing traction on the wet grass, but quickly recovered and resumed her rapid pace. He decided to end the hunt prematurely.

He threw the KA-BAR knife with unerring precision. The blade tumbled end over end and struck the woman in the back with tremendous force. She pitched forward onto the grass.

The Boogeyman stood over the woman's trembling body, admiring the way the blood seeped from the knife wound in her back. She struggled to breathe; the blade had pierced a lung.

He pulled the blade from the deep wound he had made, the metal grating sickeningly on bone, and flipped her over. The woman looked up at him with petrified eyes, snot and tears running down her face, blood dripping from her mouth. A plaintive moan escaped her lips.

The Boogeyman watched the steady rise and fall of her breasts, appreciating the dark skin of her areolas. He planted the blade between her breasts, piercing her heart and bursting through her back, burying it into the soil. The woman's pupils dilated as her muscles relaxed in death. He removed the blade from her chest, blood pooling from the wound. He put the blade to his mouth and licked some of the blood off. The hot, coppery tang thrilled his taste buds. The demon sharing his body reveled in the bloodshed.

The stunted, perverted man he had once been—appropriately named Kraven—was now fully subverted to the dark entity which had bonded to his mortal shell, filling him with its black power. Drawn to darkness from a young age, he had conducted extensive research into the black arts, discovering that the odd quirks of his personality—whether it be his obsession with inflicting pain on others (animal or human) or becoming physically aroused at the sight of spilled blood and suffering—made him a perfect vessel in which to hold the immortal power that would give him the ability to pay the world back for all the misery it had heaped upon him. Through some skullduggery and larceny, Kraven had managed to obtain pages from an ancient grimoire *Das Buch die Schatten*—pages that contained the ritual for evoking a demon from the Abyss and binding it to a human host. Kraven planned to perform the ritual on himself.

After several aborted efforts, Kraven had obtained a suitable human sacrifice, an old homeless man he had lured to his isolated house, on the outskirts of a small town, with promises of drink and drugs. After the inebriated man lapsed into unconsciousness, he had secured his hands and feet with duct tape. Kraven placed the man in the center of an inverted pentagram he had painstakingly drawn, in his own blood, on the concrete floor of the cellar, perverting the same magic Solomon had ostensibly used so long ago to protect his people in ancient Jerusalem. The future Boogeyman had sealed the unholy symbol with a circle to contain the demon, then positioned obsidian stones at each of the five points where the pentagram touched the circle, to concentrate the spiritual energy. He chalked sigils around the circle to further amplify the dark energy of the ritual.

Kraven's research had revealed that blood sacrifice was the oldest and most powerful of rituals, dating back to the dawn of humankind. The demon he sought to evoke was a creature of pain and fear and needed to be nourished before it was potent enough to cross over and manifest in a human host. The gateways between worlds were not easily unlocked.

Thirteen tallow candles had lit the room as Kraven began the ritual incantation at the stroke of midnight. He recited the archaic words in a guttural voice, speaking a language long dead and nearly forgotten, and was soon rewarded when he felt a dark presence fill the room. The candle lights changed from gold to sapphire as mystical energy was pulled into the ancient symbols, forming a bridge to the Abyss. The temperature dropped, Kraven's breath becoming visible, and the putrid smell of carrion hung heavy in the basement air. The borders between realities dissolved.

As the shadows of the cellar swelled with power, he severed the man's throat with his father's KA-BAR knife. It was a relic of the old man's time spent in the military during the Vietnam era— Kraven often wondered as to how many victims the blade had previously claimed.

The blood exploded into the air, covering Kraven's face and clothes in an unholy dark baptism. The pregnant shadows flowed from the corners of the room, resolving into a dark fog that funneled into his nose and open mouth. He felt the dark thing enter and soak into every inch of his being. The pitiful man that was Kraven was no more—only the Boogeyman remained.

Eldritch energy coursed through his veins with every heartbeat. He felt truly alive for the first time in his life as all his senses sharpened. Though the candle flames had extinguished, he could see in the dim cellar as if it were daytime. He listened through the thick cellar walls to howls of coyotes hunting in far-off mountains. The night outside beckoned to him—there was, literally, a world of potential victims awaiting him. Ignoring the gory corpse on his floor, he bounded up the stairs, threw open the door, and raced toward the forest that surrounded his home.

Since that night two years ago, he had claimed at least one victim a month, sometimes two. It became almost impossible to resist the call of the hunt, on nights of the full moon, when a primordial urge to bathe in blood would surge through his veins. He often felt like a passenger in his own body, as if it were functioning on auto-pilot, dancing to the scripted code of some mad computer technician.

Kraven tore a metal piercing from the dead woman's left

breast and placed it in his vest pocket. He then returned to the tent and painstakingly scalped the dead lover, making sure to keep the man bun intact. He made it a habit to take something personal from each of his victims as mementos of the kill. He kept the souvenirs in a large trunk in his basement, the chest laden with a sundry array of jewelry, photos, identification cards, teeth, and specimen jars containing organs suspended in formalin.

All the forest was his domain, the other animal predators becoming silent as they gave him a wide berth when he hunted. The Boogeyman had his favorite hunting locations. One site, in particular, drew his attention. There was an isolated area not far from his home, a ridge that overlooked the valley below. Young couples often congregated there in their vehicles in the evenings, drinking and listening to streaming music before fornicating. He had often driven by there as a human, always feeling a horrid mixture of jealousy and shame surface when he saw the parked vehicles. He knew what was occurring inside those vehicles, sex and joy and the intimate exchange of bodily fluids. The knowledge that no woman would ever willingly give herself to him in that manner filled Kraven with hot rage.

Instead of offering acceptance, the women he had encountered mocked his appearance. Kraven had looked at himself many times in the mirror, and a part of him understood why the women scorned him. He was tall and thickly built, but not muscular, his pale arms doughy, his gut ample, his unshaven chin sagging. His patchy brown hair was greasy and thin around a receding hairline. His dark eyes were set deep in the sockets under his bulging forehead, resembling the depictions of ancient caveman in his old schoolbooks. He dressed simply in blue jean denim overalls and brown jackets.

All of his interactions with females were stunted; they dismissed him out of hand. And now he was paying them back for their hostility and contempt…with interest.

He spent the day as he had so many times since his elevation, sitting almost comatose on the ragged sofa of his living room, biding time between kills. He didn't worry about being caught by the police or spending time in prison—he had transcended such earthly concerns. The few recollections of any clarity he retained from such torpid periods chiefly focused on the contemplation of other means of killing people, whether it be by ax, hammer, or screwdriver. The demon demanded that all the deaths occur in close physical proximity, to better experience the suffering—no guns were allowed.

Sometimes, on very rare occasions, the Boogeyman experienced the memories of the other human hosts his demon cohort had previously occupied. Vile images flashed before his eyes, terrifying the human Kraven but thrilling the demon with dark delight. In one vision, he screamed endlessly, bound in thick chains and a straitjacket on the top story of an asylum, his cries mixing with the numbing cacophony of wails from the other "patients." In another, he drowned in a lake as children laughed and jeered, a large campground visible behind them. Finally, in his third, he crept up slowly on a naked woman, his arms covered in the sleeves of a Halloween clown costume, as she combed her chestnut hair in front of a mirror. He proceeded to stab her to death with a butcher's knife, a look of disappointment and horror on the woman's reflected face as she expired. Sometimes the images mixed with those of his life as Kraven, becoming intertwined and inseparable, like a badly edited film.

The moon was full again the night following his butchering of the camp couple. The Boogeyman felt the primal call of the hunt, the demon inside him restless. What remained of the human within counseled caution, not wanting to attract the attention of law enforcement agents trailing a string of missing persons. The demon, however, demanded succor and release. The Boogeyman left his home and made his way to the ridge.

He became excited as he crashed through the woods, his thick, heavy boots mashing the long grass. Eventually, he came upon a lone car in a clearing and surveilled it from under the shadowy boughs. The engine was on and the windows were shut, covered with condensation. The Boogeyman's body filled with eager anticipation, his hand gripping the KA-BAR blade tightly.

He silently approached the vehicle with caution, a predator stalking his prey, anticipating the looks of terror on his soon-to-be victims' faces when he pounced.

It was a nice car, a newer model black Honda with four doors and painted rims. In the back seat, he saw two young people, a man and a woman, kissing and moaning as they fondled each other. The woman was a hauntingly beautiful creature with pale skin and flowing raven hair. She had removed her top and was allowing the man to manipulate her breasts under a black brassiere, her head thrown back and eyes closed in rapture. The couple was too involved in their lovemaking to notice him.

Rage and lust filled the Boogeyman. The evil entity inside resented all forms of human kindness and attraction, while the remaining sliver of Kraven's personality envied the closeness the couple shared—he had remained a virgin his entire life. Yet he now craved the woman with carnal passion, his loins throbbing to possess her.

The Boogeyman stepped forward and dug his fingers into the door frame. Metal shrieked as his muscles bunched and he tore it off, the glass panel window shattering. He threw the door aside like a child's toy. The startled man yelled in protest and raised his large fists. The Boogeyman was impressed by the man's size and physique, his biceps bulging from the sleeves of a tight designer shirt, but physical strength meant little to a supernatural being. The killer seized him by the back of the neck like an obstinate child and extricated him from the backseat. He effortlessly held the man aloft by the throat with a single hand.

The man was young, in his mid-twenties, clean-shaven and well-dressed. He tried to scream, but his throat was closed by the Boogeyman's implacable grip. The killer thrilled to the panicked fear evident in the man's wide eyes. The man futilely struck at his attacker's arm, but he might as well have been punching a marble statue. His struggles weakened as he ran out of breath.

The Boogeyman inhaled the fear, tasting it, savoring it. He noted that the woman was, surprisingly, not screaming. In fact, she was completely silent. She merely looked on from the backseat, slowly adjusting the zipper of her expensive blue jeans, a grin on her ruby lips.

The Boogeyman returned his attention to the frightened man in his hand. He drove the KA-BAR knife with awesome force through the man's sternum, smashing through the ribs and impaling the heart before severing the spine and erupting out the back. Blood sluiced from the man's mouth as his body quivered. The Boogeyman let the corpse slide off the blade before casually wiping it on the long sleeve of his brown jacket.

The Boogeyman turned to find the woman was somehow now in front of him, leaning against the driver's door window. She was short, about five feet tall, displaying sleek muscle definition with no noticeable body fat. The woman had opted not to replace the top she had presumably been wearing earlier, a decision which seemed odd given the chill in the night air. Her feet were shod in expensive black leather boots. She did not look scared. Rather, she gave him a dismissive, scornful look as she folded her arms across her ample chest.

Fury swept through the Boogeyman. Kraven had endured that evil look from women hundreds of times over the years—a look that said "Buzz off, freak! I'm not giving your fugly ass the time of day. You have ZERO chance of ever being with any woman, let alone with a knockout like me. Not even if you were the last man on the planet!" He resolved in that moment to pluck out both of her eyes and add them to his trunk collection.

He drove his blade toward the woman's torso with all the substantial speed and strength at his command. He was surprised when the blade shattered not her chest, but rather the window behind.

As he sought to extricate his hand from the spider-webbed glass panel, he felt two powerful hands seize him by the shoulders and lift him off his feet. He looked into the night sky, the full moon shining brightly through an opening in the black clouds before he was smashed down onto the hood of the car. The metal crumpled beneath him as he felt one of his ribs break from the sheer force of the impact.

The Boogeyman coughed, wondering if the broken rib had punctured his lung. He spat blood onto the windshield as he extracted himself from the metal, his breath suddenly ragged. He turned over and righted himself, planting his feet firmly on the ground in front of the bumper, only to be struck across the face by a blurring fist. His head cracked to the side as a bloody tooth flew out of his mouth. He lashed out with his blade in retaliation, but the woman moved out of the way, expertly avoiding the blow. She countered with a left cross to the side of his head that staggered him.

He stumbled away from the car, grunting as he pushed the broken rib back into place. The woman clipped him again on the back of his head and pain exploded in his skull.

Instinctually, the Boogeyman swept out with his blade, trying to create some space in which he could maneuver and bring his strength into play. The woman leapt into the air, and his blade passed harmlessly through empty air. He was ready for her when she landed.

The Boogeyman struck out with his steel-toed boot, slamming it into her chest with the force of a jackhammer just as she touched down. He both felt and heard her ribs break as the force of his kick lifted her off her feet and into the air. She landed on her back some twenty feet away.

The killer lumbered to where the woman lay on the forest grass. When she lithely rose to her feet in a sinuous movement that seemed to defy gravity, shrugging off a blow that would have killed a gorilla, the Boogeyman did not freeze in fear, as a human would have. Instead, he drove his blade into her chest, right between her breasts. A primordial sense of triumph filled the Boogeyman as his prey staggered back. He released the blade, expecting her to fall.

The pale woman did not fall. Instead, she looked the killer

dead in his blood-shot eyes. The Boogeyman was somewhat taken aback to see red light reflect from her eyes, just like those of a night animal. She snickered as she wrapped two tiny fingers and a thumb around the blade and slowly extricated it from her torso. The blade was unexplainably bloodless. She spoke, her voice hissing like leaves fluttering across a grave.

"Fiends—always trying to compensate for their minuscule penises with long blades. So predictably phallic!"

The dark woman's face twisted in macabre mirth as she laughed and crumpled the metal, like tinfoil, before carelessly tossing the wrecked weapon over her shoulder. The shadowy force that animated the Boogeyman recognized the challenge of a rival predator and rose to the fight.

The Boogeyman extended the long index and middle fingers of his right hand and focused his power into them, making them stronger than steel. He drove the fingers with all his might into the woman's left eye, pulping it and plowing through brain matter before punching out the back of her skull. The dark animus inside the killer reasoned that, while the woman had somehow been fortunate enough to survive a puncture wound to the torso, no living being could survive long with a huge hole in the head.

The Boogeyman pushed forward, trying to knock her off her feet, but the dark woman stood her ground. If she felt any pain, it did not show. Her remaining eye fixed him with a look of intense menace as she seized the wrist of his right hand in a grip of amazing strength. She slowly pulled his hand back, even as he strove to keep the fingers where they were in her head. It became an epic contest of strength between the two. And gradually, despite all his power, the Boogeyman was forced back.

She extricated his fingers and broke the wrist with a twist of her hand. Bright pain shot through the Boogeyman's brain as he stumbled back. He watched in awe as the woman's fingers became elongated and clawed like vulture talons. She lashed out with serpentine speed and severed his right hand at the wrist. A geyser of hot blood erupted from the ragged stump.

The killer fell to his knees in pain, covering the stump with his left hand, in an attempt to staunch the flow of blood. The woman gave him no respite. Even with a pulped eyeball dangling ghoulishly from her shattered orbital socket, she was able to grab the Boogeyman's other arm and fling him over her head with tremendous force. She did not let go of the arm as she threw the killer toward an ancient oak tree.

The Boogeyman felt an awful tearing sensation on his left side as he flew through the air. He smashed head-first into the thick tree trunk, the top of his skull shattering and his neck breaking with the sound of a thunderclap.

A mortal man would have been killed instantly. As it was, the Boogeyman attempted to stand, his body spasming as the shattered nerves attempted to respond to the sluggish commands of his battered brain. As he came to his knees, he was stunned to find the woman facing him, his left arm in her hands, the fingers twitching uselessly. He looked to his left side and saw viscous black blood oozing from the stump where the arm had been attached.

For the first time since his elevation, the Boogeyman knew fear.

As he watched, the dangling optic nerve contracted and twitched and retracted the woman's eyeball back into the socket. The eyeball filled with fluids and reformed as the bones of her orbital socket restructured into their original shape. The spattered blood around the socket seemed to absorb into her ashen skin. Soon she stood unscathed, with no trace of her injuries remaining.

"How?" the Boogeyman managed to mouth in utter disbelief. He now realized the true extent of her beauty, framed as she was by the light of a full moon, with unblemished skin and smooth features. The killer could only wonder as to her true age as she smiled, her red lips and bright teeth reflecting the moonlight.

And then the air filled with the stench of something long decayed and necrotic. The woman's human façade faded as her true face showed.

Long white hair flowed like a mane from atop a withered,

skull-like head, pointed wolf ears flanking either side. Her skin had become gray and leathery, stretched tight over bony cheeks and a sunken, bat nose. Smoldering red eyes beamed with unnatural light from within black sockets, set deep under a pronounced forehead. Her jaws were enlarged and filled with teeth, the upper canines grown into long, ivory fangs. The dark woman's formerly beautiful body was now elongated and warped, the skin stretched tight over wiry muscles and a long neck—a demonic nightmare brought to life.

The woman sped at him, her movement almost too fast for his eyes to follow. A terrific force struck his chest. He felt his rib-cage shatter as a vise encircled his heart.

The Boogeyman sagged to the ground, every beat of his heart pure agony. He lay supine as the woman messily extracted the organ. It pulsed erratically in her gore-slicked hand.

The Boogeyman winced as she bit into the heart, squirting foul ichor down into his eyes. The almond-sulfur stench of decay became overwhelming.

The woman laughed callously, making him feel as small and inconsequential as he had been when he bore the mortal name Kraven. All the strength fled his body with his blood.

"Mmmmm, such power!" the woman chortled, resuming her human facade. "It's been so long since I've feasted upon your kind, fiend, let alone a fiend with this much dark energy surging inside! The last fiend I can recall that rivaled your power level was berserking around Whitechapel at the end of the nineteenth century, slicing open strumpets and leaving disemboweled messes all over the borough. The fool was putting all members of the supernatural community at risk, requiring the Council to send word to me in Styria. When my servant delivered the letter sealed with their insignia, I dropped the peasant girl I was feeding on and immediately booked passage to London."

The Boogeyman's vision became clouded. He still could hear the woman's haunting voice as she prattled on with anachronistic references.

"Imagine my surprise when that fiend turned out to be a doctor to the royal family itself! Seemed he'd contracted syphilis from a street whore and gone mad from the disease. He began taking out his rage on the Whitechapel prostitutes he blamed for his distress. Oh, I can still remember the terror in the air as I walked the streets, stores closing early and peelers stationed on every block, looking for the Ripper. He was a bold fiend, taunting Scotland Yard with self-promoting letters and calling himself Jack. When he said he was 'From hell,' he was telling the truth!

"I've got to give you credit, though, you put up a much better fight than that ponce did. I confronted him as he left the scene of his latest slaughter at Miller's Court. He'd diced up the Kelly harlot and spread her parts out all over the room like he was auditioning for the Grand Guignol! What a mess he made! I picked him up, like the child he was, and flew him to a rooftop a few streets away. He was a stubborn blighter, refusing to let go of the bloody uterus souvenir he'd taken, even as I yanked his head off.

"You'd think you fiends would learn to cover your tracks better. Or, in your case, pick your victims with a little more care!" she intoned with a mocking grin. "But that demon inside you gets too greedy, no? It thrives on human misery, and its bloodlust makes my own look petty in comparison. You couldn't stop it, even as the bodies began adding up over time. The Council was tipped off by a local fey redcap, who lives at the bottom of that ridge you're so fond of dumping bodies over. Apparently, it didn't appreciate the competition. That's where I came in: A visit to the local bar, followed by a little mental domination of a lustful male, culminating in a risqué back-seat tryst that no full-blooded, demon-possessed serial killer could resist intruding on. Voila!"

The Boogeyman felt like he was being hectored by a teacher. He tried to strike her with the stump of his right arm.

The woman looked upon him with scorn as she pushed the stump away and leaned forward.

"Now, let's see what's behind the mask."

Using her free hand, she ripped away his burlap veneer. A

look of disgust came upon her face as she moved back, one hand covering her bloody mouth.

"Ugh, now I see why you had a mask on! Not much luck with the women, I gather. Not with that Frankenstein forehead and snaggle-toothed grill," she ridiculed, her silky tones brimming with contempt, thrusting her words like daggers into the Boogeyman's ego.

"Dear boy, if any of your former self remains beside that backwater, witless hellspawn you summoned, know that I've been hunting this earth for millennia. I've consumed the blood of the most fearsome beings this planet has to offer, human and inhuman. The power of that blood has made me so much more than what I was when I first rose from my grave. Talismans, spears, sunlight— the things I feared as a stripling revenant no longer affect me. You really never had a chance. Jealous, petty, insignificant, perverted misogynist—meet a true apex predator!" the dark woman roared, displaying her sharp teeth. "I'm a serial killer of serial killers."

She laughed as she finished draining his heart dry.

"The jobs from the Council keep me well fed," she proclaimed, her snakelike tongue dabbing the blood at the corner of her mouth. "It's a comforting feeling for an immortal, supernatural hitwoman to know she will always have job security. I know you fiends are compelled to keep souvenirs from your victims. I must admit, I suffer from similar compulsions, perhaps owing to the oceans of demon blood I've drunk. Guess what's going in my trunk tonight, little man?" Her eyes sparkled as she extended his desiccated heart toward him and dismissively waved bye-bye with it.

Kraven found himself alone in his shattered body as the demon fled, the fiend seeking a healthier human specimen to possess. And, as what remained of his wormy soul was sucked inexorably downward into the black vortex of Hell, Kraven caught a last glimpse of the victorious uber vampiress stomping her exquisite, leather-booted foot through his skull.

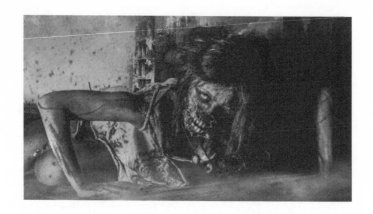

'TIL DEATH DO US PART

R.E. Sargent

CHAPTER ONE

THE BODY COLLAPSED IN THE ALLEYWAY, crimson red flowers blooming through the man's shirt in multiple places, where the bullets had pierced his flesh.

His cell phone rang, yanking Tyler Yates' attention away from the crime show he was watching. Pulling it from the pocket of his basketball shorts, Tyler looked at the display. It said "Hottie."

Tyler smiled and pressed the button to accept the call.

"Hey, sweetie! What're you up to?"

"Not much. Just seeing if you had plans tonight." His girl-friend, Tabitha Reynolds, even sounded hot on the phone. It was definitely not false advertising.

"No plans. Just got home from work an hour ago and was watching TV. Why don't you come over? I'm pretty free this week-end."

"I was hoping we could go out for dinner," Tabitha said.

Tyler looked down at his basketball shorts, thought about his plans for relaxing, and almost told her he didn't want to go out, but then thought better of it. She certainly could get any man she wanted, but he didn't want to give her any reason to *want* to.

"Sounds good, babe. Did you want to come over here, or should I meet you somewhere?"

"I'll come over."

"Perfect. I'll jump in the shower."

"See you in thirty minutes. Bye!"

Tyler ended the call and shut off the TV. He didn't feel like going out, but he knew that a relationship was a balance of give and take. It made it a little easier to say yes knowing he could sleep in tomorrow.

At thirty-two, he felt like he should have more energy. Instead, he was tired all the time, even though he was in great shape physically. He blamed it on his job. It was mentally exhausting. As a software engineer, he exercised his brain way more than he exercised his body. While he hit the gym three times a week, his brain was constantly working through complex problems, even while he was sleeping. Getting a night of peaceful sleep seemed to be a thing of the past for him. He was wondering if that would ever change.

Turning on the water in the shower, Tyler stripped and put the clothes he had been wearing in the closet. He stood under scalding water, not because he got dirty while working at his job, but more so to refresh himself.

Tabitha would want to go someplace nice, so Tyler put on a pair of blue slacks and a button-down oxford shirt. Looking at himself in the mirror, he straightened his collar and brushed his hair before putting a little product in it to keep it in place. He studied his face in the mirror: strong jaw, perfect teeth, just the right amount of maintained stubble. Then he noticed his eyes. The exhaustion he felt was painted clearly in the eyes that stared back at him. He sighed, wondering what he was doing with his life.

As he sat on the edge of the bed putting his shoes on, Tabitha walked in. Tyler had given her a key to his San Francisco Bay Area apartment after they had been dating for a couple months. He had hoped she would move in, but so far, she refused, citing various reasons. Now, after six months of dating, he wondered if they would ever be more than boyfriend and girlfriend.

"Oh good, you're ready," she said.

"Perfect timing!" Tyler ran his eyes down her short, black dress and let out a low whistle.

"Flirt."

"So? That dress looks so good on you."

"Thanks, babe."

"It would look even better on the floor, though," Tyler said, even though he knew what the response would be.

"Keep on dreaming!"

There it was. The response he had been expecting. After six months together, not only hadn't she moved in, but they also hadn't ever had sex. Not even close. Whenever their kissing started getting too hot and heavy, she would put on the brakes, hard. Tyler respected her wishes, and he certainly would wait as long as it took—because he felt she was worth it—but he was dying to take their relationship to the next level.

Pretending her comment didn't bother him—he wanted them both to enjoy the evening, after all—Tyler finished tying his shoes, put on a casual suit jacket, and grabbed the keys to his 2019 BMW i8 Roadster.

"Ready?" he asked.

"Just let me use the restroom."

While Tabitha was in the bathroom, Tyler went over to his nightstand and opened the second drawer down. Under his iPad, he found the item he had placed there three months ago. As he heard the toilet flush, he slipped it into his jacket pocket and closed the drawer.

Tabitha opened the door and came back into the room.

"Let's go!" she said.

"Where do you want to eat?"

"Do you mind traveling a bit?"

"Not at all. It's a nice evening for a drive. Where are we going?"

"Is the Moonraker okay?"

"Heck yes. I love the views there."

"Can we put the top down on the Beemer?"

"Seems like it'd be a crime not to."

CHAPTER TWO

"WHAT ARE YOU going to order?" Tabitha asked. Their table overlooked the water and the huge rock formations that jutted out from the surface. They had been there twice before, as a couple, and never tired of the view.

"I'm going with the lobster tail and ribeye. You?"

"I absolutely loved the Dungeness crab legs I had last time we came here. I think I'll have them again. Their seafood is so fresh."

The waiter showed up and took their drink order and then retreated toward the kitchen area.

"So, what's the occasion?" Tyler asked.

"For?"

"Tonight."

"Can't I just want to spend some time with my boyfriend? I've only seen you twice this week."

Tyler smiled. "I know a way we can fix that." He winked.

"I know, I know. I can move in. We've had this conversation more times than I can count."

"Yet you always have a reason why you can't...actually, they sound more like excuses."

Tabitha cocked her head and gave him a look, then started to speak. She was cut off when the waiter arrived with their drinks. After he took their order and disappeared, she started again.

"You know what, fine. Maybe I haven't been as transparent as I should have been with you, but I have my reasons."

"But that's not really fair to me, Tabitha. I like you. In fact, I've refrained from telling you, because I didn't want to scare you off, but I think I'm in love with you."

"Really?" Tabitha's eyes got misty.

"Really."

"Oh shit."

"That wasn't quite the reaction I was hoping for."

Tabitha shook her head. "Sorry. That came out wrong. I'm so flattered…and I love you too. I do."

"If you love me, then why not move in with me?"

"You want the truth?"

"I think I deserve it."

"You're right. The truth is, I'm afraid if I move in, my will-power will diminish. I'd be riding you like a kid rides the horsey carousel at the local Walmart."

"I don't see a problem with that," Tyler said, smiling, the tension from the start of the conversation dissipating.

"But I can't."

"Why not? You're a grown-ass adult."

"Okay, I'll come clean, but you have to promise not to make fun of me."

"I promise."

"I don't want to move in, 'cause I don't want to sleep with you yet. I don't want to sleep with you yet, because I want to wait until we're married—that is, if we ever take that step. I know we haven't discussed it."

Tyler's eyes widened. "Have you thought about it?"

"Yes. A lot."

"Then maybe the timing is right."

"For?"

"To get married."

"Tyler—"

"Wait!" he interrupted. "Hear me out." He reached into his jacket pocket and pulled out a small pouch. Opening the draw-strings, he dumped something into his hand, then grabbed it between his thumb and first two fingers and held it up.

"Is that what I think it is, Tyler?"

"Yes."

"How long have you had it?"

"A few months. I've just been waiting until the time was right. I figured tonight might be good since we were going out and all."

"Are you asking?"

"I'm asking."

Tabitha covered her face with her hands and let out a low squeal. "Yes. YES!"

The patrons from the nearby tables turned to look, but neither of them cared. Tyler's face lit up at his good fortune, and he slid the engagement ring on Tabitha's finger.

"So, what kind of wedding do you want?"

"The quick and easy kind. I'm not into all of that storybook crap. Let's just make it simple."

Tyler smiled. "Works for me. Now the question is when?"

"How about in three weeks? That will give us time to get our marriage license, and I can give a thirty-day notice on my place. That is, if you still want me to move in." She flashed him a mischievous grin.

"You know I do. I can't wait."

Drinks came and they ordered dinner, the conversation revolving around their upcoming nuptials. Before they realized it, the table was nothing but remnants of a meal that had become a celebration of sorts.

"Dessert?" Tyler asked.

"Tempting, but I'd better pass."

"I can always offer you dessert back at my place, if you like, since we are engaged and all now." He grinned.

"Nice try. Marry me first…then you can have all the dessert you want."

"You mean I have to wait three more weeks?" He pretended to pout.

"I'm worth it."

"I don't doubt that one bit. I'm a lucky man."

CHAPTER THREE

EXHAUSTED, TYLER SANK onto the couch. He had worked a little bit every evening over the past week, getting the apartment ready for his fiancée. He took full advantage of the weekend and did the majority of the work, making sure half the drawers were empty in the master bathroom and that half the closet was emptied out. He wanted to make it easy for Tabitha to start moving her things in anytime she wanted.

He turned on the television and started watching a crime show that was in progress. At ten p.m., the news came on, and Tyler watched a story about a man who had been murdered. The police weren't releasing all the details, but they stated the body had been torn apart, some parts missing.

"Sickos."

Tyler watched more of the story and realized the murder had happened in Salem, Oregon, which was a long way away, but definitely not far enough. He shuddered.

With work looming the next morning, he turned off the television and headed to bed. As he peeled back the covers, he thought about how, in three short weeks, he would not be climbing into this bed alone. He had never been married before and, likewise, had never lived with anyone, so this would be a new experience for him. His mind teased him with images of what he thought Tabitha looked like naked, and he imagined her stretched out across the bed, motioning for him to join her. Their wedding night could not come soon enough.

In bed, the cool fabric rubbed over his naked body and that, mixed with the thoughts of his soon-to-be wife lying naked beside him, her smooth skin backed up against him, floated him into a sensual dream, unlike he had ever had before. In the dream, she took him and used him up, until all that was left was a shaking, withered mound of flesh that was unable to move. When he awoke a couple of hours later, he couldn't help but wonder if the dream had been a good sign or an omen.

THE NEXT WEEK passed by uneventfully. Tyler worked, came home, talked to Tabitha nightly on the phone, watched television, and went to bed. For the first time ever, he realized his life was boring, and he was looking forward to sharing it with somebody. He had no trepidation about giving up his freedom. Since being on his own, he'd been muddling through life, successful and driven in his work, but unfulfilled in his personal life. Though he had never realized what was missing before, it was all too apparent now.

On Friday, when he got home from work, Tabitha was waiting for him.

He had parked his Beemer in the parking garage and rode the elevator up to his floor, tired from the long week at work, but not looking forward to spending another weekend alone. When he slid the key into the deadbolt and tried to turn it, it was unlocked. He cautiously opened the door and peered inside the living room. The lights were on, but the room was empty. He heard noises coming from the kitchen and went to investigate. When he walked around the corner, he froze, in shock.

Her back was to him as she stood over the stove. She was wearing the one apron he kept in the pantry—one that read "Will Cook For Sex"—that he used when he made his famous spaghetti sauce, because no matter what he did, he always seemed to get splatters on his shirt. He couldn't tell what she was making, but he didn't care. She wore six-inch high-heeled shoes. Her long, blond hair cascaded down her back. And underneath that apron, she was bare-assed naked.

Mouth open, Tyler must have stared at her beautiful, curvy bottom for a minute before his dry throat caused him to cough.

She whipped her head around, and he caught her ample side-boob.

"Hi, sweetie. Dinner's almost ready."

He tried to speak but couldn't.

"What was that?"

"Um…you're…naked."

She looked down.

"Why yes, yes I am."

"Not that I'm complaining, but why?"

"Preview."

"Of?"

"Of what you are getting by marrying me. Gotta keep you from changing your mind."

"That would never happen."

"Good. Now wash up. It's almost time."

"Do I get naked too?"

"Nope. This isn't about me tonight; it's all about you."

Tyler went into the bedroom and changed as quickly as he could, his mind playing over the firm flesh he had just seen standing in his kitchen. When he re-entered the room, she was sitting at the table, their plates dished and waiting. She no longer wore the apron, but in its place, she wore a red tie. And a smile.

"I didn't realize we were dressing up for dinner. Shall I go put on a tie as well?"

Tabitha smiled. "Nope. Let's eat."

Tyler slid into the chair facing her, never taking his eyes off her body.

"Hey, Mister. My eyes are up here!" She pointed to the emerald-green irises.

"You really can't expect me to focus on your face under these circumstances."

"You act like you've never seen a pair before."

"Oh, I have…just not that particular pair."

"Well, in a few weeks, they will be all yours."

Tyler exhaled deeply. "You know, it's really not nice to tease the animals."

Tabitha laughed. "Maybe not, but it's oh, so much fun!"

After dinner, Tabitha put on Tyler's robe, and they cleaned up the kitchen together. Tabitha put the leftovers away while Tyler cleaned off the dishes and racked them in the dishwasher. Then Tabitha sprayed down the kitchen counters with cleaner and wiped them off.

"It sure is easier to concentrate with you wearing something. What was that about, anyway?"

"Are you complaining?"

"No, Ma'am!"

"Okay then!"

"It just seems so unlike you."

"Just because I want to wait doesn't make me a prude. I have my reasons, but it's not that."

"So, you just wanted to torture me?"

"More like give you a sneak peek of what you are getting yourself into."

"Hopefully over and over."

"If you're good."

After dinner, Tabitha went to get dressed, and Tyler sat on the couch and turned on the TV. The news was on.

...getting reports of another murder, this one in Spring, Texas. Police sources tell us that this murder seems to be connected to the two dozen or so that have been happening all across the United States in the past month. Although police aren't releasing specifics, we are told that each of the victims were missing body parts. The FBI has taken over the investigation. A spokesman...

Tabitha appeared, dressed in a pair of pajamas, and stood between Tyler and the TV.

"Wanna watch a movie?"

"I was just watching this story on the news...people are dying..."

"Depressing stuff...let's watch a comedy."

Tabita grabbed the remote off the couch and brought up Netflix, choosing a newer movie they hadn't seen yet.

"What's with the jammies?"

"Oh, I thought it would be okay with you if I spent the night." She shrugged. "Can I?"

"Of course. But just to be transparent, where will you be sleeping?"

"The bed."

"I see. And where will I be sleeping?"

"The bed."

Tyler's eyebrows shot up.

"No funny business, Mister. You have to wait."

"But this is torture."

"I can leave if you want."

"No. Stay. Please."

"That's what I thought."

CHAPTER FOUR

TYLER OPENED HIS eyes and noticed the room was awash with light. He rolled over and looked at the clock. A little after ten a.m. He wasn't used to sleeping so late, but he had needed it.

He then remembered that Tabitha had spent the night, but there was no sign of her in the bedroom, and he could see the adjoining bathroom was empty.

His mind swept back to when they had gone to bed. At first, she had laid on one side of the bed and he on the other. Eventually, he heard her steady, even breathing and he knew she was asleep. Having her right there, but so far away, became too much for him, so he rolled toward her, scooted up against her and held her. He probably would have gotten away with it too, if his body hadn't betrayed him by responding to the feel of her firm buttocks against his groin. He remembered her waking, with a start, and telling him to put it away. Then she compromised and made him roll over, and she played big spoon instead. If he was going to get pokey, she preferred he poke empty air.

He caught her scent on the pillow next to him and wondered

if she had left. Groggily, he got out of bed, opened the bedroom door, and headed into the living room. She wasn't there. A slight breeze caught the white, cotton curtains that covered the sliding door, billowing the bottom out into the room. It was then he heard her voice. She was out on the balcony.

He walked toward the glass door, excited to see his fiancé and hoping she'd let him take her out to breakfast.

"Yes. Less than three weeks. You just need to be patient."

She was on the phone. Tyler stopped in his tracks, wanting to give her some privacy.

"I know we need this one. You've been bitching about it for months. I told you...these things take time."

Tyler cocked his head, wondering what, exactly, Tabitha was talking about. Was she referring to their wedding? Her tone seemed off. Cold. Controlled. It was not the Tabitha he knew.

"I'll give you a status update in a couple of weeks, as we get closer. Yes. Yes, I know. I understand how much is riding on this."

The breeze threw a bigger gust through the open entryway, and the curtains flipped away from the door. He saw Tabitha on the balcony, still dressed in her pajamas, her phone to her ear. The movement of the curtains caught her attention and she turned, spotting Tyler for the first time. A smile spread across her face.

"Anyway, I better go. My honey is awake and I want to spend some time with him. Yes. I understand. Okay, bye."

"Morning, Tabby."

"Morning, sweetie."

"Who was on the phone?"

"Sorry. That was my boss."

"Is everything okay?"

"Yeah. She's just nervous about a deadline."

"Well, do you need to go in?"

"Are you kidding? It's the weekend. She can get lost...I'm not dealing with it until Monday."

Tyler smiled. He had been worried for a second, but her change in tone had most likely been associated with a work call on her day off. He didn't know too much about what her job entailed at the advertising firm she worked at, as she tried to keep work things at work and was reluctant to talk about it when Tyler enquired. Luckily, Tabitha's demeanor seemed to have returned to normal, so he put the conversation he had overheard out of his mind.

"Breakfast?" he asked.

"What are you making me?"

"Nothing. I was hoping you'd let me take you out."

"As long as wherever you take me has strawberry waffles."

"Is there any other kind?"

AFTER BREAKFAST, TABITHA left. Tyler shuffled music by his favorite band, Skillet, on his iPhone, and blasted it through his Bugani Bluetooth speaker. He threw a load of laundry in the washing machine and started cleaning the bathroom, knowing he wouldn't have time to do it during the week and wanting to keep a clean place for Tabitha. No way was he going to let her walk into a gross bathroom, or any other part of the apartment.

As he wiped down the mirror, he noticed a smile on his face. He took in his features. Although he had always felt he was average looking, he never felt he was anything special. Certainly, he had lucked out with Tabitha. Never in a million years had he imagined he'd walk into Starbucks to pick up a Venti Vanilla Latte and get in line behind a Goddess. Even more mind-blowing was when she turned around and started a conversation with him, then, before she left with her Strawberry Acai Refresher with lemonade, she grabbed his phone from his hand, held it to his face to unlock it, went into his contacts, and added her name and number. Then she took it one step further and snapped a picture to add to her contact.

"It's under Tabitha," she had said. "I'll be highly disappointed if you *don't* call."

And with that, she walked out of the store, leaving him staring in disbelief. Things like that never happened to him.

It had taken him three days to get up the nerve to actually call her, for which she had immediately given him a hard time. They had gotten together for a casual dinner that night. Later, they ended up overlooking the bay and somehow, her soft, delicate hand had ended up in his. They'd been a *thing* ever since.

He watched as his smile got even bigger as he recalled the day they met. Maybe she was more than he ever thought he would have, but that didn't mean he didn't deserve her. He did. He was a good guy and he deserved good things. He definitely deserved Tabitha.

When he was done cleaning the bathroom, he moved the laundry over to the dryer and sat down on the couch. Grabbing the remote, he flipped on the TV and flicked through the channels. He stopped on the crime channel he liked and watched the last eighteen minutes of the show that was on, his guts twisting inside. The female victim had been assaulted and kidnapped and then burned alive inside the trunk of her car.

The grisly scene brought his mind back to the murders he had seen on the news...murders and mutilations. Body parts missing. Victims in multiple states. The situation had been nagging at the back of his brain, the thought of a killer traveling the country and committing these heinous acts unfathomable.

Tyler switched off the television and grabbed his laptop off the coffee table. He had to know more. Bringing up a browser, he searched for articles related to the news stories he had seen on TV. It only took a few seconds to find the first one.

When he was done with the first, he read the next, and then another. After six stories, he realized that the details were extremely limited as all of them gave the same information, but nothing more. The authorities were definitely keeping the details close to their chest. The only information available was the number of victims, their locations, and the fact the bodies had been mutilated and were missing body parts. He was unable to find out exactly what body parts were missing.

Looking deeper, Tyler flipped to the second page of results on Google and skimmed the headlines, then the third. A webpage caught his eye and he pulled it up. A murder in Bangkok that, to him, sounded similar. Was it connected? Did the U.S. authorities know about it?

Tyler imagined that a multi-state investigation was difficult, but what if this was actually a worldwide issue? A chill ran up his spine as he rubbed his right temple. Should he call the FBI and tell them about the case in Bangkok? Surely, they would already know about it, right? They were the FBI, after all.

A throbbing in the back of his head mirrored his heartbeat, and his face flushed. Feeling queasy, Tyler pulled off his shoes and laid down on the couch. Before he could make any sense of the situation, he was fast asleep.

CHAPTER FIVE

"WANT ME TO finish packing this cupboard?" Tyler asked.

They were in the kitchen of Tabitha's apartment packing up the last of everything.

"That'd be awesome. Be careful with those glasses, though. They're special to me."

Tyler wrapped each glass in bubble wrap as he placed the contents into the box. They had been working on her apartment for two days and were almost finished packing. Tyler had taken a couple of weeks off work to help her move in and so they could spend some alone time after the wedding. They still hadn't made any plans regarding a honeymoon, but they hoped to slip away for a few days to some beachside vacation rental. Sand, sun, and surf. And sex. Lots of it.

After he had taped the box closed, he wrote what the contents were on the side in black Sharpie.

"Does this one go over to the apartment or in the storage pile?"

"Storage. I figure I'll probably be storing more than I bring over. You only have so much space. One day, if we buy a house, we will have room for both of our things. Your kitchen is pretty well equipped, though, so I really don't need to bring any of this."

"This is so surreal. In a few days, you're going to be my wife. We're going to be living together."

"Yes. That's what most husbands and wives do."

"Ha, ha! Am I the only one who can't wrap my brain around this?"

"Pretty much."

"I never really thought I'd end up married."

"Too late to back out now. I'll get you all trained properly—so you'll be ready for your second wife."

"Yeah, that's a hard pass. I'll stick with one."

"Hopefully you'll still feel that way after we get married."

"Why? Are you keeping secrets from me?" he bantered.

Tabitha smiled. "Oh, you have no idea!"

They finished packing up the kitchen and loaded the last few loose items in a couple spare boxes to take to Tyler's apartment. Tabitha stepped back and took in the piles of boxes stacked around the room.

"I'm going to miss this place a little."

"Hopefully not too much."

"Probably not."

"When are the movers coming?"

"Tomorrow morning. Nine-ish."

"What say we go back to the apartment, take a quick shower, and go grab a bite to eat?"

"That's perfect. I'm starving."

"Me too."

THEY SAT AT a table in the back corner of the quaint café, both eating BLTs and potato salad. They ate silently, exhausted from the prior few days of packing and cleaning. The silence was interrupted by the waitress, who topped off their glasses of iced tea.

"Okay, so are you crashing at the apartment tonight since your place is pretty much all packed?"

"Yes. No sense in getting a hotel room."

"Works for me."

She gave him a stern look. "No funny business."

"Party pooper. We are getting married the day after tomorrow. Who will know?"

"I'll know."

"I won't tell if you don't."

"Tyler…"

"I know, I know. I'm just being a brat. I've waited this long. I can wait two more days."

"Good. I'm worth it."

"I have no doubt. Anyway, so tomorrow we clear out your apartment and get your stuff over to our place. Then the day after, we are appearing before the Justice of the Peace at what time?"

"Two thirty p.m."

"Okay, so at two thirty, we will tie the knot and then what? Go home? Get a hotel room? Go on a trip?"

"Why don't we go home and then leave the next day? I can book something tonight if you want."

"Perfect. I can't wait to get away and show off my new bride at the same time."

"Oh, there will be no showing me off. Don't even plan on leaving the room."

"Sounds like I better get some rest."

"Not a bad idea. You'll need it."

BACK AT THE apartment, they turned on the television and watched a show where crimes were solved through video footage.

When it was over, Tabitha grabbed her bag off the floor by the door and headed toward the master bedroom.

"I'm going to get in my jammies, hun."

"Are you coming back out?"

"Of course."

With the show over and Tabitha in the bedroom changing, Tyler turned to the local news channel. He caught the reporter mid-sentence talking about more murders.

...four more bodies were found this morning. Police aren't releasing the victims' names publicly yet, however, we were able to find out that one of the victims was found in Nampa, Idaho, two in Key West, Florida, and one in San Diego, California. Authorities still believe these and the other victims to all be connected, but they have declined to say how. The FBI is urging anyone with information regarding this string of murders to call their tipline at the number on the bottom of the screen...

Tyler looked up and spotted Tabitha standing at the end of the hallway, in a pair of pink silk pajamas, her eyes glued to the TV.

"You're watching this story again?"

"There were four more murders."

"It's crazy. Thank God we don't have to worry about some killer..."

"Maybe we should be...worried, that is."

"Why? Nothing is happening around here."

"I'm not so sure it matters. Distance doesn't seem to be getting in their way. And did you see? One of the victims was in San Diego. That's pretty close if you ask me."

"It'll all be over soon."

Tyler's eyebrows arched, a puzzled expression on his face.

"What's that supposed to mean?"

"Oh, I just mean that these things happen and then, all of the sudden, they stop...fade into the background, even."

"I don't see this stopping anytime soon. To me, it seems to be ramping up."

"Tyler, I think you are letting the news reports get to you. The media is being irresponsible with this...almost creating panic and chaos."

"I think people need to know this stuff. They need to be ready to protect themselves. Why are you not concerned?"

"I just don't think I'm anybody's intended victim. I lead a pretty boring life."

"But how do you know? What if the victims were chosen at random?"

"We all have to die sometime."

"That's morbid."

"It's reality, Tyler."

"But what about your friends? What about me? What if something happens to one of us?"

"I don't have any close friends. And you know I don't have any family left. All I have is you, and I won't let anything happen to you."

"You're going to protect me?" Tyler gave her a partial smile, trying to hide his amusement.

"You have no idea."

Tyler squinted his eyes at her, unsure how to take her comment.

"Anyway, hun, let's not get all bogged down with that crap. Why don't you go get ready for bed too, and then we can snuggle under a blanket and watch one more movie before we go to sleep?"

"If we watch another movie, we better do it in the bedroom, because I don't think I will make it through another one." He rubbed his right eye as if to back up his claim. "I'm exhausted."

"Works for me."

Tyler got up from the couch, turned off the television, and followed Tabitha into the bedroom. While she propped up her pillows and got in the bed, he went into the bathroom, changed into a pair of basketball shorts, and brushed his teeth.

Back in the bedroom, he slipped into bed beside Tabitha.

"So, I take it that is going to be your side of the bed from now on?" he asked.

"I hadn't really thought about it. This side just felt right."

"Then it's yours."

Tabitha grabbed the remote off the side table and turned on the television.

"What do you want to watch?" she asked.

"There are a few new action movies out."

"Perfect. Any preference?"

"You pick."

Tabitha brought up the guide and searched through the movie channels until she finally found something that looked good.

"How about this one, Ty?"

When he didn't answer, she turned toward him, only to find him already asleep. Smiling, she shut off the TV, slipped her tablet out of her purse, and picked up where she had left off reading *Widow's Point*. Five pages in, the tablet slipped from her fingers and the only noise in the room was the sound of them both breathing.

CHAPTER SIX

TYLER CLICKED THE padlock shut on the storage unit and tugged on it to make sure it was locked.

"Well, that didn't take that long. It's only..."—he looked at his watch—"...two thirty-five. I thought we'd be moving stuff into the evening."

"I don't have *that* much stuff," she said, laughing.

"Still, not bad."

"Then we are pretty much done. I'm not going to unpack the stuff at the apartment until we get back from our mini honeymoon, and I have a cleaning company going in to touch up my old apartment, so we don't have to worry about it. Looks like we have the afternoon off."

"Maybe we can get some rest and pack for our trip. Oh, shit. Did we ever book anything?" Tyler asked.

Tabitha looked sheepish. "I totally forgot to look last night, and I passed out not too long after you did. I'll book something when we get home. Then we can pack. And then we can rest up for tomorrow. It's a pretty big day."

"Yeah, it is. A wedding. OUR wedding. And a trip with you? It doesn't get any better. Plus, I'm so damn glad to be away from that stress pit they label as a job."

"You can forget all about that place, baby. Just you and me now."

BACK AT THE apartment, Tabitha took a quick shower and changed into some shorts and a white tank top. She grabbed her laptop, propped some pillows up on the bed, and made herself comfortable.

"I'm going to grab a quick shower as well, Tabby."

"Sounds good. I'll just be here researching places to go for our trip. Do you want to have a say in where we go, or shall I surprise you?"

Tyler's face lit up. "Yes, I'd love to keep it as a surprise."

"Okay, then when you get out of the bathroom, you can go watch TV, or something, in the other room. I don't want you peeking over my shoulder."

"Do you really think I'd do that?"

"Absolutely. Am I wrong?"

Tyler gave a sly smile. "Probably not."

"GO!" Tabitha pointed toward the bathroom.

Tyler started the water, stripped out of his dirty clothes, and climbed in the shower. The jets of water felt good on his back, and as soon as he was used to the temperature, he made it a little hotter. Sticking his head under the stream, he let the heat drain his tiredness away.

His mind ran back through the conversation he and Tabitha had about the murders earlier. She didn't seem concerned at all, which perplexed him. Besides their wedding, it was the only thing on his mind, and even though she wasn't worried, *he* was.

When the water started getting cold, he turned off the valves and grabbed his towel, drying off in the shower before stepping out on the mat.

Multiple victims all over the country.

He ran the towel back over his head to dry his hair a little more.

Each victim was missing at least one body part.

He stepped to the mirror and grabbed a comb off the vanity.

Which body part? Why was it such a secret?

Wearing a fresh set of clothes, Tyler exited the bathroom, kissed Tabitha on the forehead, and headed toward the living room.

"See you a little later, hun."

"Okay. I'll let you know when the trip is booked, in case you want to hang out in here after."

"Deal."

Tyler left the room and turned on the television, but his attention wasn't on the show. Fifteen minutes later, he grabbed his laptop from the side table and booted it up. There had to be more information out there somewhere.

He started with Google and found several articles on the murders. None of them told him any more than he already knew. He looked deeper. One article was more of an opinion piece, which talked about this huge conspiracy against the American people. The article had a link to a small online blog. He scanned through the paragraphs looking for anything he didn't already know. Then he spotted it.

...and although no one will confirm it, I firmly believe the body parts missing from the victims are their brains. I won't give away my source, but one of the investigation team for the Spring, Texas, murder personally told me the brain had been removed. What kind of sicko kills people and steals their brains? Did I ask if any other body parts were missing? Hell yes, I did, and the answer was a resounding "NO." That tells me only one thing. Every single one of these victims—which law enforcement themselves have labeled as

connected—are missing their brains. They have to be. If you weren't creeped the fuck out before, I bet you are now…

Tyler brought his trembling hand to his forehead and then raked it through his hair. If this information was correct, it was worse than he thought. While many serial killers took trophies, brains were not one that commonly hit the list. What was the killer doing with them? Storing them? Eating them? He shuddered.

"All booked."

Tyler looked over to find Tabitha standing in the doorway to the living room.

"Exciting!" he muttered.

"Are you okay, Tyler? You're white as a ghost."

"Yeah, I'm good. Just exhausted," he lied.

"Why don't we go to bed and get some rest? We can pack in the morning or even after we get married. It's only a two-hour drive to our destination, so there is no pressure."

Tyler took a deep breath and closed his laptop. "That sounds like a good idea. We need a little shut-eye."

As Tyler brushed his teeth, Tabitha came into the bathroom. "Are you sure you're okay? You seem…well, for lack of a better way to explain it, *off*."

Tyler paused for a moment, debating whether he should tell Tabitha what he found. He knew she didn't worry about the murders as much as he did, and he didn't want to go through another conversation about it, so he decided to keep it to himself.

"Yeah, babe, I'm good. I think it just hit me all at once."

"Okay, but if you want to talk about it, let me know."

"I will. Promise."

Tabitha bit her bottom lip and looked away. "You still want to marry me tomorrow, don't you?"

This time, there was no hesitation. "More than anything in the world."

"I was hoping that'd be your answer." She smiled and exited the bathroom, returning to the bedroom.

When he climbed into bed, Tabitha was on her side, still

wearing her pajamas, the covers pulled up to her waist. He got himself situated, facing away from her, before reaching up and clicking off the bedside lamp. Only a few seconds went by before he felt her roll over and snuggle up against him.

"Tomorrow night, *I* play big spoon," he said.

"Looking forward to it!"

In the dark, he laid awake, listening to the silence, and then, after a few minutes, Tabitha's steady breathing. She was asleep. The murders returned to his thoughts—the brains. Or rather the lack thereof. He couldn't shake the feeling of dread that crept up his spine. Was he in danger? Was Tabitha?

Finally, exhaustion took over, and Tyler could feel himself slipping over the edge into the deep, dark pool of sleep.

THE DREAM WAS not something he had ever experienced before. At least not that he ever remembered after waking up. He clawed at the bedsheets as she moved her body up and down, riding him, slowly at first, and then faster, faster. Her breath came out in quick, furious exhalations, a low moan escaping the back of her throat. As she neared climax, he felt her speed quicken and her breathing grow ragged. And then it happened. Her body stiffened, and then shuddered, as she came, the sounds emitting from her mouth loud and guttural. A side of Tabitha he had not been aware of. Except this was only a dream. Obviously, a premonition that his mind conjured up in anticipation of what their wedding night would be like. Or at least he hoped. And then it was over. She slid off of him, rolled back onto her side, and immediately fell back asleep. That was when he realized *he* wasn't. He was wide awake.

Reaching down, he touched himself to make sure. He was still erect. And he was covered in remnants of her. Rubbing the back of his neck, he couldn't sort out what had just happened. Tabitha was against sleeping together before marriage. Even the night before. Yet she had just ridden him hard. She had used him for her own pleasure and hadn't even given him a chance to be satisfied. And then she rolled over and went back to sleep. None of it made any sense.

He reached around in the bed and found his pajama bottoms curled up in a ball. He still wore the top. Extending his fingers, he felt her bare back. He lightly ran his fingers up her spine and felt only skin. Tracing the vertebrae down her back, he felt her tailbone, and then his hand brushed her bare buttocks. She was completely naked. And it hadn't been a dream. She had taken him. He didn't even know how to feel about it. And then he realized his hand was still on her butt. He paused for a moment and considered removing it out of respect, but then he remembered what she had just done to him, so he cupped her left cheek in his hand. She stirred.

"Um, Tyler?" she mumbled.

"Yeah, hun?"

"Why is your hand on my ass?"

"The better question is why is your ass bare."

He felt her jolt, and then she patted herself down. Panicked, she asked, "Where are my clothes? Oh my God, what did you do? Please tell me you didn't."

"Oh, I didn't."

"Then why am I…"

"Because *you* did."

"Huh?"

"You don't remember?"

"No."

Tyler grabbed her hand and guided it between her legs.

"OH! Holy shit!"

"Yup."

"Did we?"

"Sort of."

Tabitha sat up straight in the bed. "What do you mean, 'sort of'?"

"I thought I was dreaming, but it turns out I wasn't. I woke up with you riding me. And it was all about you."

"Oh, no. This is terrible."

"Thanks for the ego boost," he replied sarcastically.

Tabitha flicked on the lamp, on her side of the bed, and pulled the covers up over her breasts.

"You don't understand, Tyler. This is worse than you could ever imagine."

"Still hurtful."

"It's not that I don't want to have sex with you. If I could have, I would have, from the day I met you."

"Yeah, yeah, but we weren't married."

"Exactly."

"Yet tonight, that didn't matter to you."

"This wasn't me. I don't know what happened. I'm so sorry!"

"Don't be." Tyler blushed. "It was actually kind of hot."

"That's not helping!"

"I'm not sure what to say besides there's no going back. We might as well do it again, so maybe this time *I* can enjoy it too!"

"Really, Ty? That's your way of dealing with this? Suggesting we do it again?"

Tyler looked at the clock. "It's 1:23 a.m. It's our wedding day."

"Semantics."

"Okay, Tabby. What do you want me to say? It happened. I didn't do it. I'm not sure how to make this better for you. Frankly, I'm not even sure why you're making such a big deal of this."

"You wouldn't understand."

"Then explain—"

Tabitha's cell phone started ringing. She glanced at the display and her shoulders slumped.

"Oh, shit."

"Who is it?"

"My boss."

"Today? Now?"

"It's gotta be urgent or she wouldn't be calling right now. I have to get this."

Tyler just watched, his right hand rubbing the back of his neck.

"Hello?…Hi, Ivy. What can I do for you?…You do know it's the middle of the night, right?…I didn't say you were stupid…Can it wait?…We've got so much going on today, and we're leaving for a trip…It's not what you think…Okay…Yes…I understand…Hopefully we can make it quick…Okay, see you in thirty minutes."

Tabitha clicked off the phone.

"You're going to work now? In the middle of the night?"

"There's a huge issue with one of our accounts, and I need to fix something before we take off. I promise it won't take long."

"Why don't we swing by there in the morning? Before the ceremony?"

"You heard me ask if it could wait, right?"

"Yes. But—"

"But my boss is a hardass. If I don't go in, I'll be in deep shit. Just go back to sleep, Tyler. I'll be back before you know it."

"Doesn't sound like I have a choice."

"Neither do I."

"Fine. Go. Just be safe."

CHAPTER SEVEN

A NOISE IN the other room brought Tyler partially out of his slumber. The front door. Tabby was home. He let himself slip back into the inky murk of sleep, knowing she would join him in a few minutes. Fifteen minutes later, he stirred and reached for her on her side of the bed. It was still empty. Maybe he had imagined her coming home.

"Tabby?" he called, weakly.

"I'm here," she whispered, her voice wavering. She was standing at the foot of the bed.

He was alert now. "You okay?"

"No. Not really."

"What's going on? Come lay down and talk to me."

The room remained silent. He could barely make out her silhouette in the shadows. She remained at the foot of the bed. Tyler reached for the lamp switch, and the room became washed in the soft light. Startled, his breath caught in his throat and an involuntary whimper escaped.

She stood, naked, at the foot of the bed, her right hand behind her back.

"Why are you naked?"

She shook her head.

"Tab? What's going on?"

She stared at him, moisture forming in the corner of her eyes.

"You're scaring me, damnit!"

"Blood," she finally said.

"What about blood?"

"I have to keep it off my clothes."

Tyler's eyes widened, and a shriek tore from his throat when she brought her right hand from behind her back. It no longer resembled a hand. He thought of talons, but there were ten of them, about six inches long, a dark red hue at the bottom, tapering to a bright white at the tips.

Tyler scooted back against the headboard and pulled the covers up to his chin, his eyes wide.

"What the fuck, Tabitha? What is that? What are you?"

"I'm so sorry."

"Sorry? What's going on?" His voice was two octaves too high.

"I told you we had to wait."

"But we didn't."

"No, we didn't, and unfortunately, the bosses didn't like that."

"What the fuck does your boss have to do with this?"

"I'm really sorry," she repeated, moving toward the bed, the talons extended.

"STOP!" Tyler yelled, holding his hand up, as if the motion had the power to keep her at bay. "Are you going to kill me?"

Tabitha hesitated. "I don't want to."

"Then why would you?"

"It's the way things are."

"For my brains?" he asked, throwing caution to the wind.

Tabitha's posture buckled. "Brains?"

Tyler nodded.

"How did you know?"

"I'm a fairly smart guy."

"Which·is why we're in this predicament."

"Huh?"

"It's your brains that made you a target."

"What are you?" Tyler asked.

Tabitha shook her head again. "We need people like you."

"Who is we?"

Again, she shook her head.

"What is going on, Tabitha?"

"There's a reason I would not have sex with you. By doing so, I would be sealing your fate."

"How? I don't understand."

"It's what my species does."

"Your species? What are you?"

"Not human."

"Are you kidding me? I was going to marry you. And you aren't even fucking human?"

"No, but I am more loving than most humans."

"But you're going to kill me anyway?"

"I have to."

"Why?"

"It's why we came to earth. To harvest the smartest minds and take them back to our planet, to help repair our environment. Our planet is dying. In our culture, when we sleep with a man, he must die. The collection of brains is a fairly new development."

"So, you were using me this entire time?"

"No. I tried to stop it. I didn't have sex with you, because I love you. I wanted us to be together."

"But it's inevitable that we would have had sex sometime. What then?"

"Anyone we marry is exempt. You would have been spared. That's why we needed to wait."

"Why me?"

"Don't you get it? You are one of the smartest men on the planet. Have you ever checked your IQ? Probably what you call Mensa. We need experts in the fields of medical, engineering, metaphysics, science, and information technology, amongst other areas. I was sent for you. I was supposed to get your brain months ago. I kept stalling, telling them you wouldn't sleep with me. They kept telling me to try harder. They caught wind of our wedding. They controlled me last night while I was sleeping. They made me have sex with you. Then they summoned me to make sure I understood the repercussions if I didn't kill you, get your brain, and get back to the ship."

"Ship? You mean like a boat, right? You can't possibly mean…"

"I said no. They threatened me…told me that if I didn't carry out my mission, they would kill me in front of you and then kill you."

Tyler stared at her, unable to speak. Finally, the words found their way from his lips.

"So, what are you going to do?"

"What I have to."

"I'm going to die?"

"Not if I can help it."

"How can you stop this? If you don't kill me, we'll both be dead."

Her mind made up, Tabitha held out her hand, which was no longer a set of talons.

"Get dressed. There is much to do."

WITHIN FIVE MINUTES, they were in the car and exiting the parking structure.

"I hate to ask this, but how do I know you aren't taking me to them?"

Tabitha glanced over at Tyler, who was driving. His face was partially illuminated by the dash lighting.

"If I wanted you dead, you'd already be dead."

"But aren't you putting yourself at risk?"

"Yes."

"While I'm grateful, I don't want anything to happen to you. Although, I'm going to be honest, I don't know what the fuck to think right now or how to feel. Everything I thought I knew was wrong. Everything we had seems like a sham."

"I am so sorry I deceived you, Tyler. It was never my intention. You were strictly a job at first. And then you weren't. Everything changed for me in that instant, and I've been trying to figure out how to deal with it ever since."

He turned and looked at her. "Do you truly love me?"

"I meant everything I said. I still do," she said.

"I'm confused. The you I thought I knew doesn't exist. I don't even know if this is what you look like." The thought immediately registered with him, and he blinked several times, his mouth hanging open. Finally, he spoke again. "Is *this* what you really look like?"

Tabitha looked down at her knees. "No," she whispered.

"Show me your true form."

"It's not that simple."

"I have to know."

"We really don't have a true form."

"I don't understand."

"We've always just adapted to whatever life form we are around, which has been thousands over the years. It's not like you see in the movies where an alien mimics a human but later turns back into their true alien form. We don't have any such form we revert to. I will look like this until we encounter a different species and I adapt my form to be like theirs. Although this isn't what I've always looked like, it's what I look like as a human being."

Tyler drove in silence as he digested everything she said. Finally, he spoke. "So, have you ever been hideous in any of your forms? Like, was I supposed to marry the creature from the black lagoon who is hiding in a gorgeous skin suit?"

"Please," she said, letting out a soft laugh. "I'm not sure of the reference, but I can tell you I'm no creature, and I'm far from hideous. My human form is representative of the being I am, inside and out."

"Good to know." He pointed to the road in front of them. "Do you want to tell me where we are going?"

"Just keep driving. I'm trying to figure that out."

"Why don't we just head to the airport and hop a plane to somewhere far away, where they can't find us?"

"Unfortunately, that's nowhere. You know how the victims have been from all over the globe? The ship can travel to anywhere on this planet within minutes. When they identify a new donor, they travel there, drop off another being like me, and they do what they need to do. Apparently, I'm the only one who can't follow directives."

"I have to say, I'm pretty happy about that. Anyway, what about going into hiding?"

"Also impossible. The mothership can track all Brielle…that's what our species is called. They always know where we are. It's sort of like your GPS."

"Then it sounds like we're screwed," he said numbly.

When Tabitha didn't respond, Tyler looked over at the passenger seat.

"You okay?"

"Yeah. I just had an idea."

"Care to share?"

"No time. Just keep driving around until I can nail down a location." She started entering information into her iPhone.

"Is whatever you're thinking going to work?"

Tabitha looked at him. "God, I hope so."

CHAPTER EIGHT

TABITHA AND TYLER walked out of the little bungalow on Bosworth Street in Miraloma Park. They turned around to say goodbye to the man that hung back just inside the doorway, and then Tabitha approached him and wrapped her arms around him, giving him a big hug.

Back at the car, they climbed inside and Tyler started it.

"Where now?"

"I think we need to go into the belly of the beast," she said.

"You mean…"

"Yes. They won't stop looking for us. Maybe we just need to go to them. Maybe we can talk our way out of this."

Tyler glanced at her. "How confident are you that they will listen?"

"Seventeen percent."

"That's it? So you feel there is an eighty-three percent chance that we may die?" he asked, incredulously.

"At least one of us. Maybe both of us."

"And I suppose *I'm* the 'one of us' you're talking about?"

"Sadly, yes, but I wouldn't take you there if I felt there was any other way."

"Even though you're at seventeen percent?"

"Even though."

"Gee, thanks. I'm not feeling good about the odds."

"Unfortunately, they're the best odds we have. If they track us down, they won't even listen to what I have to say."

"You realize I'm putting my life in your hands, right?"

"I do. And I will do everything in my power not to let you

down."

Tyler sighed. "Is this what they mean by 'til death do us part?'"

"Try to stay positive."

"I'm trying. Anyway, where do I drive to? I can't sit here all night."

"Just move. Anywhere is fine. I will text my boss and let her know I need to see her. She'll tell us where to go. The ship is constantly moving."

"Where do they…park it? Is that the right word? Maybe land it? Does it have an invisibility cloak to keep people from seeing it?"

Tabitha looked up from her phone after sending off the text. "You've seen way too many movies."

"I'm not sure I have anything else to make assumptions off of."

"They don't bring it down into the atmosphere. Basically, they stay out of sight."

"Then how do your people get from the ship to earth?"

"We transport."

"Like in *Star Trek?*"

"Again, you and your movies and television. But I guess it's kind of like that—not with us breaking into particles and rematerializing, but more like we just appear. Obviously, we try to do so in unoccupied areas."

Tabitha's phone chimed. She pulled up the message.

"She's telling me to go back to the parking garage of the apartment and wait in the car."

"Does she know I'm with you?"

"Yeah. She said to bring you too."

"What do you want to do?"

"Follow her instructions."

"We're fucked."

Back at the complex, Tyler opened the automatic gate and pulled into the parking garage, parking in his designated space.

"What am *I* supposed to do?" he asked.

"Just follow my lead."

They sat in silence, craning their necks around, watching for someone to materialize, trying to trace down every stray noise.

Tabitha's car door was yanked open without warning, and when Tyler whipped his head around, he saw another beautiful woman standing there, this one a redhead.

"Get out," the redhead demanded, her tone low and serious.

Tabitha glanced over at Tyler, nodded, and got out of the car. He followed suit.

"You are in some serious shit. We're all going onboard." She glanced over at Tyler. "Him too."

"I can explain..." Tabitha said.

"Save it for now. The others will want to hear what you have to say."

"This wasn't her fault," Tyler piped in.

The redhead turned toward him. "You're the last person who should be talking right now. You're merely an asset."

Tyler tried to say something and found his voice was silent. He could not speak.

The lights in the garage suddenly darkened, and Tyler could barely make out the two women's faces by the glow of the red "exit" lighting. Seconds later, it was replaced by a glowing, purplish hue that seemed to come from everywhere and nowhere at all. The color twisted through the blackness, the light bright enough to cause him to squint. Then he saw the silhouettes of two figures filter through the glow, and the area they were in brightened.

Tyler looked around, not able to ascertain where they were. The walls appeared to be in flux, not really solid, yet they appeared to maintain their flatness. They were blank, no markings, no equipment or fixtures. The room, if you could call it that, was enormous, and he could not make out a ceiling. It was more like a chamber of some sort. The two figures stood before him, human shaped, androgynous, wearing white jumpsuits.

"Is this the one?" Jumpsuit One asked.

"Yes," the redhead, Ivy, said.

Jumpsuit Two remained silent, standing stiff, as if on watch.

"You did not follow your directive. You have proven yourself a liability," Jumpsuit One said. It stared at Tabitha.

Tyler looked from Tabitha, to Ivy, to the jumpsuits, his voice still unable to emit sound. Unsure of what to do, he watched.

"This one is different," Tabitha said.

"Do you really think you are the first one to fall for an asset?" Jumpsuit One asked. "It has happened before. Those who violated their directives were dealt with swiftly."

"This is on me. Let him go."

"Are you forgetting your mission? He is one of the brightest minds on this planet. We need him to fix our own. Whether or not you followed your directive, he is still an asset we need, and now that he is here, we will take care of what you should have done months ago."

Tyler tried to take a step forward, but his movements were instantly locked, as if an invisible hand held him in place. With no voice and no power to move, he blinked his eyes and watched the scene unravel.

"I'm not forgetting the mission. I'm telling you, this one is better for us alive. Don't you dare lay a hand on him."

Ivy jumped back into the conversation. "We spoke many times during your mission. While the others were carrying out their directives, you had nothing but excuses about how you had to wait…how he would not have sex with you. I mean, look at you. How could you adopt a look like that and not be able to get the asset to fuck you? What happened to you? You used to be one of our best."

"I still am. But things have changed."

"What's changed is you've gone soft," Ivy said. "I should have pulled you off of this detail months ago and took care of it myself." She walked over to Tyler and lifted his chin with her right pointer finger. "I bet you would have tapped this ass," she said, turning her body sideways and smacking herself on the rear. "I would have had you in the sack, and then had your brain in Rapto-plasm, before your body turned cold." She looked him in the eyes.

"And you would have thanked me for it."

"He wouldn't want you. He's got me."

"Well, congratulations on prolonging his death," Jumpsuit One said, "but we're out of time. Our planet won't last more than another couple of years at this rate." Turning to Jumpsuit Two, it said, "Strip him and get him ready for Ivy."

Ivy smiled and turned toward Tabitha. "Looks like I get him after all. You lose."

Jumpsuit Two grabbed Tyler and pulled him down on a couch that seemed to materialize out of the floor. Reaching for the button on Tyler's jeans, it unbuttoned them and started pulling them off, Ivy watching in delight as she licked her lips.

Tabitha moved so quickly that Ivy had no time to prepare for the collision. Tabitha smashed into her so hard that the momentum bowled Jumpsuit Two off its feet as well. As Tabitha was getting to her feet to go to Tyler, an arm wrapped around her neck and put her in a chokehold.

"Enough of this little circus," Jumpsuit One said, pulling its arm tighter against Tabitha's throat. "We don't have time to deal with this. We will take his brain, but you must be dealt with as well. I wasn't quite sure what to do with you, but you just sealed your own fate. You're a liability. You must be exterminated."

Still unable to move, Tyler watched in horror as the being's pointer finger turned into a talon-like blade, blood red with a white tip. Just as the tip pierced the flesh of Tabitha's neck, a loud shout reverberated through the chamber.

"STOP!"

All activity in the chamber halted, and all eyes turned toward the figure that floated into the room, seemingly from nowhere. It's hair was pure white, the face wrinkled beyond what any living being's should be. It wore a red robe with gold ropes around its neck that ended in tassels.

"EXPLAIN," the voice bellowed.

"She has not followed her directive. She has turned against us. She must perish," Jumpsuit One said nervously.

"BY WHOSE AUTHORITY?"

"M...mine," Jumpsuit One stuttered.

"YOU FEEL ONE OF OUR OWN MUST DIE?"

"Yes, Jandor."

"VERY WELL."

Jandor outstretched a hand, fingers lifted into the air. Jumpsuit One levitated off the ground and hung suspended from mid-air.

"DO YOU STILL FEEL ONE MUST DIE?"

"No...no, Jandor. Please. No."

"TOO LATE."

Jandor contorted the fingers on its right hand, and Jumpsuit One started to glow. Tyler had to look away as the light was blinding. The body shriveled up into a ball the size of a walnut, dimmed, grew bright again, and then exploded into particles of dust that showered the room. Tyler clamped his eyes and mouth shut and turned his head.

"ANYONE ELSE FEEL SHE SHOULD DIE?" Jandor looked at Tabitha and then glared at Ivy. Ivy rapidly shook her head.

"Come here, my child," Jandor summoned, the rumbling of the voice now gone, replaced by a more subdued whisper.

Tabitha approached Jandor.

"You have broken your covenant."

"Yes, Jandor," Tabitha said meekly.

"You shall not die, but you will no longer be able to work on this mission. You shall return home and work in the labs."

Tabitha nodded. "And him?" She glanced over at Tyler.

"Nothing has changed. We need his brain. He must be sacrificed for the good of our planet."

"Please, Jandor. He is better for us alive."

"It cannot be so, my child. Are you forgetting you slept with him? It is our way."

"Jandor, it is also our way that they will be spared if we marry them."

271

"But you never married him. You slept with him the night before you were supposed to. I know this, for it is so."

Tabitha lifted her left hand and wiggled her ring finger. "Respectfully, that is incorrect. We got married a couple of hours ago. He is my husband, and you must spare him. I love him."

Jandor was silent, the new information marinating. Then Tabitha heard the words she was dreading. "You were not married at the time you had relations. Therefore, a wedding won't save him." Jandor nodded at Jumpsuit Two, who took Tabitha's arm and held her, the grip like that of a vice. "Ivy, take him to the Fereal chamber. Tell them to move him to the front of production."

Unable to control his body, Tyler watched helplessly as Ivy led him out of the room. He turned toward Tabitha, a tear sliding from his right eye.

"I love you, Tabby. No matter what. Thanks for a great six months."

If Tabitha was capable of crying, she would have as well. "I'm so sorry, Tyler. Please forgive me. I love you too. Thanks for making me your wife." Her voice quavered.

With that, she watched Ivy lead Tyler out of the room, and once he was gone, Jumpsuit Two dragged her from the room.

Back in her quarters, unable to leave, she dry heaved and buried her face in her hands. For a moment, she was human. She had loved and been happy. She had everything she never knew she was missing. And she would spend the next five thousand years regretting the one hundred things she could have done differently.

EPILOGUE

TABITHA ENTERED THE most current findings into the massive computer system in the lab. It had been three months since the incident on the ship. It had taken them two weeks, earth time, to get back to their planet. With the harvesting of minds completed, Earth was of no further use to them. In total, they had gathered forty-seven brains, each suspended in Raptoplasm, and hooked up by nests of intricate wiring to the mainframe.

She thought back to the time she and Tyler had on Earth. It had been perfect. Those memories were something she would cherish for the rest of her life.

A movement from the other side of the lab caught her eye.

"Hey, Tabitha. I was going to grab some lunch. Want to join me?"

"That sounds great, Sasha, but could we do it tomorrow? I'm going home for lunch…maybe take a quick nap."

"Sure thing. Catch you then."

Looking at the clock on the wall, Tabitha took her lab coat off and hung it on the back of the door. She lived five minutes away, and the thought of climbing between the satin sheets and closing her eyes made her feel giddy.

Although homes on her planet were designed very differently from those on earth, she had been able to decorate to make her place resemble Tyler's apartment. It made her feel at home. She smiled as she recalled the memories again. Earth had been more of a home to her than her planet had ever been.

She slid out of her blouse and slacks and left them in a pile on the floor. Her bra and underwear followed, and she slid her smooth body between the equally smooth sheets. She stretched her toes out and propped her head up with her fingers laced behind her hair. Her breathing steadied as she relaxed, thinking about Tyler. Her thoughts were interrupted as the bathroom door opened.

"Been here long?" she asked.

"I just got here a few minutes before you."

"Well? What are you waiting for?"

Tyler eyed the clothes strewn across the bedroom floor and pulled off his robe.

"I love these *lunches* we seem to be having more and more of lately."

"Beats a dry sandwich."

"Seems like a pretty legit diet," he joked. "Skip the food and burn calories instead."

"And to think you made me wait six months! You should have proposed on the first date!"

"Hindsight," he said.

Tyler slipped into bed, and their hands found, and explored, each other. Afterward, wrapped together, they slipped into a sex coma and napped.

Later, the alarm on Tabitha's bedside table went off, and she begrudgingly pulled herself out of bed and slipped into her clothes.

"Wake up, sleepyhead," she teased, playfully kicking him with her foot.

"But I don't wanna go back to work," he grumbled, his voice muffled by the sheets.

"But you have to."

"Give me one good reason why." He blinked a few times and stretched his eyes open.

"Because, if I hadn't broken out of my room, found Jandor, and convinced it that we needed someone with your smarts to run the program, you'd be another brain in a jar. Knowledge is great, but it can only get us so far. If it feels like you weren't the right choice, it might change its mind."

Tyler sat up. "Do you always have to make so much sense? Damn you!"

"It's what I do."

"That, and what you just did…which, by the way, was amazing."

"I figure I have a lot of making up to do. I almost got you killed."

"Why, yes. Yes, you did. You might be making it up to me for the rest of your life."

Tabitha bit her lip and smiled. "I can live with that."

FROM THE RED DIRT

LP Hernandez

EAST OF DUMAS, TEXAS - 1933

I BURIED GRAMPA AS THE SUN WENT DOWN, only he didn't stay that way. Dirt so hard it nearly cracked the shovel. Haven't seen a storm cloud in months; kind of forget the way the land smells after a rain. I just remember I used to like it.

Took most of the afternoon to make the grave deep enough the coyotes couldn't get to him. They're starvin' out here like the rest of us, so I can't say I blame 'em. Daddy gave up buryin' the livestock. Wasn't much to bury anyway and the coyotes were mad with hunger. Had to put bullets in 'em and we don't have many of those left.

But it was different with Grampa.

Daddy left day before yesterday. Walked to town to buy a car so we can join up with the folks headed west. It was all the money we had. Everythin'. A life's work fit inside a coffee can, with room to spare. Maybe Grampa was waitin' for him to leave and died on purpose in his rockin' chair so his son wouldn't have to find him that way. Can't say it's much better his grandson found him.

I might've thought he was asleep or in a deep thought. The chair was rockin' with the wind just so, almost looked like he was pushing himself with the toe of his boot. It was the fly that caught my eye. I saw it crawlin' over the creases in his cheek, went straight into his mouth and he didn't flinch from it. I dropped the hammer I was carryin' and grabbed Grampa by the shoulders, shook him, prolly too hard, and his head snapped back like a broken dandelion.

Mama cried and told me to cover him up before my little sister saw. Said I could take him to the barn since there wasn't animals in there, and Daddy would handle it when he got back. But the flies didn't wait for Daddy. Mama went inside and called Jessie upstairs while I stripped the sheets from Grampa's bed. They was yellow and stank of sweat and tobacco, of whiskey spilled from a slumberin' hand. It was his smell, for better or worse, and whatever had been brewin' in his body, he didn't tell us about. He bruised easy, took a long time to sit or stand. But Grampa always said the Lord would tell him when his work was done. And so he kept workin', even when there wasn't nothin' to work. You can't make nothin' useful of dirt without rain. All you can do is move it from one place to another.

The wind tipped him halfway out of the rockin' chair when I came back to the porch. His mouth was open and there was a whole mess of flies there, dippin' in and out, goin' in dry and comin' out wet. I laid out the sheet and pulled him onto it. No way to be gentle about it and it upset the flies quite a bit. Sounded like a hornet's nest in his chest.

The worst of it was his eyes opened part way. Though I could only see the bottom half, it still felt like he was lookin' at me. Wonder what he would have thought if he could see me, eleven years old with tears in my eyes, Mama singin' a hymn to my sister in the background. I wrapped him the best I could, tyin' a knot in three places so I didn't have to see any part of him.

Grampa wasn't a large man, not that it was possible given our lack of food. But he was still too heavy for me to carry, so I had to pull him. I grabbed him around the ankles and dragged him over the porch floorboards. Then I stood for a time, breathin' hard, thinkin' about how I could get him down four stairs without damagin' him too much. Figured it would be less violent to grab him under his arms, but I couldn't stand the thought of his head restin' against my thigh, even with layers of fabric between us.

His skull thudded off of each step, a sound I'm afraid I will not be able to forget. There wasn't a cloud to block the sun, but off in the distance, in the direction of town, there was a wall of dust the color of old blood. Already, the wind was pickin' up, shootin' little needles of dirt at my neck and face. I pulled Grampa's body over the brittle grass, which crunched under my boots. The wind snaked inside the wrap, fillin' it like a ship's sail. I caught sight of him again, his mouth open with a swarm of flies sippin' whatever moisture was left on his tongue and lips.

The sound of Mama's hymn was eaten by the wind, which had eaten so much of our lives already. I shuffled faster, trippin' over my own boots a few times, tryin' to beat the dust cloud. I'd been caught outside in a dust storm before, and it gets inside your eyes, ears, even in your teeth. Worse, I think some of it got into my spirit. It was like the hopelessness abraded my soul. It killed everythin' we owned, and it was inside of me always.

I made it into the barn with Grampa's body right as the dust hit. Ran back to the house as the world went dark. Mama was asleep with Jessie, both of them snorin' right through the storm. It was just me then, sittin' in the dark with my thoughts, listenin' to the wind tear apart our family's livelihood. Kind of sounded like the ocean from a distance, though I'd only been to the coast once in my life and was probably too young to remember it.

A FEW HOURS later, the sheet, once white then yellow from Grampa's sweat, was a whole different color. Black. It was black with flies desperate to find a respite from the dust and wind. The hollow over his open mouth rippled from the inside, and I knew I could not wait for Daddy. It was an ugly sight and would get worse overnight, when there was more stirrin' than just flies. I found a spot under the dead oak tree, with the low branches I used to play on, and started diggin'. Didn't ask permission, just knew it had to be done. We could speak the words and make a marker for him after he was in the ground.

Mama saw me through the kitchen window, came out with a glass of water. She looked at the hole, about a foot deep then, and cried a bit.

"It's bad, Mama. Just keep Jessie inside."

The sun felt like a hot coal held just above my neck. The skin of my hands broke, old blisters torn open, but I heard the coyotes in the tall grass. They caught the scent of Grampa's death. I wasn't afraid of even half a dozen mangy coyotes, just one rabid one. So, I kept diggin'.

I pulled Grampa and his new cloak of flies out of the barn and dragged him back over the broken earth. The flies sought the leakin' blisters on my hands and I wanted to scream but didn't have the strength. The sun was settin' then, the coyotes in a frenzy in the field. We didn't have a dog left to chase 'em off. The last dog, Buster, ran away, Daddy said, but there was also meat in the stew that night for the first time in months.

I rolled Grampa into the grave, couldn't bring myself to arrange his body in any specific way, and just started shovelin' dirt. I did see an arm was loose of the wrap, a liver-spotted hand quickly covered with the red dirt that defined so much of his life. When it was done, and my body felt like it had been trampled to just before dyin', I ripped a few big stones from the ground and placed them atop Grampa's grave. Maybe, I thought, it would keep the coyotes busy.

I slept on the floor beside the fireplace. The stairs might as well have been a mountain. I fell asleep with coyote songs in my ears.

Don't remember dreamin'; prolly too tired.

I just remember the sound of Grampa's rockin' chair when I woke, thinkin' it must've been the wind again. Only it wasn't.

JESSIE SCREAMED, AND that woke me up the rest of the way. I ran with pins and needles in my toes to the porch. She was already gone. I heard her footsteps goin' up the stairs while Mama asked her what was wrong.

There he was, back in his chair. He wore the same overalls and the same boots as the day before. Everythin' was caked in red dirt, like it was his second skin. His head was downcast so I couldn't see his eyes.

"G-G-Grampa?" I said, halfway out the door and thinkin' about goin' back in for Daddy's rifle.

The chair moved a bit, and this time it wasn't the wind. When he lifted his head, I had to hold my hand over my mouth to keep from screamin' and felt the floor beneath my feet shift like sand. His mouth opened to speak, but only flies came out, a cloud of 'em like the puff of smoke from a train. After the flies came the soil, mostly dry and clotted, the red dirt I buried him in. My heart felt like it didn't know if it wanted to beat fast or slow, like it could go either way.

"Grampa?"

He looked at me with those dead eyes, flies expelled from his stomach, clusterin' there to lap at the moisture.

"Got…to…get ready," he said with a voice like two corn-husks rubbin' together.

He got up from his seat then and retraced the boot prints he left on the porch. There was a cigarette in his right hand, unlit, the kind he rolled himself. It was stained with the same red dirt as the rest of him. My stomach twisted when I noticed the denim around his rear was wet, and the greatest number of flies was congregatin' there. He descended the stairs like a baby learnin' its first steps, wobbly at the knees.

I didn't have a thought left. I just watched him walk away, in the direction of the barn. With our livestock dead or sold, there wasn't any work left to do, just shorin' up the house against the dust, 'til we could leave all of it behind. But that was where he headed. Think he even whistled, or tried to. Prolly couldn't because of the flies.

"What happened?" Mama asked, eyes like a barn owl.

She pinched her robe closed, worry lines carved deep into her face.

"Grampa came back."

"What?"

"He was dead. You saw it. He was dead. Had flies in his eyes and in his mouth. I-I buried him, put stones over the soil. And he's back."

"No. No. That can't be."

"It is."

We both watched as he opened the barn door and disappeared within, door closin' part way behind him.

"He came back?"

I turned to her and noticed how the shadows scarred her face. She was holdin' on by a thread. For two years, she watched the farm collapse into piles of red dirt, watched her husband bend in half from the pressure of keepin' the family together. She smiled when there wasn't cause for it, reassured me and Jessie when there was no real hope, just the memory of it. But even the strongest steel will bend under enough pressure.

"It's like the stories at church, Mama," I said.

"Church?"

"How Jesus died and came back. Remember?"

She looked off into the distance, prolly recallin' Sunday school lessons from her childhood. I didn't believe in the stories, myself, especially because of all the sufferin' God let happen to us and everyone else in the county. But it was enough for Mama, in that moment, to push her back from the brink of whatever madness she was about to dive into.

"Yes, like Jesus. I remember."

She nodded and smiled, her eyes cloudy like they was lookin' at somethin' I couldn't see.

"Take care of Jessie, okay?" I said.

She ducked back inside the house and within a few moments I heard the sound of pans clatterin'. Don't know what she could be doin' with 'em as we ain't had nothin' to cook in a pan in a long time, just beans in the pot when we can get 'em.

Used to be dew on the grass in the mornin'. Not anymore. It's just as stiff as in the daytime, after it's been cookin' under the sun. I followed the broken grass and remnants of Grampa's boot prints. What could he be doin' in the barn? There wasn't a hog to slaughter, no horse hooves to grind. All of it was gone, just the smells left behind.

There wasn't a quiet way to approach. The grass cracked and popped under my weight, like static on the radio before Daddy sold it. I grabbed the handle to slide the barn door open; barely an hour past sunrise and it burned like a hot kettle from the sun. I pulled a bit of my shirt loose of my overalls and wrapped it around my hand but still felt the heat through it.

He was standin' ten feet in front of me, facin' the other way, which was good. There was a sound of metal clankin' together as he rifled through the box of tools.

"Grampa? What are you doin'?"

It was the last question I wanted answered, but I couldn't think of a better one. How are you standing there? Aren't you dead? Those were closer to the mark, but no one teaches an eleven-year-old boy how to talk to a dead man.

"Gotta...get...ready."

"Get ready for what?"

The question hung in the air between us. Maybe it couldn't penetrate the soil still cloggin' his ears. In the absence of his speakin', there was just the sound of flies. Again, they grouped around the wet places. I'd seen plenty of dead things in my life. A calf that wandered too far from its mama and too close to a coyote that was hidin' in the grass. Doesn't take long for carrion to rot in the Texas heat. When it does, all those juices gotta go somewhere. I swallowed, but my tongue was dry as leather, as I thought about what might be goin' on inside Grampa's body.

More metal clangin' and I turned away, closed the barn door, leavin' him mostly in darkness. I didn't know what to do, not that a boy my age would have any idea. The Youngs family lived down the road two miles or so, if they hadn't left for California since the last time we spoke. They had only crops, no livestock, so when the rain stopped and the dust took its place, they had nothin' to sell. We shared what little we had, but it wasn't enough for a family to live on. Still, Mr. Youngs was a man and he would know better than me what to do.

The air outside the house smelled of somethin' cookin' and my stomach, which was pretty good at stayin' quiet, started rumblin'. I dashed up the steps, forgettin' Grampa for the moment.

Jessie sat at the table, all big-eyed with a fork in one hand and a knife in the other. There was a sizzlin' sound at the stove, where Mama tended to a skillet with her wooden spoon.

"What is it?" I asked.

"Mama's makin' breakfast!" Jessie said, nearly shoutin'.

Mama turned to me, her mouth and eyes tellin' two different stories.

"It's not much, hon, just some potatoes and a bit of dried meat. Your daddy said to save it for a special day. I, uh, don't know if that applies to today, but I didn't know what else to do."

"It smells great, Mama."

I took a seat beside Jessie and mussed her hair. At six years old, she didn't know a life on the farm that wasn't just sufferin'. She didn't know the dusty fields were once green, that the hay in the barn once had a purpose other than just for playin' on.

"How-how is he?" Mama said.

Jessie spoke before I could answer. "Grampa's all dirty!

Why'd Grampa get himself so dirty?"

"It's just a game, Jess."

"Can I play?"

I shook my head. "I don't think so. I think the game's over, but we can play another."

"Is he…" Mama began.

"I don't know, Mama. I think he needs to be where he come from. Gotta smell about him, and the flies."

Mama nodded. "Not like Jesus then?"

She turned, skillet in hand, smilin' only with her mouth.

"I don't know, Mama."

She scraped potatoes onto my plate. It was the most food I'd seen since Thanksgiving fellowship at church. When Daddy didn't have enough to tithe, we stopped goin', then most everyone left anyway. I forgot about the world while I ate, the salt burnin' my broken lips, but I'd take the pain over hunger any day. Mama had a small plate and took her time eatin', movin' the potatoes around, cuttin' 'em into smaller and smaller pieces to make 'em last. When I heard the creak of the porch steps, I shot up from the chair.

"Upstairs, Jessie," I said.

Before she could get mad or ask why, Mama nodded and led her that way.

"Tell him I love him and I'm sorry. I just can't see him," Mama said over her shoulder.

The doorknob jiggled. I opened it and backed away. Grampa stumbled inside, boots scrapin' over the floorboards. He smelled awful, like the little pond on the property after it dried up and all the fish died. The flies covered his face like a shiftin' beard. He opened his mouth, maybe to speak, but just coughed, sprayin' flies out.

His eyes looked like old milk when it gets that yellow skin on it. They were furry with flies, stuck open 'cause he couldn't blink. He held a wrench in his right hand, the big one Daddy used on the tractor. We didn't have nothin' he could use it on. I wondered if he was just retracin' his steps from life.

Grampa sat at the table, which took some effort. He sniffed Mama's potatoes, but it rattled in his throat when he did. His face and neck were swollen in places, the wrinkled skin stretched taut. There was liquid runnin' out of his ear like rust water. Tears stung my eyes and I turned away. He was like my second daddy. When Daddy was over my left shoulder teachin' me how to do somethin', Grampa was over the right sayin' not to listen to him.

"Grampa, why'd you come back?"

I accepted he was dead. His body was breakin' down in front of me. But I also accepted he was sittin' at the table smellin' Mama's potatoes like he did in life. He didn't look about to speak, so I left him there. Hadn't changed my shirt in days and my neck was grimy from sweat. Figured a wash rag and a new shirt might help me think. Daddy said he wouldn't come back without a car. I knew how much was in the coffee can. It wasn't enough. Maybe someone would take pity on him.

WHEN THE KNOCK came, I thought it was Grampa. I'd heard the chair scrape over the floorboards and the front door open a half hour before. Thought maybe he forgot how to get back inside. The girls were in the kitchen cleanin' the mess from breakfast, and so I ran to answer the knock before Jessie could.

He had backed off the porch and was standin' in the yard in front of the steps.

"Help you, mister?" I said.

He was a weathered man with a scar across his nose, like it was cut off and stitched back together. By his feet was a sack with the handle of a pot stickin' out. His clothes hung on him like he stole 'em from someone half a foot taller. The boots were mismatched and of different sizes. His cap was like the ones kids sellin' newspapers in big cities wore, and it prolly didn't do much to block the sun.

"Man of the house around?" he said.

He looked past me at the front door as Mama peeked through it, Jessie wormin' her way under her arm so she could see.

"In the field. What can I do for you?" I said.

The man glanced to the right and then behind. There wasn't nothin' livin' out that way and his smirk showed that he knew it.

"Just lookin' for work is all. If he's not here…"

There was a railroad a few miles east. On quiet nights I could hear trains thunderin' down the tracks. Sometimes it slowed if there was cattle passin' through. If it slowed enough, some of the tramps that rode the rails would hop off there. It wasn't the first time one came by askin' for work. It was how he didn't look at me, how he pinned his black overcoat to his body with one hand, like he was afraid of the wind catchin' it and me seein' somethin' I wasn't supposed to. It was the fact he danced around without speakin' it. Daddy was gone. There was no man of the house.

"Like I said, he's out in the field. Had to put an old bull down. Broke its leg."

The man looked down so I would not see him smile.

"Happy to work for supper. If he's plannin' on butcherin' it."

I gritted my teeth. "I'll be sure to tell him."

The man nodded and tipped his cap at Mama.

"Ma'am. Little lady," he said and then turned away, walkin' slow like he was underwater.

I noticed, only when he had disappeared from my line of sight, that my fingernails were carvin' sickle shapes into my palms.

"Is it okay, Joseph?" Mama asked.

I shook my head no.

"Left too quick, I think. If a starvin' man gives up easy, it's cause he's got another plan brewin'. Can you get Daddy's rifle?"

She stepped out of the house and stood beside me, lookin' at the place he disappeared.

"He took it with him."

"What?"

Mama put an arm around my shoulder, and my back stiffened

some. It wasn't a good feelin', not like it had been before.

"He had all of our money, Son. All of it. Couldn't risk losin' it."

There was little strength left in her fingers. She squeezed, tryin' to reassure, but it just reminded me of how broken she was.

"It'll be okay, Mama."

When I lie, I try to do it over important things. Our house, the paint chipped away by blowin' dust, was a gray island in a sea of brown. My first thought was to gather the girls and make a run for the Youngs property. But I had a feelin' the man hadn't gone far, was maybe waitin' just beyond the little rise in the land that met up with the dirt road. Figured it'd be better on a gray island than in a sea, where I couldn't see what was in the water.

I SAW GRAMPA by the dead oak tree. Thought he might jump back in the hole he climbed out of, but he only looked at it. The denim of his overalls was dark, and the right arm was swollen some, bulgin' against the seams of his shirt. I wanted to yell at him to just get in the hole. Had enough to worry about without my dead grampa stumblin' around the property, body balloonin' up in the heat.

I spent the whole afternoon lookin' for weapons in case the tramp came back. I would've traded everythin' in that damn coffee can to have Daddy here, with or without his rifle. The house still smelled of breakfast, but there wasn't anythin' quite so good for supper. One potato split three ways with a bit of broth spiced with the burnt bits of meat she scraped off the skillet. I had the mallet Daddy used to put down cows, but it was too heavy for me to swing. Maybe just the sight of it would be enough.

Jessie chatted while we ate, tellin' us what she thought California might be like. A family from church went that way a few months back and the daughter, who was a year older than Jessie, sent a letter talkin' about strawberries the size of a baby's fist. By the end of the meal, I was hungrier than when it started. But I would never get in the way of Jessie dreamin' out loud. It's just tellin' yourself stories, which we all needed then.

Mama sent Jessie up to get ready for bed. It was still light, but the shadows were stretched out and I could hear coyotes, likely gettin' stirred up from Grampa's death smell.

"What're you gonna do with that, Joseph?" Mama asked, nodding at the mallet.

"Hopefully nothin'. If need be, I'll do like Daddy showed me."

"It's not right. You're just a boy."

"There's no right or wrong about it, Mama. I don't need to kill him. I just need to keep him from gettin' to Jessie. If he makes it past me, that'll be your job."

Mama nodded. She rummaged through a drawer next to the sink and pulled out a knife then dropped it in the pocket of her apron.

"Leave the window open in case you need to jump," I said.

We hugged for a long time. I felt the warmth of her tears soak into my shirt, though I didn't hear her cry.

"It'll be okay, Mama. Maybe Daddy will come drivin' up in a car tonight."

It wasn't a lie. Just tellin' myself a story.

"Maybe so," Mama said.

I PULLED A chair up to the window in the sittin' room. I cracked it a bit and listened to the sounds of the day givin' way to night. Figured I would hear him before I saw him, the grass crunchin' under his mismatched boots. It was so dark at night, even with a half moon and no clouds. From where I sat, all I could see was shadows, and all of 'em looked like the tramp with the stupid hat.

An hour after dark, I had to pinch myself to keep from noddin' off. I got up from the chair and walked around the room, checking the lock on the door at the back of the house. I suppose if I was the tramp, I would likely use that door instead of the one I guarded. I'd wedged a chair under the doorknob, but it wouldn't survive a couple of good kicks.

I imagined how it would go down between the tramp and me. I'd hold the mallet with one hand up near the head of it and the other grippin' the handle. If I could jab it at his stomach, I could stun him, knock the air out of his lungs. After that I didn't know. Couldn't do much else with the mallet that wouldn't haunt me for the rest of my life.

I snapped my eyes open, only then realizin' I'd drifted into a dream. My chin rested on my forearms and a bit of drool was leakin' out the side of my mouth. Why was I awake? Some sound I heard on the edge of the dream, but it planted itself in that part of my mind, and I couldn't recall it.

My eyes adjusted to the dark some, enough so I could tell the shapes apart. I put my ear next to the openin' and listened for the sound to come again. It did after a few seconds, voices. Not one voice. Voices.

I stood up, mallet in hand. Felt impossible to wield, like I was a kid playin' knight with a man's sword.

"Your daddy cut up that bull?" the tramp said, not hidin' anymore.

I didn't know what to say. Maybe I could make my voice deeper, but I don't think it would fool him.

He laughed. "I didn't think so. I think your daddy is dead or gone away. That makes you the man of the house now. Isn't that right?"

I opened my mouth but didn't have any words ready.

"Oh, come on. I can see you in there. Holdin' somethin', it looks like." .

I gripped the mallet tighter.

"Hope it's bulletproof."

Some of the strength bled out of my legs.

"Now I know you ain't got much. Barely got four walls and a roof. Wouldn't be worth it to rob you. What if I just take shelter for the night? Think your mama would mind the company?"

"Go to hell!" I yelled.

"Ha, ha! There he is!"

There was a sound of the doorknob rattlin' behind me.

"Sorry, brought a friend with me. Hope that's okay. That's Long Jake back there. Don't know how he got the nickname. He ain't exactly tall. Gotta nasty case of syphilis, though. Maybe Long is referrin' to somethin' else," the tramp said, laughing again.

The door shuddered from an impact.

"And if I'm keepin' your mama company, I guess Long Jake will have to make do with the little lady."

The door shuddered again.

"Well, that's rude of me, isn't it? I can see you, but you can't see me? You know, it's awful dark in there. Care for a little light?"

There was a brief spark and then the flame grew. He stood off to the side of the porch steps some, holdin' a bottle up near his face, a burnin' rag hangin' out of it.

"Think I could make it through that open window up there?"

He held the bottle back like he was gonna throw it.

"No!" I yelled.

I ran to the front door and grabbed the knob, not really thinkin' about it. I unlocked it but didn't open it. It was what he wanted. He wanted me to come out. The back door rattled again, the wood soundin' like it was splinterin' some. I couldn't fight 'em both off, maybe not at all, and definitely not runnin' from one to the other.

"Fire's gettin' hot over here, young man," the tramp said.

The door behind shook, chair bucklin'. Then it went quiet for a moment. Felt like a long time but probably wasn't. Then a scream. Thought Long Jake might be gettin' ready to bust through, but it wasn't that kind of scream. I backed away from the front door and took a couple steps toward the other man. Another scream and I started runnin'.

The tramps was fightin' behind the house. No idea why, but it was the best I could hope for. I kicked aside the broken chair and pressed my nose to the window. It wasn't the tramp. I opened the door and stepped outside. My eyes adjusted some, not enough to see color, but one man was on the ground with his hand up, the other standin' over him.

"Grampa?" I said.

"N-n-no!" the other man yelled, scootin' backwards.

The smell hit me then and it felt like my stomach flipped upside down. I covered my mouth, but the smell changed the taste on my tongue to somethin' rotten. Grampa lifted the wrench with his left hand. In life, he was right-handed, but the right arm was swole like it was about to pop. He brought the wrench down, not fast but it was heavy. The man on the ground seemed injured already, and he hid behind his arm instead of deflectin' the blow. The wrench caught him in the teeth, and the next scream was choked with blood.

I just stood there, not knowin' what to do. Long Jake coughed blood and prolly any teeth he had left. He was lookin' at the blood spillin' on his chest and not at the wrench Grampa held above his head.

Two quick explosions. The wrench fell out of Grampa's hand. The tramp with the stupid hat was standin' about ten feet away. Didn't bring the fire with him.

"Grampa!"

I ran a few steps toward him, but the odor drove me back. Grampa looked at his belly, touched it with his fingers. The smell of gun smoke mixed with the stench of rot. I dropped to my knees and vomited my supper.

Click

Click

The tramp flipped his gun around so that the grip was facin' out. He walked toward Grampa, and I realized I couldn't lift the mallet. My hands felt like they wasn't mine anymore, like I couldn't control 'em. I was about to watch Grampa die for a second time.

"Guess you wasn't lyin' about your daddy. What the fuck is wrong with him? Smells worse than pig shit."

The tramp reared back at the same time Grampa turned to face him. I couldn't see Grampa well in the dark, just the shape of him, but the tramp saw him just fine.

"W-what? W-what the fuck?"

He took a step back as Grampa came toward him. The tramp tripped, stumblin' backwards, gun slippin' from his fingers. Grampa stood over him. He touched his belly, probed the exit wound with his fingers.

"What the fuck?" the tramp said again, boots comin' free as he scooted.

Grampa's hand came loose of his stomach with a wet, suckin' sound. Looked like he had a mound of mashed potatoes in his hand, but they was black and the smell got worse real quick. Grampa collapsed onto the tramp, who wouldn't stop screamin'. He beat Grampa in the head with open palms, but I doubt Grampa could feel it. Long Jake was sittin' upright, touchin' the ruins of his mouth.

The tramp found his gun and prolly was about to use it. He opened his mouth to scream, but it ended quick, as Grampa shoved the handful of whatever he pulled out of his stomach into the tramp's mouth. Grampa pinched the tramp's nostrils and hovered just over him. The tramp gurgled and thrashed, suckin' the rotten entrails into his lungs. Grampa's face was just a couple inches from the tramp's. Then they was connected by a black stream of clotted flies and filth, as more of what was rotten in his belly was expelled, fillin' the tramp's mouth.

Long Jake was standin'. He looked at the wrench and then at Grampa. Couldn't see his eyes in the dark. Couldn't guess what he was thinkin', jaw hangin' onto the skull by sinew, his buddy chokin' to death just a few feet from him. He didn't look at me. He didn't look at the house. He walked into the tall, dry grass, trailin' blood.

The tramp's arm was movin', but his legs was still. He wasn't fightin' anymore, just wavin' his hand like shooin' a fly. Plenty of those around him. That stopped after a few seconds, and then it was quiet again. Three souls and I was the only one breathin'.

Coyote yaps came soon after from the tall, dry grass. A couple more screams, not a whole lot behind 'em.

"Grampa?" I said.

I couldn't bring myself to touch him, to come any closer. I could still smell him.

I didn't even thank him as he stood, the river of gore between his mouth and the dead tramp's snappin'. He walked forward, into the night, in the direction of the dead oak tree. To the red dirt that defined so much of his life.

I called to him again, but he didn't turn back. His head was angled at the sky listenin' to somethin' I couldn't hear, the Lord I imagine, tellin' him his work was done.

No coyote songs that night. They was too busy eatin'. When I woke the next mornin', there wasn't a whole lot left to bury.

MAMA AND ME didn't tell Daddy the truth of what happened, not the whole truth. Even the part about the tramps nearly broke him, and there's only so many times you can break a man before he can't right himself. Grampa was a hero. Took down two thugs with just a wrench, sacrificin' himself in the process. Daddy didn't need to know the other part, about how Grampa came back. It made it harder to leave, though, knowin' Grampa was in the dirt we put in the rearview mirror of Daddy's Ford. I just hoped he'd stay there.

THE SHOW MUST GO ON

Bridgett Nelson

We are each our own devil, and we make this world our hell.
—Oscar Wilde, "The Duchess of Padua"

PROLOGUE

1949, Manhattan

LANA SUNK WEARILY INTO THE RATTY, wine-colored couch in her dressing room and slipped off the black torture devices surrounding her dainty feet. She wasn't sure how a human foot was supposed to fit comfortably into those pointy-toed monstrosities; they'd probably give her the same unsightly bunions that had disfigured her roommate's feet—bunions caused by her many years en pointe in the corps de ballet with the American Ballet Theater.

As she gently rubbed away the soreness, one by one, her fellow chorus girls leaned into the room to tell her goodnight. Lana knew she needed to head home, too, but she was in no rush to get back to the dump where she lived in the Bronx. Though she genuinely liked her two roommates, the apartment itself was full of mold and the temperature never seemed to go above fifty-eight degrees in the winter, despite the constant rumbling of the antiquated furnace. It was so small—six hundred square feet—the trio of young women were forced to separate the living room into three, jail cell-like bedrooms, using stained sheets as room dividers. Bringing a lover home was awkward, to say the least. Unfortunately, it was all she could afford, even splitting the monthly rent three ways. Being a chorus girl in a Broadway production, even a popular show, didn't pay much money. But someday soon...

Exhausted after two very strenuous performances, a matinee earlier in the afternoon and another that evening, Lana rested her head on the back of the couch and closed her eyes. Immediately, her thoughts strayed to the dead girls.

She'd never had a choice. Not really. The entertainment industry was cut-throat. If she was ever going to become a Broadway leading lady, she had to take out the competition. And she did. Deciding to start small, Lana befriended Jean, an actress with a modest but pivotal role in the production. She didn't want to attract unnecessary attention and figured an up-and-coming actress's death was less likely to garner intense scrutiny than that of a full-fledged star.

Lana became close to the petite brunette by faking enthusiasm for Jean's love of jazz music. The two women spent many hours together at the Birdland Jazz Club, which was located just north of West 52nd Street in Manhattan. By the time she finally killed Jean, Lana was beyond tired of the cobalt blue and white (complete with dreadful, dangling gold fringe) décor of the bar. Determined to put this poor, deluded woman—whose taste in music was questionable, at best—out of her misery, Lana had spent an entire morning alone, in her grimy kitchenette, whipping up different varieties of cookies. But her cookies contained that little something special—rat poison. Every tenant in her rodent-infested building kept the toxic powder on hand, so she had no trouble finding what she needed. Once the cookies had finished baking, she placed them in a pretty, white wicker basket and left them at Jean's front door; then she went on her merry way. Jean's body was discovered by her mother the very next day. If the theater gossip was true—and in Lana's experience, it always was—Jean had died on her kitchen floor with bloody froth oozing from her mouth.

Lana wasn't selected for Jean's role.

After licking her emotional wounds for several weeks, while also waiting for the drama surrounding Jean's unexpected death to die down, Lana then focused her attention on Marlene. Marlene was a marginally famous singer and actress whose role in the play was just as crucial as Jean's, but bigger and better.

The entire cast knew of Marlene's penchant for women; her lesbianism was the worst-kept secret in the New York City theater community. Lana used the information to her advantage, putting her scantily clad body in Marlene's direct line of sight every chance she got. Subtle smiles, and perfectly timed secret glances, had Marlene eating from Lana's palm in mere weeks. Though Lana preferred men, she quickly learned that making love to a woman had its advantages—everything was gentle, soft, and liquid. And Marlene certainly knew what she was doing; fucking a gorgeous actress every day certainly wasn't a hardship for Lana.

They didn't share their relationship with the rest of the cast, per Lana's request. As she explained to Marlene, she didn't want anyone to think she was "fucking her way to the top." Marlene laughed at her rationale, knowing intuitively that Lana was very talented and would eventually land a better role, but pragmatically agreed to keep things quiet.

One night, after a romantic dinner in Marlene's apartment, Lana crushed up two Seconal tablets she'd found in the medicine cabinet and stirred them into Marlene's Pinot. Within twenty minutes, Marlene was fast asleep, giving Lana the opportunity to smother her to death with a sheathed-in-silk pillow. It was surprisingly easy. She spent the rest of the evening eliminating all traces of herself from Marlene's home.

Although Marlene didn't have family in the area, her corpse was found the following afternoon. When she didn't show up for their daily rehearsal, the director sent a lackey to her apartment. The building's doorman was unable to raise her via the telephone, so he unlocked her door to perform a wellness check and discovered her already decomposing body lying twisted among the red silk sheets of her bed. A bottle of barbiturates sitting on her nightstand—placed there by Lana—led the medical examiner to rule Marlene's death an accidental overdose. Within two days, the case was closed and her body was cremated.

Lana wasn't selected for Marlene's role, either.

Feeling hurt and slightly reckless—Lana was pissed her hard work was helping other actresses further their careers—she decided to focus on the lead actress's understudy, Vivian. Just one day after setting her sight on the curvy blonde, the two women were alone and hustling down the theater's steep stairwell, offering Lana the perfect opportunity. She gave Viv a gentle nudge and watched her stumble—her long, shapely limbs flailing frantically as she cartwheeled down the steps—and land with a loud crunch on the landing. Even from a distance, Lana could tell Vivian's neck was broken—her pretty face was pushed into the hardwood floor, despite the fact she was lying on her back. Hiding her smile, Lana ran back to her dressing room, where she fell into a peaceful slumber on the sofa—until a piercing scream alerted her Vivian's body had been discovered.

She was still waiting to hear who would replace Vivian as Lauren's understudy.

While Lana had been daydreaming about her victims, the theater had gradually quieted; aside from the janitorial staff, she might be the only person left inside. She stood, grimacing at the pain in her tender feet, and walked behind the privacy screen to change out of her costume. As she buttoned up her cheap, cotton dress, she heard a knock at the door.

A male voice boomed, "Miss Turnell, you still in here?"

"Yes," she responded quizzically, peeking around the screen. Her eyes widened, and her heart rate tripled, when she realized Ritchie Callisto, the show's producer, was framed in the doorway of her dressing room. Not only was he here, a place he'd never stepped foot in before, but he was smiling...at her.

Ritchie Callisto was smiling at her!

She quickly pulled on her winter boots, the aches and pains in her feet all but forgotten, and walked toward the man with her hand extended. "To what do I owe the pleasure, Mr. Callisto?"

Gripping her hand between his cool, dry palms, he replied, "I'm not going to beat around the bush, Miss Turnell. It's late and I'm sure you'd like to get home and rest. I have a work-related proposition for you."

Smiling politely while feeling shivers of pleasure race down her spine, Lana nodded her head and responded politely, "I'm listening."

"As you probably know, we've had our fair share of staffing issues following some very unfortunate and untimely deaths within the cast. Tonight, Lauren was called back to Minnesota to be with her father, who is critically ill. She has asked for a month's leave."

"I'm so sorry to hear that." Lana coughed theatrically to cover the giggle that bubbled up in her throat.

"The director told me you've never missed a practice or performance and that you've managed to learn every speaking part in the play. Is this information correct?" He gazed hopefully at her.

"Indeed, it is. I like to be prepared." Was he going to offer her the understudy position, or the actual lead? This was huge!

"That is such a relief! He mentioned you also have a lovely voice. We were hoping you'd be so kind as to fill in for Lauren during her extended absence, Lana. You would, of course, receive her weekly paycheck during the month she's away, and it would be considered a huge favor to us—something we'll look very kindly upon in the future when considering casting for upcoming productions. Obviously, it's not easy to find a replacement who already knows the role, especially after Vivian passed away last week, God rest her soul." He stopped talking for a moment, crossed himself, and then turned back to her. "We figured when Lauren returns, you could become her permanent understudy. So, what do you say, Lana?"

Fuck that. Lauren will be my understudy.

"I would say, Mr. Callisto, you can absolutely count on me."

"Excellent!" Looking at his watch, he began backing out of the room. "Why don't you come in an hour early tomorrow and we'll get the paperwork taken care of? Then you can get fitted for your new costumes. Does that work for you?"

Unable to contain her smile, Lana replied, "Of course. Thank you so much, Mr. Callisto. You won't regret this!"

"You're very welcome, Miss Turnell. I know you won't let us down." With that, he turned and walked away. Once she was sure he was out of earshot, Lana threw her arms in the air, jumped up and down, and squealed with delight. Finally, finally, her dreams were coming true. She'd worked so hard, even selling her soul to the devil—metaphorically speaking, of course—when she'd been forced to kill those three women. Yet on this perfectly ordinary Tuesday evening, during a cold, blustery January, Lana's entire world had forever changed. She suddenly couldn't wait to get home and share the news with her roommates.

Wrapping her scarf around her neck and sliding on her too-thin coat, she grabbed her handbag and ran outside. The wind was frigid against her bare legs as she walked toward the subway station, but she didn't care. Instead, she pondered the possibility of getting her own place with her increased income and excitedly wondered what the next day would bring. Her mind clicked through the cast, silently determining who would be jealous when they heard the news of her impending stardom. Lost deeply within her thoughts, Lana neither saw, nor heard, the out-of-control car careening toward her as she trudged along the crosswalk. She didn't feel the brutal impact and never knew what hit her. By the time her body forcefully hit the ground, deep layers of her smooth skin peeled away as she skidded across the rough blacktop, Lana was already dead. Just as quickly as her star had begun to sparkle, it violently burned out on the street fronting the Lyric Theater.

CHAPTER ONE

AVA LOOKED AT herself in the lighted mirror, puckered her full, Cupid-bow lips, and blew herself a kiss. The hair stylist and make-up artist had just left; she'd been buffed, plucked, waxed, and beautified for over two hours, including a quick dive in the spray tanning booth. Her hair now hung down her back in shiny, ebony curls, and her flawless porcelain skin glowed—a faint pink blush gracing her chiseled cheekbones. Her trademark, though, the feature for which she had no doubt helped make her famous, was her large, round, celery-green eyes. According to the *New York Times*, they were "MESMERIZING" and "MAGNETIC." She made the color pop even more by using complementary shadows in shades of lavender, violet, and aubergine. Naïve, she was not. She knew her strengths and played to them.

"Thirty minutes until curtain, Ava!" an unknown man yelled into her dressing room, causing her toned body to flinch. Nervous electricity shot down her spine. She still couldn't wrap her mind around the fact she was the lead actress in the prodigious Broadway musical production, *Sizzle*, which was playing in the most infamous and sought-after theater on the Great White Way. Most people would probably consider her good fortune nothing but luck...yet Ava had worked her ass off for the past decade, taking endless acting and vocal classes, working her way up through the ranks, and sleeping with powerful directors and producers when necessary. Again, she was a woman who knew her strengths. Now that she'd reached the summit, she'd be damned if she'd let anyone stand in her way.

She slowly finished her lukewarm green tea and slipped into the sleeveless, fuchsia gown with the big bow covering her bottom...the gaudy one her character wore in the opening number.

Ava then pulled on the matching, full-length opera gloves, which ended at her bicep, along with the rest of her jewelry and accessories. Finally, being the diligent performer she was, she ran through her vocal warming exercises.

At the same time the disembodied voice yelled, "Fifteen minutes!" from the hallway, her make-up artist strolled back into Ava's room and worked her magic, expertly righting any wrongs which had occurred in the past hour. She finished by adding a thick coat of Ava's signature lipstick, MAC's Ruby Woo. After recapping the tube, she gave Ava a once over, nodded in approval, and moved toward the door, calling out, "Break a leg, Ava. We're all rooting for you and Ian!"

Hearing Ian's name, Ava blushed. Her leading man was one of the most beautiful creatures she'd ever laid eyes on. She was determined to make him hers—hopefully tonight in her king-sized bed. Or on the countertop. Wherever.

"FIVE MINUTES!"

Taking a deep, calming breath, Ava slipped on her white ballet flats, walked out of her dressing room…and into the rest of her suddenly charmed life.

"YOU WERE SO great, Ms. Babineaux! We loved the show!"

Ava smiled at the overly excited, frumpy woman standing before her, offered her thanks, and signed the crumpled program she was handed. She silently wished she could quit signing autographs and get to the opening night party at the Plaza Hotel. Unfortunately, dozens of fans were waiting at the side door she always used. Though she definitely didn't want to get a bitchy reputation, she made a note to herself to use a different exit next time. Ava hid her impatience, like the professional performer she was, and slipped on an enigmatic smile. Thirty minutes later, one of her many male fans hailed her a cab. She climbed inside, gave her driver the address, and sat back with a Cheshire cat grin. She was finally on her way to Ian and the rest of the cast.

"WELL DONE, MS. Babineaux, or should I say, 'the brilliant ingénue, the bright, shining star of *Sizzle*.'" Ian tapped his wine glass to hers, his eyes twinkling, a devilish smile highlighting his rugged good looks. To Ava, he looked like Heath Ledger—only better.

"Hmm, let's go with the star thing. It has a nice ring," Ava deadpanned. "And we mustn't overlook all the mentions you received in the opening night reviews, Mr. MacKenzie. What was that one line? I believe it was, 'Ian MacKenzie is the next Marlon Brando, with his smooth tenor vocals and brooding good looks.'"

Ian stared deeply into her green eyes with his Hershey chocolate ones before finally responding, "I mean, what can I say? They're not wrong." He chuckled, shrugged his shoulders, and said in a nonchalant voice, "Face it, beautiful, we're going places."

Letting out an inebriated whoop, Ava replied, "Hell yeah, we are! I'm so excited to see how things progress with the show. This is a dream come true for me, and it's just as sweet as I'd always imagined." Ian wrapped his arm around her shoulders, and she happily nestled into the cozy little niche created.

The two stars of *Sizzle*, dressed to the nines, sat in the corner booth of The Champagne Bar at the Plaza Hotel. Though they ignored the stares, the couple was garnering quite a bit of attention. Ava knew just how striking they looked together. He, with his blond curls, brown eyes, and tanned skin, and Ava, with her porcelain complexion, hair so black it sometimes looked blue, and those dazzling green eyes. Together, they were an entertainment journalist's wet dream.

Breaking her reverie, Ian said in a mocking voice, "Might I suggest you not get too comfortable, love? You know the Lyric Theater killer is probably coming for you." He guffawed and then took a big gulp of his white wine before motioning to the hovering waiter for another.

Suddenly losing her celebratory high, she turned her head to look up at his face and asked, "What the hell are you talking about, Ian? That's really not funny."

"Don't be silly. You know exactly what I'm talking about, Ava."

"No, I really don't."

"You haven't heard?" he asked.

"Heard what? You're driving me crazy. Tell me," she huffed, moving his arm off her shoulder.

Clearing his throat, he began, "For the past fifty or so years, several leading ladies—I believe the number is four—have mysteriously disappeared, never to be heard from again. The last place they were all seen was inside the Lyric. Not a single person, in all these decades, has ever discovered what happened to them. Neither has anyone been held accountable for their disappearance." Ian stopped talking and nodded his head in thanks to the waiter, who had just refreshed his wine goblet. He then focused his warm gaze back at Ava. "Seriously, you've never heard about this? They've even documented the disappearances on several television shows." Ian sat back in his seat. "It haunts the theater community to this day."

Ava sat, stunned and disconcerted, for several seconds…then crumpled into fits of laughter. "Good one, Ian. Trying to pull one over on me already, eh? I may be the new girl, but I'm not that gullible."

Ian leaned forward, his cocoa eyes serious. "Ava, I'm not joking. I actually remember the last disappearance. It happened around the same time I started my acting career. The actress's name was Nancy…Nora…something." He picked up his phone and did a quick search. "Natalie! Her name was Natalie," he said excitedly as he passed Ava his phone. She hesitantly took it from his warm hand and reluctantly read the article.

Natalie Woody.

As she scrolled through the article, she found the other women's names: Marilyn Morris, Ginger Ralston, Audrey Hollister, and Rita Haycourt. All four women had begun highly successful runs as the leading ladies at the Lyric Theater—and all four had disappeared shortly thereafter, without a trace. The disappearances started in 1950 with Marilyn and ended in 1989 with Natalie.

"This, this is terrible, Ian. Why didn't anyone tell me?"

"It's not something anyone in the theater world likes to discuss...it's our dirty little secret. The less attention it receives, the better. But Ava, I'm sure you're perfectly safe. I just mentioned it so you'd be aware of your surroundings," he responded, clearing his throat. "It's always better to be safe than sorry. Plus, I'd be, well, I'd be devastated if anything happened to you."

Her fiery annoyance diminished by Ian's sweet words, Ava picked up her glass and knocked back the rest of the crisp wine. The cool liquid soothed her parched throat. She wiped the corners of her mouth daintily on the white linen napkin, tossed it onto the tabletop, and scooted herself out of the booth. Standing, she looked down at Ian's handsome face and asked, "Want to go to my place for a nightcap?"

"I thought you'd never ask," Ian replied, wearing a large, toothy grin.

CHAPTER TWO

DEEP IN THE heart of the Lyric Theater, long after the cleaning crew had abandoned their carts and locked up for the night, a dark shadow passed through the aisles, reflected only by the LED light strips which lined the carpet on either side. It disappeared for a few seconds, only to reappear at the center of the stage—the ill-defined outline vaguely resembling that of a voluptuous woman. If one listened closely, they could often hear the faint, but undeniable, sound of feminine sobbing. The problem was people never looked or listened closely, and the shadow went largely unnoticed, much to its dismay.

For decades now, the shadow had been "haunting" this theater—silently commiserating with the performers as they came…and then went; watching brilliant shows…and some real stinkers; and reveling in the feeling of being a part of it all. Even though it wasn't. Over the years, the music style had changed, the costumes had become skimpier, sex and cursing became less taboo, and the shadow had been around to see, and judge, it all.

The shadow's incorporeal body disappeared from the stage and materialized as a dusty oval inside its old dressing room—the last place the shadow had ever felt any semblance of happiness. The space looked nothing like it did in 1949. Back then, the room was little more than a storage closet with cement floors and cheap, wood paneling on the walls. The heating system was always on the fritz, so the shadow froze during the late fall and throughout winter's duration. Though air conditioning units were available in the forties, the Lyric did without. Heat exhaustion and dehydration were very common problems for actors during the summer months. Despite it all, the shadow guessed there wasn't a single performer who would have changed a thing about their experience at the Lyric.

Now, decades later, the room boasted hardwood floors, drywall, and central air and heating. There was a beautiful make-up table, big enough for three actors to use at once, and an attached lighted mirror. Plush furniture, paintings, even a small kitchen area, which contained a mini-fridge, a microwave, and a Keurig coffee maker, completed the area. And this was just one of the many lowly chorus girls' dressing rooms.

The black particles, which made up the shadow's "body," dissipated once again, and haphazardly reunited in the lead actress's dressing room. This space was, for all intents and purposes, an apartment—a home away from home for the worthy leading lady. And someday, Lana promised herself, as her particles shifted and shimmered, it would all be hers.

She had no memory of dying on that long ago day in 1949. One minute she was walking across the street, and the next, she was frantically running around the stage in the Lyric, panicked, and screaming for the actors to help her. Not a single person glanced her way. Lana had no way of knowing that almost a week had passed since the freak accident that took her life. Scared and desperately confused, she ran to her dressing room and looked in the mirror. There was nothing to see except a very faint charcoal haze. She looked like a ghost who had died in a fire—sooty and dirty. Her confusion and fear were deep-rooted, like a malignant tumor. Gradually, small chunks of her memory returned, but she still wasn't sure what she was. Or why she seemed to be stuck inside the Lyric day in and day out, year after year.

One night, long after the cast and crew had left for the day, and a little over a year after Lana's gory death, she heard a voice whispering into her ear. She was sitting on the edge of the stage, her shadowy legs dangling over the edge. Unsure what she'd heard, Lana jumped up, turning her misty head left and right, but saw absolutely nothing. Shrugging her shoulders, she sat back down and began humming the songs from the musical she was hired for in 1949. She still remembered all the lyrics to every song.

"Lana, my child—do you still long for fame and fortune?" The voice inside her head had a hissing quality, nearly snake-like but edged with a guttural growl that cut through her brain like a knife. It was the voice of a monster in a horror movie.

"Of course, I do. That's all I've ever wanted." At this point, Lana didn't really give a shit who she was talking to—he couldn't possibly hurt her further. She was already dead and so fucking miserable.

"You can still have everything, Lana. All your heart's desires. Just do what you did when you were alive and KILL. Make sacrifices to me, your eternal father."

Intrigued, Lana asked the demon a question and listened with rapt attention to the answer.

CHAPTER THREE

LIFE WAS SWEET for Ava. *Sizzle* was breaking box-office records every single night, and there was already extensive Tony nomination buzz. Her love life with Ian was out of this world—as were the orgasms. She was even receiving movie scripts from major Hollywood directors. Ava couldn't remember a time when she felt happier or more fulfilled.

Glancing at the time on her phone, she realized she was going to be late if she didn't get out of the theater soon. Grabbing her clothes, she went into the bathroom to change. When she came back out, she wiped off the heavy stage make-up, which made her look ghastly in natural lighting, and reapplied it with a more subtle hand. Feeling as though she should text Ian and let him know she was running a little behind, she reached down to grab her cell and realized it wasn't there. She could have sworn she'd left it lying on the make-up table. She shifted the make-up palettes around to make sure it wasn't hidden beneath one, looked under the table, then stood and walked around the five hundred square foot room. Her phone was definitely missing. Had someone come in while she was in the bathroom and stolen it? *Oh God, it wasn't even locked.*

Ava began to panic, thinking about the graphic pictures stored on that phone and what they might do to her blossoming career. Unnerved, she grabbed her handbag and coat, took one final glance around the room, and glimpsed her phone lying on the table exactly where she thought she'd left it. *What the actual fuck?* There was no way someone could have snuck into the room and returned the phone. She'd been right there. It was impossible. Had the phone been lying there the whole time? Shaking her head, she wondered if it was time to see the doctor for some meds. She was clearly losing it.

FEELING THE SUN shining on her face, Ava opened her eyes.

Knowing it was Monday, her day off, she stretched, feeling positively feline and sexy on her Egyptian combed cotton sheets. She'd splurged and ordered them directly from Italy the month before. Looking at her phone, she realized it was only a little after eight. Feeling indulgent, she rolled over and shut her eyes, planning to sleep for another hour. Ian chose that moment to walk into the bedroom.

"Ava, we need to talk." His voice sounded cold and robotic.

Not liking his tone and worried about being dumped, Ava sat up, gripping the sheet to her naked chest. "What's wrong?"

"You know Goddamned well what's wrong. Don't try to act innocent."

Anxiety ground through her core as she racked her brain trying to think what she could have done last night that would rate this kind of ire from the always mellow Ian. Ironically enough, she couldn't remember last night. At all. The last thing she remembered was finding her phone and the feeling of relief that it hadn't been stolen. The rest of the night was completely blank.

"Did I get drunk? I mean, I don't really feel great this morning, but it doesn't feel like a hangover at all—more like the flu." The achiness had hit her in waves when she sat up in bed. "To be honest, I...I can't remember much about last night."

"No, you weren't drunk, which, frankly, makes what you did even worse." Ian avoided looking at her. "I find it very hard to believe you can't remember anything. Seems like a pretty convenient excuse."

"I'm not lying. I wouldn't do that to you. I remember being at the Lyric, thinking I'd misplaced my phone, and the rest of the night is completely missing." She shook her head and rubbed her temples, as if that would somehow help her remember.

"If you can't admit what you did, I don't know how we're supposed to work through it, Ava. You hurt and embarrassed me."

"Ian, please. Please look at me." Her voice quivered.

When she finally had his full attention, she stared into his eyes and said, "I swear on my career I do not remember what happened last night. There is a huge gap in my memory. I remember searching for my phone in the dressing room, then finding it exactly where I thought I'd put it in the first place." She paused. "Oh, and I remember thinking to myself I needed to see my doc because I was obviously letting life stressors get to me. Everything after that is gone. I am not lying to you, Ian. Please, please believe me."

Seeing the fear and confusion in her eyes, Ian found himself softening. He reached out and gripped her slender hand, a small smile curving his lips.

"I do wish you'd tell me what it is I did, though. You're worrying me," Ava pleaded gently.

"You were meeting me and some of the other *Sizzle* cast at the 40/40 Club. You had to stay over because John wanted to discuss a couple changes to the opening number," Ian replied, letting out a tired sigh.

Nodding her head, Ava agreed, "Yes, I remember all that. It's what happened after I left the theater that's giving me problems."

"You were pretty late getting to the club. When you finally arrived, you looked...different, somehow. I'm not sure what you did with your make-up, but your entire face shape seemed off. When you started talking, though, that's when I knew something weird was going on. Babe, you had a southern accent."

"What the hell?" Ava quietly murmured. She'd grown up in Vermont. Confused, she continued listening intently to Ian's memories of the events.

"Honestly, I figured you were just putting on a show for everyone, acting. But then you started hitting on every guy—and girl—who came to our table. Babe, you kissed several of our cast mates. If that wasn't bad enough, you asked our blatantly homosexual waiter to come home with us for a threesome. Needless to say, he wasn't interested." Ian's cheeks flushed during his retelling of her horrid behavior. "When I finally got you home, you stripped off all your clothes, collapsed on the bed, and then screamed half the night. I think you were having nightmares. I kept trying to wake you up but couldn't. You sounded absolutely terrified. I stayed awake in the living room so I could keep an eye on you. I haven't had any sleep yet, but when I heard you moving around a few minutes ago, I figured it was time to talk."

"My God, Ian, I'm so sorry, and horribly embarrassed. I don't even know what to say," Ava said tearfully.

"Were you on something, Ava? Did you take something before you left the theater?"

"Not that I remember. But obviously, that means nothing in the face of my actions last night. I'm as confused as you are."

"Would you see your doctor if I called and made an appointment?" he asked worriedly.

Nodding, she answered, "I think I need to."

"Okay, I'll make the call while you get your shower. Sound good?"

"Yeah…yeah. That's fine. I feel terrible anyway," Ava whispered, though her mind was elsewhere. Hearing Ian's story sent a stab of fear and dread down her spine. A sense of doom settled in her gut. Something was very, very wrong.

CHAPTER FOUR

LANA TURNELL GREW up on a farm located in the foothills of the Appalachian Mountains, deep in the heart of Tennessee. She couldn't wait to leave. As soon as she turned eighteen, she packed her meager possessions and took a bus to New York City. The first few nights she was there, she slept on a bench in Central Park. Eventually, she found a job as a waitress at a small diner and responded to an ad requesting a third roommate in a cheap, Bronx walk-up.

She was blessed with a beautiful singing voice, though where it came from, Lana never figured out. It sure as hell wasn't from her mama or papa. She sang twice every Sunday, and every other Wednesday evening in the church choir—not because she gave a shit about God or religion, but because she reveled in the admiration her voice brought her. When she sang, not one person in their rural town remembered she was poor and uneducated. Instead, they were awed by her talent, referring to it as a "gift from God." She was more inclined to believe it was just the shape and size of her vocal cords, mouth, throat, and nasal cavities…but what did she know? In her free time, when she wasn't cleaning out animal stalls or helping Mama with the baking, she taught herself the dances she'd seen the girls at school doing, when she bothered to go.

Lana worked hard to lose her accent upon arriving in New York. She realized immediately how much it made her stand out, and not in a good way. She began mimicking her roommates' New England speech patterns and then practiced on her customers at the diner. Before long, the southern twang was gone, except when she was excited, angry, or drunk. Then traces would creep back in.

When she was twenty years old, two full years after arriving in New York City, Lana landed a role on off-Broadway. It wasn't a speaking role—she was basically just stage filler—but it was Broadway. From there, she was eventually hired as a chorus girl. Although it was a step in the right direction, things weren't happening fast enough. That's when her latent killing talents decided to make themselves known.

And then…then…after all that hard work and all those struggles, she had finally landed a lead role, only to be violently killed less than fifteen minutes later. Being stuck in the Lyric Theater for eternity told her all she needed to know: she was in hell. Forever watching other women achieve their dreams, while she blew around the theater like filthy dust.

Then she'd heard the voice. The voice which informed her all was not lost or hopeless. Lana simply needed to kill five leading ladies, one per decade. She obviously had no issue with that. In 1981, while watching the news in one of the chorus girl's dressing rooms, she learned of the newly coined phrase which precisely defined her previous life—Lana was a serial killer. So, killing one person per decade? Puh-leeze. She could do it in her sleep.

That thought stopped her in her tracks.

She didn't eat. She didn't sleep. She was nothing more than floating dust particles with a consciousness. How the hell was she supposed to kill a woman when she was incorporeal? The answer, when it finally came, shocked the hell right out of her; or not. Lana Turnell, after all, was full of fire and brimstone.

CHAPTER FIVE

AVA PUT ON a burst of speed as she finished her twenty-minute run on the treadmill. Afterward, she picked up a towel and wiped the moisture from her face and neck, then guzzled a bottle of water. In the shower, her lavender-scented body wash helped relax her racing mind.

Her doctor had found nothing. She'd even performed an MRI of Ava's head to make sure a mass wasn't causing personality changes. Thankfully, her brain looked perfectly normal, as did every other body part. After exhausting all diagnostics and finding nothing, the doctor kindly suggested it was likely stress and started Ava on an anti-anxiety medication. That was three weeks ago. Since then, Ava had blacked out two more times, absolutely scaring the shit out of Ian, and upon hearing about her actions later, scaring herself, too.

During the first blackout, she'd lured Ian to the rooftop lounge in their building, where she proceeded to stand on the ledge and dance wildly, the southern accent once again making an appearance. Ian didn't need to remind her she could have fallen thirty stories to a very grisly death.

The second blackout occurred during a matinee performance of *Sizzle*—in front of a live audience. During the middle of the show, her voice changed, becoming lower, a mezzo soprano instead of a full spinto. Although the audience didn't seem to notice, the cast certainly did. Thankfully, it was very short-lived, but it freaked the hell out of Ava. She refused to let anything threaten her hard-earned career. To make matters worse, after every blackout she'd been deathly sick the next day, achy and lethargic, like she was coming down with the flu. Whatever this was, it was knocking her on her ass.

And though she hadn't told Ian yet, she thought she was being watched—all the time. She kept their blinds and curtains closed, even during the day, yet it didn't help. The disconcerting feeling of menacing, greedy eyes staring into her soul remained. The paranoid feelings were, oddly enough, even worse at the theater. It was affecting her focus, causing her to flub lines during rehearsals. Something needed to change. She didn't feel like herself at all. Instead, she felt quite distinctly like a person she would never normally care to know: cruel, crass, and vulgar, with a penchant for the extreme.

Ava walked to her closet and opened the door, critically eyeing her wardrobe. Ian was taking her out to dinner at the latest Manhattan hot spot. After selecting a black, body-hugging, Dolce and Gabbana turtleneck midi-dress, she placed it on her bed and went into the bathroom to blow dry and style her hair. When she walked back out, her green eyes had become blank and soulless. Her hair, usually worn long, with soft waves framing her face, was pinned up in a decidedly fifties-inspired look. She glanced at the outfit she'd selected, frowned, and hung it back in the closet, choosing instead a red rockabilly swing dress, with capped sleeves and black and white polka dots on the bodice. Sliding her feet into black stilettos, she wrapped the straps around her ankles and fastened them securely. She left her skin unadorned, adding only some mascara and a matte, retro-red liquid lipstick. Grabbing her clutch, she headed to the elevator. When she exited the building, she asked the doorman to get her a cab.

"Of course, Ms. Babineaux," he said cordially, tipping his hat in her direction and quickly taking in her appearance. "Heading to a costume party?"

"No, you imbecile, I'm not. Why are you even talking to me?"

Shock spread across the man's bloated features. "My apologies, Ms. Babineaux. Please forgive me. It won't happen again." He awkwardly assisted her into the taxi, which had pulled up to the curb, and then silently mouthed, "Fuck you," as she sped off into the growing dusk. He shook his head and let out a disappointed sigh. She'd always been so polite before, too.

IAN'S FACE SHOWED his obvious shock as he glimpsed his girl-friend strolling toward him. Immediately, based on her appearance, he suspected she was in the midst of a black-out. She would never go out dressed like that…unless it was Halloween. Instead of leading her into the restaurant, where their table was ready and waiting, he tucked his hand into hers and said, "Hey, babe. This crazy place got our reservation mixed up and they don't have a table for us right now. Why don't we go home, order in some of your favorite Thai food, and watch a movie? I'll even rub your feet," he sing-songed.

"What incompetence!" she yelled, a southern lilt threading through her words. "I'll have a word with the maître d'." Before Ian could respond, Ava had haughtily walked in the front door of the establishment and, already, he could hear her shouting. He sighed and his shoulders slumped. It was going to be a long night.

CHAPTER SIX

THE FIRST TIME Lana saw her, in the early spring of 1950, she was enamored. Marilyn was a beautiful platinum blonde whose childlike innocence enchanted all who knew her. Her smile lit up the entire stage. After carefully watching her for several weeks, Lana greedily selected Marilyn as her first sacrifice. The creepy de-mon voice had informed her that she would take on various aspects of each of the women she'd murdered. But the very best part of this deal? After she'd sacrificed the fifth and final woman to the demon, he promised she would become corporeal again. There was still a very real possibility of stardom. For this reason, Lana chose her candidates carefully. She considered their performance talents, their physical beauty and charm, their intelligence, and their ability to make their cast and crew love them. Marilyn met each and every criterion, and then some. She was perfect.

Lana, always the sadist, loved toying with her sacrifices before killing them. She often moved their possessions, leaving them in bizarre places. Wheedling her way into their dreams, she created the most violent, gory nightmares they'd ever experienced. And, like the demon she apparently was, she frequently possessed their bodies. She didn't have the power to stay within them for long, usually just a few hours, but fuck, it was fun. Even better, the possession had the added benefit of (usually) making them feel really sick the next day— something about her essence poisoned their bodies. Lana was like a virus, growing, mutating, and feeding off her hosts.

Poor Marilyn. She was ready to commit herself into the psych ward before she died. Lana's games seemed to affect her more than most. When she finally put Marilyn out of her misery, Lana actually felt as though she was doing the woman a favor.

The night it happened, Marilyn asked the piano player to stay for a few minutes after the show. She wanted to practice a certain verse in her ballad, one which had been giving her trouble. After running through it until she had it down, the musician left, but Marilyn did not. She sat on the piano bench, let out a loud sigh, and started pecking random keys. Completely lost in her thoughts, she never sensed the menacing blanket-shaped shadow slowly wrapping itself around her petite form—until she registered the intense stinging of her skin dissolving. Then the screaming began. It went on and on as Lana absorbed her body, layer by slow layer, until eventually, not a single skin cell of Marilyn's remained.

CHAPTER SEVEN

AVA AND IAN stood outside the theater signing autographs. Ava couldn't wait to finish up so they could go home and properly cel-ebrate their three-month anniversary—and that included toys and a sexy new teddy she'd purchased earlier that afternoon at Sugar Cookies, a luxury lingerie boutique. She was dying to see his ex-pression when he finally saw her body in that little slip of material. Her private shopping assistant had assured her she looked smoking hot.

After finishing up, the couple made their way down West 43rd Street. Ava hailed a cab, anxious to get home, but Ian, mellow as always, asked, "Why don't we walk for a little while? Get some fresh air and enjoy each other's company?" Unable to say no to the man, Ava shooed the cab away and began strolling down the street arm in arm with her love.

Ian was being unusually quiet for a man who wanted to chat. "Everything okay, babe?" she gently coaxed.

"Everything is perfect. I've just been trying to figure out how to tell the love of my life I was chosen as the lead in the *Gwendy's Button Box* film." He looked at her and gave the cheesy grin she loved so much.

She stopped walking and turned to stare at him. He stared back, waiting. Without any warning, she let out a squeal and jumped into his arms, wrapping her legs around his waist. "Ian, this is the best news I could have possibly heard. Congratulations times a thousand, baby! I'm so proud of you," she squealed before plac-ing her lips against his and passionately kissing the man who meant so very much to her. Cars honked their horns and several people catcalled, but it didn't faze the happy couple at all. When they fi-nally broke apart and began walking down the street, Ava gently bumped her hip against Ian's and teased, "I knew you'd get it."

"Filming starts next summer, which works out well. By that time, we'll both be ready to move on from *Sizzle*. So, what do you say, Ava. Want to move to L.A. with me?"

"Of course, I do! And I'll show you just how much when we get ho…" She paused momentarily before her face twisted in frus-tration. "Shit! I left your little surprise in my dressing room. I tell you what—you go ahead home while I run back and grab the bag. I'll meet you there in just a few minutes."

"I don't like that, Ava. It's late and…"

Ava cut him off, "Oh hush. There are people everywhere. We're only a couple blocks from the theater. I can have the bag and be in a taxi in less than ten minutes. It's perfectly safe."

"All right, then," he reluctantly relented. "But be careful, and stay alert. I'll see you back at the apartment. This surprise better be worth it, woman."

"Oh, I think you'll be pleased," Ava smirked as she began walking backward down the sidewalk. "See you in a few!" With a final wave, she turned and sauntered down the street.

AVA PUT HER key in the front door, figuring it would be quicker and safer to enter there, as opposed to the performer's entrance at the rear. A few recessed lights were strategically lit throughout the lobby, but shadows largely dominated the space. As Ava made her way through the theater, walking slowly down the aisles, which were lit only by LED strip lights, she could readily admit this place was spooky as fuck after hours. She'd never been in the building when it was this dark and silent. Where the hell was the cleaning crew?

Reaching the entrance to her dressing room, she used a different key to unlock the door, flipped on the light, and walked inside. No sooner had she picked up the bag—which was exactly where she had left it, sitting on her rustic, weathered gray coffee table—than the door slammed shut behind her. Ava jumped, dropping the bag of sex-time goodies on the floor. Hoping it was just a member of the cleaning crew, she yelled out a timid, "Hello?" Hearing nothing, she walked to the door and gripped the levered handle. It wouldn't turn. She heaved her weight against the metal exit. It didn't budge. She was stuck.

Panicked, she began pounding on the door, screaming. A couple minutes later, feeling tired and frustrated, Ava walked to the couch and dejectedly sat down. Ian was waiting for her. Thinking of him, knowing how worried he would be, she pulled her phone from her handbag and began to text him a message requesting help. The screen of her phone kept fading in and out, like a satellite television when rain clouds were blocking the signal. Just before she hit send, the screen turned black and died, despite having full charge. "What the fuck is going on?" she mumbled to herself, trying to stay rational and not let unrealistic fears overtake her. There had to be someone around who could help her. Suddenly feeling desperate, she pounded and clawed at the door until her knuckles were bloody and her nails were ripped, also oozing red.

Panting from her exertions, Ava walked to the stainless steel fridge in her kitchenette and pulled out a chilled bottled water. Twisting off the top, she chugged half its contents while standing there. Leaving the bottle sitting on the counter, she walked to the Mac laptop she kept on a corner desk for the sole purpose of researching her roles. Perhaps she could send Ian an email or Facebook message. The water in her belly shifted and gurgled when she plopped onto the desk chair. Seconds later, her hopes were shattered when she tried to turn the machine on and nothing happened. She knew it wasn't the battery, as the machine was currently plugged in and charging. "What is happening?" she yelled out, her voice echoing through the room.

Frustrated, she pushed the chair back from the desk and began pacing the room's perimeter. There had to be an answer to this problem...but what? Ava never gave up—ever—and she'd find a solution, even if it took all night. *Think, Ava, think!* If she didn't show up at their apartment soon, she knew Ian would come looking for her. Maybe she should just lock herself in the bathroom, hunker down, and wait for him to arrive. Satisfied with her plan, she grabbed her purse, along with the bottle of water she'd left on the counter, and headed toward the attached bathroom.

As Ava walked by the large, antique mirror she had installed behind the couch, she glimpsed something out of the corner of her eye. Pausing, she turned to the left and studied the mirror. At first, she saw nothing—just her luxurious dressing room reflected in the glass. But then…then she discerned something which caused her eyes to widen in shock and fear. Directly behind her, rising from the ground like a hazy mist, was a menacing blanket of black. It was huge…at least ten feet tall, and equally as wide. When she noticed the top of the "blanket" curving toward her, adrenaline sent her darting toward the bathroom, but the thick, almost opaque wall somehow gave her a shove—one hard enough to knock her flat on her back, sprawled across the hardwood floor.

Before she could even attempt to stand, the blanket covered her body, stealing the breath from her lungs. Whatever it was, it had weight. She felt it wrapping itself around her, literally lifting her body from the floor, and tucking itself underneath. She was virtually cocooned in its embrace. Ava felt oddly comforted and warm, like a swaddled baby—until the burning started. At first her skin felt sunburned, tingling and sensitive to any type of pressure, but it became progressively worse as the seconds passed. Tortured, Ava screamed in pain and terror. She thrust her arms and legs into the mist, hoping to find a way to escape, but the blackness just stretched and grew, accommodating her every movement. She felt as though she was encased in mutant silly putty.

As the acid ate through her eyelids, Ava felt her iconic green eyes pop inside their sockets. The pain was indescribable—unlike anything she'd ever felt. Immediately, she sensed the mist blanket sucking up the liquefied remains. She breathed in the particles and could feel them ulcerating her lungs, making her cough uncontrollably. The black mist also entered her mouth, rapidly making its way from one end of her digestive system to the other, consuming her body from the inside out.

Slowly, it devoured her frame. Although Ava had no idea how much time had passed, she was fairly certain she could hear Ian banging on the door and screaming for somebody to help. Ava tried to call out to him, but her vocal cords had already been destroyed.

Long before the acid reached her arteries and ultimately killed her, Ava's sanity had broken. Her mind couldn't conceive of the hell her body was enduring or the fact that this was actually the end of her very short life. She was still so young; she'd never really given death any real consideration—it was something that should only happen to the elderly, after they had lived a long, productive, and happy life. Ava couldn't help but ponder the unfairness of the situation.

The pain was unending and excruciating. Her nerve endings throbbed with the agony of the assault. When the mist sucked up her spurting arterial blood, Ava was already blind, deaf, without a nose to smell or a tongue to taste, and her psyche was shattered. That didn't prevent her from feeling the life force flowing out of her body, though—and it was terrifying. Thankfully, the fear didn't last, as she was dead seconds later. Thirty minutes after her soul departed the physical world, her body was nothing more than a beautiful memory. The ravenous black mist quietly dissipated. It was as though neither woman had ever been there at all.

IAN FRANTICALLY BANGED on the door, yelling for Ava. He was petrified. No matter what he or the cleaning crew attempted, even picking the lock, it wouldn't budge. The door swung inward, so they didn't have access to the hinges or pins. He didn't know what the hell was going on, but he knew it wasn't good. Ian slid down the wall until his butt hit the floor, rested his elbows on his knees, ran his hands through his hair, and cried. He never should have let her come back to this place, with its fucked-up history, all alone. If anything happened to her, he'd never forgive himself. Ava meant the world to him.

Suddenly, without any fanfare, the door crashed to the ground, stirring up a cloud of dust. It left a gaping entrance into

Ava's dressing room. The cleaning crew backed timidly away, but Ian stood and ran frantically inside, his head turning right and left as he searched for his partner. Though she didn't seem to be there, her handbag was on the floor, its contents spilled and spread haphazardly around. A half-full water bottle was lying on its side near the bathroom door. And there, by the couch, was the item she'd come back for. It was still sitting upright; a little white bag with elegant black lettering, which read "Sugar Cookies Lingerie."

Tears rolling down his face, Ian yelled to the cleaners to call 911, then picked up the bag and sat on Ava's plush white couch. Pulling out the black and metallic gold tissue paper, he peered inside and saw a beautiful red negligee. Ava knew how much he loved seeing her in the color red. He pulled the silky material out, held it to his face, and sobbed. Ian sensed, deep in his heart, he was never going to see her again, no matter what the police might do. Decades from now, she'd just be another of the Lyric Theater's missing women.

CHAPTER EIGHT

LANA COULDN'T BELIEVE the changes in the city since she'd last walked its busy streets in her very own body. Everything seemed bigger, taller, more glamorous, and, oddly enough, dirtier. The energy was the same though—a constant thrum of electricity that coursed through every single New Yorker. There was a reason people came here to live—that energy was addictive.

She had stayed in her particle form long enough to escape Ava's nosy lover, but as soon as she was outside, in the alleyway behind the Lyric, she transformed. Though she still had her own physical features, there was an essence inside her of each of the women she'd sacrificed. Lana now had Marilyn's infamous wiggle when she walked, Ginger's innocence, Audrey's sophistication, Rita's confidence, Natalie's sweetness, and Ava's charisma. She was the whole package.

Before she'd escaped Ava's dressing room, she'd swiped her wallet. Inside, she found over eleven hundred dollars in cash. Tossing the credit cards and the leather pouch which held them in a nearby dumpster, she headed to the nearest luxury hotel. Lana could not wait to crawl between crisp, cool sheets and sleep in a bed for the first time in over five decades.

THE NEXT MORNING, Lana bounded out of bed before dawn, made some calls, set up some appointments, and reveled in the hottest, steamiest, most luxurious shower she'd ever experienced. Body wash and loofahs? Who knew! She refused to waste one minute of this second chance. Lana knew all too well how quickly it could be taken away.

She called the concierge, gave him her clothing sizes, and asked if a shopper could pick her up an elegant, yet casual, dress, a set of undergarments, and appropriate shoes. She also requested some red lipstick. After being assured they could have something for her within the hour, Lana then put in a call to the kitchen. After skimming the menu, she chose pancakes with strawberries and whipped cream, and a pot of strong, black coffee. While she was waiting for her food, she sampled the little bottles of lotions, perfumes, and powders supplied by the hotel. Once her perfect skin was moisturized and pampered, she turned on the television and quickly became overwhelmed by all the channels. She did manage to find a program which grabbed her attention—it was called *Fear Factor*. Those Madagascar hissing cockroaches…yuck! Lana literally shed tears of joy as she devoured her first real meal in more than fifty years. A girl could get used to this.

About forty minutes after she'd placed her clothing order, there was a loud knock at her door. A short time later, she was dressed…and looked like a million bucks. The shopper had chosen an indigo blue fit and flare dress, with a high neckline and three-quarter puff sleeves. It was relatively short, hitting several inches above her knee, but Lana didn't mind. She had great legs, may as well show them off. The soft knit material was comfortable and flowed beautifully against her trim body. The color looked gorgeous with her pale skin and auburn hair. The dress had been paired with nude suede pumps, which had three-inch block heels. Feeling confident and stylish, Lana tucked what was left of her cash into her bra, grabbed the key card to her room, and hurried outside to make her 8:30 appointment.

SHE WALKED INTO the lobby of the building and was immediately awed by its size and grand appearance. The floor to ceiling, milk bottle–shaped windows were a sight to behold. As she rode the elevator to her designated floor, she nervously smoothed her dress and tried to check her appearance in the reflective metal of the lift.

She'd made an appointment with a talent agency—the same one she knew Ava used. Lana only hoped they'd find her worthy enough to take on as a client. She was beyond anxious to get back on the big stage.

When she entered the office, the receptionist looked up, eyed her critically, and gave a stiff smile. "May I help you?" Her nameplate read Mitzi Martin. *Jesus, people actually named their daughters Mitzi? Morons.*

"Yes, I'm Lana Turnell. I have an 8:30 appointment with Fred Asher," she replied haughtily. *Thank you, Rita, for giving me your confidence…literally.* She glared at the unfortunately named receptionist, who rapidly realized her place and looked away, then took a seat in the waiting lounge. Five minutes later, she was escorted to Mr. Asher's office. The views from this high up caused an innocent sense of wonder inside Lana. It was so incredibly beautiful.

When Mr. Asher walked in, she gracefully lifted herself from the chair, gave him her most winning smile, and politely shook his clammy hand. Within ten minutes, she knew she had this man wrapped around her little finger. She was sitting on the edge of his desk, regaling him with one of her funny anecdotes, when she happened to glance out the window. Despite her shock, she couldn't help but shake her head and smirk. *Well done, Satan. Fucking bravo, asshole.*

Lana wasn't stupid, so it didn't take her long to understand what was happening—to see her life laid out exactly like the empty fucking hole it was, full of endless misery and useless sacrifices made to an evil force she didn't understand. The demon had fucked her over. He'd given her only the briefest taste of how sweet this life could be. And now he was taking it away…again. But what could she do? Not a Goddamned thing. She was well-ensconced in her little slice of hell. Always on the outside looking in—forever forced to watch actresses rise to fame and success on Broadway, while she could only hope for brief, hours-long interludes of that same life, every fifty years. Enough to make her crave it even more. Though she hadn't before, Lana suddenly believed wholeheartedly in karma.

Heading toward the north tower, at an incredible speed, was a huge Boeing 767 aircraft. Lana and Fred were sitting in an office on the ninety-seventh floor of the World Trade Center. The date was September 11, 2001.

Just before the plane made impact, Lana muttered, "Fuck my life." And then the world exploded.

EPILOGUE

2021: Present Day

TONIGHT ON *Dateline: Secrets Uncovered*, we'll be looking at a bizarre mystery that spans more than seven decades, and centers around one of the most iconic buildings in New York City's Great White Way—the Lyric Theater.

Built in 1903, many believe the theater has been a hotspot for supernatural activity. Beginning in 1950, one short year after a random chorus girl was accidentally killed by a car just feet away from the theater's front doors, things have been, well, shall we say…peculiar. Seven women, all famous on the Broadway stage, have disappeared, never to be heard from again. All are assumed to be dead, though their bodies have never been found.

There seems to be a pattern, though, as each woman disappeared approximately ten years after the one before her. In fact, Greta Garbry went missing just six months ago, almost ten years, to the day, following the disappearance of Veronica LaBlanc in 2011. Greta's family and friends are frantic to find her. Though her family assured authorities she didn't suffer from any mental illnesses, several people, who wish to remain anonymous, have shared with us that Greta had been acting oddly in the months leading up to her disappearance, oftentimes behaving like a completely different person.

So, what is happening to these women? Are they willingly leaving their seemingly perfect lives behind? Is there an elderly serial killer on the loose? A copycat? Or could there be, like many believe, a supernatural element involved?

Over the next hour, we'll be interviewing friends and family of the lost celebrities, including Ian MacKenzie, the boyfriend of *Sizzle* sensation, Ava Babineaux, who disappeared on September 10, 2001, just one day before the World Trade Center towers tragically fell. Could she have been lost in the rubble? Ian says otherwise. This is a man who is firmly part of the supernatural cohort, and tonight, he's going to publicly share Ava's confounding story, for the very first time.

I'm Keith Morrison and we'll let you form your own opinions as we investigate the Lyric Theater mysteries tonight…on *Dateline*.

ABOUT THE AUTHORS

RENEE M.P.T. KRAY grew up in Michigan with eight siblings and several really dumb dogs. Having been homeschooled from a young age, she was able to experiment with writing and quickly fell in love with the art. She earned a BA in literature from Ave Maria University, her MFA in English and Creative Writing from Southern New Hampshire University, and has self-published two collections of short stories: *Think Again: A Captivating Compendium* and *Restless: A Year of Ghost Stories*. However, none of these pursuits have been as challenging as trying to get her pug, Potato, to stop eating dirt. Find out more about Renee at www.reneemptkray.com.

JEREMY MEGARGEE has always loved dark fiction. He cut his teeth on R.L Stine's Goosebumps series as a child, and a fascination with Stephen King's work followed later in life. Jeremy weaves his tales of personal horror from Martinsburg, West Virginia, with his cat, Lazarus, acting as his muse/familiar. Find out more about Jeremy at www.facebook.com/JMHorrorFiction.

SCOTTY MILDER is a writer, filmmaker, and film educator living in Albuquerque, New Mexico. He received his MFA in Screenwriting from Boston University, and his award-winning short films have screened at festivals all over the world, including the Cannes Short Film Corner, Cinequest, the Dead By Dawn Festival of Horror, HollyShorts, and the H.P. Lovecraft Film Festival and CthulhuCon. His independent feature film *Dead Billy* is available to stream on Amazon.com and Google Play.

His short fiction has appeared or will appear in *Dark Moon Digest*, *KZine*, *Lovecraftiana Magazine*, as well as anthologies from Dark Peninsula Press, Sinister Smile Press, Dark Ink Books, Little Demon Books, and others.

Scotty teaches screenwriting and film production at Santa Fe Community College, Sol Acting Studios, and The Seattle Film Institute. He is also the co-creator and cohost of The Weirdest Thing history podcast, with actor and theatre artist Amelia Ampuero.

Find out more about Scotty at www.scottymilder.com or www.facebook.com/scottymilderwrites. He's also on Instagram at @scottypotty2317.

STEVEN PAJAK is the author of novels such as the U.S. Marshal Jack Monroe series and the Mad Swine trilogy, as well as short stories and novellas. When not writing, Steven works as an administrator at a university. He continues to be an avid reader of Stephen King and Dean Koontz, John Saul, Richard Matheson, and many other favorite authors in the horror, suspense, thriller, and general fiction genres. Steven lives in the Chicagoland area with his wife and two teens. Find out more about Steven at www.stevenpajak.com.

BARRY CHARMAN is a writer living in North London. He has been published in various magazines, including *Ambit*, *Firewords Quarterly*, *The Ghastling* and *Popshot Quarterly*. He has had poems published online and in print, most recently in *The Literary Hatchet* and *The Linnet's Wings*. Find out more about Barry through his blog at www.barrycharman.blogspot.co.uk.

RED LAGOE, author of *Lucid Screams* and *Dismal Dreams*, enjoys spewing her horror-ridden mind onto the page every chance she gets. When she's not writing, she can be found under dark skies with a telescope, dabbling in amateur astronomy. Find out more about Red at www.redlagoe.com.

RICHARD CLIVE is a writer, journalist, and editor living in the medieval town of Conwy, North Wales, with his wife, daughter, and pet Labrador. Richard studied film and scriptwriting in Manchester and describes himself as a horror and science fiction writer. His passions include books, old horror movies, long walks, and tea. Find out more about Richard at www.facebook.com/richard.clive.332.

DAVID ANTHONY was born and raised in Southwest Michigan but now resides in the Pacific Northwest with his wife and daughter. Having been a fan of dark fiction all his life, he now writes horror, sci-fi, and fantasy of the darker varieties. His stories can be found in several anthologies and magazines, including: "The Thing in the Corner," published in *Lovecraft eZine*, issue 36, and "The Contractors," published in *Crime Syndicate Magazine*, issue 3. Find out more about David at www.davidaanthony.wordpress.com.

KRISTAL STITTLE was born and raised in Toronto, Canada, where she still lives with her cat, although she's known to frequently flee to the lakes and forests of Muskoka. Trained in 3D animation, she continues to paint and illustrate regularly while dabbling in photography whenever she's not writing. She's the author of the zombie Survival Instinct series, and the thriller *Merciless*, as well as many short stories. You can find her on Twitter @KristalStittle, where she's probably lurking in the comments of her favorite horror authors' posts. Find out more about Kristal at www.kristalstittle.com.

SCOTT HARPER grew up watching Hammer horror flicks and reading Marvel black-and-white monster magazines. His stories have appeared in numerous speculative fiction venues, including volumes three and four of the Better Off Dead Series. Now a full-time writer, he dedicates himself to continuing the horror legacies enshrined by Bram Stoker, John Steakley, and Marv Wolfman. Find out more about Scott at www.scottharpermacabremaestro.com.

R.E. SARGENT is the author of several novels, as well as a handful of novelettes. R.E.'s novels include *Relative Terror* and The Fury-Scorned series. At a young age, R.E. fell in love with books. While many of the other kids were playing sports, he was reading as many books as he could. He quickly got hooked on mysteries and suspense. It was his love of books and storytelling that led to his passion for writing. One of his biggest inspirations is Dean Koontz. R.E. currently lives in Oregon with his wife and their two fur-children, Riley and Mason. Riley is a Chocolate Lab and Mason is a Bernese Mountain Dog. Find out more about R.E. at www.resargent.com.

LP HERNANDEZ is a writer of horror and speculative fiction. His work is featured in many anthologies and collections, including *Lockdown Horror* from Black Hare Press, *A Monster Told Me Bedtime Stories* from Soteira Press, and *Forgotten Ones* from Eerie River Press. Several of his stories have been adapted as audio dramas by The NoSleep Podcast, and he was awarded second place in the 2019 Writer's Digest Annual Writing Competition for genre fiction. When not writing he serves as a medical administrative officer in the Air Force. He also loves his family, heavy metal, and a crisp high five. Find out more about LP at www.lphernandez.com.

BRIDGETT NELSON is a registered nurse, turned horror author. Her story, "Political Suicide" is featured as part of the horror anthology, *If I Die Before I Wake - Volume 3: Tales of Deadly Women and Retribution*; her story, "Invader", is included in *If I Die Before I Wake - Volume 4: Tales of Nightmare Creatures*; and she contributed the final chapter/epilogue to *Devil's Gulch: A Collaborative Horror Experience*. Bridgett is a proud member of the Horror Writer's Association.

She lives in West Virginia with her husband, Doug; her teenagers, Parker & Autumn; her three pugs, Bodhi, Harlow, and Dexter Morgan, and her frequently aroused, 180-pound St. Bernard, Sal—who has WAY more followers on Instagram than she does.

Bridgett thoroughly enjoys writing, mainly because wearing a bra is not required. She also really likes tarantulas. A lot. Find out more about Bridgett at www.bridgettnelson.com.

MORE FROM SINISTER SMILE PRESS

THE BETTER OFF DEAD SERIES

Do you love IF I DIE BEFORE I WAKE – The Better Off Dead Series? The Better Off Dead Series delves into the farthest corners of your mind, where your deepest, darkest fears lurk. These masters of horror will haunt your dreams and stalk your nightmares, taking you to the edge of sanity before pushing you to the brink of madness! Read the rest of the series now!

If I Die Before I Wake Volume 1: Tales of Karma and Fear
If I Die Before I Wake Volume 2: Tales of Supernatural Horror
If I Die Before I Wake Volume 3: Tales of Deadly Women and Retribution
If I Die Before I Wake Volume 4: Tales of Nightmare Creatures
If I Die Before I Wake Volume 5: Tales of the Otherworldly and Undead
If I Die Before I Wake Volume 6: Tales of the Dark Deep (12/6/2021)

LET THE BODIES HIT THE FLOOR SERIES

Let the Bodies Hit the Floor is the latest series from Sinister Smile Press, the creators of The Better Off Dead series. These volumes bring you the very best in horror/slasher/stalker/serial killer crime fiction. The more vicious and bloodier, the better. So, put on your pee-pee pants, because you're in for one hell of a dark, sinister journey.

A Pile of Bodies, A Pile of Heads Volume 1 (9/6/2021)
A Pile of Bodies, A Pile of Heads Volume 2 (9/20/2021)

SINISTER SUPERNATURAL STORIES SERIES

The Sinister Supernatural Stories series brings you delicious horror that focuses on elements of the supernatural. Pull up a chair and dig in, but never after dark— everyone knows bad things always happen after dark.

Screaming in the Night: Sinister Supernatural Stories Volume 1 (3/7/2022)

NOVELS

Devil's Gulch: A Collaborative Horror Experience

Sinister Smile Press

Horror Themed Anthologies
and Collaborative Novels

Creating Nightmares is our Business...
and business is good!

Made in the USA
Middletown, DE
20 July 2021